James Girls 2

What's Done in The Dark

F.J. Stevens

JAMES GIRLS 2

ISBN: 978-0-692-93507-1

Dedication

To my family. My angels watching over me and riding with me every day, your love and encouragement keeps me going.

Acknowledgements

This second endeavor was an enormous undertaking and I would be remiss if I did not acknowledge those who helped me bring this story to light.

My editor, Rob Bignell; my cover artist, web designer and creative partner Thomas Holmes. Joy Bhatacharee, Kariz Marcel, Rik Hall, you all are exceptional at what you do and continue to make this process so much easier for me.

Lori, Olivia, Sydney, Shelley, Aiko and Lauren I thank you for your time and your invaluable feedback on the story.

I thank you all, sincerely for being who you are and enabling me to do what I love to do. You mean the world.– F.J.

Prologue

Sitting on the sofa, tearful and drowning his latest sorrows in expensive vintage cognac, Ray couldn't help thinking, *What the fuck is it all for?* It was all over. Everything. Carlita didn't love him anymore. Missy surely hated him. She wasn't taking his phone calls. Probably laying up with some fuck. And pretty soon the pics, the *private* pics, for his and Carlita's eyes only, would hit the news. Then the videotape. Then it would be all over.

The day before, he'd called the blackmailers' bluff. Mostly because he didn't have the one point two million they demanded, but it didn't matter much now. Everything was about to be exposed. Maybe that was a good thing, he thought. Trying to keep up the façade was wearing him thin. Pretending to give a damn about Missy was getting old, and loving Carlita behind closed doors made them both miserable.

All he wanted was Carlita. To walk a city block and hold her hand. To sit in the middle of a crowded restaurant and feed her from his fork, letting the whole world know he was his, or she was hers, or...whatever the case. But that wasn't his reality.

The reality was Raymond Coleman was a championship winning, hall of fame contending former NFL playing superstar with a reputation to protect and a fast crumbling empire he was desperately trying to save. Coming out of the closet, which he wasn't even sure he was in, would surely ruin him and any chance of scoring a deal lucrative enough to get the IRS, the mob and his soon to be second bitch of an ex-wife, Missy off his ass.

He sat in the same spot for hours. Sun up to sundown. Nightfall to dawn. Drinking glass after glass of the brown liquor, trying desperately to come up with a plan. He'd tried everything. Liquidated everything. Borrowed from everyone he could and still was nowhere closer to a solution than the day the gangsters showed up at his front door to call in their loan.

Earlier that day he'd taken the last of his cash and tried to run it up at the craps table in the new Maryland casino. But that plan failed miserably. He ended up owing his buddy Roman an extra $20,000 after the casino manager cornered him mid-stream at a urinal and demanded that he settle his marker. *Prick.*

Leaving town wasn't an option. They'd only find him, or even worse, hurt the people he left behind. His children. His parents. He couldn't risk it. Missy was his last resort, but she was ignoring him. He'd called all night and texted her all morning and nothing. She stood to lose just as much as he, but for some reason she didn't seem to care. *Heartless bitch.*

So he sat and drank and sulked until everything was foggy. His eyes were heavy. He needed to sleep. Maybe the answers would come in the morning. Too tired to hike the stairs, he pulled his feet up onto the sofa and closed his eyes.

Two hours later, he awoke half off the sofa and still fully dressed. His arm had not yet awakened, his foot ached, and his eyes were practically glued shut. Blurry vision came into focus, and he jumped to attention when he saw Giovanni sitting in an armchair across the room, looking particularly unforgiving.

Giovanni's right hand man, Rob, stood close by his side. All six-foot-eight, 300 pounds of him with one hand clasping his left wrist, his left hand holding a sleek .45 caliber Beretta with a silencer attached. Both hands donned thick black leather gloves.

Ray's life flashed before him. Mostly the end of it. He pictured the barrels of both men's guns raised and aimed squarely at his chest. His arms flailing as he attempted to shield himself from the onslaught of hollowpoints. A coroner pushing a gurney out of his front door, past a dozen news reporters and paparazzi. His poor, grief-stricken mother crying over his grave.

He knew it was the end, and there wasn't a single fucking thing he could do about it. He'd tried. Giovanni didn't need to say a word. Although the sadistic, Napoleonic little runt would never resist the urge to hear the sound of his own voice. To intimidate one last time.

"So Ray. You ard veddy hard man to keep up with. Yes?"

Ray swallowed hard. "Yeah. Hey listen, Giovanni, man I swear…"

"Shut the fuck up nigga!" Rob yelled as he chambered a round and aimed for Ray's head.

Ray cowered in his seat with his hands raised, "Ok, ok, ok! I can get the money Gi. Really man. Just give me a couple days."

Giovanni smirked and addressed him in his thick Sicilian accent. "Aye. I tole you it's not about the mawney no more. I givva you time. I givva you mor'd time. You disappear. You make a…uh…how do you say…an *assa-hole* outta me. So…" He shrugged. "Your'd time iz up."

Rays eyes welled. It was time. He panicked. "Wait, Gi. Come on man. Please. I'm beggin you man. I can fix this."

Giovanni's face remained expressionless. Not a trace of compassion. He didn't even look angry. Business as usual. Unlike his protégé. Rob was clearly agitated. Jumpy even. He rocked from side to side. He snarled at Ray, occasionally biting at his bottom lip and shaking his head. Ray could almost hear his thoughts.

So focused on Rob, he didn't hear anything Giovanni was saying. He wiped the tears that escape his eyes. Then he braced himself. Manned up, so to speak. "So I guess there's nothing I can say to change your mind?" He looked at Giovanni and then at Rob. Searching for an out. Something. Anything. There was nothing. He sighed. "Fuck it. Just do it. Just get it over with." Then he closed his eyes tightly, waiting for a *pop* and maybe a white light. Hoping to God it would be instant. Quick and painless.

Rob walked over and put the gun to his temple. "He said, get up!"

Ray sat there with his eyes still closed tight. In a crackling voice he murmured. "Come on man. Just do it! Just fuckin do it!"

Rob grabbed him by the arm and yanked him to his feet. "Man, get the fuck up!" He pushed Ray toward the foyer and to the stairs. "Come on nigga. Up the steps! Let's go!" Giovanni trailed close behind.

Ray stumbled up the stairs on shaky legs, with one eye half open, afraid of the *pop* that would surely come to the back of his head at any minute. Rob followed him close with the gun at his back. Giovanni walked behind them singing something loudly in Italian. Being purposefully creepy. When they reached the top of the stairs, Rays eyes bulged. "Wait, what the fuck is that?!"

Giovanni responded, matter-of-factly. "That? That izza how you die."

Ray looked at Giovanni, then over at Rob, then he yelled, "The fuck it is."

He pushed Rob hard knocking him into the bannister and nearly down the steps. Rob grabbed the bannister to break his fall. Ray dashed past him, getting halfway down the stairs before Giovanni tripped him, causing him to fall hard on his chest before tumbling down to the second landing. Giovanni pulled his gun from his waist and walked slowly down the stairs. He knelt beside Ray and pushed the barrel to his nose. "Back up the steps. Don't make a this so hard."

Ray sobbed. "Come on Gi man. Not like this. You can't do me like *this*. Just shoot me, man. Just shoot me. Please." Rays eyes were fixated on the thick rope with the noose tied to the bannister. "I'm not doing this."

Rob lifted himself from the floor, grabbed Ray by the shirt and drew his fist back. Giovanni yelled, "Naw!" Rob grimaced, as he held his fist back. He wanted one good hit. Just one.

Giovanni pulled an envelope from his jacket. "Ray. You havva no choice. You owe me mawney. I will get my mawney. One way, or the awther way. I could not get it the one way... so I get it the awther."

"But if you just..."

Giovanni raised a hand. Shushing his captive. "I deeg around a little beet. I find outta you have pawlicy. Ten million. You owe me only two. You familee gets the rest. Eveddy one iza happy. Eazy peazy. My fidend, you die either way. This way izza better. For'd me. For'd your familee. Jawst get the rope, Ray."

At that point, both Rob and Giovanni's guns were pointed at his head. Ray didn't care. They were gonna kill him anyway.

Why should he do this crazy shit? He'd rather be shot. He took a firm stance. Ready to die. "No! I won't do it! You can't make me do this. You may as well kill me right now cause I ain't fuckin doin it." Then he took off running down the long hall.

His captors watched, half amused, as he tried the bedroom doors, yanking at the handles and slamming into the heavy doors with his good shoulder. They were all locked. Every room except the bathroom. He ran inside and locked the door behind him. Surprised they didn't give chase, he yelled, "You motherfuckers may as well kill me now cause I ain't fuckin doin it!"

Rob bit his bottom lip. He was just itching to put a hot one in Ray's ass. But he had orders. Giovanni sucked his teeth, tired of fuckin around. He pushed his gun back into his waistband and handed Rob the envelope. Rob knelt and pushed it under the bathroom door.

Ray broke the seal and pulled the contents of the envelope. His eyes welled and soon the tears rolled in a steady stream before they fell to the marble tile below him. One by one, he pulled out photographs of the people he loved most. Ray Jr., 7 years old, sitting on his bike, the spitting image of his father. Little Gabriella, 4 years old, in pigtails holding Penny, a beautiful brown doll fashioned in her image, a birthday gift from daddy. Ray's parents sitting in their old fishing boat on the lake behind their home. And last there was a picture of Missy lying on the beach in a string bikini.

Ray opened the bathroom door and slowly stepped out. He whimpered and he sobbed. Giovanni was unmoved by his tears. It was time to get it over with. He had places to be. "Bottom line my fidend. You die. Or eveddyone dies. It is your'd choice." He lifted his arm and pulled back the sleeve of his jacket to check his watch. "I will givva you a second to think about."

Ray took that second. He looked over at Rob who was standing close, still clasping his gun. Still mean muggin. Just looking for a reason to take him down so he could make his way to his family. Ray shuddered at the thought. His family. His innocent children. His parents. They didn't deserve to die at the hands of animals because of his mistakes. Even Missy. He couldn't let them go down.

He willed himself over to the bannister, legs trembling, palms sweating, trying to swallow down the bile that had risen to his throat. He reached down and pulled the rope up, his stomach churned. He held the thick noose in his hand. Once more he turned to look at his executioners. They stood behind him, stone-faced.

Ray pulled the noose over his head and took a deep breath, just before throwing up at Rob's feet.

"Ahhh shit! My fuckin shoes! You muthafu…I should– "

"Aye!" Giovanni yelled. "We do not havva the time for this. Ray. Do not make me ask you again. Your'd family depends on this. Come on. Let's go."

"Yeah let's go nigga." Rob snarled as he wiped the side of his shoe on Ray's pant leg. "Get yo ass up."

Ray wiped his mouth with his sleeve and slowly pulled himself back up to the railing. He held on to it tightly with both hands, rocking back and forth and crying. Trying to work up the nerve. He could feel their eyes at the back of his head; hear their heavy, impatient sighs as he ever so slowly lifted a leg up and over the railing. He looked down at the floor beneath.

Suddenly he thought, what if the rope gave way? He'd hit that marble table and then the hard marble floor. What if he didn't die? He pictured Rob and Giovanni looking down at him, laughing at the bloody disfigured mess. They'd probably shoot him anyway. To finish the job. No. He couldn't do it. He'd rather be shot. He turned around, "Listen Gi…". Before he could gather his next thought, Rob shoved him over the edge.

I'm Coming Home

After a failed attempt to retrieve her children from Missy's house, Brenda's homecoming was becoming quite the disappointment. Eager to put a smile on her face, David made a couple quick calls and instead of heading home he decided to take her on an impromptu, parole compliant honeymoon weekend.

They newlyweds spent two glorious days and nights at The Lands. A plush five-star resort and spa in a wealthy suburb of Washington, DC. Two days of couples massages, meals prepared by world renowned chefs, long romantic walks around the beautifully landscaped compound. They laid poolside sipping exotic cocktails and soaking in the first warm rays of the summer season. It was just what Brenda needed to cleanse the jail from her psyche.

After a decadent champagne brunch, and one last dip in the dreamy lagoon style swimming oasis, the happy couple packed it in and hit the highway. Headed home.

Brenda's first time driving up and into a gated community was an experience. Security greeted them with a smile. "Good afternoon Mr. and Mrs. Cohen." She smiled. It was the first time someone had referred to her by her new married name. It felt strange, but good.

Brenda could hardly contain her excitement, as they pulled into the circular driveway and parked in front of the four car garage. Dave hopped out and walked over to open her door. "My lady." She stepped out of the car, removed her sunglasses and looked up at what was easily the most magnificent home she'd ever seen outside of a television set.

She turned to David. "Is...is this our house?"

He smiled. "Yes, it's our house."

"The whole thing?"

He laughed. "Yes, baby the whole thing. Come on."

He took her hand and led her over to a short brick staircase between two vast white columns. Brenda stood behind him, anxiously waiting as Dave pulled a single key from his jacket pocket and slid it inside the lock. He pushed open the front door and hoisted her up into his arms, which made her a little uncomfortable, considering she was just about twice his size, but it was nice. He carried her over the threshold and eased her back onto her feet. "Welcome home, Mrs. Cohen."

There was no concealing the joy she felt when she looked up at high vaulted ceilings and around at twelve thousand square feet of empty space. She wrapped her arms tightly around his neck and kissed him softly on the lips. "I love you sooooooo much."

David returned the soft smooch and smiled. "I love you more. Now come on and let me show you the rest of the house."

They explored every inch of the home. It was massive, unfurnished and screaming for Brenda's decorating flair – six large bedrooms, five baths, and an enormous basement with a state of the art theater room and wet bar. The kitchen was what she was most impressed with: Italian marble countertops and modern stainless steel fixtures; two sub-zero refrigerators that were already stocked; a double Viking range with professional grade cookware hanging overhead. She couldn't wait to get some of those fancy pots and pans moving on that stove.

Glass collapsible doors in the living room opened to the most fabulous backyard retreat. To the right, a stone pavilion shielding a full outdoor kitchen with bar seating and a fireplace for cozy entertaining. Ahead, a glass tiled illusion pool overlooking three acres of immaculately landscaped greenery and blooming gardens.

"Dave?"

"Yes."

"This is amazing."

He smiled, knowing he'd saved the very best for last. He

took her hand and led her up the winding staircase, down the long hall and into the most magnificent, most luxurious room in the house. The master suite. It was the only furnished room in the house. Brenda gasped when Dave opened the double doors.

The room was illuminated by the flickering light and glimmering reflections from an elaborate crystal chandelier that hung at its center. Beneath the lighting, a king-size four poster bed, beautifully dressed in her favorite royal purple silk, to match draperies that hung from floor to ceiling windows on either side of the room. Off to her left was a huge walk in master closet and to her right the master his and her bath.

Brenda stood in awe. She walked over to the bed and ran her hand across the plush duvet. "This is...like..fit for royalty or something."

Dave walked up behind her and kissed her on the back of the neck. "Exactly. For a queen." He pulled her around to him and planted one on her lips. "Now, can I have you?"

Brenda had managed to stave him off the entire honeymoon weekend. She told him that she didn't want their first time to be in a strange hotel room, she wanted to make love for the first time in their marital bed. Good one. But bullshit. She was just too afraid to be with him.

Kissing and necking in the visiting hall of the Fluvanna State prison was titillating and exciting, but being with him? *Really* being with him? That was something entirely different. She'd only been with one man her entire life and the thought of getting to know another – in *that* way – scarifying. She needed a minute.

She gently nudged him away as she thought on a response. "Babe. I'm kinda sweaty. Do you mind if I take a shower first?"

Dave was only mildly disappointed. As bad as he wanted to push her down on that bed, to finally ravage her sexy, voluptuous, BBW curves...as badly as he wanted to sample her sweet nectar, they were home now. There was plenty of time for that. And the waiting heightened the excitement a bit, so he pulled back and smiled. "Of course. You'll find everything you need in the bath. I'm going downstairs to get dinner started."

"Dinner? You're cooking?"

"Something like that." He pecked her softly on the lips and retreated from the room.

Brenda thought of the one time she let Melvin make a meal. The house smelled of burned chicken grease and bad cabbage for days. But she'd gladly consume whatever Dave had on the menu, if it bought her more time.

When Dave left the room Brenda breathed a heavy, albeit temporary sigh of relief. She knew there was only a matter of time, probably minutes before he'd be back at her. Grabbing at her, kissing on her. Sending surges through her in places no man but Melvin had ever had pleasure of. She was unnerved. Unsettled….unsure.

She enjoyed every single kiss; relished in every second of his touch. That is…until it was over. Then the guilt set in. Somehow she felt she was betraying Melvin with every indulgence. She knew in her mind that was ridiculous, David was her husband after all, but her heart hadn't caught up to her head yet, and for a moment she was sad.

There she was, posted up in a mini mansion, riding shotgun in a new convertible S Class Mercedes with more money at her disposal than she'd ever had. Well…legit money. And all she could think of was her late husband. This was the dream he'd promised her. It was the life he wanted her to have. Having it now was incredibly bitter sweet.

She loved Dave. There was no question about it. But it was different. Very different. David was her knight in shining armor, but Melvin was the love of her life. She tried to put Melvin out of her mind and focus on the husband at hand. It was only right.

She walked into the closet and stood undressing in the full length mirror. Examining every curve. She suddenly felt fat, although she was at least 30 pounds lighter than she was when David first professed his love for her curves. In fact, he'd mentioned on several occasions that she was losing too much weight, and he couldn't wait to get her home to fatten her up. Still, *err* body knew white boys like em pale and thin as a rail. So she'd tried her best to get in shape before she came home to him.

She stepped into the shower and turned it on. The force

from the raining showerhead above was so strong it nearly ruined her freshly coifed curls. She jumped out and away, shaking her head vigorously so that her entire head wouldn't absorb the water. She checked the drawers, no shower cap, a huge problem. So she wrapped her head in a towel and figured out how to work the front facing shower head and stand at an angle that didn't eviscerate her entire salon experience.

After lathering with a heavenly scented soap from an automatic dispenser, she took the cover off her razor and went to work. She had more than her share of peach fuzz north of her ankles and since err body knew white boys like em hairless and careless, it would be a little while before she was honeymoon ready.

Over the shins and up the thighs, she glided the blades until she was baby bottom smooth. Just as she neared the crease of her inner thigh, David called out to her from the doorway, "Don't you dare."

Startled, Brenda dropped the razor on the floor. She stood there naked, feeling more exposed than she ever had. She crossed her arms to her chest, barely covering nipples on her ample triple D bosom. "David. You could have knocked, you scared me."

He smiled, "So I have to knock to come into my own bathroom? With my own wife?"

Just then Brenda realized how silly she must have sounded. She *was* his wife. It was time to get over herself. Seriously. But she'd never been naked in front of another man. Not one without a stethoscope and a PhD. It was incredibly awkward.

Dave undressed slowly, down to his bare ass. He stood for a moment, staring at his new bride. As happy and as horny as he'd ever been. Fully erect. Drinking her completely in. He moved toward her, and as he approached Brenda was filled with an interesting mix of dread, shame, excitement and surprise. She couldn't help thinking, *Oh, shit it's big. Err body got that one wrong.*

He pulled the shower head from the wall and rinsed the suds from her body. Starting at her shoulders, then down her back and over her legs. He gently pulled her arms away from her chest and washed the suds away, down her torso and over her thighs. Then he parted her legs with one of his, and turned the showerhead upward into her most tender places.

She flinched when the force of the water hit her spot. He let the water jets linger for a while before he backed her into the cold stone tile, dropped the showerhead to the ground and knelt in front of her. Seconds later as she took in two fists full of his soft black hair she thought, *ooh, yesss, they got this one right*.

After a while...a good while...Brenda's moans intensified and Dave sensed she was near climax so he stopped abruptly and pulled himself back up. Before she could protest, he hushed her with a kiss and hoisted her up on the wall. He pulled her down onto him. Despite the wetness, there was considerable tightness, a feeling he hadn't experienced in some time.

He pulled back and pushed forward gently, slowly, going in just a little deeper. She whispered, "Wait."

He pushed her forward slightly as he pulled away. "Do you want me to stop?"

"God no."

He grinned and then he kissed her, giving her his tongue as a subtle distraction, as he grabbed her hips and pulled her back onto him.

Brenda gasped as her sweet fortress was finally breached and she received him fully. Nothing outside a specula had been inside her body for over three years, and until that moment she didn't realize how much she'd missed sex.

He held her by the waist, as he began to bounce her up and down, slowly and rhythmically; getting more and more turned on by the sweet slapping sounds of their wet flesh. Dave never missed a bounce or a beat as he walked her out of the shower and into the bedroom.

He laid her down on the bed and pushed her legs back. Then he put one arm on the bed for more leverage, as he entered her again. Again she gasped and then whispered, "I love you."

He made long slow strokes inside her, in every direction hitting every spot. Nothing like the fast and furious pounding she'd seen the white guys do to the white girls in the movies.

Amazing.

He turned her over onto her stomach, and he sighed. "Damn."

She looked back at him over her shoulder. "What? What's wrong?"

"Your ass."

"What's wrong with my ass?" She panicked.

"Nothing's wrong. Baby. I love your ass." He took a cheek in each hand and shook it hard. "I fuckin LOVE your ASS!" He growled as it wiggled and jiggled, then he buried his face into it. She squealed, as he tickled her senses with his lithe fingers and long hot tongue. He pleasured her for a few minutes with his tongue before he rose and entered her again.

In and out he thrust and pulled as her fleshy backside bounced up and down, turning him on more and more. He reached around her waist and down into her soft mound. Massaging her gently with his forefinger and thumb as he penetrated her deeper from behind.

He moaned, "Ummm. Brenda."

"Yes baby?"

"I love you."

"I love you, too."

He pushed deeper. "You love me?"

She gripped the sheets in both hands and pulled at them with every thrust. "God yessss. Yes, baby. I love you so much."

He began to pump harder and faster. The pounding she'd seen in the movies. But it was good. Really good. It turned her on. She could feel him pulsating, which caused an even more intense sensation inside of her.

She moaned. "Babe, I think I'm about to cum."

Dave grabbed onto her shoulders as he pumped away. "Yeah, baby I'm about to cum."

"No! I'm gonna cum."

"Yeah, I'm cumming! Oh shit I'm cumming!"

He held onto her tightly. Their moans meshed, and they came to a near simultaneous climax.

Brenda stared back at him, in complete awe. He was not

what she expected…at all. She thought, *oh my God, I love himmm!* David looked up at her lovingly as he laid on her back still panting and waiting for the tingles in his groin and the weakness in his legs to subside. He bit her lightly on the shoulder, "Girl… I knew you'd be good. And sweet. I fuckin love you, you know that?"

She turned to face him and they kissed. Sweet soft kisses of consummation. Gone were the guilty feelings about Melvin. Brenda just wanted to be loved and so far David was doing a bang up job at it.

He gave her one last kiss before sliding off of her and into the closet. He walked back over to her with two plush terry bathrobes. "Here, put this on. I have a little surprise for you downstairs."

She cooed. "Ooh I love surprises."

They walked down the stairs hand in hand. Brenda's nostrils were accosted by a most familiar, most heavenly scent. She smiled wide as Dave led her into the kitchen and pulled out her stool at the far end of the island. He took his seat at the other. The table was covered with brown paper and a small ice bucket at either end with three bottles of ice cold imported beer. In the middle was a large round wooden crate with exactly what she'd been waiting for, for three long years.

She couldn't believe he remembered. Jumbo, extra seasoning and extra hot. Apparently Joe's Crab Shack delivered. Brenda was in sheer bliss. And that's just where she intended to take her new husband to…but later.

The Shake Down

The accounts were getting low. Lower than they'd been since her first few years out of college. Now she was eating into her savings. The money her estranged father left in the will. It wouldn't be long until it was gone. All of it. Because it still wasn't enough to pay her debt.

The greedy little Italian man demanded one hundred thousand dollars. On that day. And a hundred, $100 bills on the first of each month, until Ray's debt was paid. He introduced himself as Little Gi and nodded to his associate, Big Rob, an imposing mammoth of a man with a creepy smirk that made her skin crawl. When he informed her that she was still responsible for her late husband's gambling debts to his late father Giovanni, Missy was stunned.

At first she laughed at his proposal. "Are you kidding me? My husband – and believe me, I use that term very loosely – is dead. I have absolutely nothing to do with his debt or any arrangement he had with you or your father. So if that's all…" She rose from her seat to show the silly, greasy little man the door, but he didn't budge. Instead he pulled a manila envelope from his jacket pocket and tore into its seal. Then he laid out several photographs on the coffee table.

The first photo was of Brandy, Missy's nineteen-year old niece and adopted daughter, walking to class at the Georgetown campus. Next was Mandy, her eight-year old niece (also adopted when their mother, Brenda, Missy's sister was so unfortunate to be sentenced to prison) at soccer practice at her boarding school. The last photo was of Misa, Missy's beautiful three-year old baby grand-niece that she adopted from Brandy soon after her birth.

Gi gave an intimate and very disturbing account of what

he'd do to each of her girls if the money was not received on time and if she attempted to engage law enforcement of any kind. And so, like clockwork, every first of every month Missy drove to a little Bodega in Old Towne Virginia and pushed a thick envelope through a mail slot at the back door.

Several months had passed since that fateful meeting and bills were piling up left and right. The mortgage, the credit cards, the leases on the office space and the cars. Both Mandy and Brandy's tuition. All past due. Her weekly massages, hair and nail appointments, retail therapy sessions, were all a thing of the past. She was near survival mode.

After the extortion payment, there was just enough money left to pay the bills at the house and for one of the cars. The others would have to go back to the dealership. She was two months behind on Mandy's tuition, and they'd already threatened to cancel her enrollment. Brandy's college tuition was coming due. Even with the scholarship, tuition at Georgetown was steep.

Before her hardships, Missy couldn't remember the last time she'd balanced a checkbook, checked a bank statement, or even looked at a receipt, but these days she was scrimping and penny pinching within an inch of her life.

Business had been slow the last couple of quarters, and she suspected Matt was doing his own thing on the side. She'd lost several major clients in as many months without notice or cause, and a bankruptcy filing was likely, if not inevitable.

With no reprieve in sight, Missy knew the smart thing to do was sell the house. Sell and move back into her rental property in DC. It wasn't an ideal situation, but she could make a few bucks on the sale and there was enough room at the DC apartment for the girls. The property was in Adams Morgan, a good neighborhood, close enough to good schools. It was the only play. The only thing that made sense. But she still wasn't ready. Not just yet.

The doorbell rang, breaking Missy from her worrisome thoughts. She wiped her hands with a kitchen towel and walked into to the foyer. She peered out of the window and squealed before snatching the front door open.

"Brandy! What are you doing here? I thought you weren't coming home until next week? How'd you get here?"

Brandy stood in the doorway, stunning but breezy in a long white tank dress and sky high espadrilles from the latest Louboutin collection, her long bright red wavy hair cascading down the front into her cleavage. She struggled with several large shopping bags. "I decided to come back a little early since my roommate was leaving earlier. Didn't really want to fly back home alone. I took a taxi from the airport."

The cab driver walked up the driveway carrying more shopping bags and one of the large vintage suitcases Missy loaned her for her trip.

Missy took a few shopping bags off Brandy's hands. "Did they let you exchange your ticket?"

"No. I had to buy another ticket. Do you know they charged me full price? Thirteen hundred dollars. Crazy."

Missy nearly gasped at the thought. The girl had just wasted over $2000 on airline tickets. "Brandy, you really should have called me before you did that. And when did you go shopping?"

"Oh. I stopped off at Tysons Corner on the way back."

"Girl, you flew into Baltimore, that is *not* on your way back."

"Well…not really but kinda. The cabbie didn't mind waiting for me outside. Can you pay him? He said he'd a take credit card. Mine's maxed."

"Maxed? Brandy, I gave you that card for emergencies. There's a $10,000 limit!"

"I know but after the airport lost my luggage…"

"Your luggage?! My Louis Vuitton! Brandy that luggage is priceless. I told you not to…"

"I know Aunt Missy, I'm so sorry. But it wasn't my fault. I didn't have time to send it ahead and they wouldn't let me carry it on the plane with all my other stuff. I filed a claim. They said they'll reimburse you for it."

Missy's nostrils flared. That luggage was her first luxury purchase. It cost her nearly two month's pay. Brandy begged and pleaded to use it and promised she'd ship it ahead so she wouldn't have to travel with it. The girl was way too spoiled for her own good. In trying to give her "the best," Missy has created a credit card-wielding, label-whoring monster, and she had no idea how she was gonna reign her back in. But considering her current financial condition, she'd have to try.

After the testy cabbie swiped Missy's Amex for the $170 fare, Missy slammed the door shut. "OK, Brandy. You and I need to have a talk."

Brandy noted the serious tone and frowned. Not in the mood for it. "Auntieeeee, can it wait? I'm so tired. And hungry. It smells good in here. What's cooking?" She walked into the kitchen.

Missy followed. "No, actually it can't wait. I need to tell you…"

"Ooh!" Brandy squealed. "You made gumbo?! I haven't had this in so loooong." She pulled the lid off of a stock pot of seafood gumbo and took in the aroma. "Is it almost ready?"

"Almost. Have a seat."

"Umh! I can't wait!" Brandy picked up the glass of champagne sitting on the counter and took a sip. "Umh. This is good. You should put a little orange juice in it, though."

Missy snatched the glass away from her. "Girl! Give me that! What is wrong with you?"

Brandy scowled. "You do realize I've been drinking mimosas like all summer long. The legal drinking age in Europe is eighteen, thank-you-very-much."

"Yeah well welcome back to America. Where you need to be twenty-one to sip with me. So how was your trip?"

"It was nice. I worked a lot so I didn't get out as much as I wanted, but we got some partying time in."

"I'm not talkin about partying, Brandy. Did you get to see the sights? Did you go to any of the places on the list we talked about? How was your host family? Let me see your pictures? And why haven't you been calling me?"

"Dang auntie. One question at a time. I need to charge my phone first. My host family was nice. I kinda got the impression they've never really been around black people."

"Why do you say that?"

"Nothing specific, really. It's just a feeling. They were really nice and pleasant. They just asked a lot of *culturally specific* questions. Seemed borderline fascinated with me, you know."

"Yes, trust me, I know. Anybody touch your hair?"

"You know they did. The mother. Real sneaky like, too." They laughed. "But other than that, it was all good. Between work and my friends, I wasn't there that much anyway. When did Elizabeth leave?"

"This morning."

"How was she?"

"Fine. Quiet. She spent most of her time working, with her friends and family here. We didn't spend that much time together but I thought she was a nice enough girl. It was nice to have a reason to use my French. You really should learn Brandy. I keep telling you that."

"I speaky the Española. That is enough."

"Cualquier chica."

Brandy laughed. "Si." She perched herself up on a stool at the island in front of Missy's laptop. "What's this? You're on Tinder?"

"No. Not really. Carmen set up that profile. I have no interest in Internet dating. Bunch of desperate women and horny men telling a bunch of lies. No thank you."

"Why not? I know you need some by now."

Missy frowned. "Little girl. I hope you don't think I'm about to sit here with you and discuss my *needs*. Don't *you* worry about my needs. I'm fine."

"Umh hmm. I'm just saying. You look a little wound up. Maybe you could use someone to *unwind* you." She held out her arms and gyrated on her stool. A little too well for Missy's taste.

"Brandy, cut it out."

"Ok, ok."

"Actually Carmen did approach me with another idea for a reality show. She seems to think finding me a man would make for interesting television."

Brandy squealed. "Ooh! *Black Love*?! That's my SHOW! Oh

you gotta do it, Auntie!"

"Child, please."

"Why not?"

"Because I'm not crazy."

"What's crazy about it? You get on TV. You get *crazy* paid, and you might even get you a man outta the deal. Hmm. Sounds like a win win to me."

"Well, we could use the money. That's for sure." Missy suddenly realized she was thinking out loud.

Brandy looked at her, puzzled. "We need money?"

Missy noted the worry on her baby girl's face and decided it wasn't quite the time to break the news. "Oh, no. No. I just meant…it would be good to put a little more away for a rainy day. You know how I am about savings."

"Yes, unfortunately I do. Well my vote is for *Black Love*. They be havin some fine brothas on *there*. Here look." Brandy pulled up the website and scrolled through the last season's contestants. Sexy chocolate masculinity in every shade. "Look, they even let a white boy in last season." She maximized a pic of a scruffy thirty something white guy who closely resembled Bradley Cooper. Missy's favorite mister from the "flipside."

Missy smiled wide and mumbled, "Now that is some sexy white chocolate right there. Might make a sistah wanna switch sides"

Amused, Brandy hollered. "Ahhhhh! I know that's right, Auntie. Get down with that *swirl girl*! Seriously though, you should do this. At least give it some thought. You never know. What do you have to lose."

Missy grunted. "Hmm, Nothing much. Just my dignity. Self-respect. My good name…"

"Auntee…"

"I'm serious. After that mess Carmen pulled with Aunt Pat and PJ, I don't know if I can trust her with my life on television."

Brandy laughed. "Well I don't blame you because that *was* a flaming hot mess. Carmen is a flaming hot mess. How are you even still friends with her?"

"Why do you say that?"

"Because you always tell me how you don't do drama and how everybody is not my friend. Carmen is nothing BUT drama and she hasn't exactly been the best friend to you over the years. Your words, not mine. You might wanna start takin your own advice. That lady is not your friend. Everybody sees it."

"Who's everybody?"

"Ev-er-y-bo-dy. Me, Aunt Pat, PJ. Anybody who's got eyes. You buy a new car, she gets a new car. You move to Great Falls she moves to Great Falls. Now she dyed her hair blonde. Everything is a competition with her. Always has been, You've said it yourself. She's phony and she's a slick talker. I still can't believe she talked Aunt Pat into doing that show. PJ I get, but Aunt Pat?"

"Yeah, I know. I'm still confused about that one."

"I'm surprised she still has her job. Double the damn rainbow. She could have got somebody killed with that."

"Stop cursing girl."

"I'm sorry, I just don't like the chic."

"Well you don't have to like the chic. She's not your friend."

"She ain't yours either."

"Brandy…lay off. Carmen and I have been friends since we were kids. She's been there for me through everything. The good, bad and all of the ugliness. She's not perfect but—"

Brandy interrupted. "Anywaaay, back to Black Love. I really think you should do it. I know you don't care for reality TV, but this show is way different. I mean don't get me wrong, there's drama. I think there always has to be drama to keep people watching, but it's not your typical reality show with all the fighting and cursing and foolishness." She laughed. "Now that I think about it, that's probably why nobody watched it last season but me."

"Reality TV is reality TV. It's all a bunch of foolishness if you ask me. I'll pass."

"Ok, suit yourself. I'm going up to take a shower and unpack. I'll be back down in a little bit." She hopped down off of the high stool. "Oh, what did you need to talk to me about?"

"Nothing. It's not important. Go up and get yourself

squared away. Dinner'll be ready in a few."

"Ok." Brandy kissed Missy on the cheek, stole another sip of champagne, and ran up the stairs before Missy could whack her on the behind with her towel. Missy smiled, as she watched her beautiful little daughter-niece skip happily up the stairs with at least a mortgage worth of shopping bags in her arms. *Brat.*

She couldn't help marveling at how far her baby girl had come and how well she was doing in just a couple years. After Brenda went to jail, Brandy's spirit was completely broken. When Misa was born, she fell into an even deeper depression. It took a lot of time and love and a lot of therapy, mostly retail, to bring her out of her sadness, but she'd blossomed into a strong, beautiful and mature young woman with so much love and light, despite the horrible things she'd endured.

Missy thought that taking Misa and raising her as her own was the absolute right thing to do. It was best for everyone. Brandy didn't miss a beat. She finished high school at Missy's alma mater, Georgetown Day School, and was doing excellent at the university. She'd just completed a European exchange program and a summer internship in France. Everything was all right…almost.

The rice just needed to simmer a few more minutes, and dinner would be ready. Missy poured another flute full of champagne and walked back over to her laptop to finish scanning the website.

Brandy was 100% correct on two things. Those men *were fine*…and she needed some. Bad. It had been many moons since she had gotten some. Well…something *good* and she'd become way, *way* too familiar with her showerhead as of late. Something had to give. Then there was the money. It was way less than she would have imagined for TV, but everything could be negotiated. So she grabbed her cell and made the call. Just to hear Carmen out. What could it hurt.

Double the Rainbow

The first wedding season post passing of the gay marriage bill, Pat squared was still going strong with Ahmed, the pot-bellied Persian and Consuela, the Mexican mamacita. Carmen, anxious to pitch the next greatest reality show to her bosses, threw out an idea – an elaborate, gay, double church wedding ceremony on live national television. Ratings gold!

Carmen, Missy's BFF had been an associate producer at BET Studios for nearly 10 years, but it wasn't until she pitched this reality show did the executives take notice.

The new show would be called *Double the Rainbow*. Six episodes leading up to the over the top double gay wedding involving a mother and son. The mother, a lesbian ex-con rumored to be one of the biggest gangsters the city has ever known, was marrying her former cell mate who happened to be the daughter of an alleged member of a Mexican drug cartel. The son was a fabulously fly transgender male who owned a hip DC hair salon financed by his fiancé, a successful Persian businessman whose sexuality had caused a major uproar in his community.

The show was dynamic, on trend with current events, and completely ripe for controversy. It was sure to a be a sensation. The network execs were all in and as soon as she got the green light Carmen ventured into the hood looking for Aunt Pat and PJ to get them on board.

PJ's eyes were all aglitter while Aunt Pat's impassioned expletive laced decline was a mere starting point for the negotiation in Carmen's eyes. She was going to get them on that show. Hook or crook.

She offered money. *No!* She came back the next day with an

offer for more money. *Fuck no!* On the third attempt she doubled the second offer, added a production credit and limited editing privileges…to which a very frustrated Aunt Pat replied, through clenched teeth. "Carmen if you don't get the fuck out my face with that shit!" Carmen quickly retreated. Back to her drawing board.

She spent days trying to figure out what it would take to get Aunt Pat in the game. It wasn't until she promised PJ a pitch meeting with the execs for his very own show that she got the greenlight on hers. Somehow PJ had convinced his mother and Double the Rainbow was a go.

*****

Aunt Pat grew more and more on edge with each day of taping. The cameramen were pushy *and* nosy. She had no privacy. They were nipping at her heels with microphones and subtle direction from the time she woke up to the time she pulled the covers back over her head. She could barely take a piss without a chaperone.

If it weren't for PJ and his reality star aspirations- and the subtle guilt trip he laid on her- she would have told Carmen just what she could do with those got-damn cameras. Two days of constant whining and reasoning had broken her down.

PJ pleaded, "Maaaaa! I'm trending on social media right now! My Snapchat is lit and my You Tube tutorials have gone viral! Freakin Rihanna just retweeted my post! Ma! We gotta strike while the iron's hot!"

Aunt Pat had no clue what any of that meant, but she could see it was important to him. So she signed on for something she had no idea would bring her business to a near standstill.

No one would come within a mile of the television cameras following her. They wouldn't even talk on the phone. So money was hangin out on the streets. She couldn't collect and she couldn't conduct. Not the girls, the guns, the dope. Too much exposure. The only legit business she was able to conduct herself, was the bar and that was the least lucrative business in her crooked enterprise.

Three weeks before the wedding, she was a nervous wreck. She couldn't wait to get the shit over with. So she could get back to business. Consuela was behaving strangely, buggin about her wedding gown and her newly dyed blonde hair, which was more orange than blonde thanks to a bad drugstore coloring kit.

PJ's husband-to-be was doling out unwelcomed fashion tips. He'd sent Aunt Pat several suits from his personal stylist, and she promptly called PJ to come over and pick them up. "You tell that fat towel head muthafucka I already know how to dress myself," she said. "And if he send me another muthafuckin suit, they gon bury *his* ass in it."

PJ responded with a "Dang ma, it is so not that serious. He was just trying to help. I'll just take em back."

The truth was, Aunt Pat was terrified of what was about to go down. Beside the fact that it would play out on live national television, it would be her third marriage. She'd sworn years ago that she'd never marry again. Marriage changed everything. Both times before, she thought she'd married her best friend, and it all went to shit. Fast. And both times it ended in tragedy. She was cursed.

She and Consuela were in a perfect place with each other. Consuela didn't ask too many questions. She cooked and cleaned and took care of the house. The sex was still good. She never asked for anything except more time. And Aunt Pat gave it to her, whenever she could. Everything was good. Better than good. And Pat just knew that as soon a she put a ring on it, for the whole world to see, everything would change. She had bad vibes about the whole thing.

PJ, on the other hand, was over the moon. His final fitting was in a week, and ever since Bruce the Olympian turned trans, everyone was suddenly and very specifically in the transgender business. Now all of the major fashion houses, the cosmetic and hair care conglomerates were on board with the new revolution, and thanks to some top notch promotion from the network, "Miss P" was in very high demand.

When news of the show was "leaked," the House of Versace

reached out to PJ personally to custom make his gown. MAC, L'Oréal, Revlon and even Cover Girl were clamoring for sponsorship and to do PJ's makeup for the wedding. L'Oréal offered to do a limited release makeup line in his honor.

PJ couldn't have been happier with his newfound fame…and money. No more hustling luxury goods or trolling for sugar daddies on The Hill, he was about to be a star! They hadn't even finished filming and were already in negotiation for PJ's spin off reality show, *Miss P's World*. Six episodes of highly orchestrated drama and celebrity cameos in his downtown DC beauty salon. It was all so exciting!

The day of the wedding…the grooms were impeccably dressed in custom Ceruti and Hugo Boss tuxedos. Consuela's over-the-top ruffle laden gown was done by a Mexican designer who had just won a reality show design contest, and PJ…well, PJ was very clearly intended to be the star of the show.

PJ's one-of-a-kind creation of Chantilly lace, silk taffeta and Swarovski crystals took twelve of Versace's best seamstresses in Milan a total of 200 hours to make, and it weighed in at whopping 53 pounds. It put Missy's wedding gown to complete shame. A very important note.

The wedding ceremony was held in one of the biggest gay-friendly churches in the Dupont Circle neighborhood of DC, officiated by Pastor Jackson, a highly controversial transgender minister that frequently trended on social media for her outrageous commentary as well as her outfits.

The wedding party and the guests were mostly other reality stars and there was endless rainbow themed décor throughout the church, from the flowers to draperies to the lighting. It was a complete and utter circus and the eclectic mix of parishioners loved every minute of it. The network predicted the ratings to break records. And they did. For more reasons that they'd hoped.

The grand entrances were made. First Ahmed in a well fitted conservative black tux and a freshly painted on hairline, then Aunt Pat in a white tux with a rainbow colored necktie and matching pocket square. Their respective groomsmen in matching ensembles took their places at the dual altars. The over the top bridesmaids followed, dancing in to Sylvester's cult hit *You Make Me Feel.* The cameras panned in on Aunt Pat just as she mouthed, *This is the gayest shit I ever seen.*

When their spectacle was done and the bridal parties were in place, the music stopped. The crowd was instructed to their feet and trumpets sounded from behind the massive double doors. Seconds later, the doors flung open and in marched a full ten-piece mariachi band in colorful garb playing a traditional Mexican wedding song. One by one the trumpeters and violinists and guitarists blew and strummed themselves down the aisle as a stodgy brown fellow in a sombrero and thick mustache sang operatic from behind a podium at the head of the church.

The music changed, upping the tempo, and Consuela – and all of her ruffles – meandered down the aisle, rolling her tongue and shimmying like Charro. The entire church joined in the fun, dancing and clapping her all the way down to the altar. *Buenos tiempos.*

Then, there was the moment of truth. The moment everyone was waiting for. The very first transgender bride to hit the television waves. Patrick James, aka PJ, aka Miss P, was a six-foot-three vision of loveliness, sparkling in bejeweled floor length couture and over a half million dollars in custom diamonds from Cheryl Jones of New York. His signature long locks snatched in an immaculate bun, his face beat within an inch of life and Fantasia sang acapella as he made his way to the alter wearing the fiercest resting bitch face for the photogs.

Miss Jackson began with a speech about unconditional love and acceptance. She quoted scriptures about love and judgment, some of the great speeches of our time, and ended with the sentiments of the White House. There wasn't a dry eye in the house.

Each couple recited their vows, all of which were prewritten, prearranged and preapproved by the show's producers. PJ's dramatic, tearful and colorful vow would provide sound bites for years to come.

Before pronouncing the couple's matrimony, Miss Jackson

made the obligatory call for objections.

"If anyone has any reason why this man and this man and this woman and this woman should not be joined together in matrimony…may you speak now…right now…or forever hold your peace."

The church was eerily quiet for over five hundred guests. The pause was unusually long, as if some sort of protest was anticipated. The double doors to the church sprang open, and there stood a tall, dark and gorgeous Mexican, later identified as Hector, Consuela's first husband and father of her five children – the husband who abandoned her and took her children when she was sentenced to seven years in prison for drug trafficking. He yelled, "I object!" in a thick accent.

The crowd turned and gasped, as he made his way down the long isle, swiftly and singing in Spanish, what would later be revealed as he and Consuela's wedding song.

Aunt Pat was looking at Consuela, who was looking at Hector with tearful eyes. PJ was looking at Aunt Pat, awaiting some sort of a signal. Ahmed was looking nervous because he knew something was about to go down. Something not good. Something he did not want to be a part of.

Hector stopped at the altar and reached out for Consuela's hand. She reached out to him, turning to Aunt Pat and before she could utter what was certain to be an apology for leaving her bride at the altar, PJ yelled, "Oh HELL no!" snatched her by the hair, and tossed her off the stage. Aunt Pat jumped down and grabbed Hector by his beautiful jet black hair and went to work on his face as Ahmed ran backstage to the dressing room for cover.

The wedding of the century was a complete and utter catastrophe. A brawl that pit bridesmaids against bridesmaids and groomsmen against groomsmen. Families ran from the audience to the stage to rescue their people as others ran for the door. Punches were thrown, a couple of knives were pulled, and one shot was fired into the air, shattering a skylight that rained down shards of stained glass into the church.

At the point the gun shot was heard, the live broadcast was

interrupted by the network. They quickly cut to commercial. The show was over. But it was only the beginning.

Familiar Faces

She saw him for the third time in a month, pulling his son out of his car seat and taking his little hand. Walking him across the street, up the staircase and into the Mt. Calvary Church's daycare facility. Yes, she watched every time. It was hard not to. But she took care not to be seen. As soon as the doors closed behind them she drove away.

Talib Jr. looked so much like Tay it made Brandy sad. Ever since that day she spotted him walking into the church, memories of the time they shared flooded her mind. The good and bad. From the day she punched him for grazing her on the behind, to the fiery birthday dinner that ultimately tore them apart. Nearly three years and countless meaningless affairs later, Brandy James was still undeniably in love with her first and only love.

The next morning, she found herself at the same spot. Parked across the street from the church. Waiting to catch a glimpse. One last glimpse of him and then she'd stop taking the drive, five miles out of her way to downtown.

She checked her watch. It was half past eight. He was late, and now so was she. Suddenly she felt foolish. Stalker-ish. She started the car and threw it in reverse, slamming into a car behind her. *Shit!*

A beautiful new seven series BMW, fresh with temporary registration tags was attempting to pull into the space behind her, as she was backing up. She put her car in park and grabbed the insurance card from the glove box. When she got out of the car, a young Trump-looking yuppie was already standing there fuming and surveying the damage to his new ride.

"You stupid bitch! Look what you did to my car!"

Brandy frowned, "Bitch? Who are you calling a bitch?!"

"Do we have a problem here?" Tay walked up behind the man and put a hand on his shoulder.

The man was startled and turned to him. "Dude, look at my car! She backed into my fuckin car! You saw it!"

"No, *dude*. What I saw was you pulling in and driving into *her* car."

The man pulled his cell phone. "Yeah well, we'll let the police decide."

"That's fine. You can give them your version, and *we* can tell him what *really* happened. It's up to you. Or you can go on about your business. Fix your car, and she'll fix hers. No harm, no foul."

Looking into Tay's eyes, the man sensed that going on about his business would be the safest course of action. So he turned and got back into his car. Tay turned to Brandy. "Are you all right?"

She nodded. Then he walked back over to the man who was sitting in his car, still fuming and waiting for them to step out of his way so he could leave. Tay reached into his car and grabbed him by his necktie, pulling his head outside the window. He whispered, "And don't you ever call a black woman a bitch. Do you understand me? *Dude?*"

The man nodded. "Yeah man."

Tay took Brandy's hand, and they stepped out of the way to let him pass. He peeled away quickly without looking back. They laughed.

Tay leaned against her car. "You know that was your fault, right?"

"I know. And I feel bad."

"Don't. He shouldn't have called you a bitch."

"No, he shouldn't have. Thanks for coming to my rescue."

"It was my pleasure. Although you're the last person that needs to be rescued."

"True that. One more bitch and I would have socked his ass in the face."

"Oh, believe me, I know. So…how long were you gonna

stalk me before you said hello?"

Brandy was caught off guard by the comment. She didn't have a comeback. "What?"

"What? You heard me. How many white Bentley coupes do you think there are in this neighborhood? I could spot you from a mile away, girl."

Brandy laughed. "Nobody's stalking you. I was just dropping my friend off at work."

"Oh yeah, what friend is that? I know everybody that works here."

"I don't have to explain myself to you."

"You're right. You don't."

"So where's your baby's mother?" Brandy regretted the question as soon as it hit the air.

Tay hesitated for a second. "I don't know. At home with her new baby I guess. I have custody of my son. Unofficially. He lives with me."

"Oh."

"Yeah but I wouldn't have it any other way. I love my little man."

"That's good. I always knew you'd make a good father." She felt herself getting a little emotional. "Well let me go. I'm already late for class."

"Oh, where are you in school?"

"Georgetown."

"Whoohoo. G'town. Somebody got some money."

"Shut up. I'm mostly on scholarships. It's still expensive, though."

"I'm sure." There was a second of awkward silence before Brandy decided to make her exit. "Well, Tay I really do have to go before I miss my first class. It was good to see you."

She turned and reached for her car door. He took her hand. "Wait. Can I call you sometime? This weekend?"

"I'm...I'm going out of town tomorrow and..."

"Brandy. Please."

She could see the desperation in his eyes. He missed her. And she missed him too, desperately. But too much had happened. Way too much to come back from. She thought, *why did I even come here?* "Tay. I'm sorry. I gotta go." She hurriedly jumped into her car and pulled away. In the rear view she could see him, still standing there in the parking space watching as she drove away.

She thought it was time to finally move on. Really move on. She saw him. They talked. She got what she needed. Closure.

Sick and Tied

David laid back with his arms outstretched as Brenda bounced up and down on him. looking back at him over her shoulder. The sight of her fleshy backside jumping and jiggling had him going, as usual. He didn't want it to end. He never wanted it to end, but her legs were beginning to cramp, so she decided to make it end.

She rested on her knees and slid slowly back upon him. He moaned as her warmth completely enveloped him. She bent over as far as she could. so he could see as much as he could as she slowly pulled herself up and thrust herself back down upon his manhood. She moaned. The moans were soft at first. Soft and sexy. Then they became louder and more intense. Dave was responding to the breathy sounds. Soon he started moving with her. Thrusting himself up when she came down. Grabbing her by the waist and squeezing it tight and he pushed and pulled her in the direction he desperately needed her to go. She could feel him pulsating inside her. It was time. She was ready. He thrust harder and a little faster. She felt the throb. He slowed the rhythm. "Damn baby. I could be inside you all day."

She rolled an eye. *Fuck*. Plan C. She cried out. "Ooh baby. Yes. Yes. Fuck me all day. I want you to fuck me all dayyyyy."

Dave perked up at the thought. He gripped her hips and thrust hard. "That's what you want? Huh baby?"

"Yess baby. That's what I want. Um hmm. Umh hmm. Yesss baby." She went on moaning and carrying on until she felt the "O" would be justified. "Wait. I'm cummin. Ahh baby I'm cummin...YESSSSSS!" Then she shuddered and fell limp on his legs. "That was so good."

"I know...why'd you stop? I was about to cum." She knew

that was a lie. He whined. "I wanna cum baby. Come here."

He slid his body out from under hers and crawled up behind her. Then he nudged her back down onto the bed, onto her stomach, and pushed himself back inside.

It's not like it didn't feel good to her. But after over an hour of holding her legs in positions they weren't meant to, and straddling him in a reverse cowgirl so he could get the view he wanted, she was tired and ready to stop. David was an animal, and he wanted it every day. E-ver-y sing-le day. And although the sex was amazing, and Dave made her feel like no one else could, he was kill-ing her.

Brenda was a happy homemaker, expected to perform her wifely duties at whim to compensate for her luxurious life as the wife of one of the most successful trial attorneys in the city. It was an unspoken rule. Every day, seven days a week, Dave wanted a healthy breakfast, a lengthy lay, and a gourmet meal on the table when he got home from work.

She obliged, happily in the beginning but after a few months the June Cleaver routine was starting to get old. She'd been doing that all her life, and as strangely as it sounded to every one she talked to about it, she wanted something more. But for the moment, all she wanted was her horny husband to hurry up and cum so he could roll the hell off of her.

So she started to gyrate her hips, grinding back on him hoping it would speed up his process. She pulled herself up to her knees and threw it back on him so strong that her big cocoa brown cheeks clapped together swallowing him up, pulling him into her and turning him on even more. Two minutes in, and they were moving rhythmically together. He lifted a leg and pulled her cheeks open, hitting a sensitive spot inside her, making her wet all over again. *Dammit.*

Brenda was back in the game, moaning and frowning and feeling the tingling sensation coming on. She looked back at David who was also frowning at her ass at it moved. "I fucking love this big ass!" He hit another spot. She was almost there. Then David shuddered, and it was over. *Damn!* she thought, he *would* cum now.

He laid on top of her back waiting for his tingles to subside. Then he kissed her softly on her back while he jiggled her booty with one hand. "So, what's for breakfast, baby?"

Brenda looked back at him. Mildly disgusted. He was barely out of her before he was putting in his breakfast order. "Um, can you give me a minute?" she said. "It's 7:30 on a Saturday morning." She pulled herself from underneath him and moved back to her side of the bed.

"Ooh was that an eye roll, sister girl?"

She turned to look at him and show him what a real eye roll was before she turned back over to face the wall."

"Ok…did I do something wrong?"

She sighed. "No. You didn't do anything."

"Ok, then what's wrong with you?"

She sat quietly for a moment before she answered. "I miss my kids, David. I mean I really miss my kids." She began to sob into her pillow.

He scooched over to her and rubbed her back. "I know you do, babe. I told you that we can take it back to court whenever you're ready. I never understood why you dropped the case in the first place. They're *your* children. Your sister has no right to keep them."

"I know. I think it's time now. I'm ready."

He kissed her on the shoulder. "Well then it's a done deal. We'll file the paperwork first thing on Monday." Then he slid out of bed and walked into bathroom.

Brenda laid for a moment, thinking about her children, of how wonderful it would be for them to come home. To have their laughter fill the big empty house. She missed them terribly. David yelled from the shower. "Babe! Do we have any fruit downstairs? You think you can whip up some crepes? I have to go into the office this morning, and I need to get a move on."

Annoyed, Brenda snatched her robe from a nearby armchair and threw it on. "Yeah." Then she headed downstairs to her duties. Slamming pots around she mumbled to herself, *Fuck him, feed him and see him off to his wonderful career while I sit home and twiddle my damn thumbs, just waiting for him to come home so we could do this shit all over again. I'm gettin real tired of this shit.*

"What was that babe?" Dave took his seat at the head of the table and waited to be served.

She sat his plate in front of him and swallowed her words. "Nuthin."

Black Love

Missy walked into the meeting with extreme trepidation. She wasn't sure about this reality show nonsense, especially after the *Double the Rainbow* fiasco. But she needed the money. They were offering her a low six figures for six weeks of taping and a two-part reunion special. Not a bad haul. Plus, Carmen had creative control and assured her that she wouldn't let her look crazy on TV. All things considered, she figured, she could at least hear their pitch.

For a BET production, the meeting was conspicuously white, which was more than a little bit bothersome, but Carmen was at the head of the table so that put Missy a little more at ease.

They went through their ideas for the show, most of which seemed to be the formula for every other dating show on television. A dozen men competing for one woman's affections with the winner riding off into the sunset with her. Cookie cutter love competition. But the producers insisted that there would be a twist that none of the contestants would expect. Not even Missy, the star of the show was privy until it was revealed on the first day of taping.

Pen and contract in hand, Missy was beginning to feel uneasy again. *A twist?* That didn't sit right with her at all. But those were the terms. Take them or leave them. And take them she would. She gave Carmen a very knowing, *you better not screw me* glare before she signed on the dotted line and snatched up the advance check. So it was a done deal. Production was to begin in a couple of weeks.

The next morning, Missy woke in a panic. *What the fuck have I done!* She dressed hurriedly and headed into DC to her attorney's office, unannounced. After he perused the contract and explained what she already knew, he laughed, suggested she figure out how to live with the choice she made, and advised her to never to bring him another contract she'd already signed.

Disappointed and somewhat embarrassed, she left Herbert Anderson Esq.'s office and headed over to the northeast quadrant of the city. Back to BET Studios.

"Is Carmen in?"

Carmen's assistant looked up from her personal call. "Yeah, she's in a meeting, but she should be out in a few minutes. You can wait in her office if you want."

"Thanks."

As she sat at the edge of the comfy armchair with a $5 latte in one hand and a $30,000 check in the other, Missy went over and over in her head what she could possible say to Carmen to get out of the foolishness she'd signed up for. She wanted out. Not now, but right now. It just wasn't worth it. Not even for the money.

Carmen walked in all smiles. "Hey gurrrl," she sang as she took her chair. "We were just meeting about you. What's going on?"

The fantastically logical and brilliantly persuasive speech Missy had just rehearsed went straight out the window. She threw the check on Carmen's desk. "I can't do this."

Carmen smiled, picked up the check and placed it back in front of her. "Girl bye." Then she turned to her computer, effectively dismissing her friend.

Missy's face was serious. She pushed the check back over to Carmen. "I'm serious. I can't do this. So you can take this check back. Do whatever you have to do. I don't care. But I'm not doing it."

Carmen sighed and turned back around. She pushed the check back over to Missy. "Girl, you better cash this damn check and get your mind right. You know you need this money. "

"You can't pay me enough money to make a fool of myself. Ruin my reputation and embarrass my family. A *second* time. So go back and tell your boss or whoever you need to tell, I'm not for sale." She flipped the check back over to Carmen. It landed on the floor.

"Really."

"Yes, really."

"Missy I don't have the time or the patience for your drama this morning. You signed a contract, and you accepted payment. It's a done deal. So I suggest you go have yourself a mimosa or a Xanax or whatever it is you think you need to do to get over your little nerves."

"Excuse me?!" Missy gave her friend a death glare. She'd recently shared that her doctor prescribed a low dose of Xanax for her anxiety attacks. But Missy was too nervous to take them. Carmen could be a little insensitive at times, borderline petty, but this was a particularly low blow. She snatched her purse from the desk and stood. "Goodbye Carmen."

"No wait! Ok, look. I'm sorry. Ok? I'm sorry." She reached over the desk for Missy's hand. "Come on. Sit back down. Please."

Missy took her seat, silently and reluctantly.

"Look I don't wanna fight with you. Seriously. You're just putting me in a bad spot, Missy. I need you to wrap your head around what's going on here. You can't just walk away. These guys have already spent tens of thousands of dollars on rentals and leases and pre-production. Things are already in motion."

"It's been like twenty-four hours."

"What can I say? Things move fast around here."

"Carmen please. I'm begging you. I don't wanna do this. Be a friend."

"What the hell do you think I'm doing? Why don't *you* be a friend!"

'Me?"

"Yes *you*. Missy I brought the show to the producers. Sold them on it. Negotiated a higher salary for you than anyone's ever gotten on this network. I fought like hell for the EP spot so that I could have creative control. You think I did all of that for me? And what happens when I go to them now and tell them that my best friend that I fought tooth and nail for is backing out of the deal with two weeks to production? What happens to me? After they sue your beautiful ass into bankruptcy for all the money they've spent, which they *will* do, what happens to me? My career? My reputation? Have you thought about that?"

Missy rolled her eyes and looked away. Truth was she hadn't thought about it. Would they really sue? Like really? The very last thing she needed in her life was to owe somebody else some money. And maybe she *was* being a little selfish. She could have just said no when Carmen asked her the first time. But the money sounded good. She knew that backing out now would be disastrous. But she just couldn't live with things as they were. "Ok. Now if I do this…"

"*When* you do this?

"*IF* I do this, I'm gonna need a few more things, just to get comfortable."

"A few things like what?"

"Well it ain't no Xanax."

Carmen laughed. "Ok, ok. Go head girl, I'm listening."

Idle Hands

"Can we talk?"

"Of course." Dave muttered as he shoved a piece of buttery corn muffin into his mouth. What's on your mind babe?"

"How's your food?"

"It's perfect, as always." He smiled. "The way to my heart."

Brenda smiled. "Good. How about your drink?"

"The drink is great. I love it when you experiment."

"Well that's what I wanted to talk to you about?"

"Drinks?"

"No…well yeah. I mean the whole thing. Everything. Food, drink. I wanna open a restaurant."

Dave nearly choked on his bread. He grabbed his water goblet and took a sip before clearing his throat. "A what?"

"Nothing big. Just a small little soul food spot. Somewhere in the city. I've done the research. I've crunched the numbers. Right now the restaurant market is –"

"Brenda, do you have any idea what it takes to run a restaurant?"

"No…but…"

"Exactly. I know you love to cook, but t's not just about cooking babe."

"I know that David." She threw her napkin on the table and huffed. "I'm not a complete idiot."

"No one said you were an idiot. But restaurants are a really fickle business. You can't just think –"

"I need something to do!"

"What?"

"I NEED something to do."

"You have plenty to do around here."

"Like what?"

"What do you mean like what? Are you kidding? Like taking care of this house. Like taking care of your husband."

"The house is immaculate, your meals are prepared, I show you affection whenever you ask and I still have…like a whole day to waste."

"So taking care of me is a waste?"

"You know that's not what I meant." She picked up her plate and walked to the kitchen. "I just need something for me."

Dave picked up his plate and followed her. "What do you mean something for you? Brenda I thought we agreed. You said you loved being a housewife."

"I do. I mean I did David…but…"

"Am I not enough for you? Is this not enough for you? I work hard everyday, sacrificing so I can give you the best life possible and –"

"That's just it! You work everyday. You have your practice. You went to college and law school and passed the bar. You're doing what you planned for in life. You're living your dream. And what do I have? Besides a busy husband and an empty house."

"I really can't believe what I'm hearing from you right now. I give you everything. Everything."

"And I appreciate everything you do, I promise you. I do. I don't take our life for granted. Dave, I love you and I'll always be here for you when you need me. I hope you know that. But this…" She waved her hands over the stove of pots and pans with the carefully prepared samples of what she planned to offer. "…this here is *my* dream."

He sighed. "Brenda…"

"Just think about it. Ok? Promise me that you'll think about it." She kissed him sofly on the lips and turned back to her pots. She bent over to pick up a towel that had fallen to the floor. Pink lace panties peeked out from the hem of her short dress.

She was barely upright before Dave pounced. He unzipped his pants, pulled her panties to the side and bent her over a bar stool. "I'd much rather be thinking about this."

The Diss-Connect

Aunt Pat was working overtime. Double time to get her mind off her troubles and to get back everything she'd lost. Fuckin with PJ and that wack ass reality show; trying to be a *good supportive* mother...he'd hit stardom, and she'd lost everything else that mattered in her life.

Consuela was gone. Gone back to her husband and children. Last she'd heard, they'd remarried and moved back to Brooklyn. She was also rumored to be eight months pregnant, which was interesting considering they'd only parted ways seven months before. So Pat was left alone and lonely, with a bunch of unanswered questions she'd probably never get answers to. That wasn't exactly PJ's fault, but opening herself up to get played on live national television was.

Even worse than that, or, at least equally as bad, she lost her main connect, the Peruvians. It took years to cultivate a relationship with her Peruvian connection and just like that, it was done.

After all she'd gone through. All the scheming and planning, the expensive trips to Peru, masquerading as her own sidekick for over a year to prove that a woman could negotiate in a man's world. Considerable time and effort spent and still no dice. They wanted nothing to do with her.

It was only after she orchestrated a fake assassination attempt on the mother of a high ranking lieutenant in the organization that she was able to get a seat at their table.

She stuck a knife deep into the chest of the fake attacker – who wasn't privy to the fact that she'd actually be stabbed as part of the plan, but was aptly compensated for her pain and suffering – and after Mrs. Bravado relayed the heroic events to her son,

Aunt Pat was owed a debt that she collected on as soon as she got out the joint.

Dope. Not just dope but *good* dope. The Peruvian's product was so good junkies were suspended in mid-air all over town. She was makin good money. Not quite the empire she'd built back in '88 but damn close. Territory in three quadrants of the city on lock. Money flowing to and through the downtown strip club, the funeral home in Bmore and her new sports bar over on the northeast side.

Clean money was wired monthly to the Caymans where she was building her retirement home. She planned to visit it as soon as she got off papers. Which was a whole other thing. She was back on probation after getting arrested for assaulting Consuela's husband. He didn't press charges, but the DA refused to let her walk away clean since it was all on TV.

So before the show, everything was as good as it could possibly get and now it was all shot to shit. Suddenly she was bad for business. The Peruvians sent that message through one of their minions, and just like that, all ties with the organization were severed. Everything grinded to a halt, and she was feverishly looking for a new connect to feed the cities need before she lost her territory and clientele.

She and her business partner, Rocky, a tall lanky, heavily pierced and tatted woman of a particular age, took a trip up to New York. They needed to reconnect with the last connect until they could find a better one.

Two years prior, when they informed Imelda Santos that they no longer needed her services, it was a less than pleasant exchange, to say the least. With an overflow of mostly powerful estrogen in the room, things got way past heated. Insults were thrown, guns were drawn, and Rocky inadvertently took a bullet in the thigh when Imelda's daughter, a fiery little half-Columbian, half-Dominican pistol named Peta, jumped the proverbial…and the literal…gun.

It took all the composure either of the boss ladies could muster not to start a full-fledged war right there in the back of the restaurant. In the end, the ladies came to an agreeable split but before Aunt Pat walked and Rocky limped out, Imelda shouted in her thick Columbian accent, "Jou'll be back." And back they were. With their tails between their legs willing to make whatever deal they could to keep their businesses afloat. All because of a fucking TV show. *Unbelievable.*

They took the Acela train up to Penn Station, then took a gypsy cab into Queens. Aunt Pat tapped lightly on the back door of the La Casa Empanada and "Pistol Peta" let them in. Peta and Rocky locked eyes until Aunt Pat signaled for Rocky to stand down. Peta led them into the kitchen where Imelda stood over a large stock pot, stirring it slowly and humming. Without looking up from her pot, she addressed her guests. "I see, jou're back."

Aunt Pat responded, "Hello Imelda."

Imelda replaced the lid on her pot and removed her apron. She instructed Peta to look after her pot before she walked away, over to the table where Aunt Pat and Rocky sat. She stood over them. "I want double the original price."

Aunt Pat leaned back in the chair and crossed her legs. She paused for a few seconds and sighed. "Imelda that's crazy."

Imelda shrugged and smirked. "Columbia has a shortage in product and now I am forced to go through mi primo in Guatemala, so my cost is more."

"Come on. I ain't payin double. Mark it up, fifty percent. At fifty percent we can deal."

"This is not a negotiation, Patricia. Double. And jou'll take it. Ju have no place else to go."

She was right. And besides, Aunt Pat knew it would be temporary. Imelda was just a placeholder until she could find better. "I guess you have a deal. Same arrangement as before." They shook hands before Aunt Pat and Rocky saw themselves out.

Rocky was seething. They were barely out the door before she popped off. "What the fuck, Pat? How we gon make money with that shit? Her shit ain't even that good!"

Pat lit up a cigar and took a pull. "What, you got a better option? You think she was gon make that shit easy for us?"

"Nah but I'm sayin--"

"Stop worryin. We on short time with her. You know that. She knows that. For now, we just need to put some product on the street to keep them corners up. As long as we can pay our people. We'll just take the hit for a minute while we figure it out."

"That's easy for you to say. I ain't got what you got, Pat."

"Ok, but I got *you*. You know that, right?"

"Yeah I know. I'm just sayin. I just hate to give that up to that bitch tho. Imelda takin advantage, Pat. And I wish you let me pop that lil bitch Peta. Real talk. Imma shoot that bitch soon as we finish our business. I swear to God."

Aunt Pat laughed. "Rocky, that beef is squashed. Let it go."

"Yeah. I'll let it go. After she gets shot."

"Whatever man. Let's go get something to eat so we can get the fuck outta this town."

"I thought you sad we was goin to Brooklyn."

"Nah. I changed my mind. We got bigger fish to fry right now. Another time."

Buyer's Remorse

Every day of the next two weeks was sheer torture. Missy had second and third thoughts about going through with the show. Nightmares of strange men's hands all over her body and teeny tiny festering herpes sores from all the kissing. Though Carmen assured her that STD testing was required, nothing is ever foolproof.

She cringed at the thought of the scathing reviews and all of the negative commentary that would inevitably pop up on social media. The Bossip's and the Huffington's. Mediatakeout. *Oh God, Wendy Williams*, she thought. After the scandal with Ray, she wasn't sure she could stomach anymore bad press. The trolls on Twitter were relentless.

Carmen had done her level best to make Missy comfortable with the situation. She saw to it that Missy had control of her wardrobe and styling, something she insisted on after her first meeting with the show's stylist. Missy didn't even wait for the woman to get out of the door before she dialed Carmen up.

"Carmen, what the hell?!"

"What? What's wrong?"

"What's wrong?!"

"Yes, Missy. What's wrong now?"

"What's wrong is I'm standing in a dressing room with three full racks of cheap prom gowns and skin tight, fuck-em-girl party dresses? And your girl just laid a hot pink lace front wig across my bed. I already told you, you are not about to have me looking crazy on national television. I did not sign up for Hip Hop Hoes or Big Booty Wives or any of that other garbage. I am not a THOT, Carmen!"

Carmen replied, half distracted with her online flirtations. "I know you ain't no THOT, you a queen, boo."

"Carmen, please don't play with me. And do not patronize me."

"I'm not."

"Good. And since you seem to have not gotten the memo the first time, I am NOT to be made into some stereotypical lip smackin, neck rollin, sassy ass angry black woman…"

"Ok."

"…I am NOT to be made into some…damn hoochie mama spouting foolishness for hashtags on social media."

"Right.'

"NO perpetuated stereotypes of any kind, Carmen. I'm serious. Are we clear?"

"Uh huh."

"Are you even listening to me?"

Carmen giggled and hit send on a sexy selfie. "Yes, girl I'm listening. I heard you."

"Then what did I say?"

"You said you not a THOT and you not gon…roll your neck for hashtags."

"That's not really what I said…but you get the point. Honestly, I can just style myself. I know what I want to wear, just send me your budget and I'll work it out."

"Ok, that's fine."

"And call that girl back here to pick up these damn strip mall clothes."

"Don't worry. I got you."

Missy hung up the phone relieved. She could rest a little easier knowing she wouldn't be the latest, greatest, disgrace to the black race. To Missy, image was everything and maintaining control over *that* was key. She fully intended to be represented as her authentic self – an educated, classy, sophisticated, proud, beautiful black business woman to be reckoned with, revered and respected.

Missy also wanted to preapprove the contestants, a hard fought battle that she lost. Not only could she not approve them, she would not meet any of them until the first day of taping.

Carmen assured her that was standard protocol for the show and non-negotiable. Not even *she* could change that. But it was a small price to pay. After all, how bad could they be?

In the end, the ladies came to a relatively amicable agreement, to just have each other's back. Carmen would protect her from all the foolishness and Missy would give Carmen good TV for her resume. A little smart, a little flirty, a little sexy. A little drama for the ratings. She had a few things in mind. The games were about to begin.

Over the Rainbow

The network was fined heftily by the FCC, several arrests were made after the show, and the deal for *PJ's World* fell through, but PJ was still on top of the universe. He'd signed an exclusive and very lucrative deal with MAC cosmetics, and thanks to his flawless cocoa brown skin, which was part genetics and part weekly collagen facials, he was being courted by Dove to endorse a new skincare line.

The checks were coming in regularly. He'd just completed an epic photo shoot for Ebony Magazine, gracing the cover with some of the best who'd ever done it in a wig and false lashes. Famous transgenders of color representing several generations of beauty and courage; from the incomparable and impossibly stunning Rupaul to the beautiful Laverne Cox who was breaking barriers all throughout the entertainment industry.

In less than six months, Miss P was virtually a household name without ever singing a song, bouncing a ball or otherwise displaying a talent for anything more than being a tea spilling, messy hot label whore with a slick mouth and a snarky attitude.

Fresh off a weekend vacation with some of his reality star buddies in Cancun, he decided to stop over at the bar to check on his mother. At 8:30 on a Friday night, it was virtually empty. No food. No music. Not even the faintest trace of hookah. Just a couple crouched low in dark corner and a skinny young white girl dancing offbeat to the music in her head. Rocky was in her usual position, leaning back on a corner of the bar, nursing her cognac and watching sports on TV.

"Hey Rocky, How you doin boo?" He reached over the bar and gave her a hug.

"Waddup big time. Where you been at?"

"Oh you know. Here, there, a little bitta everywhere. Just flew in from Cancun this morning."

"All right now. I see you…lookin good."

"Thanks doll." He flipped his hair to one side. "It's what I do." Rocky shook her head and they laughed. "Where's my mother?"

"Downstairs. I think she got company though."

PJ snorted. "Hmm." He walked to the back and down the stairs to the basement, just passing a young nubile girl with long blue hair and a Coke bottle shape, who was smiling and adjusting her tube top. Aunt Pat was just coming out of the bathroom."

"Hey *ma.*"

"Oh, hey PJ. Wassup?"

"Got yourself a new one, huh."

Aunt Pat smiled. "Yeah she new."

"She's cute."

"She aaight. Nuttin serious. So what's up with you?"

"Nothing much. Just got back from Cancun with the housewives."

"Hmm. Must be nice."

He smiled. "I'm enjoying it. I can't lie. So, what's goin on around here? It's like empty on a Friday night. And who's the white girl? One of yours?"

"Skinny? Blonde?"

"Yeah."

"Nah she ain't mine. She's been coming in regular, though. Gettin wasted and closing the bar down. Neighborhood's changing."

"I see. Where's the party at? It's like dead up there."

"Well, business been a little slow. You know that shit goes in cycles, though. It'll pick back up."

"Yeah, it's slow all right. I might have to do a few appearances or something. Get some of my friends to come through."

"Nah don't worry about it. I'm good."

"If you say so."

"I do."

"Ok. So have you heard from your *ex*? Ole fat face...black bean burrito-eatin ass. I tried to drag that bitch. I hope I see her ass again."

"No boy. I ain't heard from Consuela. And I'm puttin that shit behind me. All of it. Her. That fuckin TV show. I got more important shit to worry about."

"Worry? What you got to worry about? Ma, what's going on?"

"Nothin just business. Did you get everything straightened out with Ahmed?"

"Yeah. He's letting me keep the house, my cars, my ring and of course the shop. But other than that, we're done."

"You ok with that?"

"Oh I'm fine. He's still a little shaken up though."

Aunt Pat laughed. "Yeah, I'll bet. James Girls a lil too much for him huh?"

PJ shook his head. "I guess so. I think he was ok until you shot that gun. Ma. That was wildly unnecessary. Why in the world would you -- "

"Look I ain't gon keep explainin myself. I was mad. Nobody got hurt..."

"Actually they did."

"Well nobody got shot."

PJ laughed. "I really can't with you." He slung his signature pashmina over his shoulder, replaced his sunglasses and pulled his latest designer satchel back into the crook of his arm. Then he peered at his mother through the top of his sunglasses. "Are you just gonna stand there or are you gonna see me out?"

Aunt Pat followed him up the stairs. "Boy don't make me slap you."

"Always the threats of violence from you. You've really got some anger issues mother. Maybe I should call your probation officer?"

"Maybe I should call you an ambulance."

PJ shrieked. "That is no way to talk to your beloved only child."

"Whatever. Now get on outta here PJ. I got a lotta shit to

do today."

"I'm going. No need to push. PJ has a full schedule today himself." He stopped short of the door, did a bit of a half twirl and looked around the near empty bar. "Are you *sure* you don't need anything? I'm more than happy to help you mother."

"No PJ! I done told you now, I'm good."

Aunt Pat was anything but good. Business was slow, and the bar was losing money by the day. She'd just sold off the strip club for pennies on the dollar. The funeral home was still making a little money, but that was a joint venture with her Baltimore cousins, so the profits there were shared and her cut minimal. To top it all off, her banker in the Cayman's had been busted for his laundering practices and every dime of her "retirement" was tied up in the investigation.

She ushered PJ out of her bar with the question on the tip of her tongue. PJ could probably solve her problems with the short stroke of a pen. A simple phone call to one of his new friends. But she couldn't bring herself to ask. For the all the years she was away and all the shit he'd been through while she was gone, she wouldn't dare ask him for help. Or for anything. She was still trying to make up for what she'd done to his life. But she needed help from somewhere.

Imelda's shit quality dope was only making things worse. She could barely give it away, which meant she could barely pay her workers. And workers only stayed loyal when they were being fed. She knew it was only a matter of time before somebody stepped up and challenged her for her corners.

People were walking away from her left and right and even Rocky was starting to mouth off. Pat didn't blame her. She had a family to feed. Something had to give. And soon.

Insecurr

Dave had been spending more and more time at work, leaving Brenda at home to her own devices – cooking, journaling, and watching way too much television. In just a few short months, she'd gained back most of the weight she'd lost in prison, and although it had fallen in the ideal places for a sistah – tits, hips and ass – she was increasingly self-conscious about his feelings.

He complimented her often, but somehow she never really believed he was that into the whole curvy woman thing, especially since he'd only dated model types before her. She'd done her fair share of cyber stalking her husband before they wed, and of all the pictures on his social media, there was not one pic of one woman with as much as a hip bone to hold on to. His mother, Evelyn pretty much confirmed her suspicions on an impromptu visit to the house one morning when she just happened to mention that Brenda was not his "usual" type.

Evelyn Cohen was a mean old lady who probably used to be a mean little girl, and she was clearly on the warpath because her only son turned up with a new black wife on his arm. Brenda understood her frustration, but she had no intention of being disrespected.

Evelyn caught Brenda in the kitchen cleaning. As she knelt down on the floor scrubbing tile in a pair of cut offs, a ragged tee and a headscarf, Biggie Smalls blasted through Bose stereo speakers, and Brenda rapped the lyrics to "Gimme Da Loot" word for word. Loud. She nearly fell over when Evelyn appeared in the doorway.

"Good morning dear. Did I catch you at a bad time?" Evelyn said.

Brenda recognized Evelyn immediately from her pictures.

Mortified, she pulled the scarf from her head and scrambled for her iPod to switch it off - before Evelyn got a chance to hear Lil Kim's sexcapades. "No. Of course not. Mrs. Cohen. Hi." She quickly washed and dried her hands before extending them. "It's so nice to finally meet you. How'd you get in?"

"The door was unlocked dear."

"Oh. Dave must have forgotten to lock it. He just left for work."

"Yes, I know that dear. I'm here to see you."

Brenda wasn't sure how many more "dear's" she was gonna be before she had to kick this uppity old lady up outta her house. "Here to see me? Ok. Can I offer you something to drink? Eat? I made breakfast this morning —"

"No, thank you dear. I really just came to see you for myself. David sees fit to keep you away from his family, so if the mountain won't come to Mohamed…or Mahalia."

Mahalia? Did this bitch just… Brenda inhaled and closed her eyes for just a second. She opened them and feigned a smile. "I've been asking him when we were going to meet. He's just been so busy at the office lately that—"

"So tell me…" Evelyn interrupted as she surveyed Brenda from head to toe, making things very uncomfortable. "…how did you meet my David?"

Brenda was caught completely off guard. She had no idea what Dave had already told her. "Work. I retained his services for estate planning when my husband died a few years ago. We became friends and…things just progressed from there."

Evelyn pursed her thin, rouged lips. "I see."

Brenda couldn't tell if she bought the story or not. She spent the better part of another hour trying to redeem herself from the less than stellar first impression, but to no avail. Clearly Evelyn had already decided she didn't like her, even before she walked in on Brenda's gangster rap karaoke session.

After answering a series of invasive questions, from fertility to her plans to convert — or not to convert — to Judaism, Brenda was finally done with her. It was time for her monster-in-law to get the hell on. "Oh! You know what?" Brenda said. "I *completely* forgot I promised Dave I'd bring him lunch today."

"Oh, well I'll go in with you. We can take my car. I so rarely get to see my son now that he's *married*. "Evelyn smiled. "My dear, you must let him up for air sometime." That tickled her. She let out a loud, cackling laugh.

Brenda breathed slowly in and out before she handed Evelyn her expensive purse and replied. "Actually I have to run a few errands first Mrs. Cohen. But I'll be sure to let him know that you stopped by. I'll ask him to call you."

Evelyn took the hint. "Please see to it that you do. It was lovely chatting with you dear. I'll be in touch."

She pushed the stool back under the island, placed her Chanel on her forearm and headed back out to her car. Brenda slammed the door, just hard enough to send a message.

*****

After she finished her cleaning, Brenda pulled together a picnic basket, a cute outfit and headed into DC to surprise her hard working husband. She hadn't seen his new office and decided today was as good a day as any to introduce herself to his colleagues.

When she arrived at the building, she was already impressed. He'd moved from his father's office on Capitol Hill and rented prime office space on K St. in northwest DC, where the movers, shakers and policy makers held court.

The lobby in the building was massive with marble from floor to ceiling, modern sculptures and art deco lighting. Her footsteps echoed loudly when she walked through. The security guard directed her to Cohen and Associates on the 10th floor.

When she stepped off the elevator she was again, impressed by the digs. Fancy contemporary furniture. The firm's name mounted high on a wall behind an empty reception desk.

She walked around, peering into offices and conference rooms until she reached the largest office at the far end of a long corridor. It was the only one with privacy glass. She smiled at the fancy marble nameplate with gold embossed lettering. *David M.*

Cohen, Esquire, and beneath his name, *Founding Partner*. Her husband. How did she get so lucky to be with this man?

A sudden loud cackling from the other side of the door broke her from her thoughts. She turned the handle and walked in, startling David and a scantily clad, pale, freckled-faced, *I Love Lucy* lookin red head sitting on the edge of his desk.

"Brenda!" Dave sprang from his chair and hurried over to her. "Sweetheart, what a pleasant surprise." He kissed her cheek. "Is everything all right? What are you doing here?"

Brenda looked over to the redhead. Nary a trace of a smile on her face. "Everything's fine. What are *you* doing here?"

Dave ignored the comment. He seemed a little too nervous for Brenda's taste. "Hunny, this is Meredith, my paralegal. I told you about her."

"No, actually you didn't."

Lucy hopped her skinny ass down from his desk and onto her stilettos. Her shift dress was practically painted on, and her cardigan, at least a size too small. Certainly too small to conceal her inappropriate-for-the-office freckled cleavage. She extended her hand. "Pleasure to finally meet you, Brenda."

Brenda extended hers, halfheartedly. "Mrs. Cohen."

Dave smiled nervously trying to think of a way to break the tension. He didn't quite recognize the look on Brenda's face, but he knew it was nothing good. He lifted the basket from Brenda's hand. "Oh! You brought me lunch?! Hunny, that was so thoughtful of you. I was just about to order in."

Meredith looked at Dave and then back at Brenda. She smiled. "I'll leave you two alone. It was very nice to meet you, *Mrs. Cohen.*" Brenda grunted. Meredith headed toward the door but stopped before closing it. "Oh and Dave, I'll be back over in a bit. We really need to go over your *briefs.*"

It was all Brenda could do not to snatch her skinny smug ass by her thin red ponytail. Meredith walked across the hall to her office. Brenda watched, as she removed her too tight sweater, pulled down her hair and shook it loose. She sat on top of her desk, seductively crossing her long legs, knowing she was being watched.

Brenda turned back to Dave. "Who the fuck is she?!"

"Oh. Come on Brenda. I just told you, she's my paralegal."
He walked over and hugged her from behind. "*Sweetheart*. Don't
do that."

"Do what?"

"Play the jealous wife. It's unnecessary. You know I don't
want nobody but you, boo." He slapped her hard on the ass and
shook it to make it jiggle.

Brenda pulled away. She really wasn't in the mood to be
patronized by his wigga nonsense. "Dave, stop it."

He slapped it again and shook it up it down making it clap
together in her flimsy dress, trapping the thin silk fabric between
her massive cheeks. He bit his bottom lip. "Damn girl. What
imma do wit all dat ass?"

"Dave!"

He walked over to the door and closed the blinds. Then he
walked back over to her and pushed her forward, over onto his
desk, sweeping all of its contents to the floor.

"Dave no."

He pulled her dress above her waist and lifted one of her
legs on top of his desk.

She pulled her leg back down. "Do you allow all of your
paralegals to call you by your nickname?"

He lifted it again. "It's a very informal office environment."
Then he knelt, pulled her panties to the side and buried his face
into her ass. Once again she was silenced by his long tongue and
lithe fingers. He brought her to orgasm quickly then he stood
and unbuckled his belt, dropping his pants to the floor.

He entered her quickly, intentionally riding the tail end of
her orgasmic wave. Sliding in, out and around the most sensitive
spots within her as she tried to squirm away from him, moaning
for him to stop. That always made him crazy. In the best way.
He reached an especially sensitive place within her and she called
out. "Oh! Ok, don't stop. Don't stop baby. You gon make me
cum again. Oooh. Yesss. Please don't stop."

He stopped. And backed away from her. She looked back at
him and whined. "What? I told you not to stop."

He smiled. "Beg for it."

"What?"

"If you want it, beg for it."

"What? No."

"Well then." He reached down and pulled at his trousers.

She cried. "OK, please!"

"Please what?

"Pleeease put it back in."

"Put what back in?"

"What?"

"Put WHAT back in."

She smiled. Amused, a little irritated and a lot horny. "That big white dick."

He smiled wide and dropped his pants back to the floor. Then he eased himself back inside and gave her one hard thrust. She yelled out, "Oh!" He pulled out and thrust again. She moaned. "Shiiit." He thrust again, and she yelled "Ahhh!" The more she yelled, the harder and faster he penetrated, deep thrusts in search of that G-spot, and another orgasm. He hit the spot. She called out to him. Screams of ecstasy that could be heard through the halls of the near empty office space. Certainly across the way where Lucy would be listening.

Dave released deep inside her. When he stopped shaking, he kissed her on the back of the neck and gave her ass a hard slap. "Now what's in the basket, baby?"

Brenda rolled her eyes. Slightly annoyed with his usual post-orgasm demands. He was barely out of her and already asking to be fed. She lifted herself from the desk, pulled up her panties and smoothed down her dress. "Lobster rolls, arugula salad, and pecan tarts for dessert."

"Oh, babe, you're too good to me." He pulled up his pants and kissed her hard on the lips. "Thanks I'll see you at home." He walked around to the other side of his desk, hit the intercom and summoned Lucy. "Hey, Mer, can you bring in those briefs now? And grab me a Coke from the kitchen please. Thanks."

He walked into his executive bathroom and closed the door behind him. Brenda walked over and stood outside the door. She leaned against it. "Babe. I made this lunch for us. I thought we could go over to the square and have a little picnic."

He opened the door, freshened and neatened. "Brenda, you surprised me at work. I planned on ordering lunch in. I have a ton of work to do. Deadlines to meet. I'll be home around eight." He kissed her on the forehead, as Meredith walked in and took her seat on the other side of his desk.

Brenda walked into the bathroom to pull herself together. She could hear Dave ask Lucy through the door, "Lobster roll?" When she walked out of the bathroom there they were, enjoying the romantic picnic lunch she prepared.

As much as she wanted to snatch the rolls out of their mouths, throw them back in her basket, and walk the hell out, she knew better. She had evolved from that young girl that popped off for any little thing. The one who'd sling a bitch across the floor for even eyeballing her man too hard. *That* girl, though she could still be summoned if absolutely necessary, had been suppressed in prison and a much subtler, sophisticated woman had emerged. One that was more rational and thoughtful, with her anger appropriately managed thanks to a jailhouse therapist.

But this day, her patience was being tested. Something wasn't right. It just didn't *feel* right. One thing was for sure and two for certain. Dave had better not be playing her for a fool, and Lil Lucy had better watch her damn step. Brenda's antennae were up again. And that was never a good sign.

Showtime

The first day of taping came quickly. Carmen scouted locations for a solid week and found one of the most magnificent venues in the city – The Mansion on O St., a 30,000 square foot, hundred-room luxury boutique hotel, slash museum in the Dupont Circle historic district in Washington, DC. It was grand and interesting and eclectic with its themed bedrooms, hidden doors and secret passageways. The place had so much charm, it was its own character on the show.

The show was to begin with the contestants. They'd already been prepped by the producers. They'd already taped and re-taped their official introductions to the world. You know, the green screen chatter. And they were already getting acquainted with one another over cocktails in the parlor. It was a little early in the day for libation, but Carmen thought that it would loosen them up enough to get them into their carefully crafted, lightly scripted characters.

The network sent a car to pick Missy up. She was dressed smartly but sexy in a white Kato sheath dress with peplum detail. Though she was completely covered in white crepe, there was no concealing her ample assets. She wore white, pointed stilettos with a gold heel, perfectly complimented by her African-inspired gold wire necklaces and bangles. Her freshly highlighted honey blonde hair was straightened and pulled to her back and the bronzy makeup gave her a sun kissed glow that complimented her full red lips. *Classy. Sophisticated. Beautiful.*

On the ride from Great Falls to Dupont Circle, she sipped her complimentary rosé and allowed her mind to wander a bit. Where in the hell were they taking her, and why did everything have to be such a big secret? Who were these men, and where did they find them? She thought, they'd better be just as fine as the one's she'd seen on the website or it was Carmen's ass. Missy had already warned Carmen that if she had to go through with this nonsense she'd better have some wicked eye candy to help her pass the time. Carmen pinky swore the guys were just her type.

The car pulled onto a narrow one-way street and parked in front of the mansion. Missy recognized it immediately. She and Carmen had attended a couple of cocktail parties there, and she loved the place. *Good choice Carmen,* she thought. She took one last sip of champagne, freshened up her red lip and put her game face on as she waited for the driver to come around to her door.

Cameras captured her from every angle, as she stepped out of the fancy white stretch Rolls with authority. She sauntered up the staircase, into the mansion and over to the parlor where 12 very eager and slightly intoxicated contestants stood, waiting to see who they were competing for.

When Missy walked into the parlor, there was a collective gasp, followed by hysterical laughter. The guys were slapping high fives and licking their chops. Missy smiled nervously, as she surveyed the room thinking, *Oh. My God. I am going to KILL Carmen!*

Intuition

Brenda walked out of the office building and over to the park. The weather was near perfect. 82 degrees and partly sunny, almost no humidity, which was odd for late-summer in DC, but most welcomed for a nice stroll in the park. She picked up a chili dog and a bag of Doritos from the food truck at the corner, and after walking around for a few ticks, she found a seat on a bench beside an elderly gentlemen feeding pigeons and talking to himself. He looked a little parched so she offered him her bottle of water. He didn't thank her after he took it, but that was ok.

He drank the bottle down completely and got up, walked over the recycling bin, and threw it in. Then he took his seat at the end of the bench and continued breaking off crumbs from a piece of stale bread. He wore a suit and overcoat, both of which were tattered and soiled but his hands and nails were oddly clean. His hair and beard was long and gray but neatly combed back. Frederick Douglas style. He mumbled. "You better protect yourself."

Is he talking to me? "Excuse me? Are you talking to me?"

"Always protect yourself. They'll use you. Lie to you. They'll tell you they love you, but they don't. They never do. You gotta be smart. Protect yourself. Whitey don't give a damn about you. You'll see. All you have to do is open your eyes. You'll see."

Brenda sat for a while listening to the rantings of the old guy...and thinking. Something wasn't right. Despite the spectacular sexcapade that had just taken place, something about the visit didn't seem right. Their body language? Lucy's attitude. Women don't behave that way unless something's going on...or unless they want it to be. Dave seemed nervous, too. Too nervous. And why was the office so empty?

Her mind raced. Her appetite was suddenly lost. She offered the old guy her hot dog and chips. He declined. "I don't eat that crap. You shouldn't either. That's what they want you to do." So she threw them in the trash and walked back across the street to the office.

She walked past the security desk toward the elevator and the guard yelled out. "Ma'am! Ma'am! I'm gonna need to see some ID."

"Oh, no. I'm just going back up to my husband's office for a sec."

"I'm sorry ma'am, I'm still going to need your ID."

"What? I'm just going up to the 10th floor? You just showed me up there an hour ago."

"Its policy. I need to see your ID, and I need you to sign in again." He pointed to a clipboard on the small desk beside the large desk.

Brenda sucked her teeth before she pulled her ID from her wallet and handed it to him. She signed the stupid clipboard and slammed it back down on the counter before walking toward the elevators. He stopped her again. "Ma'am, who are you going to see?"

She grit her teeth. "I just *told* you, my husband. David Cohen. He has a law practice on the 10th floor."

"Oh, Mrs. Cohen. I'll have to call up first."

"What! Call him?" She put her ID back in her wallet, her wallet back in her purse, and headed to the elevator. By the time the security officer called out to her again the elevator doors were closing. She stepped off on 10 and walked the same path as before, past the empty reception desk, the big kitchen and conference rooms. Past a half dozen offices with glass doors. The blinds on David's office were still closed. She opened the door...and dropped her purse.

"What the fuck?!"

****

Brenda rushed over to his desk and snatched Lucy by her

65

thin red pony tail, bringing her nasty ass up off the floor and to a semi standing position, just high enough for a closed fist punch square in the face. And then another. Lucy's lip spat blood and Dave, after getting his pants back up, grabbed her arm and tried to pull her back. Brenda threw Lucy across the floor and unloaded on him southpaw style. A hard right to his side and an overhand left to his jaw. He fell back into his chair – the same chair in which he was just seated comfortably enjoying a blow job from his paralegal. He raised his hands in an attempt to shield himself from the massively painful blows. "Brenda! Stop! Wait."

She didn't heed his cry but instead continued to unload on him until the security officer pulled her off. She screamed, "I fuckin knew it! I knew it! You motherfucker!" She yelled back at the guard, "Get off me! Get the fuck off of me! Get your hands off me! Get off!"

Dave shook her, as she screamed repeatedly for someone to get off of her. She was wet with sweat, tears streaming from her closed eyes. "Brenda! Hunny wake up! Wake up!" She opened her eyes and the sight of him infuriated her. Reflex kicked in. She punched him hard in the jaw.

Don't Taze Me Bro!

Brandy walked out of class frustrated and bogged down with two weeks' worth of assignments. Trig and Poli Sci. Her worst subjects. She decided to call it a day, head home and spend the rest of it at the pool drinking some of her aunt Missy's good white wine from one of Misa's kiddie cups. Just in case.

She stepped out into the unusually hot September sunshine and noticed Tay sitting on a bench across the way. He stood when he saw her and walked over, grabbing her books to save them from dropping to the ground. She grimaced. "What are you doing here?"

"You know what I'm doing here. I miss you. And I'm not letting you run me away again. Brandy, I *know* you miss me, too. So let's just stop playing this —"

"You're not listening to me!" she screamed. "I can't do this with you again Tay. I can't." She sobbed. Tay dropped the books to the ground and pulled her close to him. He held her tightly as she tried to wriggle free."

"No. Tay let me go."

"Babe stop. I just want to talk to you."

"Just…get off of me."

He pulled her closer, and she shoved him hard. "Get off me!"

Two campus police cars drove up flashing their lights. An overzealous officer jumped out and grabbed Tay by the arm while the other questioned Brandy. "Ma'am, are you a student here?"

"What? Am I a student here? You see a man grab me, and the first question you ask is am I a student here? What if I wasn't? Would you still help me?"

Tay snatched his arm away from the cop, "Exactly. Man, get your hands off me." Moments later, two DC police cars pulled beside them, sirens wailing.

The first two officers out of the car walked over to Tay. "What's the problem here?"

The overzealous campus officer spoke first. "This guy was manhandling this woman here, and we were trying to figure out what was going on."

Brandy scowled at him. "No, you were trying to figure out if the black folks belonged at Georgetown." She turned to the cop. "Look, sir, I'm a student at Georgetown." She pulled her wallet from her bag. "This is my student ID, this is my boyfriend, I was upset about something, and he was just trying to console me. End of story. Everything's fine."

The DC cop turned to Tay, "Sir, can I see your ID please?"

Brandy yelled, "What do you need his ID for? I just told you…"

"Ma'am! Please step BACK! Sir your ID please?"

Tay shook his head. "Brandy calm down, please. Officer, my wallet is in my back pocket."

The officer reached into Tay's pocket. "No wallet." His partner pulled out the cuffs. Looks like you're goin with us."

The officer fastened the cuffs tightly and pulled him toward the squad car as Tay yelled. "Wait! I must have dropped it. It probably fell out in the car. Sir, just let me go to my car."

Brandy yelled at the officer, "Wait, what are you arresting him for! He didn't do anything!"

She walked up to him, and he pulled out his taser. "Ma'am I won't tell you again! Back off!"

Fearing she would be tased, Tay yelled, "Brandy!" The officer turned the taser on him and hit him with the full 50,000 volts, as Brandy screamed bloody murder. Several students filmed with their phones, as Tay fell limp to the ground, shaking and disoriented from the shock. Brandy attempted to run to him and another officer pulled his gun on her, forcing her to the ground.

Terrified, she laid there crying and watching helplessly, as they dragged Tay across the yard. He yelled as they shoved him forcefully into the back of the squad car. "Brandy, go and get TJ for me! He has to be picked up by six o'clock! Ask for Ms. Mae and Xavier. Please!"

As a lady cop held her on the ground with a knee planted firmly in her back, she yelled back at him, "Ok!" *Wait, what did he just ask me?*

The Twist

The working title of the show was "Black Love: The X Factor," and the twist – one of them – was that all of the contestants were ex-boyfriends of the subject. There was no open call for auditions, as is the typical practice, these gentlemen were all contacted by the show and informed that an ex-girlfriend was looking for love on television. They were offered a pretty decent stipend for their participation and most of them agreed for one reason or another. Money being the one reason and fame being another.

After the first day of taping, 16 long hours of fake smiles and phony conversation with men she'd had no intention of ever seeing again, Missy was exhausted. She couldn't even wait to get home to call Carmen's ass. She'd sent her several texts earlier that day that went unanswered. So she left a voice message:

This is the twist? Chucky? Are you serious? How about you stop ducking my calls and be a woman about yours for once! Call me back!

Just before midnight, Carmen rang her phone. Missy looked at it, and sent it to voice mail. This was not a discussion she was going to have over the phone. She listened to the message:

Missy, first I want to apologize for keeping you in the dark. I had strict orders from the top guys to keep it close. They wanted to make sure that your on camera reaction was authentic. I promise you that's it. No more surprises. Anything else you'll be the first to know. You have my word. Please don't be mad. Second, you are going to have to stay at the mansion. You can't leave at night and go home, you have to stay there. It's in your contract. You knew that. I'll send a car for you in the morning. And call me if you need anything. Love you!

Missy rolled her eyes at the phone. That bullshit apology was not going to fly.

The next morning, she waltzed into the BET Studios early and unannounced. She walked right into Carmen's office, slamming the door behind her. "Really Carmen? Really? Chucky?"

Startled, Carmen quickly, and somewhat suspiciously closed her laptop. "Missy. Hey! What are you doing here? Did you get my message?"

"Yes I got your message. What did you do steal my goddamn phone book? How'd you get in touch with all of them? Carmen, how could you call Chucky in for this?"

Carmen shrugged and smiled. "Well...he *is* your ex isn't he?"

Missy dropped her purse on top of the desk and sat in the chair across from Carmen. "That's not funny. I told you how things ended. Chucky made his decision to go on about his life, and I'm fine with that. Why would you bring him here? And what happened to his wife anyway?"

Carmen smiled. "Aahhhh. So you care?"

"I didn't say that. I mean, he's on a television dating show, and he's not wearing a ring. Where's his wife?"

"Why didn't you ask him? Didn't you get a chance to talk to him yesterday?"

"No I didn't, smart ass. We don't have our 'date' until today. I went out with Xander and Andre yesterday."

"Ooh!" Carmen cooed. "How'd that go? How's *Xander*?"

Missy's demeanor changed suddenly. She even lit up a little. "Gurl. Xander. Whoo chile! He is still fine as all get out. Beautiful smile, body for days, but still a bit of a jerk."

"A jerk with more money now..."

"...but a jerk just the same. I'm getting rid of him early."

"And Andre?"

"Still as loud and ignorant as he ever was. You know I never could take him anywhere."

"Ooh girl I remember. Big, loud and ghetto. A real live hood nigga. I remember he smoked *so much weed* back in the day."

"And the day hasn't changed."

"How do you know?"

"You can tell by his lips."

"Oh yeah…true. You used to tell something else about those big lips…and a few other big body parts if I remember correctly."

"Yeah…he was king ding-a-ling all right. But the minute he hopped up off me he'd say something so goddam dumb…girl, I just wanted to muzzle him."

Carmen laughed. "I hear you. But you sure you wouldn't wanna sample that…just one more time?"

"Hell no! He's gotta go too." She smiled. "So I'm not tempted."

Carmen smirked. "Um hmm. So you just cuttin em back huh girl. I heard you eliminated two already. Which ones?"

"Ian and Hector."

"Ooh Hector. The craaaazy lat-in-o. "I swear I thought that papichulo was gon kill you girl. He was definitely obsessed with you. I can't lie, I was kinda scared of him."

"*Exactly* so why would you call him here?! You know he's crazy!"

Carmen laughed hysterically at Missy's frustration. "Aaahh! I'm sorry girl. I thought it would be good TV! We needed a little Goya spice up in there."

"You are such a sellout."

"I am not a sellout. I just have a job to do."

"Whatever. So where's Chucky's wife?"

"Well, I don't know if it's my place to be divulging folks' personal business all willy nilly…"

Missy glared at her. "Bitch…"

"Ok, ok. She left him."

"Whaaaat? Are you serious?"

"Yeap. Last year after his show got canceled. She took the baby, all the money she could get her hands on, and left. That domestic abuse scandal really messed him up, too. They canceled his stand up tour and the movie special. The Comedy Club let him go. His career is really drying up. Trust me, he jumped at this opportunity."

"Domestic abuse? Chucky?"

"Well…alleged. She dropped the charges against him."

"Wow. That's definitely not the Chucky I know. But then again…what do I know. Look who *I* married."

"Okay." Carmen looked down at her watch. "Missy it's almost eight o'clock. You already late for taping. You want a ride back over to the mansion?

"No, I drove."

"Ok, but remember, you have to stay there. Leaving is a breach of your contract. They have to film everything. Sunrise to moonlight. I explained that to you already."

"Yeah, yeah I know. You know you owe me one for this."

"Owe you? I'm paying you handsomely for this little adventure, sweetie."

"No sweetie. That check is cute, not handsome. Not yet." She grabbed her purse and mumbled as she walked out of the office. *Got me spending 40 damn days and nights in a house with all those fools. I did not sign up for this.*

Missy left, headed for Dupont Circle. Dreading another day of taping. This day the producers had her going on an outing. A fancy dinner with Chucky and one of her college exes, Daryl, another wealthy, highly educated, devastatingly handsome JERK who preferred blondes. Usually the ditzy white ones. Another ex she'd written off a long time ago and hoped she'd never see again.

So there she was, sitting at a dinner table asking a bunch of scripted questions that she already had answers to, waiting for something "spontaneous" to happen. It was all so stupid. But she smiled and played the part for the cameras as best she could.

"So Daryl, it's been a good while since we dated. Tell me what would you do to make our *second* first date special?"

Daryl used the question as his opportunity to plug his Internet company and brag about his life. His second first date included a helicopter ride to his lake house in Shenandoah Valley. A gourmet dinner prepared by his personal chef, a full body Swedish massage by his Swedish masseur, and a private serenade from his very good friend, Johnny Gill, as they sipped Perrier Jouet under the stars.

He used impeccable grammar and perfect diction when he spoke; all the while Chucky was mocking him and making faces behind his back. Missy could hardly keep her composure, and when Daryl turned to Chucky, his expression suddenly serious as he cooed, "Dayum, can I go?" Missy and the entire crew broke out into hysterical laughter. So much so that it stalled the taping for a while. Daryl was seething but kept his cool.

When the tape rolled again, Missy posed the same question to Chucky. He took her hand and stared intently into her eyes.

"All jokes aside. All that extravagant stuff is cool. But we been there and done that, right baby girl? Kristal in the bubble bath. Penthouse suites at the Beverly Wilshire. Top back on the Maybach and shopping on Rodeo Drive. That's old."

Daryl sighed loudly and took a sip of his brandy, which made Chucky smile because he'd clearly gotten under his skin.

Chucky cleared his throat loudly and looked directly at Daryl. "Like I was sayin. It's been done playa." He turned back to Missy. "This nigga wanna *hire* somebody to cook for you and *rub* on you and sing to you." He looked back at Daryl and scoffed. "Lame." Then he looked back and Missy. "As for me? My second first date? I'm goin old school wit it. I'd take you to Trios for some chicken cheesesteaks wit errything on em, pick up a bottle of that good Moet Rose you used to like, a couple red cups and take you out to Gravelly Point by the airport. I would lay out a blanket underneath the stars, give you a good ole foot rub while we sip, and talk and watch the planes come in over the Potomac. Just like we used to do back in the day. Before all the money and the fame and the drama. When we ain't have nuttin but us. You remember that?"

Missy smiled, reminiscing on the fun she had with Chucky. It was always so easy with him. "I do."

He smirked at Daryl, reached out and stroked Missy's cheek. "Then I'd take you back to my grandmamma house and knock da BOTTOM out dat pussy!"

Missy spit out her water, and the cameraman nearly dropped

the camera he was laughing so hard. "I think we'll have to bleep that," he said. Even Daryl got a giggle. Chucky, the breakout star of the show, won the producers and Missy over that night, and at the elimination ceremony he received his flute full of champagne, signifying his move on to the next round.

Chucky was in it to win it, and although Missy was slightly mortified by his latest antics, she didn't much mind. She needed her bottom knocked out.

Inquiring Minds

"What the hell! What'd you hit me for?!" Dave grabbed his face.

Brenda turned over and rubbed his face. "I...I'm sorry. I didn't mean to hit you."

He stretched his jaw. "Yeah, well you hit me pretty good for someone who didn't mean it. What the hell were you dreaming about?"

"What?"

"Nothing. Your mom stopped by this morning."

"Really?"

"Really. We talked for a bit."

"About?"

"She asked how we met. I told her you handled my husband's estate after he died."

"Why'd you tell her that?"

"Well I didn't know what to say. I didn't know what you'd already told her. What *did* you tell her?"

"The truth."

"Seriously?"

"Brenda, your case made the news. She knew I represented you."

"And what did she say?"

Dave laughed. "What does it matter. I'm a grown ass man. I don't answer to her."

"So she hates me."

"Noooo. No she doesn't hate you."

"Well she definitely doesn't like me."

"What did she say to you?"

"That she doesn't like me."

"What?"

"No. She didn't actually say that. Well not in so many words. You know what. Never mind about that. Who is Meredith?"

"Who?"

"MER-e-dith. Who is she?"

"She's my paralegal and an old friend of the family. I've known her for years. How'd she come up?"

"How do you think she came up? After your mother surveyed my fat ass bent over scrubbing the floor like the help, she just happened to mention that I *must be special* because I was so *vastly different* from the other girls you've dated."

"Mother said that?"

"Yes mother did. So you dated Meredith?"

"No. I mean…yeah we hung out a couple times back in college. Mostly because our parents thought it was a good idea for us to connect. It didn't work."

"Um hmm. Imma need you to define *hung out.*

"Brenda…baby. Meredith is a friend and a colleague. That is it. You have absolutely nothing to worry about. I promise you. I am head over heels in love with my beautiful brown wife."

"Why do I have to be your brown wife? Why can't I just be your beautiful wife?"

"You're both. Now come over here and gimme summa dat brown suga."

She pushed him off of her. "Dave, come on. Stop it."

"Brenda there's nothing going on between me and Meredith. Don't you trust me?"

"Yeah I trust you…but…."

"But what?"

"I don't know. I know you said you were ok with it but…"

"Ok with what?"

"Me not…you know. Giving you head. It's just…I just never really liked it."

"Oh. Are we back to that again? I told you it was ok. It's not a big deal."

"Yeah but I know how white guys really like it…and them white girls love to do it and…"

"Do you hear yourself? Do you know how silly you sound?

You've really got to stop with these stereotypes. What if I did that to you? What if I brought you a fried chicken dinner with red Kool-Aid and watermelon for dessert?"

"I'd probably give you some head."

They both laughed.

"Seriously. Baby. You are the only girl for me."

"Woman."

"Yes, woman. And I like my woman like my coffee. Strong, black and full bodied." He slapped her on the ass. "Now get your fat ass over here and sit on my face."

"Ok now that's too much…"

He kissed her softly on the lips for every letter. "P. H. A. T."

She smiled. "I see somebody's been reading the Urban Dictionary again." She climbed on top of him and smothered him with her boobage. Then they spent the next hour making love. As per the norm, he released, shook her bottom and inquired about breakfast. She threw on her robe and made her way to the kitchen.

As she flipped his omelet and poured a steaming cup of his freshly ground Blue Bourban coffee, she reflected on her dream. It was just so damned vivid. Dave was clearly playing down his involvement with the redhead because Evil-Lyn had a completely different story to tell. But that wasn't it. Something else was up with this lady. Brenda's intuition had never once failed her. It was kicking her in the teeth, and it was not to be ignored. There was only one thing to do. She picked up her cell and went into the pantry.

"Hey Aunt Pat. Can you come over later? I need your help. No, I can't talk right now. I'll tell you later. Ok, I'll see you soon."

Brenda was fit-na get some answers. She just hoped that this was the one time her intuition was wrong.

*****

Aunt Pat pulled up to the house in her "vintage" red pick-up truck, which was actually less vintage and more "old." Her thin legs peeking from underneath cargo shorts and inside tan suede work boots. Her muscular, heavily tatted arms peeked out from the short sleeves of her signature plaid button-up. She was one handsome dude if Brenda had ever seen one, imposing, with a stern look on her face. Always. She ignored the lighted doorbell and knocked hard on the door. Brenda opened it and greeted her with a big hug. "Hey my favorite aunt in the whole wide world. It's been too long since I've seen you."

Aunt Pat looked up and around. "Damn girl. This a nice ass house. I ain't know you was livin like *this*. What your husband into? I know he ain't rollin like this off no legal retainers."

Brenda giggled at her aunt's cynicism. She was suspicious of everything. "I'll just take that as a compliment, Aunt Pat. Actually, Dave is doing pretty well. He picked up a lot of new clients after my trial."

"Why? He lost your case."

"I mean…yeah but he still did a good job. And word gets around town. He's a good lawyer."

"If you say so. So what is it you called me all the way out here for?"

Brenda gave her the whole lowdown. Told her she needed to know exactly who Meredith was and what she and Dave were up to. Brenda gave her Meredith's cell phone number, which she'd lifted from Dave's phone and a photo she'd printed from the firm's website.

Aunt Pat looked at the photo and laughed. "She kinda looks like a young Lucille Ball."

Brenda giggled. "Yes! I thought Lucy as soon as I saw her picture."

"She pretty."

"You think so?"

"I mean…in a weird kinda way. She kinda like one of those old pinup girls in one of them old Coca Cola ads. That odd type beauty."

"I guess."

"You really think he fuckin wit her?"

"I don't know what I think. Maybe."

"Well how far you want me to go with this?"

"As far as you can. I want everything you can get. How long you think it'll take?"

"I don't know. Imma drop it off to my man today. I'll let you know when I have somethin."

"Fair enough. You staying for lunch?"

"Nah, I got elsewhere to be. You be good baby girl. And keep your eyes open." She looked around the house again as she headed for the door. "Yeah. You keep them eyes open."

Brenda shook her head. "Thanks Auntie. Love you."

"Love you too baby."

Aunt Pat pimped back to her truck and sped down the driveway. Brenda sipped her tea feeling a little more at ease. If anyone could get answers it was her Auntee. So, for the time being she would go on as if everything was all right. As far as Dave would know she'd taken him at his word and everything was. Brenda certainly hoped it was. With everything she'd been through she didn't need no more surprises. But she braced herself...just in case.

T.J.

Getting arrested on a Friday afternoon usually meant you were in for the weekend, and for Tay it was no exception. Brandy called Missy crying hysterically and asked her to meet her at the police station. She didn't explain why. "Aunt Missy, it's an emergency! I'm at the 9th District police station. Please meet me here and I need an attorney! Please hurry, I'll explain when you get here."

Missy was in full panic mode. She called Herbert to meet her at the station and sent Carmen a text to let her know that she was leaving the house for a while. When they walked in the front door of the precinct, Brandy stood at the front desk, the back of her pants covered in grass stains, in a heated exchange with a desk officer, well on her way to being arrested.

Missy called out to her, "Brandy! What's going on?!"

"Oh Aunt Missy, I'm glad you made it!" She hugged her. "They locked Tay up at my school this morning!"

"Who?"

"Tay! He was just there to talk and then I got upset and then he grabbed me and the campus police came then the regular police came and they tased him and I tried to stop them but they pulled their gun on me and–"

'Wait, wait, Brandy slow down. They pulled a gun on you?!"

Brandy calmed down and gave Missy the whole story. Herbert walked over to the girls. "Ladies, it's after five o'clock. Unfortunately, there's nothing more we can do today. I'll be back for his hearing first thing Monday morning."

Missy gave him a hug. "Thanks for coming down, Herb. I owe you one."

"No no, we're even now. I'll talk to you tomorrow."

Brandy interrupted. "Wait, Mr. Anderson. I can't talk to him until Monday?"

"I'm afraid not, hunny. Not unless he calls you."

"Fuck!"

Missy snapped, "Brandy!"

"Oh I'm sorry. I'm sorry. Aunt Missy I gotta go."

"What? Go where?"

"Just something I gotta do, and I'm already late. I'll talk to you later!"

Missy stood there more confused than ever, wondering what the hell was going on with Brandy. They definitely needed to have a talk.

Brandy tore out of the precinct and ran to her car. It was already 5:35, and rush hour traffic in Georgetown was always brutal. After some strategic maneuvering, she finally pulled into the parking lot at the daycare at 6:12, just before the 15-minute grace period was up. She walked inside the church and followed the signs downstairs to the basement where the daycare was located.

There were three classrooms, all of them empty. She turned around when she heard a door opening, and out of the bathroom walked a sixty-something woman holding a gorgeous little brown boy with curly brown hair who looked almost identical to Misa.

Brandy walked up to them. "Ms. Mae?"

"Yes can I help you?"

"Yes, I'm here for TJ. Tay…I mean Talib asked me to pick him up. He was held up at work."

"I see. Do you have the safe word?"

"Safe word?"

"Anyone picking up a child other than a parent must be on a pre-approved list or give us a safe word. Since there's no one currently on TJ's list you must have the safe word."

"I…I'm sorry. Maybe he forgot. I don't have it."

"Then I'm sorry."

"Well he asked me to ask for an Xavier."

"That's the word. Let me get his jacket."

Ms. Mae put TJ in Brandy's arms and walked into the classroom. TJ reached out for Brandy's earring and pulled it out.

She grabbed it before it fell and put it into her pocket. He smiled wide with little white teeth resembling chicklets. "Hi. What's your name?"

Brandy couldn't help but smile back. This was one of the cutest kids she'd seen, besides Misa, and his smile was infectious. "It's Brandy. What's *your* name?"

"My name is Talib Ahmad Mbungalo, Jr. but everyone calls me TJ. I am four years old. My address is 1212 2nd Street Norf Eest Washeengton Dee Cee, and my phone number is five five five…"

Ms. Mae came back with a small blue and red backpack with Elmo on the front and a tickle me Elmo doll peeking out from the top, the same one Misa slept with every night. "TJ, remember you're only supposed to say that if you're lost. Right?"

He threw both of his arms in the air as if he'd just won a race. "Yeah!"

"That's right!" Ms. Mae turned to Brandy. "We're working on that."

Brandy grinned. "He's so smart."

"Yeah he is. Everybody loves him here. So, are you related?"

"No, I'm a friend of Talib's."

"Oh ok. You know I had to make sure you wasn't comin up here for his mother. She's been banned from here. Tay don't want her anywhere near TJ. And I don't blame him." She whispered, "I think she on that stuff. But you ain't hear that from me."

Brandy smiled at the old lady who clearly wanted to spill the tea. She was tempted to pick her for more information, but decided against it. What would be the point? "No, I didn't hear that from you. Thank you Ms. Mae."

She took the backpack and handed TJ his doll. Misa's car seat was in the trunk, so they were all set.

The long ride home started out a little awkward. Brandy wasn't exactly a kid person. But this little boy was too cute to resist.

"Hey, TJ."

"Yes, Miss Brandy?"

"Do you know the Barney song?"

TJ held up is hands and shouted, "Yeah!"

They sang it all the way home. All the way up to her front door where Missy stood, waiting for her.

"Brandy, who is this child?"

"*This* is TJ! Can you say hi to Miss Missy?"

TJ raised his little brow and smiled. "Missy Missy? What kinda name is that?!"

The ladies smiled. He was awful cute.

"I'm going to take him into Misa's room. I'll be back." Brandy gave him a few toys to occupy himself and walked back out to the kitchen where Missy was busy preparing dinner, chopping vegetables, a little too loudly. She didn't look happy.

"So, that's Tay's child. Misa's cousin," Missy said. She dropped her knife on the counter. "Brandy what are you doing?"

Brandy shrugged. "Tay asked me to pick him up."

"You? Why?"

"Uhhh because I was standing right there…and he was like being arrested…like after lying on the ground, trying to shake off the electric shock from a taser…"

"You know what I mean. Why is he here now? Where is that girl, his mother?"

"I don't know. He said he has full custody. I guess they don't deal anymore. It's fine."

"It's absolutely not fine. Brandy don't get mixed up with this boy and his baby. I worked too hard to make sure that you and Misa have every opportunity to be a success and I'm not letting you throw all of that away because this boy tracked you down."

"Throw what away? I'm not getting *mixed up* with anything. I am just babysitting for a friend for the weekend. Doing a favor. Besides I'm the whole reason he's in trouble."

"Oh please. Don't fall for that nonsense. *He's* the reason he's in trouble. He shouldn't have been at the school in the first place."

Brandy sighed. "Be that as it may, I'm doing this. I promised him. After this weekend, you won't have to worry about it. All right?"

Missy shook her head. "Misa's at Annabelle's for the weekend, and I have to go back to the mansion to tape this stupid show, so you're on your own, little girl. Think you can handle it?"

"Of course I can handle it. I have Misa all the time."

"Actually you don't. You play with Misa sometimes. There is a difference."

"Aunt Missy, I said I got it. Go on back to DC and do your thing. We'll be fine."

"Um hmm. Then you can finish dinner." She picked up her purse and keys from the table. "Call me if you need me. I'll see you back at the jail first thing Monday morning. And watch that child, Brandy."

As soon as Missy closed the door, Brandy rolled her eyes and went back to TJ who'd somehow managed to open his backpack and empty the contents of a cherry red juice box all over the light carpet.

Brandy grimaced and mumbled. "Shit." Then she took the juice box from his hand and gushed. "We'll just have to blame that one on cousin Misa, huh TJ?"

He threw his hands in the air. "Yeah!"

To Go Cups

The room was dark. Quiet, except for the purring motor of the ceiling fan overhead. Missy heard footsteps in the hall. She pulled her sleep mask up and grabbed her cell from the nightstand. It was 1:16 in the morning, and someone was lurking outside her door. She knew it was gonna happen. That's why she told Carmen she didn't want to stay nights at the mansion. Ex-lovers, alcohol and machismo did not mix well.

Chucky, Brian and Jamal were the last three in the house, and she was supposed to eliminate one of them the next day. She couldn't wait either. Missy had had more than enough of *Black Love*, Carmen and the pushy cameramen. Even Chucky and his on camera antics were getting on her nerves. He was a joker but lately he had been going so far over the top Missy couldn't tell if it was about winning her or him trying to get his own show. She had a good mind to send him home just to teach his cocky ass a lesson.

After dealing with all of Brandy's drama, Missy got back to the mansion just in time for a late dinner. The guys had already been throwing back shots and reminiscing about the days of old. She walked in just in time to catch their googly eyes and get grilled about who she loved more. That was her cue. She ordered a white wine to go and took her dinner plate back to her room. She left the drunken men to their drunken nonsense and turned in early, but clearly somebody didn't get the I-don't-wanna-be-bothered memo. She had a trick for somebody's ass, too.

Her keychain-sized pepper spray had just enough fume left to take a motherfucker down. They could try it if they wanted. First person that crossed her threshold was definitely getting a face full of fire.

The footsteps went past her room and down the hall. She thought, *Oh they're probably just going to the bathroom or something.* She waited a few minutes before turning over to go back to sleep. No sooner than her head hit her pillow she heard footsteps again.

"Hello?" she shouted. There was nothing. She shifted around in the bed, trying to find a comfortable spot. Her damp, silk nightie was sticking to her back even though the room was cool. For a split second she thought *early menopause?* Then she shuddered and quickly put it out of her mind, along with the thought of looking tired on camera if she didn't hurry up and get some sleep. So she turned up the dial on the overhead ceiling fan and replaced her sleep mask before tucking in.

Missy was fast asleep in minutes. Giving him a prime opportunity to sneak in undetected. He slid a credit card into the narrow space and pulled back the latch before he twisted the knob and quietly opened the door to her room. Missy was near REM sleep, and the ceiling fan whirled fast, so she didn't hear a sound as he tiptoed over to her bed.

He whispered, "Missy. Hey Missy…" He touched her shoulder, startling her so that she jumped up, pushed him back and grabbed the keychain from the nightstand. She flipped the top on the container and sprayed everything it had. Problem was, the ceiling fan blew half its contacts back in her direction.

She fell out of bed onto the floor. They rolled around on the carpet screaming, coughing and gagging until she managed to pull herself up and run into the bathroom. When he heard the water running he jumped up and ran in behind her. She flushed her eyes in the sink and he in the bathtub.

They conversed between coughs.

"Goddamn girl. You crazy or what?"

"Chucky, how did you get in my room! The door was locked."

"I needed to see you."

"Yeah, well look how well that turned out. Do you know what time it is?"

"Yes the only time the damn cameras are turned off. Shit. My fuckin face is on fire."

They looked at each other through painful, blurry, squinty eyes. Missy coughed and laughed. "Lord have mercy. How'd I manage to spray *myself* in the face?"

Chucky laughed. "Yeah one good squirt, and it was over for the both of us. Oh wait. That sounded kinda good, didn't it?"

"Shut up, nasty."

They sat in the bathroom long enough for the burning to subside. Chucky took her hand and led her back out into the bedroom. "You hungry?"

"Not really. It's almost 2 a.m."

"Yes you are. You ate that nasty tuna salad for dinner. You *know* you hungry."

She laughed. "OK yeah kinda."

"Wanna go for a ride?"

"A ride?"

"Yeah a ride. My car's parked in the garage over on 21st."

"You know we're not supposed to leave the house."

He snickered. "Psssht. You scared? Get a dog. We outta here."

They tiptoed down the stairs, past the other bedrooms.

When they got to the front door Chucky stopped. "Oh wait. I forgot something."

"Come on Chucky it's late. I'm not trying to be out fooling with you all night. We start taping in like five hours."

"I know, just hush. Wait right here."

She whispered, "Hurry up!"

He walked over to the parlor, tugged at the side of a giant mirror and pulled it back. Then he slipped into a passageway behind it. A few moments later he jumped out from behind that mirror carrying two bottles of champagne. "Ok let's go."

"Chucky! You can just take these peoples stuff like that!"

"Shh! They can put it on my tab. Let's go."

They exited the mansion quietly and walked the couple blocks to his car. It was a beautiful summer night. The air was still and the bright full moon was sorta romantic. Chucky put on the latest D'Angelo cd and pulled back the panoramic moon roof on his Porsche before they set off to who knows where.

They drove into Dupont Circle taking the P street exit, then took a left back over to Que St.

Missy squealed, "Trios?!"

He smiled. "Hellz yeah!"

He walked over to her door and ushered her out. They walked into the old carry out just in the nick of time. The owner was just about to close up shop. "Heeey Chucky! Wassup man? They dapped it up. "It's good to see you."

"Wassup Mark. Long time." He looked over at Missy. "This my wife Missy."

Missy gave Chucky a side eye before she extended her hand. "Hello Mark."

"Hey, yeah I remember Missy. Fine self. What ya'll up to? I was just about to close up."

"We just out rollin. You already know what I want. A whole chicken and cheese wit errythang."

"That's wassup." Mark yelled to the back, "Aye Black! Let me get a whole chicken jont wit errything,"

Black yelled back, "I just cleaned the grill man I'm boutta go home!"

"Well fire it back up! We got some VIP's in the house!"

Minutes later Mark handed them a brown paper bag with their cheesesteaks and a few complimentary goodies. They hopped back in the Porsche and hit the road. Chucky cranked the music back up as they drove well over the speed limit, under the tunnel toward the highway. Missy hadn't felt so free in a long time. She smiled when she saw the sign for Gravelly Point.

Chucky pulled off the highway and into a parking space on the empty lot. He grabbed the bags, the wine and a blanket from the back and they settled onto a spot close to the water. Just like old times.

Chucky popped the cork on one of his *hot* bottles of cold champagne and poured two healthy cups.

"Where'd you get to go cups?"

"Girl, you know I stay ready."

"Apparently so." She took a bite of her sandwich, the cheese stringing from the end of the bun to her lips. "Ummm! I haven't had one of these in so looong."

Chucky bit down into his and closed his eyes. "I know, it's good right."

"Yes, exactly like I remember it."

Chucky smacked his tongue a couple times. "Man, this champagne is boss! What is it?" He picked up the bottle and examined the label. "Salon Les…les..I can't pronounce this shit. But it's good as a mofo."

She grabbed the bottle from his hand. "Salon Les Mesnit. And your ass is going to jail. Do you know how much this cost?"

He took another swallow and answered, nonchalantly. "Nope."

Missy shook her head. "It's a vintage…$500 a bottle, maybe more."

"Got dam! No wonder it's so good! Well it's open now." He playfully raised his brows up and down. "*We* might as well drink up."

"Oh no. I don't have anything to do with this."

"So you gon tell on me?"

She turned her head.

"I knew you was a snitch."

"Shut up Chucky."

"Come here."

"What?"

"Come here girl. Gimme dem feet."

She quickly kicked off her sandals and obliged him. Chucky gave a killer foot massage. Which usually led to *other* things. This night would be no different. He gave her a good five minutes of sensual, expertly pressure pointed massage before he started to venture above her ankles. He caressed her calf and then pressed his long strong fingers into her thighs. Outer, then inner, then up and into the places she was longing for him to go. Places he hadn't been in two years, nine months and ten or 20 days. But who was counting.

She moaned softly and smiled. "So are we going back your *grand mamma's* house?"

He climbed slowly on top of her and whispered. "Who

needs a house?"

Grateful

The rain washed over the city in buckets. Torrential downpours began in the early morning, and loud thunder woke Brenda from a dream where she stood in her mother's kitchen helping her wash the collard greens for Sunday dinner. Brenda tried to plead her case to Betty; to profess her love. Even asked for her blessing. But Betty wasn't having it. She stood over the stove grunting, frowning and turning her chicken.

"Girl you better wake up. I don't care what you say. That white boy ain't right. What he want witchu anyway? A maid? Hmm. Educated white man. Jewish at that. He just gon come get a nigga and marry her outta jail? Bullshit. Hand me that bowl over there."

"But ma. You don't understand. He's not like that. He loves me. And I love him!"

"Brenda! Wake up!"

Dave shook her arm. "Brenda! Wake up! I'm gonna be late for my meeting. I need my breakfast."

Brenda opened her eyes. And rolled them closed again. "Dave! Can you for once do something for yourself?! What am I to you your cook? Your fuckin maid?!"

There was an uncomfortable silence. He looked at her, puzzled. "Where'd that come from?"

Brenda sat silently.

"Fine. I guess I'll grab something on the way." He stormed out of the room, slamming the door behind him.

Her first instinct was to stop him. Run after him and apologize. Dave didn't deserve to be snapped on. He'd been nothing but good to her since the day they met. He loved her, and he'd given her a good life. Still she let him go, if only to make it clear that she *wasn't* his maid, or is cook, or his fuckin concubine. She had a mind and feelings and she needed more out of life than to serve her husband, as his mother so eloquently intimated during her visit.

She went back to sleep and slept through the morning, for once. She hadn't done that the entire time they'd been married. If he was up she was up, sexing or cooking, sometimes both, at the same time. Sex stopped being sexy. It was borderline objectifying. Fetishistic almost. Brenda couldn't tell if it was attraction or a weird fascination he had for her. It's not that she didn't think she was sexy or worth a man's adoration, but…there was something off about the whole thing.

She picked up the phone and dialed Aunt Pat.

"Good afternoon my most favorite auntie in the whole wide world who handles all things big and small."

Aunt Pat answered, dryly, "Wuddyu want?"

"Dang, why I gotta want somethin?"

"Cause you just said I'm your favorite aunt that handles all things big and small. Obviously you need me to handle somethin. What is it?"

"Where's your man on the investigation?"

"Um hmm. I don't know yet. He text me last week. Said he might have somethin, but he ain't hit me back yet. I'll call him today."

"Cool. So other than that. How's everything goin in your world? You talked to Connie?"

"Why the fuck y'all keep askin me about her? No! I ain't talked to her since the show."

"Ok ok. Don't bite my head off. Geez. I don't wanna hold you up. Just let me know what you find out.

"I already told you I would."

Brenda walked out onto the veranda. She stood there leaning against the wrought iron railing, sipping a mimosa and looking out onto the beautiful landscape. Gorgeousness. Perfectly landscaped gardens to the right. Olympic sized swimming pool on the left. Below her a motor court with her beautiful new custom BMW and Dave's expensive toy cars.

She turned around and peered back into her bedroom, in all its grandness. Fine furnishings and luxurious linens. Expensive jewels and trinkets lined the dressers. A massive walk in closet housed a wardrobe befitting Hollywood royalty. Far surpassing her old Ridgewood walk in, jam packed with designer sneakers, red bottoms and stretch jeans. Louis bags in every design. Hood couture.

These days she was stepping lively in Giuseppe Zanotti and Brian Atwood. Frocks from Alexander Wang, Balmain and Lanvin. Bags by Celine and Bottega Venetta. No more bamboo earrings, flawed tennis bracelets and hot Rolexes from the back of a truck. Now there were vintage Chanel brooches and baubles by Bvlgari; his and hers Audemars timepieces from the royal collection.

Brenda lived like a queen. Better than she'd ever imagined. Certainly better than she did when she was in the "life". And it was all because of her husband. Her hard working, adoring new husband who wanted nothing more than to love his wife and to be taken care of.

She thought back to the day they met at the jailhouse. How slovenly he was and how nervous she was about letting him take her case. Then she thought of the next time she saw him in his GQ best, polished and poised, ready to take on the world to set her free. Dave was truly her white knight on a white horse. He'd found her, rescued her, and loved her back to life. He saw past her past and loved her for exactly who she was. Clearly. He loved her.

The longer she sat and sipped and reflected on all the good that David Cohen had brought to her life, the guiltier she felt. For doubting him. He'd done nothing wrong. Nothing at all. Never given her a reason to believe anything other than what he'd said and who he'd been to her. So what, he wanted to jiggle her ass a little. It was a great ass, who could blame him? He loved her cooking so much that he wanted it every day. He wanted a housewife to be there to take care of his needs and he would love and spoil her completely rotten in return. Was that really *so* wrong?

For all of his hard work and sacrifice, all the long hours and time away from home, all Dave wanted was to make love to his wife often and be fed. For her to be supportive and available and present when he needed her. The same thing any man wants. Every man wants. She felt foolish.

Aunt Pat's phone went straight to voicemail. "Hey, this is Brenda. About that thing. Just call it off. Ok. Oh and thanks. Bye."

Baby Mama Drama

The door shook so hard Brandy thought it would come down. Keisha screamed at the tippy top of her lungs for someone to "open the muufuckin door!" Brandy hadn't planned to open it, or even acknowledge Keshia's craziness, but somehow TJ managed to slip out of bed and down the hall before she could catch him. He ran as fast as his little feet would carry him, yelling, "Mommy! Mommy!" By the time Brandy reached him, he'd already opened the door and let *mommy* in.

Keisha walked right in, right past TJ without so much as a nod in his direction. "Where Tay at?"

She looked bad. *Real bad,* Brandy thought. She'd lost a ton of weight and her face was jaunt. She'd always been known for having a ginormous butt, but that was gone. So were her hips. And the hair around the perimeter of her head.

What was left of her hair was in a messy pony tail. Her leggings were so stretched out they were nearly see through, and her T-shirt was dirty and slouching at the neckline. She wore house slippers that had seen way too much of the outdoors. And then there was this weird smell about her, a stench that Brandy couldn't quite place, but it was a drug for sure. Whatever she had gotten hold of, had pretty good hold on her. It was kinda sad...but Brandy wasn't sad at all. She just shook her head thinking how real karma could be. "So you're not even gonna speak to your son?"

Keisha looked down at TJ for a moment before she picked him up and perched him on her frail hip. "Yeah. Where Tay at?"

"He's at work," Brandy said. "What can I do for you?"

"What can you do for me? Pshhh. Girl please. What he got you in here babysittin? You know he don't really fuck wit you right. He just need a baby sitter. He'll let anybody watch TJ. You ain't special."

"What do you want Keisha."

"I want my money. Tay told me he would give me fifty dollars so I can get my medicine. Just til my check come."

"Well he's not here so you have to come back later."

"Well if you give it to me he can just give it back to you. Then I won't have to come back and bother y'all."

Brandy frowned. "What? I don't have any money to give you."

"You be fakin like shit. You *know* you got money." She sighed. "Anywayyy. So what y'all supposed to be back together now?"

Brandy sighed, "Not that it's any of your business, but no. We're just friends. I'm just here doin him a favor."

"Ya'll might as well get back together. Ion want his lame ass no more. I mean…don't get me wrong. The dick is good. It's big or whateva. But I'm over it. I'll let you have him back." She clapped her hands together and laughed. "For fifty dollars."

Brandy balled her fists at her sides. Tired of hearing Keshia's dumb voice. Ready to knock the nonsense right out of her knotty head. "Keshia I swear if you don't…"

"Ooh." Keisha put TJ back down on the floor. "Tay got it lookin real nice up in here. I ain't been in here in a minute. New furniture. New carpet." She walked around the room. She went over to Tay's bedroom and peeked in. "Same old sheets though." She smiled at Brandy. "I need to use the bathroom." She walked into the bathroom and closed the door.

Brandy looked at her watch. It was almost eight o'clock, time for Tay to get home so she could get the hell out of there and away from his baby mama drama. She'd done her good deed, and there was no way was she about to get mixed back up with Keisha's crazy ass. That chapter was closed.

Keisha lingered in the bathroom for quite a while. TJ sat on the sofa nodding, so Brandy picked him up and carried him back to his room. Just as she tucked him in she heard Keisha yell. "Tell Tay I said I'll holla at him later." And the door slammed shut.

She walked out to the living room and locked the door before returning to TJ's side.

Twenty minutes later, Tay walked into the bedroom where Brandy laid sleeping with TJ in her arms. He kissed them both on the forehead. "Hey."

She opened her eyes. "Hey." Then eased carefully out of bed so as not to awaken the peacefully sleeping toddler. They walked back out into the living room.

"I'm sorry I'm late. Work was crazy today and thank God my car was still parked on the street. I just knew it was gonna be towed. Thank you for taking care of him, Brandy. I don't know what I would have done without you this weekend."

"You don't have to thank me. I was happy to do it for you."

"I didn't get a chance to thank your aunt for sending the lawyer to get me out this morning. Will you leave her number for me? And I really appreciate you getting TJ to school today. And I'll reimburse you for the clothes you bought him. And... "

"Tay. It's ok. I told you, I was more than happy to help."

"I know, I just can't thank you enough. How was your weekend? How'd TJ do?"

"Our weekend was great. TJ's a sweetheart. He was fine."

"I think he likes you. You know he can be really funny with new people."

She smiled. "I'll bet he can. I like him, too."

"I didn't even think y'all were in here. All the lights were off and I didn't see your car."

"My car's parked right out front."

"Uh...no. It's not."

Brandy ran over to the window. "Oh my God!" She ran back into the kitchen where she left the keys, and her purse, and her cell phone. Everything was gone. "Oh my God. Oh. My. God. That bitch stole my shit!"

"Who?!"

"Keisha!"

"You let Keisha in here?!"

"What? Yeah she said she was picking up money from you."

"Keisha is not supposed to be within a thousand yards of

this house, me or TJ."

"Well how the FUCK was I supposed to know that, Tay?! That's *your* baby mama drama! I just got here! Shit!"

"Ok, calm down…"

"Calm down?! She has my car! My purse! My credit cards! My license! Oh my god ALL my personal information."

Tay stood there feeling helpless and exasperated. It definitely was not how he planned to start anew with the woman he loved. But he was gonna fix it. Keisha had wreaked enough havoc on his life and he was going to put a stop to the bullshit once and for all.

"Hello, police? I need to report a robbery."

Sweet Thang

Half-eaten subs, red cups, and an insanely expensive half-empty champagne bottle was strewn about on the grass. Chucky pulled one side of the blanket over them, completely shielding them from the elements, and any voyeurs that happened to be out taking a predawn jog.

Once he had her completely naked, he dove in face first, relishing in her scent and her sweetness. The soft sexy way she called his name when it was gettin really good to her. Chucky was an expert on all things Missy. He knew where all the buttons were and what call would get a response.

A soft kiss on the left side of her neck made her hair stand on end. A gentle nibble on her left nipple made her wince, but if you pushed them together and licked them both back and forth, she'd release for you. When she arched her back and parted her legs, she wanted your face below her navel, and if you got the perfect combination of finger-tongue thrusting, there would be multiple breaches of her dam, which not only inflated egos but made for a deliciously juicy night of lovemaking.

On top of all that, she was a FREAK. Costumes, role play, in the sunshine or the rain, everything was game. Missy was hands down, without a doubt the best piece-a-pussy he ever had, and the kicker was he was totally, completely and irreversibly in love with her. It didn't get better than her, and he'd had plenty to compare her to.

Under the shield of the thick blanket, he'd managed to wriggle off every item of clothing. He'd given her everything he'd been saving up for her for three years. She winced, released and the dam was breached, so it was time. He climbed up on top and inside. She gasped at his fullness, and he closed his eyes, as he tried to maintain his composure, find his rhythm. "Damn girl, you boutta make me cum already."

He was determined not to let it beat him. Once he pulled it together, he was ready. He pushed her legs back and stood on his hands and toes and he dropped himself inside her, slowly, so she could watch. She always liked to. He went in deeper and deeper as she opened to him, hungrily receiving every inch of him. They were both completely naked and dripping wet from the intense heat radiating from under the heavy blanket. The sound of their moans echoed into the dawn.

He dropped to his knees and pushed one of her legs back before he entered her again. He cradled her head with one hand, kissing her passionately and with the other he held the back of her knee, controlling her openness. He pushed her thigh over and down, allowing himself to penetrate deeper inside and then he pulled it back up, closer to his body to create a little more friction, gyrating his hips, moving in, out and around her, hitting her sweetest spots.

Missy felt a sudden shift in his rhythm and his pulsating veins, which only excited her more. Then she began to Kegel him on into his release, contracting her muscles on his outstroke.

"Um. That's right baby. Cum for me," she moaned loudly.

"Shit. Baby you bout ta make me cum. I'm bout ta cum. I'm bout ta.." Just as he released, the roaring engine of a low flying jet drowned their sounds. Chucky hadn't been with a woman in a while, and what better way to get back into the game than wrapped up inside the only woman he'd ever loved.

The orgasm was intense and emotional for the both of them. For a while, they lay there with her legs still wrapped tightly around his waist, and he still nestled in her warmth. He planted soft sweet kisses over her entire face as he professed his love to her in true Chuck nasty fashion. "Damn girl. Pussy make a nigga wanna stalk."

Missy laughed until she could hardly breathe. Chucky could always come up with a good one.

He smiled. "You laughin. I'm dead ass. This is it. It's us now."

"Whatever Chucky."

"You think I'm jokin. I'm not playing no more games with you, Missy. Or my life. Once we get this stupid game show shit over with, Imma cash my check, get you a ring as big as I can afford, and we gon make this shit official."

She grinned at the thought. "Really?"

"Yes really. You know I love you. And you already know *he* love you."

"*He* who?"

She felt him stiffening inside her. He gave her one good thrust. "Him."

Chucky reached underneath her to grasp her bottom and gave her his tongue as he thrust again, and again. Slowly and deliberately, searching for that spot.

Her soft moans filled the air and excited him all the more. The sound of her voice. His name on her lips. Everything felt right. She rubbed his back. He kissed her face. It was wet. Her tears were all the confirmation he needed. He was finally home.

"Yeah, baby. This right here. This is mine. I ain't goin nowhere baby. You ain't goin nowhere. We home." He pushed back her leg and put his back into it. "I'm home right."

She cried out, "Yes."

He went in deeper. "It's mine right?"

"Yes!"

"Um hmm. That's right."

As Chucky worked her over, Missy opened to him completely. The sex was as good as it had ever been. Chucky really knew how to move his body. He knew how to work her body. He knew exactly how to please. She'd already released twice, and he was still plunging away, whispering softly in her ear, "I love it when you cum for me, baby."

She responded, nearly breathless, "I love it when you make me cum."

Chucky was a selfless lover. He'd do most anything to please her. She wanted to return the favor. She gently pushed at his chest, "Turn over." She pushed him up and rolled him onto his back so she could mount him properly. Then she gripped his manhood and guided it back inside. Sliding up and down, varying speed, motion and tension.

Chucky bit his bottom lip and grunted. "Fuck." He held her breasts in his hands tweaking hard nipples, causing her to moan. He thrust upward as she descended…downward, consuming every inch of him. He grabbed her hips and shuddered. Another jet flew overhead drowning their sounds. When it passed there was quiet and then…

"Park Police! Show me your hands!"

*****

Missy laid there stark naked and *completely* mortified. Not to mention sweaty and dripping of Chucky's love. Chucky had tossed both their clothes outside the blanket, so there was no way to retrieve them without at least one of them being exposed. It was an impossible situation.

Still under the shield of the blanket, they heard the car doors open and close.

Missy whispered. "Oh my God. We're going to jail. Chucky, we're going to jail. Go get my clothes."

He half laughed. "*You* go get em." She sighed. He sensed she wasn't in the mood for jokes. "Ok, ok. I'll handle this."

He eased out from under the blanket and stood tall. "Officer, I can explain."

An hour later, Carmen was at the police station picking them up. Chucky walked out smiling, but Missy was still a little shaken up, embarrassed, and a dreadful mess with bags under her eyes and her hair matted on top of her head. She tried to avoid Carmen's gaze, to no avail.

"Y'all *nasty*," Carmen teased.

Chucky smiled and humped the air.

Missy rolled her eyes. "Can you just take us back to his car please?"

"Oh, so I don't get a thank you for getting out of my bed at the crack of damn dawn and driving 35 miles to rescue you two dirty delinquents? No respect." She leaned over in Chucky's direction. "Was it worth it?"

He exaggerated a wink, and Missy yelled. "Carmen!"

Carmen laughed. "What?! I'm just playin. Look, I did what I could, but y'all know I ain't gon be able to keep this quiet. Don't be surprised if you hear about it once the show comes out. I talked to the officer, and he agreed to let you both off with citations for the litter. The lewd and lascivious behavior and disturbing the PEACE charge..." She glared at Chucky. "...have been dropped. Chucky why would you ask an officer to stop looking at your dick?

"Cause he was looking at my dick!"

Missy rolled her eyes. "Jesus Christ. Can we just go, please!"

Carmen giggled. "I'm ready. Oh, and one last thing, you've been banned from Gravelly Point. Officer Simms says if he catches either one of you there again you're going to jail."

Chucky yelled, "Say what?! Give up the Point? Oh nah, you can forget that shit. No deal. No deal." He looked at Missy. "We gotta fight this shit baby. You ridin or what?"

She scowled at him. "Do you EVER stop playing?" She jumped in the front seat of the car and slammed the door shut as Carmen and Chucky stood on the outside, looking at each other like two scolded toddlers.

Missy and Chucky rode back to the mansion in complete silence, and the ride was doubly painful because they were stuck in early morning rush hour traffic. Before they left the precinct Missy made it very clear that she'd had more than enough of his antics. She just wanted a shower and some sleep, but unfortunately they were already late to start their taping so not only would she be spending the day faking on camera, she'd look haggard doing it. She thought, *What the hell am I doing?*

De-Classified

Her headaches were getting worse by the day. Between the money and the bullshit with Connie, Aunt Pat had a lot on her mind. She thought it was stress. But maybe something more. She hated doctors, but the bootleg Percocet's stopped working a week ago and the pain was so extreme her vision was getting blurry. That couldn't be good.

She laid back in her chair with a cold compress on her forehead. The room was dark and quiet. The sound of her cell phone ringing instantly sent her head pounding again. She snatched it up and answered with her eyes closed.

"Hello."

"What it do, Miss Pat."

"Oh. Hey Lance."

"Did I catch you at a bad time? You sound kinda…out of it?"

"Nah, I'm good, what you got for me?"

"I didn't find a whole lot on the lady, Meredith. But I got some interesting stuff on your boy."

"Interesting?"

"Yeah. I just got back from public records. I think your boy livin foul. Real foul."

Too Late to 'Pologize

Missy opened the front door. "Hey. Why are you knocking? Where are your keys? What's wrong?"

Brandy mumbled as she walked past her, "Nothing. I lost my keys." She ran up the stairs. Missy called out. "Brandy!"

Before Missy could get the front door closed there was another knock. She opened it. "Yes?"

"Melissa James?"

"Yes, I'm Melissa James."

A wily millennial with long disheveled hair passed her a thick white envelope. "You've just been served. Have a good afternoon, ma'am."

Missy watched as the messenger hurried back down the driveway to his teeny blue Smart car and sped away. Missy smiled thinking how strange it must be to drive the little contraption.

The return address was from Cohen and Associates. She tore into the envelope and pulled out a thick stack of papers stapled at the top. Then she laughed. *Really?*

After she gathered her thoughts a bit, Missy walked upstairs to Brandy's room. She knocked a couple times before turning the knob and walking in.

Brandy lay across her bed with her headphones on, humming. She looked up at Missy's stern expression and switched her music off. "Hey."

"Hey sweetie." She squinted. "Those are some really nice headphones. When'd you get those?"

"Neiman's. The other day."

"I didn't know Prada made headphones."

Me neither. I saw them on the mannequin and the salesperson said they had them in gold. So I got them. Nice, right?"

"Yeah, but was there something *wrong* with the really expensive apple headphones I bought you for Christmas?"

"Huh?"

"Never mind. Can you just take them off for a second?"

Brandy pulled her headphones off and laid them on her bed. "What's going on?"

"I just got something in the mail that we need to discuss."

"Ugh. Aunt Missy I had a really long day today and I'm really tired. Can it wait?"

"No, actually it can't."

Missy handed her the stack. Brandy looked at the first page. "Oh, wow. Really." She threw it on the bed and put her headphones back on.

Missy pulled them back off. "Sweetie we have to talk about this. Now I've backed off when it comes to your mother. I haven't pressed the issue, but like it or not it has to be addressed."

"Actually it doesn't. I'm an adult, over the age of 18. This is about Mandy. My name is nowhere on that piece of paper."

"Your mother wants her *children*. Not her child."

"In that case, she probably wants her *grandchild*, too."

"Well now, that's never going to happen."

"Exactly. She can't come now and try to reclaim anybody. We've done just fine without her all these years. She's remarried now. She can start a whole new family with that white man."

"Brandy."

"I'm not talking about this anymore, Aunt Missy. I'm done." She reached for her headphones.

Missy grabbed them and tossed them behind her. "No, let's be fair now. She did come for you when she got home. The same day as a matter of fact. She came here several times, and you refused to speak to her."

"I said I'm not talking about this."

"When you finally spoke to her, you completely flipped on her, Brandy. You looked her in the eye and told her that you hated her. You told her that she was the reason Mandy was messed up and that everyone was better off without her."

Brandy screamed, "You act like I lied! We *are* better off without her. All of us!" Heavy tears dropped from her eyes. "Two years she was gone, Aunt Missy. We didn't get to see her face once. Never once heard her voice and she comes back like *I'm home?*! Married to some white man and ready to make a family?! Fuck her!"

"Bran—"

"No! I mean it. I don't want nuthin to do with her! And I'll take Mandy away myself before I let her get near her again!" Brandy ran into her bathroom and slammed the door shut.

Missy's heart broke, as she stood outside listening to Brandy's sobs. She wanted to go in, but figured it better to leave her alone, for a little while at least. Maybe she needed a good cry. She had a right to be angry. But Brenda had a right to her feelings too.

Missy regretted not intervening before. She knew it was selfish of her not to step in. But truthfully, she didn't want to give up her girls any more than they wanted to go. Misa was hers, free and clear, adopted shortly after her birth. Brandy was of age, so the decision was hers, but Mandy was vulnerable, fully subject to the agreement she'd made to give her back to Brenda as soon as she was released from prison.

Missy knew full well that if Brandy hadn't stepped in and put Brenda on a major guilt trip, she would have lost Mandy for sure. Mandy helped the cause by screaming bloody murder every time Brenda came near her, but Missy added insult to injury when Brenda pleaded for her to step in and do the "right thing." Missy responded, "Well Brenda if they don't want to be with you. I mean…you do want what's best for them, don't you? Do you really think that uprooting them from a life they've grown comfortable with is the best thing right now?"

Brenda stood in Missy's foyer with pleading eyes focused intently on Brandy and a grip firmly on Mandy's hand. She just wanted her children back. Like they agreed. But Brandy's eyes were cold. Mandy screamed and pulled away from her. Missy stood wait, no doubt hoping she'd give up walk away. And she did.

Feeling defeated, unwanted and unwelcome, she finally let go of Mandy's hand. Mandy threw her arms around Missy's waist. Her crying stopped immediately. Brenda's silent cries went unnoticed as she turned and walked away from her children. Again.

A week later, Missy received a call from her lawyer. Brenda had dropped her custody suit. At the time, Missy convinced herself that it was the right thing, mainly by her own self-serving, clichéd reasoning. *Everything happens for a reason. If Brenda were meant to get the girls back she'd have them. If she really wanted them she would have fought harder.* Bullshit.

Ever since the day Brenda left her house, Missy's life had gone on a complete downward spiral. It started with the smallest thing. A call from her contractor telling her that there was a crack in the foundation of her beautiful new home. Thirty thousand. A call from her accountant telling her that her business was being audited. The end result, Matt was doing some shady accounting, and she was now partially liable for more than $200,000 in back taxes. Lastly and most horribly, a visit from a slick little greaseball making threats against her family and demanding a million for some shit she had absolutely nothing to do with.

Missy's entire world was crumbling slowly, and she couldn't help thinking, maybe, if she started trying to make some of the wrong things right in her life, then just maybe she could undo some of the craziness. So she decided to give Brenda a call. Tomorrow.

Ride Wit Me

Brandy had been ignoring his calls. His texts. Emails. She didn't want to hear nothing from Tay except "We found your car, and your purse is still inside." She felt foolish for even starting with him again. All that drama. Keisha's crazy crackhead ass. She was lucky, Aunt Missy was so busy with her show she didn't even ask about the car. Brandy prayed they'd find the damn thing before she got wise. But with Keisha there was no telling what would happen.

She laid in bed, staring at the ceiling a full twenty minutes after her alarm had gone off, contemplating whether or not to go to class. She hated to have to take an Uber all the way into the city, but missing her exam was not an option. So she peeled herself out of her comfortable bed, turned on her favorite morning radio station and hit the shower.

After her shower, there was just enough time for a quick breakfast, then she'd call the car share service and jump into her clothes. Her phone rang. She glanced over at it, *Tay.* She ignored it, again. Aunt Missy yelled upstairs, "Brandy I'm gone! Have a good day!" Moments later, a car horn blared from outside in the driveway. She walked over to her window, rolled her eyes hard and chuckled.

"Boy, what are you doin here?" she yelled from her bedroom window.

Tay yelled up to her. "Hurry up and get dressed. You wanna be late for school?"

She smiled. That's exactly what he used to say to her every morning when he called to wake her up for school. He'd call her at 7 a.m. sharp, rushing her to get ready, and then he'd still show up late, which made them both late for class. Everyday.

She grabbed her robe from the back of the bedroom door and walked downstairs. Tay sat on the hood of his car. Smiling. Flashing his perfect whites. Dressed in denim, a black leather jacket and matching black leather boots. Smelling good, on purpose.

"What are you doing here?"

"You cold?"

"Huh?"

He looked down. Her nipples were at attention, protruding through the thin fabric of her silk robe. She folded her arms over her chest. "What are you doing here?"

"I just told you. I'm here to take you to class. Today's the day for your big exam, right?"

"Yes, but you really didn't have to drive way out here to…"

"Brandy, it's no trouble. And it's the least I could do. I'm really sorry about your car. I'm sorry about everything. If I could…"

She raised a hand. "Don't worry about it. It's not your fault. Have you heard from Keisha?"

"Nobody's heard from her."

"Well I haven't told my aunt yet. I'm really hoping they'll find it before she finds out it's missing. But anyway…" She gave him a coy smile. "…you wanna come inside and wait while I get dressed?

"Nah."

Surprised and mildly disappointed she inquired. "Why not?"

Tay nodded to the backseat of his car. TJ was strapped in his booster seat fast asleep. "And traffic's gonna be a beast on I66, so we need to get movin. I don't want you to be late for class."

"Um hmm. Well it wouldn't be the first time."

"Yeah, yeah, whatever. Now go get dressed, lil girl."

To that she unfolded her arms, allowing her robe to gape open, giving him the slightest peek of her black lacy bra and panty set. Then she smirked. "Little girl? Trust me, there's no little girl here."

Tay tried to conceal his grin, and his growing excitement, as she turned to walk away. The wind blew through her robe lifting it high enough for him to scale her shapely brown legs, thick thighs and her booty bouncing almost out of her panties with each exaggerated step she took toward the house. She glanced back at him before she entered the house. He caught it and waited for her to get inside before he stood and adjusted himself.

Tay sighed, and laughed and thought to himself. *Damn Brandy. This gon be a long ass ride.*

Low Blows

The next morning her phone rang early. Missy answered with her sleep mask still firmly in place to block out the strong morning sun.

"Hel...Hello."

"Missy what are you DOING? How many times do I have to tell you that you cannot go home after taping? This costs us time and money! I can't keep covering for you."

"Carmen, listen. My kids come first. Brandy needed me, and I went home. I planned to come back, but then it got late and..."

"I sent a car for you. It should be there at seven."

"I'm perfectly capable of driving myself.

"No, you're not. Please, just be ready at seven."

"Fine."

Missy showered and dressed in a hurry. She grabbed her coffee and ran for the door. "Brandy I'm gone! Have a good day!" she yelled up the stairs before she rushed out to the town car. Brandy's little boyfriend pulled into the driveway, as her driver backed out. Missy pretended not to see him. She made a mental note to speak with Brandy about him as soon as she got back home. Brandy had come too far to get mixed up in his foolishness. He'd have to go.

Traffic on the 166 Interstate going east was murder in the morning. But it did give her time to catch up on her reading. She'd barely cracked the latest from her book of the month club, and this morning was as good as any. Fishing through her briefcase for her paperback, she ran across the envelope with the custody papers. She thought of Brenda.

She picked up her phone and stared at the number for some time before she got the courage to hit the dial. The phone rang once and then it went to voice mail. She hung up and dialed again. Again the call was forwarded to voice mail. Missy didn't leave a message.

She sat staring out of the window as the car slow-crawled through morning traffic. Brenda was mad. Obviously. And rightfully. Missy thought she had every right to be. The agreement wasn't kept. All the woman wanted was what she was promised – her children. Not only was she denied them, she was humiliated and hung out to dry.

As hard as it would be, Missy planned to fix it and do what she could to make up for the lost time. Brandy would prove difficult for sure but at the very least she would send Mandy back home to be with her mother. It was the right thing. The only thing.

Missy wanted to do things right. Have everything official, at least in the very beginning. There was way too much bad blood for another handshake situation, so Missy thought it was actually good that the lawyers were already involved. They could quickly hammer things out – the exchange of custody, the visitation. Make the transition as smooth as possible.

With at least another half hour on the trip to DC, she decided to read through the complaint and see what Brenda had in mind, to see where they could start. She pulled the petition from the envelope and flipped through.

The first few pages, standard enough. She was going for full custody of Mandy. To be expected. No biggie. But the more she read the more incensed she became. Brenda had lost her fuckin mind.

As was written, Brenda wasn't just going for Mandy, she wanted Misa, too. She was contesting Misa's adoption, citing Brandy was coerced into giving her child away. She detailed that Brandy was a minor at the time her child was taken, and at that time Missy was not yet her legal guardian. She cited Missy as unfit to parent, as she was financially incapable of taking care of the children.

There was a smaller envelope in the bottom of the bigger one, the contents of which were clearly not a part of the official complaint. Inside was a copy of Mandy's last three behavioral evaluations, the withdrawal documents from her boarding school, enrollment records for her new school and several collection notices for unpaid tuition from both schools. It was pretty clear to see that Missy had removed Misa from the more expensive school, enrolled her into a less expensive, lesser accredited school and Mandy was regressing as a result. That's how it looked at least. That's the narrative Brenda would use.

Along with Mandy's documents, there was a notice of default from Missy's mortgage company, confirmation of the voluntary repossession from the Mercedes dealership, and several bank statements with overdrawn balances highlighted in bright neon green. Stuck to the bank statements was a yellow Post-it note with familiar handwriting:

Melissa,

I see times are tough, but the children shouldn't have to suffer. Wouldn't you agree? I want my babies back. Give them up now or prepare for a fight. If you can afford it.

-Mrs. Brenda Cohen

Missy flipped the papers onto the floor and laughed. She thought, *Really*. She sat back and pondered the entire situation. From the day she opened that jail letter with Brenda literally BEGGING her to take the children in, to the present day where she was being attacked and berated, simply for doing what she was asked to do.

Pretty soon the laugh turned to a smirk, and the smirk to a frown. The more she thought on it, the angrier she got. She had a good mind to call Brenda's ungrateful ass back and let her have it. How DARE she come at her this way? She thought, *I take care of your kids like you BEGGED me to, and now I'm the fucking villain? I didn't turn your kids against you, YOU DID! I didn't send you to jail, YOU DID! That was YOUR LIFE! YOU chose to marry a fucking drug dealer and raise your kids up in that bullshit life. That was YOU! Not ME!*

By the time they arrived at The Mansion, Missy had worked herself up into a real tizzy. All of her compassion and charitable thinking had gone by the wayside. She was ready to get the day done so she could go and see her lawyer. Money may have been limited but Missy had enough political capital stored up to pull a few favors, gratis, so if her little sister thought she was going to muscle her just because she'd come into a little money, she was sadly fucking mistaken. She'd better be prepared to fight, because no one was going to take her girls away. *Not even their mother.*

The Chosen Few

Brian, Jamal and Chucky were the three men left standing after all of the shenanigans. Missy had been wined and dined, courted, and even proposed to. She'd been subjected to so much hamming and fighting and pettiness that she couldn't wait for the show to come to an end.

She was tempted to send Chucky's ass packing after the stunt he pulled with the police officer, but she'd already been instructed to keep him around.

At the elimination ceremony, she was instructed to ask each of the guys why they thought they should stay in the competition. Their responses ranged from the ridiculous to the sublime.

Brian was a psychologist, a handsome light caramel brother with thick wavy black hair, perfect brows and an incredible gift of gab. The man could talk you into or out of anything…which was the reason he and Missy didn't work. One of them anyway. She always felt like she was being manipulated. He was so charming and easy. He spoke softly though his voice was deep. Smiled wide with perfect whites and always looked you intently in the eye. Subtle suggestions, hints, subliminals. Sentences ending with "for your own good" and "you'll thank me later." Kinda like a pimp. And it was effective because in the end he was always the one getting what he wanted.

He was a selfish lover with an impressive package, and a social butterfly with more "friends" than she could count. At first she found him challenging, but it wasn't long before the chase became exasperating. He was just too much work. She knew he loved her, in his own way, but he was a player – a player that was not quite ready to give up the game. So she left him, his friends, and his games in New York.

Seeing him again was a bit of a treat. He'd aged well. Other than a little salt and pepper gray in his full beard, he looked exactly the same. His body was still lean and tight. She'd noticed that while they were lounging at the pool. He still said all the right things at the right time. All of the time. He'd charmed his way through to the end game, and his reason for staying was that he wanted another opportunity to make a life with the most remarkable woman he'd ever known and been so foolish to let slip away. God had given him another chance, and if she'd have him he promised not waste it. He wanted to show her what happy looked like, what it felt and tasted like.

His words were so eloquent and so sincere that she had to snap herself out of the trance that he'd put her in. When he finished speaking, Jamal was on one side of him mean muggin and Chucky was giving him the screw face from the other side. Neither of them impressed by his heartfelt display.

Chucky mumbled, "Bamma ass been rehearsin that corny shit all week."

Jamal stood there looking slightly uncomfortable in the tight suit jacket that Carmen insisted he wear to dress up his baggy jeans, Timberland boots, tank top and the signature baseball cap he wore turned to the back. He'd only made it through because she liked looking at him. All six feet, six inches and nearly three hundred pounds of massively yummy muscular fineness. He was a retired NFL fullback and rapper out of West Philly, a one-hit wonder that was at the height of his career when they dated but still desperately trying to ride that ten-year-old wave.

When asked why he thought he should stay, he rapped his response to the sound of the percussion created by beating on his right thigh with his right hand and his chest with his left. An original love rap from J'Mally Mal, peppered with profanity that had to be bleeped about every third word. It was awful and embarrassing for everyone, but plenty good for TV, and incredibly it would become J'Mally's second hit on I-tunes.

When Jamal was done he smiled, triumphantly. Missy stood silent. Chucky frowned then mumbled, "The *fuck*?" The set erupted into laughter.

When everyone was composed, Missy directed the question to Chucky. He took a moment to gather hs thoughts. "Look I don't have no *poetry* to recite or no whack ass rhymes to spit…All I have is me. Just me. The same me I've always been. The me that has loved you from the moment you told me I was a degenerate little cretin that wasn't worth your time." Missy smiled. He smiled back. "After I looked the word up, and reflected on it, I decided to go about the business of changing your mind about me. The business of becoming a man that was worth your time. I pulled my pants up. Stopped huggin the block. Went back to school and got my diploma. Started chasin my dreams. I made a success of my life. That was all you, Missy. No one has ever made me feel more like a somebody than you. You encouraged me. Saw the good in me. You taught me to dream bigger and to reach higher. And no matter what happens, tonight, I will forever love you for that."

Missy's tried hard to suck in a tear that threatened to fall from the corner of her right eye. He continued.

"So I stand here before you, being here for you and only you. Unlike some other people up here on this platform…" He glared at Brian. "…I'm not living with my pregnant baby mama. Pictures all on Instagram kissing her on her belly. Buncha Picture People photos at the mall. Whole family dressed alike in all white. I'm just sayin." Brian sighed and rolled an eye. Chucky continued.

"Then you got another one up here, profile on homothug.com. Hangin at The Mill over on 8th street. Lookin for a few good men." He shook his head at Jamal. "Yeah nigga, I looked you up. Gay much?"

Jamal lunged at Chucky, and security snatched him up just in time. "Fuck you nigga! You tryna call me gay?! I will *kill* you fuck nigga! I'll fuckin kill you!" Jamal was a big boy, so it took four security officers to keep him away from Chucky, who was standing just a few feet away with his guards up, feigning machismo but secretly terrified of the beast trying to get loose.

The officers dragged Jamal out of the parlor kicking and screaming while Chucky continued to taunt. "Aye Mal, man it ain't nuttin wrong wit bein gay. Go ahead and own that shit duke. Taste da muufuckin rainbow."

The cameras kept rolling. Missy was outdone. She wasn't sure what to say, but the director signaled for her to keep it moving. She turned to Brian. "So is it true?"

He stood silent for a moment and then decided to fess up. Sorta. "I'm sorry Missy." He walked over to her and gave her a kiss on the cheek. Then he turned and walked off set. His game was over.

Chucky smirked. He stood in front of her and grabbed her hands. "So, you see. It's just me. Just me and you, baby girl. Just like it's s'posed to be." He leaned in for a victory kiss…

"You sure about that man?" a voice called out from the heavens. Actually, it was an amplifier projecting the voice from across the room. Missy and Chucky turned in the direction of the voice, and in walked Kevin Clark, Missy's ex that she was *this* close to marrying.

Chucky looked up at her, then back at Kevin, then over to the executive producer, who was sitting in a director's chair and smiling like a Cheshire cat. He turned back to Missy. "What is this shit?"

She looked down at Chucky and shrugged. "What? I don't know."

Shady Business

Chucky grabbed Missy's hand, and they walked off set. After a heated argument that ended with him accusing her of playing games, he stormed out of The Mansion and headed over to BET studios to Carmen's office.

He walked past the receptionist and burst into her office, slamming the door behind him.

Carmen looked up from her computer and quickly shut it down. "Hey. What you doin here?"

"Don't fuckin act like you don't know what's goin on. I know you pullin strings over here. Fuck is Kevin doin in the house, Carmen?"

"Kevin? Kevin Clark?"

He glared at her.

"I didn't know he was coming on. He turned us down when we asked."

"Well apparently he had a change of heart."

"Seriously? Wow. I didn't know. I promise you." She smiled. "But I did just get an email telling me that you caused the last two guys to walk off set? They had to drag Jamal off set? What happened?"

"Carmen, you know those niggas wasn't there for Missy. One of em still with his baby mama and the other one fuckin with boys."

She leaned back in her armchair. "Chucky. Come on. What difference does that make? It's reality TV. At the end of the day, you know you the only one that got a chance with her. We're just trying to make good television. You takin this shit way too serious, baby boy."

"*I'm* taking it too serious?"

"Yes. Yes, you are. Keepin it one hundred, Missy ain't on here trying to find love anyway. She here cause she need the money. Same as you."

"I'm not here for no money…"

"Yeah, ok whatever but she is. My girl gotta lotta shit on her plate right now. Obviously shit y'all ain't talked about. Gettin her to come on this show was like pullin teeth. Then when she found out you were in the mix she really flipped. To tell the truth, that's how I knew y'all had unfinished business. Otherwise she wouldn't have been that upset. Look, Chucky, she loves you, and if you want her, get her. I put you in position. You already hit it didn't you? So now it's up to you to close the deal. Kevin Clark is a non muthafuckin factor. Missy don't want him. She never really did. She said he had nervous, sweaty hands. And his dick was too small."

Chucky raised a brow. "Whaaat?"

"Yeah. No chemistry. She just wanted the status, but then she changed her mind and went with the better option. Ray."

"Hmm."

"You almost made the cut. Your hat was in the ring for a minute. If you would have asked her to marry you instead of giving her a key to your place, who knows? But *you* fucked that up."

"Is that right?"

"Yeah. Anyway. So this is how it's gon go. We got one more show to tape. The finale. You guys will each get a date and then we'll have the final elimination ceremony. We can't tell Missy who to choose, of course, but trust me when I tell you, you got this on lock. Now go handle your business, black man. Go get your girl."

Chucky rose from his seat and walked out without another word. Carmen was full of shit, he thought. And messy. A terrible friend. But she was right about one thing. Kevin Clark was a non-factor, and he definitely wasn't letting him stand in the way of his new life with Missy.

*****

Meanwhile, back at the ranch, Missy and Kevin were at the bar having drinks. As soon as Chucky stormed out, Kevin took his opportunity for some alone time with his favorite girl, the girl he should have married, and would have married if she'd only given him a chance.

Kevin was newly divorced, and he'd left the political arena to start his entertainment law practice. Partnered with two other high powered Hollywood attorneys, he'd built a lucrative business and was back in DC to open their Georgetown branch.

Missy had followed Kevin's "situation" and career for some time. He'd divorced his wife a little over a year prior, and in that short span he'd made an incredible new life for himself, recently gracing the cover of Black Enterprise with his partners and ranking high up on the list of Ebony's most eligible bachelors. He looked good, too, better than she remembered. New money would do that.

No more off-the-rack suits and discount designer shoes. He wasn't living off an honest politician's salary anymore. He was racking up billable hours on some of Hollywood's most elite entertainers and according to him he was working with a realtor and looking to close on a twelve thousand square foot home in Fairfax. Little Kevin Clark was definitely living the life and if she'd allow herself to fantasize...

A pang of guilt fell upon her for even entertaining Kevin. As much as Chucky infuriated her, she couldn't deny how much she loved him, how happy and alive he made her feel, how much she enjoyed just being able to be herself when she was with him. He was a little down on his luck at the moment, but he had what it took to bounce back. About that she wasn't worried at all. And though it was good seeing Kevin again, she knew he wasn't the one for her. She'd play this stupid show to the end and pick the one she loved. Ride off into the sunset...or whatever.

Chucky walked into the parlor with a whole new attitude. Much more pleasant than when he left. She and Kevin were finishing their last drink for the evening and engrossed in conversation about nothing in particular. Chucky walked over, extended his hand and formally introduced himself. "Hi, Kevin. I'm sure you know by now, I'm Chucky Wilson, we never formally met. Good to meet you man."

Kevin gripped his hand firmly, "Likewise."

"Good. Well we have an early day of shooting tomorrow so if you kids don't mind, I'm gonna excuse myself for the evening."

Missy looked puzzled. "You're leaving?"

"Yeah. I need my beauty rest." He kissed Missy softly on the cheek. "You kids don't stay up too late. Have a good night." He patted Kevin on the shoulder and walked away.

Missy replied, still confused. "Oh…ok. Goodnight."

Kevin was also a bit taken aback, all things considered. But he was happy to be given more time alone with his girl. Shortly after Chucky retired, Missy attempted to follow suit, but Kevin convinced her to stay for one more drink. And then another. And a shot. He even jumped behind the bar to make her one of his famous Long Island iced teas, the one with the hint of peach flavor that always took her a little too far over the edge.

The next morning, her eyes were nearly glued shut. Her head was heavy, and she was completely naked, sweating under her thick terry bathrobe. She picked up her cell phone. It was 8:13, thirteen minutes after the time she was scheduled to be in hair and makeup. There were several missed calls from Carmen, the producer and Chucky.

She ran to the bathroom and disrobed, bumping into a wall and various furniture along the way. As soon as she reached the cold marble she fell to her knees and hugged the toilet. Her mouth and eyes watered, and it seemed everything she'd had the night before came up.

The hangover was epic, easily the worst she'd had and she'd had many. She managed to climb into the shower and cleanse, wetting her hair under the showerhead, despite the stylist's plea not to. By the time she pulled herself out, it was too late for hair and makeup so she decided to try to pull it together herself.

She squeezed a little setting lotion into her hands and worked it through her wet hair. Then she bent down and put a dryer to it to set it in, trying to achieve that perfect beach wave, that bed head made famous by Carrie Bradshaw.

She slathered moisturizer on her face and applied concealer, a little more than usual to mask the unusually dark circles under her eyes, and a little more gloss to moisturize unusually dry, cracked lips. She applied her foundation heavier than normal. For the cameras. A little blush to color her cheeks. Then she grabbed an eyeliner pen and a mascara wand.

With a queasy stomach and an unsteady hand, she did her best. It would have to do. There were only two more shows to tape and she was ready to get back home to her kids and her life.

Around 9:15, she emerged from her room. She walked out into the parlor. "Sorry guys. I'm ready now."

The entire crew stopped and stared. Kevin and Chucky were chatting away at a table in the corner. They looked up at her, standing in the doorway. Silenced. In complete and utter awe of the vision that stood before them. The expression on Chucky's face was most telling. He looked up at her and smiled. "The *fuck* happened to you?"

*****

Taping was delayed for a bit as the crew tried to compose themselves from laughter. Mortified, Missy ran from the room. Back to her suite. Chucky ran after her. Laughter could be heard in the distance.

She slammed the door on him, and he jiggled the knob. "Missy! I'm sorry!"

She screamed from behind her bedroom door. "ASSHOLE! I have never been so embarrassed in my LIFE!"

Chucky laughed. "Babe, I said I'm sorry. I didn't mean to…you just caught me off guard."

"Chucky WHY would you embarrass me like that?!"

"Come on now. You know I was just playin witchu."

She scrubbed the crooked liner and clumped mascara from her eyes. "I'm done with this shit. I'm going home."

"Missy…"

"I'm GOING HOME!"

"Missy will you open the door? Please?"

"Go away."

"Missyyyy."

"I said go AWAY, Chucky!" She gagged and grabbed a nearby wastepaper basket. He could hear her heaving through the door.

"Are you ok?"

"I'm fine. Just go." She threw up again.

"Girl if you don't open up this damn door…"

After a few moments of silence, she crawled over the door and unlocked it.

Chucky turned the latch and walked in as she stumbled back over to the bed. He frowned. "You look like you still drunk?"

She held her head in her hands. "I feel like it."

"What did you drink?"

"Just a couple martinis. And a Long Island."

"Mixin that light and that dark." Chucky shook his head. "Get you every time."

"But I didn't really drink that much."

"Apparently you didn't have to. Lightweight."

"Shut up."

"So what y'all talk about last night, while I was gone?"

"None of your business. You shouldn't have left."

"I had business to handle."

"Um hmm. So did he."

"Don't play with me, Missy."

She tried to giggle, but her head was pounding too heavy. "Can you hand me my purse please. I need to take an Advil."

"Nah, you need a BC powder for that."

"Well I don't have a BC powder."

"You want me to go and get you one?"

"No. I want you to hand me my purse. And that bottled water over on the desk."

He obliged. She took the pills and laid down on the bed. Both of their phones chimed. Chucky looked at his. "It's Carmen. She said taping is suspended for today."

"Good."

"Yeah, that works for me. I got shit to do today anyway. You need me to get anything else?"

"Yes."

"What?"

"Out of my room."

He laughed. "Ok. Ok, I see how you do me. But that's aight. I'm gladly leaving. Cause baby girl...yo ass need some beauty rest."

She laughed and threw her pillow at his head. "Kiss my ass, Chucky."

"Oh I will." He winked. "Later."

He retreated from the room smiling. Glad to have the day off. He had a long errand to run.

Missy swallowed her pain medicine. As soon as the water hit her empty stomach she threw it back up. Her head ached and her vision was blurry. Sweat dripped from her forehead though she was freezing cold. She pulled the covers up to her neck and closed her eyes. *What the hell is going on with me?*

For the Best

Brandy called twenty minutes after his workday began, hoping to get his voicemail. She got it.

Hey Tay. I know you're at work right now. I don't want to interrupt your day, I just called to tell you that I really appreciate you picking me up for school the other day. You got me there on time, I passed my exam so everything's good with that. But I've been thinking. Thinking a lot about...I dunno, about everything. I just don't think it's a good idea for us to keep seeing each other. At least not right now. I have so much going on right now. I just don't think it's a good time to, you know, start something. And this has nothing to do with you. You've been great. It's...well...I hope you understand. Ok. Take care.

Five minutes later, her phone started ringing off the hook. Tay called from his cell. Then he called from his job. Over the next couple of hours several calls came in from numbers she didn't recognize. She sent them all to voice mail.

Of all the calls there was only one message left. She listened, reluctantly.

Hey. I didn't want to leave a message. I'd rather speak to you in person, Brandy, but I see you're not going to answer your phone. I'm sad to hear that message. I thought we were coming to a good place. But I understand. I really don't have much more to say other than...if you should change your mind, I'm here. I'll always be here. Take care of yourself, too.

There was a long pause at the end of the message and then the call disconnected.

Brandy hated leaving a breakup voice mail message as much as Tay hated hearing it. But it had to be done. He was getting too attached. She was getting too involved. And the drama he brought to the table was not something she could sign up for.

The shit was already costing her. Charges to her credit cards.

Days sitting in vital records and the Social Security Administration and the DMV for new identification. The car was still missing. No telling when they'd find it and what condition it would be in. And she just knew that it would only be a matter of time before she had to put hands on Keisha's ass. It was all too much. Way too much. So she was done and it was for the best. She kept telling herself, *it's for the best.*

The Finale

Chucky and Kevin stood in their designated spots in the middle of the parlor, awaiting Missy's grand entrance. She walked in and turned heads. For all the right reasons.

Missy picked out a killer outfit for her finale. A teal sequined gown by Marc Bauer and silver strappy stilettos by Celine. Her hair pulled backed into a loose chignon and her makeup sultry. Smoky eyes and a bold crimson lip with a hint of gloss at the center pout.

Her finalists were also impeccably dressed in designer tuxedos from Hugo Boss. Chucky dressed his down with a tee and black leather Chuck Taylors while Kevin was positively debonair with an Italian silk diamond point bowtie and Tom Ford wingtips. Somehow he got the teal memo because his bowtie and pocket square matched her dress perfectly, much to Chucky's irritation.

Missy took her place on the elevated platform. Her head still ached. Her lips were cracked and dry as sandpaper under the mounds of lipstick. She looked fantastic but felt shittier than a neighborhood dog park.

Her final dates did nothing to help her situation. Earlier that day Chucky surprised her with a day of Go Kart racing, bison burges and fries. Kevin planned a romantic sunset river boat ride on the Potomac as they dined on his favorite, Indian cuisine. By the time she returned to the mansion to tape the elimination, she realized that a lingering hangover and a day filled with varying degrees of motion sickness, greasy foods and spices was quite the recipe for a disaster.

All she wanted was for the day to be over so she could collect her last paycheck and get the hell back to VA. But her queasy stomach and swollen colon had other plans. Three bathroom trips into the show, she needed her makeup retouched and fresh undergarments. She asked the director if they could reshoot later but was informed that the shoot was costing by the minute, they were well over budget and that any further expenses would come out of her pay. So she did her best to suck it up and stick it out.

She was given her lines the night before and was too sick to study. So there were many takes. Kevin was poised as always. Chucky was growing more restless with every take, telling jokes to keep the mood light and keep his nerves in check. He'd been confident the entire show about is chances at taking the prize but lately...not so much. Kevin made him nervous, and after leaving them that night Missy had been acting strangely. A little distant. He didn't quite know what to make of it.

Missy didn't like being told who to pick. She knew who she wanted. Why should the show have a say in who she was going to be with, either way? After spending weeks rehearsing lines and reshooting spontaneous conflict from multiple angles, she'd learned just how little reality there really was in reality tv. It was fascinating but disappointing. She'd never look at those shows the same.

Take seventeen and she had her lines down pat. The producers got the reactions they wanted, from every angle they needed and Black Love: The Ex Factor was done. She was immediately shuffled out of the parlor to do her last round of interviews, then out of mansion and back to reality. Real reality. In four weeks, they'd tape the reunion special, she'd collect her final pay and get on with the business of figuring out what the hell she had just done to her life.

No Regrets

For weeks, insults and accusations were thrown about in affidavits and more complaints. Missy's poor finances, Brenda's alleged criminal history. According to the one complaint, Missy was near destitute after paying restitution to the government for tax evasion. In another, Brenda was second-in-command of a criminal enterprise with her first husband. Cases for neglect were made on both sides. Brenda's prison stint, Missy sending Mandy away to boarding school. Brenda's failure to have Mandy's autism diagnosis timely. The battle had gotten nasty…and expensive. Missy had used all of her favors. All but one.

With the legal fees coming due, her finances were tighter than ever. She'd already begun moving things slowly back into the apartment in Adam's Morgan. The house was on the market but she didn't have any offers. She desperately needed to sell before foreclosure.

Breaking the news to Brandy wasn't going to be easy. Missy had spoiled her so, that the level of scaling back that was necessary would surely be a culture shock. The Benz had already been sent back to the dealership, and Missy's newest, most precious Maserati SUV would be picked up by week's end. The Bentley was the only car that was paid for and with that, they were going to be a one car household for a while; which meant that Brandy would be on public transit for a while. It was hardly the life they'd grown accustomed to. But it was their new reality, and the sooner they acclimated, the better.

Dear Mama

November 28. There was a light snowfall in the early morning. Predictions for heavy snowstorms later in the day. The air was frigid at 36 degrees, so Brenda bundled up good. She grabbed the heavy floor-length sable and matching hat, the thick cashmere scarf with matching gloves. She headed out early to avoid the rush hour traffic, which was sure to be twice as bad with slippery roads.

Nearly two hours later, she turned into the driveway, through the massive wrought iron gates and made her way around to the far east side of the property. She pulled over, parked half on the lawn and grabbed the bouquet of roses from the back seat. It was the first time Brenda had been back to the cemetery since Betty was buried.

Betty's birthday had always been their own little holiday. Ever since she could afford to, she made a huge deal of it. Elaborate family dinners and plenty of gifts. Mostly cash. Betty's favorite. She'd always given her a mixed bouquet with lots of pink roses. Today would be no different. Just nicer roses.

She'd forgotten exactly where the headstone was, so she had to walk around a little. She walked slowly, half dreading her destination. Reading grave markers along the way. Admiring the creativity of some and raising a discerning, slightly judgmental brow at others. She almost laughed aloud when she reflected on the mammoth, massively tacky memorial she'd bought for her husband. Everything but the kitchen sink. That's what they put on it. His picture, the children's names, their handprints. And that was just on the front. There was a memorial bench, a marble urn and an eternal flame. The funeral home worked her over good. *Fuckers.*

A half hour later, still no Betty James. *Where is she?* Brenda closed her eyes and thought back to the funeral. Driving into the cemetery. *Funeral home to the right. Family cars parked ahead. Left turn right there.* Betty's grave was on the west side of the cemetery, not the east. So she pulled her scarf over her face to shield from the cold wind and headed back to the car.

The wind picked up and soon there were mild flurries of snow. There wouldn't be much time before the storm. She drove to the other side of the grounds and parked on the road next to a cedar tree. It was all coming back to her.

The cemetery was empty except for one worker tearing down a tent, a slow moving truck laying salt on the roadway, and a woman crouched over, sitting on a memorial bench somewhere in Betty's area. Brenda walked over looking for her mother's heart shaped headstone. There were several.

"Missy?" Brenda called out when she recognized her. Missy sat on the bench opposite Betty's headstone. She wore a white parka with the hood pulled over her head and a scarf covering her face. But Brenda could tell.

"Yes."

Brenda sat down next to her. There was an extremely awkward silence. She looked over at Missy. Her eyes were red and puffy. Her cheeks rosy from the bitter cold. Mascara streaked her face. "I guess we should talk."

Missy looked up and scowled. "I would...but I don't think I can't *afford it.*"

"Look Missy, I had to do what I had to do, ok. I want my kids!"

Missy wiped her face with her scarf. "Do you mind if I just sit here for a second, and mourn my mother? In peace? Do you think I could do that?"

Brenda hushed and they sat for a little while, in silence. Missy started to cry again. She sighed before she spoke through her tears. Her voice cracked. "I miss her, Brenda. You got to spend so much time with her."

Brenda didn't say a word. She wasn't really sure what to say. Nothing seemed the most appropriate.

"I can't even remember the last time I saw her smile. Or heard her laugh. She was so funny. I missed so much time with her Brenda. It hurts."

Brenda took Missy's hand. "I know."

A few quiet minutes and a few more tears later, Brenda walked over to the headstone and arranged her roses in the urn with Missy's lilies. She sat back on the bench next to Missy, who was still sniffling and wiping away tears.

"I...I gotta go." Missy stood and walked down the short hill toward the road. Brenda didn't stop her.

Minutes later, the snow fell heavy, covering the grass and the road. She'd planned to hit the grocery store and head home before the roads got too bad. But walking away was hard. She felt, like she was leaving Betty again. Leaving her behind. She realized that was crazy thinking, yet her feet wouldn't move from the bench. A half hour and a couple inches, or so of snowfall later, the pickup truck pulled over next to her. The driver yelled out, "Ma'am, I'm sorry but we're closing now. Locking the gates. You'll need to make your way out now."

Brenda nodded. She walked over to the headstone and touched it, as she prayed and cried a little more. Then she plucked one rose and one lily from the bouquet and headed back to her car.

The road was still slippery despite the salt the truck had just dropped, so she drove slowly, carefully down the hill. She rounded the turn for the exit and noticed a lone car in the parking lot of the funeral home. A beautiful white Maserati SUV. Had to be Missy's. She turned onto the lot and pulled in next to it.

Missy didn't notice her. She had her head down on the steering wheel and her body shuddered. The right front tire was flat. Brenda stepped out of her car. She walked up to Missy's window and tapped it, startling her.

Brenda walked around and hopped in the passenger side.

"You ok?"

"No." She cried. Brenda sat there for a moment, then she pulled Missy close and put her head on her chest. She held her big sister in silence and allowed her time to purge. To get everything out. When Missy raised up and dried her tears she looked Brenda in the eye. "I miss you."

Brenda felt a lump forming in her throat, and it burned to hold back. She grabbed Missy and hugged her tight. "I miss you, too."

They sat in the cold car and cried until several inches of snow had fallen. Brenda looked up and came to her senses. "Girl we gotta get outta this damn blizzard."

"I know. I already called roadside assistance."

"How long ago?"

"Almost two hours now."

"Two hours? We might as well just change it ourselves. Open the hatch."

"What?"

"Open. The. Hatch."

Missy hit the button, and Brenda walked to the back of the car. Seconds later she came back to the window. "You don't have a spare."

"What?"

"You don't have a spare tire."

"I don't know."

"No, I wasn't asking. I'm telling you, you don't!"

"Oh."

"Oh? What was roadside assistance gonna do?"

"Brenda, I don't know. Give me a new tire I guess."

Brenda frowned, "What? Missy. Just call them back and cancel."

"Why?"

"Because we don't have time to sit out here and wait to see if they gon show. These people are ready to close the gates and put us outta here. I'll take you home, and we can pick up your car later."

"Leave my car here, in the cemetery?"

"Well it's that or leave *you* here in the cemetery?"

"Ok, ok."

The undertaker came out onto the parking lot. He walked up to the window. "Ladies, is everything all right? We're closing up early today. Oh, you've got a flat. Pop the trunk."

Brenda answered dryly. "She doesn't have a spare."

He frowned. "What?"

Brenda shook her head and smiled. "That's what I said. Is it all right if we just leave the car here and pick it up tomorrow?"

"They're calling for a lot of snow tonight. We'll probably be closed tomorrow but the next day is fine, or just as soon as you can."

"Ok great, and it won't be towed or anything?"

"No, of course not. I'm going right in to let my manager know what's happening. The car will be fine ma'am."

"We'll be back as soon as we can. Thank you sir."

"No problem. The roads are gettin pretty bad. You ladies get home safe."

"We will, thanks." She looked at Missy. "You ready?"

"Yeah, just let me grab a couple things from the back.' Missy rifled through some bags and put one together for the road. She walked over to Brenda's ride. A brand new 8 series BMW coupe. metallic gray with white perforated leather interior, Brenda's initials expertly stitched into the headrests and woven into the rugs. *Impressive*, she thought. She opened the back door and set the bag on the seat.

"Missy." Brenda popped the trunk. "Would you mind putting that in the trunk. My white seats…"

Missy hesitated for a second before she grabbed her bag. "Yeah, sure." She closed the trunk and got in. "This car is gorgeous."

"Thanks, it was a gift from my husband."

"Oh. Special occasion?"

"No, not really. He just buys me things."

"Uhm. Must be nice."

Brenda smiled. "Yes…it is. He surprises me with things all the time."

She couldn't resist the urge to brag a bit. Dave was her knight in shining armor and she didn't see any reason to conceal it, or even play it down.

As Brenda spoke loudly and proudly of her lavish new life,

Missy couldn't help admiring the flawless emerald cut diamond dangling on her ring finger. The matching diamond tennis bracelet and the full length sable draped over her shoulders. She thought, *this car has got to be worth hundred thousand*. "So, I saw the address on the complaint. You live in McLean now? Crest Lane?"

"Yes, and I love it there. Dave bought the house as a surprise for me before I came home."

"Niiice. That's a pretty ritzy neighborhood."

Brenda responded, nonchalantly. "Yeah. It's a nice enough neighborhood."

On the slippery ride to Missy's house, the girls had a chance to catch up. Traffic on the I66 was a parking lot. It took nearly two hours for what was typically a half hour drive.

Brenda got around to asking the questions again. "What was your problem with ma? Why did you leave?" Missy decided it was time to answer, though she knew it was a risk. After all, Betty wasn't there to defend herself. Brenda just might feel a certain way about that. She'd probably take it to heart. Possibly push her out of the car into the snow. But she needed to get it off her chest. Once and for all. It was time to tell the truth. The whole of it. Come what may.

Belle Grey

Brenda sat quietly for a moment before she spoke. "I guess I can see how that would change things between you two. Ma *was* a little money hungry. I can't lie about that. But I still don't see you giving up on her the way you did."

"Brenda, I was raped."

"What?"

"Do you remember my old roommate Jennifer?"

"She raped you?"

"No. Listen. Jennifer's mother Edwina was my mentor in college."

"Her *mother* raped you?!"

"Damn Brenda no! Listen! Eddie was a wealthy DC socialite. She came up from the streets. Met and married a rich white man and settled in Georgetown. Well she heard from Jennifer that I was having money problems. I was actually about to get kicked out of school when she came up with a solution to all my money problems. She set me up with this woman in New York. Belle Grey. I'll never forget her. I thought she was the most beautiful woman I had ever seen in my life. She was charming, and glamorous and…I swear that woman could sell ice to an Eskimo."

"But what does she…"

"Brenda, please."

"Ok."

"I was told that Belle was a former runway model and had her own modeling agency, but after a few photo shoots and networking events, I found out her real story. She ran a high-end escort service and recruited her girls through the phony modeling agency. She baited me in with a couple well-paying modeling gigs, which turned out to be nothing more than shoots for pictures to solicit to her customers. Then she cut me a check for the rest of my tuition."

Brenda pursed her lips and mumbled, "Um hmm."

"Well the money was essentially a down payment on her investment. My blonde hair and blue eyes would make us rich, she said. Well we didn't get that far. She sent me to a house on Long Island. It was a pretty big house. Not quite a mansion...but close. I can still remember being overwhelmed by the smell of jasmine when the client, Jeremy, opened the door. He was white and really tall, actually handsome. He was well-dressed and well-mannered. You know, rich. He invited me into his dining area where we ate a four-course meal and drank plenty of wine. I kept checking my watch. Belle said I had to stay for two hours, so I was intent on making sure I didn't stay a minute more. Belle kept emphasizing that sometimes the clients just wanted someone to talk to. Not every one of them wanted sex every time. Some of them just wanted to play out a fantasy or indulge in a weird fetish or two, but sex wasn't necessarily part of the deal."

"Necessarily."

"Right. She'd even shared some of her own personal stories of guys just wanting to smell her feet or have her cook and clean for them in the nude for a thousand bucks an hour. I'd been hoping the whole time I'd be so lucky. But no matter what happened, he'd paid for two hours of my time so..."

"You had to do what you had to do."

"Exactly. I swear I tried to waste as much of his time as possible. I excused myself to the ladies room a couple times, but then I was like damn I don't want him thinking..."

"You was takin a shit break?"

Missy burst out laughing. "Well yeah."

"You had the bubble guts."

"Brenda..."

"You was prairie doggin?"

"Brenda! Can you be serious. Please."

Brenda giggled. "Ok, ok. Sorry."

"Anyway. By the time we talked and flirted and drank wine

and had all four courses, I looked up and had like fifteen minutes left on the clock. How much was he going to want from me in fifteen minutes? I felt like I was home free at that point. Five minutes later Jeremy stood from the table, he walked over to me and took my hand. He lead me over into the living room and into his arms. We danced to a tune he was humming. He turned me around and pulled me close to him. I could feel his hard-on. But I wasn't alarmed, I just politely told him that my time was up, and I thanked him for a lovely dinner. He kissed my neck, and I can't lie. I was a little aroused, but still ready to leave while I was ahead and still had my clothes on. He kissed me soflty on the lips and informed me that he'd arranged for another hour of my time. I asked if I could call Belle to confirm, and he said yes. He showed me to the phone which was in his parlor, along with several of his friends. Friends that looked as young as sixteen and as old as seventy five. Needless to say, there was no phone and no escaping what was about to happen to me. A fantasy, involving a house nigger."

Brenda brought her hands to her face. Bracing herself for what was to come.

Missy paused for a second. The memories flooded back to her. She was almost too choked up to speak. But she sucked back the tears and continued. "They let me go at midnight as promised. I won't go into everything that happened…but a few weeks later my period was late."

"Oh my God."

"Yeah. Belle sent me to this house, with this nurse. She told me it was still early enough that it would be quick and easy. I went to sleep on a table and woke up in a hospital bed. Something went wrong, so the nurse panicked and called an ambulance, but she left me there on the table bleeding. The whole ordeal left me traumatized and pretty much sterile from all the internal scarring that woman did when she placed whatever it was she used inside my body."

"Wow. Missy, I'm so sorry that happened."

"Yeah, me too. So little sister you can imagine how I felt when I found out that Betty lied to me about my father for all those years. When I found out that he never left me like she said; *she* was the one who ran him off but she still managed to cash the checks he sent me every month and not say a word about it. Brenda, my father was a doctor. He was a somebody. A wealthy man who wanted me in his life and would have gladly paid for my college. So everything I went through when I was in New York…" She swallowed hard and wiped a tear. "…all that shit was for nothing. All of the struggling. The scheming and stealing. It was all for nothing."

"Missy there had to be.."

"She made me think my father didn't WANT ME! Brenda, she never even told me when he died."

Brenda sat silently for a moment. Thinking there had to be more to it than what she was being told because what she was hearing didn't sound like Betty at all. "Look, I'm not gon pretend I know how you feel…"

"Don't. Because you had your father your whole life so no, you definitely do not know how I feel."

"That's what I just said Missy, I don't know. But what I do know is that mama loved you. Shit, she loved you the most. She would never have done anything to intentionally hurt you, of all people. So I don't buy it. She had to have her reasons. I know you cool with your stepmother now, but know that there's two, maybe three sides to every story."

"Yeah, well one of those sides got me raped and left me sterile. Sooo."

Brenda sighed. "Well I'm glad you finally told me."

"So am I. There's more to it…of course…but that's the jist. That's why I left. Do I regret it now? Absolutely. But trust me when I tell you I felt I was more than justified."

"We all have regrets big sis. Lord knows *I* know. But you can't let that shit eat you up. I mean…what's done is done. You just gotta figure out how to deal and move on. That's all you can do."

"I suppose.' She sighed. 'I need a drink."

"I know, right. You wanna stop and get something?"

"No, I have plenty at the house. You wanna come over and

have a drink?"

"Nah I gotta hurry up and get home before I *can't* get home."

"Yeah, these roads are a mess. Raincheck?"

"Absolutely." Brenda smiled. "So...are we like...sisters again?"

"We never stopped being that."

"I mean for real sisters. Like borrow your lipstick, cornrow your hair, cuss out your boyfriend for you, sisters.

Missy laughed. "Yes, but on one condition. No, actually two."

"What are those?

"Cook for me."

"Oh, girl. Done. Easy. Now, what's the other?"

"Drop the suit. We can work this out. Out of court. I don't want to fight with you anymore. You should be with your girls. You are a *good* mother, Brenda. And they need you."

Brenda swallowed down hard. Tears filled her eyes. She reached out and grabbed Missy's hand. "Thank you." She sniffled. Thank you."

Missy clasped her fingers through Brenda's and held on to her hand. "You don't have to thank me. I love you baby sis."

"I love you more."

Brenda turned into Missy's driveway and parked. She pulled Missy in and hugged her tight. More than three years had gone by without one kind word, let alone an embrace. The burden of the senseless grudge had weighed heavily on them both. Seemed like the sisters were destined for a relationship rife with chaos, turmoil, and competition. Neither wanted it that way. But that's just the way it always was.

But for whatever tomorrow would bring them, tonight they'd found a common place where love, truth and sisterhood trumped all things. A new beginning. Yet again.

Talk to Me

Rocky walked down to the basement carrying the night deposit bag with the days take. Dreading giving Aunt Pat the receipts for the pitiful take on a Friday night. She heard the noises from the hall. She walked over to the bathroom and knocked.

"Hey. Pat. You ok in there?"

Aunt Pat yelled back through the door. "Yeah. Go'on back upstairs. I'll be up there in a minute."

Rocky hung back. Pat was definitely not ok. And if anyone could see that, it was Rocky. A couple flushes and Aunt Pat walked out holding a napkin to her mouth. She jumped.

"Fuck! Rocky you scared the shit outta me!"

"I'm sorry."

"I thought I told you I was coming upstairs."

"I know but…Pat, how long we gon pretend nothing's wrong?"

Aunt Pat rolled her eyes and walked behind the bar. "What you talkin bout?"

"I'm talkin bout *you*. You ain't been eatin. So ion know what you in there throwin up. You losin weight. What you'on think nobody can see that? I'm your best friend Pat. Come on now. Talk to me."

Aunt Pat grumbled. "Ain't nuttin to talk about."

Pat stood for a moment, waiting for a real answer. It didn't come. She threw the bag up on the bar. "Well here's the receipts for tonight. I'm goin home. You good?"

"I'm good. Goodnight Rocky."

Rocky shook her head, disappointed that her friend wouldn't confide in her. Something was clearly wrong. But what could she do. If Pat wasn't willing to talk to her. She decided to let it go. For now.

Rocky didn't get halfway back up the stairs before she heard a loud crash. She ran back downstairs to find Aunt Pat laying in a mess of broken glass. Apparently she had fallen into the stacked wine glasses that were left to dry behind the bar.

She ran over to help Pat up. "*Now* will you talk to me?"

Head of the Class

Missy pulled up to the house, eyes bucked wide. She thought, *this* is Brenda's house? What did Brenda know about French architecture? And how could they afford it on a trial lawyers pay?

Brenda opened the front door and smiled. A victorious one. Not that she reveled in her sister's financial misfortune, but it was kinda nice, for once, to be on top. To be the sister who had it all. For once. It was nice.

Missy looked up and around, the house was more awesome inside than even she imagined. She kissed Brenda on the cheek. "Hey babe. Your house is like. Wow. It's…it's really nice."

Brenda took that as a huge compliment because Missy so rarely gave them. "Hey sissy. You are just in time for lunch. Come on in the kitchen."

She led her into the foyer, through the living area. She walked slowly so Missy could drink it all in. "We're thinking of changing the décor a bit."

"Why? What's wrong with the décor? Wait..is that a.."

"Steinway. Yes, Dave plays casually," she lied. "Let's go to the kitchen. I made us a little surf and turf. Something light."

Brenda took care to prepare a meal fit for queens. Something a bit unexpected. Lobster Bruschetta, Kobe Pepper Filet Mignon bites and twice baked mini potatoes with smoked herb gouda. For dessert there was a decadent strawberry cheesecake trifle. She'd spent the last two days googling and testing recipes.

When Missy saw the magnificent spread, she pouted and whined. "Noooo. Brenda. Where's my fried chicken? Where's my macaroni and cheeeese? And my purple Kool-Aid with the sliced lemon?"

"Sorry sis. I don't eat like that anymore," she lied again. "Now grab that pitcher and that bottle for me please. It's a beautiful day out. We're taking this poolside."

She led Missy to their newly decorated outdoor area. An elaborate party space with a full gourmet kitchen, dining space and a sundeck patio for lounging poolside. She never spent any time out there. It was just another opportunity to show Missy how well she lived. Little ghetto Brenda, livin lovely while her bourgeois', high fallutin, high saditty big sister was just barely makin do. The tables had definitely turned. Not that Brenda was happy about it. Happy was way too strong a word.

Brenda popped the top on a bottle of chilled Perrier Jouet and poured it slowly into the half pitcher of freshly squeezed O.J.

Missy smiled, "Expensive mimosa."

Brenda grinned. "Nothing's too good for my big sister."

Missy took a sip and closed her eyes as she reveled in the best damned mimosa she'd ever tasted. "So what did you need to talk to me about?"

"Head."

"What?"

Brenda poured herself a glass of the expensive concoction and proceeded to empty a miniature bottle of Stoli vodka inside. "That's what I needed to talk to you about." She passed Missy a small bottle. "Stoli?"

"No, thank you." She scowled, as Brenda stirred the vodka in with her finger. "And you're ruining that perfectly good mimosa."

"Tend to your own damn drink, Missy."

"Whatever. What do you mean, head? What are you talking about?"

Brenda sighed. "You gon make me spell it out."

"What? Brenda, I really don't have the time."

"Okaaayyy. Ok, ok. I never told you this before. Don't really know why I'm telling you this nowww…but…"

"But what?"

Brenda pouted. "I don't know how to give head."

Missy nearly choked on her drink. She giggled. "What? Are

you kidding me?"

"No, I'm not. And stop laughing."

She tried. "Ok, wait, wait, wait. Seriously. You don't give head? Why not?!"

Brenda shrugged. "Ion no. I just don't. I never really liked it, I guess."

"You guess you never really liked it. Well did Melvin like it? Does that fine ass white man you married like it? Shit I know *he* does."

"Well...Melvin didn't really care. I mean, I did it a few times with him...and I guess I was kinda bad at it...kinda on purpose." Brenda smiled "Like really bad. Like scrape-some-skin-off-it-with-my-front-teeth-so-you-won't-ask-me-to-do-that-shit-ever-again bad."

Missy shook her head and laughed. "Girl. I can't even believe you're my sister. So what about Dave?"

"He say he don't mind.... but –"

"That's bullshit."

"I know, right!"

"Did you do him?"

"I tried. Once. But it was hard."

"His dick?"

"No! Well yes...but no, I don't mean it like that..."

"Girl, if you don't hurry up and tell me what's going on. I don't have all day to be out here foolin with you."

"Ok." Brenda sighed. "It's *pink.*"

"What!?" Missy laughed so hard she had to sit her drink down to keep it from dropping to the ground. She reared back in her chair and held her stomach. "His DICK?!?!"

"YES! Ok yes his dick. It's pink." She grimaced. "Pink and tan. With like a fat, pink mushroom on the top. And I ain't puttin that shit in my mouth."

The look of disgust on Brenda's face as she described her husband's member sent Missy over the side of the lounger in an absolute FIT of laughter. She nearly rolled into the pool. "Girl! Stop! Oh Lord! My stomach hurts."

Brenda sucked her teeth. "I'm glad you think my life is so

funny. Cause I damn sure don't. This shit is serious Missy."

Missy's laughter was contagious. Brenda tried to stifle her giggles but decided to just get it on out of her system. It really was funny. "Come on Missy, seriously," she whined. "What do I doooo?"

"Why you askin *me*?"

"*Bitch*." Brenda gave her big sister, the self-proclaimed *head doctor* a very serious side eye. "Don't act like I ain't seen your nasty ass in action. And for the record, I am STILL traumatized."

"Yeah, well. That's what you get for bustin in my room unannounced."

"Ok, never mind that. What can I do? Missy I have to figure this out. He's just being nice right now, but I know he wants it. I found a video in the DVD player."

"Porn?"

Yeah, *Deep Throat 7*. Not a nigga in sight. Nothin but skinny, big titty white girls suckin dicks and feelin on each other."

"Ok. Well you *did* marry a white man, Brenda."

"Yeah. I did."

Missy smiled. "Not that there's anything *wrong* with it."

"Shut up."

"All right look, you just gotta put mind over matter. Don't even think about it. Just close your eyes, hold your nose and go in. You know, like when you jump in a pool. Oh, wait! I forgot. You can't swim either! Aaaahhhh!" Missy laughed until she snorted.

"See. I knew you was gon clown me. You ain't no damn help." Frustrated, Brenda got up to clear the table.

"No, wait. Sit down girl. I'm listening. It's just a trip. You were married all those years, and now you married to that fine ass *white* boy, and you don't give head? That's crazy to me."

"But why is that so crazy? Why can't I just not like to give head."

"Well, do you *get* it?"

"Of course I *get* it. That's different."

Missy chuckled. "Different, how? Girl, never mind. But whatever. You got any bananas around here? Or cucumbers or something?"

"What? No! I know you don't think I'm bout to sit here and watch you suck on no damn fruit!"

"Ok, then what exactly is it that you want me to do?"

"Just forget it. Nothing."

They sat for a few moments in silence with Missy still amused and Brenda a little annoyed. Missy's wheels started turning. "Awwwwww…girl I think I might have the answer to your problems."

"Really? What?"

"Um hmm! I have to go home and look for it. Hopefully I didn't put it in storage or accidentally throw it out. It's gotta be in one of those boxes in the basement."

"What?!"

"I have an instructional video. I used it a few years ago when I was trying to seduce Chucky."

"You needed a video for that?"

"No. I really didn't. But I wanted to step up my game. It's called *The Art of Fellatio*…"

"Really Missy. A help-you-suck-a-dick video?"

"No. Uh uh. No." Missy waved her index finger at her little sister and smirked. "See… you look at me strangely. You think it's a silly notion. You don't *believe*. But you haven't seen the video. Let me tell you somethin. I, Melissa Delores James, was once the head doctor…"

Brenda laughed. "Oh, here we go…"

"No. I'm serious. You know that's what I called myself. But now? Right now? Today? After watching A.O.F? Oh, hunny. I am a valeDICKtorian. I am aHEAD of the class. I am the head motherfucking MAS-tuh."

"Shut UP!"

"Oh and with the help of A.O.F., you too can leave em stuck on stupid. Sittin outside your house, stalkin you at your job and shit. Tying strings around your ring finger while you sleep to check the ring size. Calling home to the wife like 'Lookit, I ain't never comin home no more.'"

Brenda laughed, hard and gave her big sister a double high

five. "You play too much."

By the time Missy was done, Brenda felt like she'd just been sold on one of those late night infomercials. The Head Master. $19.95 plus shipping and handling. Brenda couldn't wait to get her hands on the video. She didn't need to create a stalker and she already had the ring. She just wanted to keep her husband.

Party Ova

Man, Missy wasn't playin about this video, Brenda thought as she watched a hefty Yugoslavian woman with a thick accent perform oral on a gorgeous dark haired Adonis that she introduced as her husband, Dmitry. *She must have tricked him with that technique,* Brenda thought.

Brenda watched the video five times, fast forwarding, rewinding and playing it back in slow motion. She didn't want to miss a single angle or facial expression. How did *that* woman get *that* dick all the way down her throat like that? Anka bent over backward and you could actually see it in her throat like one of those sword swallowing carnival freaks. She was amazing, All Brenda could think was if she could make Dave respond like Dmitry did when he climaxed...Lucy could hang it up. She'd be filing an unemployment claim in no time.

As per Anka's instruction she had a frankfurter, a medium-sized curved banana, a regular and an English cucumber. She was to start from smallest to the largest and by the end of the video Anka guaranteed that she'd be able to make them disappear into the depths of her throat; down to the trachea. Or your money back. Brenda wondered how many actually asked for their money back.

She called David earlier that day and told him to come directly home; she had an extra special surprise for him. When he arrived he could smell dinner from outside the front door, all of his favorite salty buttery rich soul foods. All the things that tasted so good but were oh so bad. Fried chicken, fried cabbage, four cheese macaroni and hot buttered biscuits. For desert, there was heavy butter-crusted peach cobbler a la mode.

By the time Dave came in, Brenda had already had a few

shots. They were kicking in fast, too. Though she'd been known to throw back a few in her day, she hadn't had much more than an occasional mimosa since she came home from prison.

They enjoyed the heavy dinner, dessert, and a good hour of scintillating conversation over a few more martinis. By the time they were done with dessert, Brenda was all but wasted.

She was nothing but smiles, as she put on her seduction routine, teasing and taunting Dave in red patent pumps and skin tight cut offs, braless in a thin white tank that highlighted erect nipples. She licked her glossed red lips and made promises of a night to remember, through a series of giggles and drunken hiccups.

Dave was feeling his third martini, too. Being totally taken in by his sexy bride, as she walked back and forth in front of him, exaggerating each step to make all the loose body parts jiggle, like he liked. She stopped and stood directly in front of him with her back to him, peering seductively over her shoulder.

Dave liked the view from behind the most. Her small waist led down to the most perfect ass he'd ever been so close to. He'd had just about enough of her teasing so he stood up, pulled her close to him and whispered in her ear, "Let's get this party started, baby."

He turned her around to face him and gave her his tongue, enjoying the taste of her sticky cherry flavored gloss. They kissed hungrily and pawed at each other, frantically tugging at each other's zippers. He pushed her down on the table and peeled her out of the short shorts that barely contained her ample apple bottom. Then he parted her legs and buried his face inside her.

She began to get comfortable, relaxing into it for a bit before it dawned on her that she'd veered from her plan. "No!"

She kicked him off of her so hard he fell over the dining chair behind him. He laid there on the floor, stunned. "Brenda what the..."

"I said n...no!" She hiccupped and walked over to him. "It's my turn. Lay down!"

He looked up at her, a little puzzled, but he followed her instruction anyway. He laid back as she straddled him clumsily and tugged on his belt. Suddenly she stood up again. "Wait! Wait one m...minute. I'll be back." She returned with the bucket of ice cream and threw it on the floor beside him before she dropped back down to her knees.

She fumbled with his belt again for a minute, and he tried to assist, eager to get things going. She popped him on the hand. "I got it!" She pulled away his belt and threw it to the side then she snapped the buttons on his shirt exposing his chest. She licked a nipple and reached out for the ice cream, grabbing a heaping handful from the bucket and slapping it on his chest.

He winced. "Ahh! Babe that's cold."

"Shuuut uuup. Just lemme do this." She sopped up the ice cream...and a little of his sweat. Once it was all gone she pulled at his pants. He reached down to help and she yelled at him. "I said stop it! Let me do it!"

He held his hands back. "Ok, ok!"

So she continued, pulling his pants down to his ankles and then his briefs. She reached into the bucket again and he yelled "Ok, wait a minute...I think I might need to..."

She slapped another handful down into his crotch. He yelled, "Oh shit! Babe!"

She yelled, "Shut up!" and went in, first licking the ice cream that had fallen to the inside of his leg. She sopped it up, along with his man sweat. Kinda gross. But she kept going, thinking of the video and how he'd respond once she put the real moves on him. Just like Vlad did. And then she'd have him in the palm of her hands.

She took him with the palm of her hand and stroked him in all his stickiness. He moaned, as she cleaned up the rest of the ice cream and a little more man sweat with her tongue. She looked up at his penis, erect and pink, dripping with the ice cream.

In that moment, she realized that there were two things that should never go together. Sweet musk and sweet milk. Her stomach turned. She threw up all over him.

*****

Over the next week, Brenda was up every morning, early. His breakfast was ready, his clothes were laid out neatly on the bed, his briefcase and keys sat by the front door so he wouldn't have to look for them, and any other thing she could think he needed before he could even ask. She was positively mortified thinking of him cleaning vomit from balls while she laid on the floor, still stinking of vodka and the vomit that she fell in. She didn't even remember getting into bed that night. She woke up the next morning, completely hung over, but completely clean and tucked in.

Dave begged her to stop apologizing, said it was fine, he knew she was just drunk and to forget about it. Still she wondered. He'd barely touched her since.

He was acting strangely. He'd been home a lot less. Leaving earlier in the morning and coming in later. A sudden business trip. She couldn't help wondering if she'd lost. If Lucy had won. There was only one way to find out.

The Reunion

Lights. Camera. Fight! Andre had Ian on the floor in a headlock. Ian was nearly asleep when security finally pried Andre's arm from around his neck. The cameras kept rolling. The audience egged Andre on. Ian asked for it.

After a cooling off period, they allowed the gentleman to return to the stage. Carmen sat pretty in the hosts armchair.

"So, Andre. Why did you get so angry?"

"Cause. Bamma muufucka always lookin down on somebody. Keep callin me a thug and shit." He looked directly at Ian, who sat across the stage on another sofa. "I don't give a fuck where you went to school or how much money you got. N*gga, you keep talkin to me like you crazy, imma *show* you what a thug do."

Ian rolled his eyes to the side, trying to conceal the terror Andre had just put in them. There was a cut under his eye, his throat was raw, and his raised collar couldn't hide the bruise Andre's forearm made at the front of his neck. Dodging Andre's icy threatening glares, he didn't speak another word the entire show.

Missy sat on the gaudy gold throne – a stupid prop Carmen insisted on – and shook her head. The foolishness seemed unending, and Carmen instructed them to capture it all. The f-bombs, n-bombs, the threats of bodily harm. Two fights had broken out, and Andre had thrown a wad of cash across the stage to show Ian he "gets money." It was a circus, and if not for her contractual obligation, she would have walked off set at the first sign of nonsense.

Once the riff raff segment was done the finalists were introduced. Kevin first. He walked out with Obama swagger in his custom tailored suit and Italian wingtips. His Rolex shining almost as bright as his bleached white veneers. He was clean shaven and smelled of success. Wearing the Cartier cologne that he knew Missy liked. She smiled and he smiled.

"Good evening, Missy. Great to see you again." He kissed her on both cheeks and took his seat. "You're stunning as usual."

She blushed, unintentionally. "Thank you for the compliment Kevin. It's good to see you as well."

Carmen salivated at the subtle, but obvious flirtation. Their chemistry was undeniable. Chucky noticed as well. From back stage.

"So, Kevin. The vote was close. You lost the fan vote by less than a 1 percent margin. How do you feel about that?"

He unbuttoned his jacket, crossed a leg over and leaned back on the sofa. "Well Carmen, the rules are the rules. I lost. Fair and square and I'll take it like a gentleman." He smiled. "It's just unfortunate that the decision wasn't left to the lovely lady here. I suspect things would have turned out a little differently. If you know what I mean."

Missy's smile faded, and Carmen's widened. Both wanting to know where he was going with it. Carmen asked, "No, Kevin I actually don't. Care to elaborate?"

Missy leaned forward in her chair, "Carmen…"

"No Missy, let him finish his thought. Kevin. Please. Continue."

"Well it's quite obvious Melissa and I have chemistry. Undeniable chemistry. But more than that. I love her. I've always loved her. She knows that. This little game here…I mean…it's what it is. A game. Nothing to do with our reality."

Carmen grinned. "*Your* reality?"

Missy had enough. She could just imagine Chucky going off back stage, and the last thing she wanted was another fight. "Kevin. Stop it. Ok?"

"Stop what? Wanting you? Loving you? You didn't tell me to stop that night."

She frowned. "What?! Wait…"

Kevin was suddenly serious. He leaned forward on the sofa

to make his appeal to her. "Missy, I've thought of nothing and no one but you since the last night we were together. Your smile. Your smell. Your touch…"

"My touch? Kevin I never touched you."

"Come on babe…"

"I NEVER TOUCHED YOU!"

Carmen smirked, as she looked over at the quarreling former lovers. Kevin's little revelation was an unexpected treat. She couldn't have written it better. She knew things were about to get turned up. She looked into the camera straight ahead of her. "We're gonna go to commercial while we sort this out. We'll be right back."

The director shouted, "Stand by!"

Missy stood from her chair. "Kevin what the hell!"

Chucky came flying from the corner and connected with Kevin's jaw. *Whap!* "Lyin Muthafucka!"

Kevin fell hard to the ground. Missy toppled over, as she tried to grab Chucky's arm to prevent him from landing another blow to his head. Carmen signaled for the cameras to keep rolling, as security zeroed in on Chucky. Once again the crowd was in an uproar. Andre ran from the front row and tackled Ian, who sat on the other side of the room. Security was split between the two altercations and trying to stave off another one from erupting between two groups of rowdy girls in the audience. It was complete pandemonium. Just what Carmen ordered.

Chucky cocked his fist back, as Kevin raised his arms to shield his face. Missy yelled, "Chucky stop!"

He turned to her suddenly, "Stop! You tellin me to stop?! You fuckin this nigga?!"

She was horrified. Through clenched teeth she whispered, "Really Chucky?"

He broke away from security and stormed off the set fuming and swearing, but Missy refused to chase. Carmen chased him down like a hound, with cameras following closely behind. She turned to Mike, the camera guy. "Turn up the mics and stay on him. I want everything."

Mike was at Chucky's heels, capturing his every move,

including the hole he punched in a set wall. A second camera focused in on Missy kneeling at Kevin's side, tending to his bruised face.

When Carmen reached Chucky's dressing room he was pacing the floor, trying to calm himself down. He raised a hand. "Don't even start."

"Start what? I don't blame you for punching him. He had no business puttin Missy on blast like that."

"What? You think she—"

"No. That's not what I'm sayin."

"I ain't goin back out there, so don't even ask."

"You have to go back out there."

"I don't have to do shit."

"Chucky—"

"No!"

"You know I hate to pull the E. P. card, Chucky…" Carmen shrugged. "…but I kinda gotta."

"Get the fuck out my face with that shit, Carmen. I'M NOT GOING BACK OUT THERE."

"Well if you wanna get paid you will."

"It ain't even worth it." He finally stopped pacing and sat. "You think she fucked him?"

"No. No! Come on, that's stupid. Kevin just wants to be extra for TV. And he didn't actually say that."

"Yeah he did."

"Well…not verbatim."

"He ain't have to say it *verbatim*. He said it. ON fuckin camera. Bitch ass."

"You know your girl. You trust your girl. Let it go Chucky."

He sat, still fuming. She gave him a minute before going back in. "Chucky this shoot is costing by the minute. We gon shoot this with or without you and if you don't come back out, not only will you not get paid, the network will probably file a suit against you. And it won't be a thing I can do to help you. Did you spend the advance?"

He didn't speak.

"You won the show, you won the girl, and you're contracted

to be out on that stage with her. You can say whatever you want. Do whatever you want. You just gotta get your ass out there and do it on camera. Come on now. What you gon do?"

He waved her off. "I'll be out there in a minute."

She waited until she turned her back to smile. Then she motioned to Mike to head back out to the stage.

Head Doctor

Brenda decided to give it another go. She hopped in the shower, packed up the picnic basket and hit the highway, headed to downtown DC.

During the drive she focused on nothing but good things. The good days with Dave, the direction her life was going. She'd long ago blocked out the bad – death, prison, losing her children's love. There was nothing she could do to change the bad, but she could make the good exponentially better, starting with keeping her husband happy.

She signed in with security in the lobby and headed up to the 10th floor. She walked off of elevator smiling and carrying her basket of treats, excited to see her husband and make up for the morning tiff.

Once again the office was empty. Quiet. No one at the reception desk. As she walked the hall the offices were also empty. Strange. Halfway down the hall she nearly bumped into Lucy who was walking out of the kitchen with a fresh cup of coffee in a tight pencil skirt, tight cardigan, and push up bra. They greeted each other through squinted eyes and pursed lips.

"Brenda."

"Meredith."

Meredith walked ahead, back into her office and shut the door. A little too loud for Brenda's taste. *Did she just slam her door?* Brenda walked into Dave's office. He was sitting at his desk with his head in his hands. It took a moment for him to notice she was there.

"Brenda, what are you doing here?"

She noticed the pained look on his face. "Is everything ok?"

"Oh yeah. Yeah. Everything's fine. What's up?"

She smiled wide. "Nothing's *up*. I just wanted to see you. Things have been a little off between us lately. So I wanted to do something nice for you. Is that ok?"

She set the basket on his desk and pulled the flap back. All of his favorites. Crispy Cajun fried chicken, chilled Amish potato salad, sautéed kale and warm honey cornbread.

He gazed at her lovingly and smiled. "Babe. This is so awesome. Thank you. I really needed this today."

"Rough day?"

"Like you wouldn't believe."

"Well, I have just the thing to fix all that."

Brenda walked over to the door and turned the lock. Dave smiled wide. "What are you doing?"

"Locking a lock."

"I see that. Whyyyy."

She walked back over to his desk. "So I can share what I learned in class?"

"What?"

She pulled the tie on her wrap dress and dropped it to the floor, revealing a white corseted teddy with matching garters and hose. She pulled him to his feet, unzipped his pants and let them fall to the floor. Then she fell to her knees.

Brenda faced the pale beast head on. Without the slightest reservation. Then she proceeded to put every instruction from *The Art of Fellatio* into practice.

Up against the wall, sitting in his chair, lying down on the sofa. She took him in and stopped just short of his climax. He pleaded with her to allow him to release. Each time, she whispered, "Not yet."

Finally, she asked him to stand in front of the sofa. She walked around to the back of it and bent over backward, arching her back over it. Her head hung off of it, a foot shy of the floor. "Come here."

Dave held himself in his hand. "Are you serious?"

She smiled. "*Cum*. Here."

He grabbed on to the back of the sofa and eased himself down to her. She received every inch of him into her mouth, allowing him to disappear into her throat, fully, wholly and quite easily. Just like the practice fruit, after many hours of practice.

Dave was dumfounded at the level of skill she displayed, considering how awful she was on her first attempt. The head was next level. Powerful. Like nothing he'd ever had. It shifted his perspective on their life together. It was *that* serious.

After a strong half hour of the tantric tongue teasing Dave released and as soon as he was at the ready again, he gave Brenda a session that she would never forget, pulling out a few tricks and treats of his own.

They made love in every corner of the office. Exploring each other. Experiencing love to a whole new height. Brenda couldn't have been happier, sitting atop her husband. Her breasts held firmly in his hands, as she stared in his eyes and moaned his name. She gyrated her ample hips. Willing him to his finish within her warmth. She felt him beginning to pulsate. He grabbed her hips, as she pulled away. "No baby I'm about to –"

Brenda quickly dismounted, pulled herself down and him into her mouth. He tried to pull away, but she held him down firmly by his hips to keep him inside. Another 30 seconds of learned lip-tongue manipulation, and it was over. Dave grabbed a handful of her hair and released heavy from his loins; a tear from his eye and a holler that seemed to shake the glass on the door. "Gawwwd DAMN Brenda! Whoo hoooooo!"

Brenda grinned from ear to ear, as she watched him roll and squirm around on the carpet. She tried to touch him. He pushed her away, curling up into a ball and whimpering like a newborn puppy.

She crawled over to him and teased. "So you're just gonna lay there in the fetal position huh? Come over here and hold me."

His breathing was heavy and his heart still raced. "Ok...wait, wait. Please. Give me a sec."

Ignoring him, she turned him over, pulled his arm around her neck and rested her head on his chest. They laid for a few moments. Quietly. Both of them spent, with aching jaws and sore limbs. Slight rug burns and post orgasm throbs still lingering from a marathon session that redefined it all.

In each others arms, they could feel a shift happening. Something…spiritual. Cosmic maybe. A heightened awareness of one another. It was odd and comforting. Satisfying. For Dave especially. If he wasn't sure before, he was on that day. Brenda was everything. The one. The one to spend the rest of his days with. The one to bear his beautiful babies. No one would stand in the way of that. Not Meredith. Not his overbearing mother. No one.

Lying on the plush carpeting, they held one another and kissed. Eyes open. Each stroking the other's face and hair. Taking each other in as they never had. A silent but mutual recommittal to their lives together. It was powerful and emotional. The first time they'd truly made love.

Suddenly, Dave took her face in his hands. "Where. Did you learn. To give head like that?!" He kissed her hard on the lips. "*Fuck*!"

Brenda smiled triumphantly. "*The Art. Of. Fellatio.*"

"The what?"

"My sister gave me an instructional video. I'd say it works."

"You're goddamn right it works! I could do a testimonial."

"Shut up."

"I'm not kidding. Brenda. That could save lives. Families. I mean seriously. There would be no more divorce."

She laughed. "Come on let's eat, before your cornbread gets too cold."

As he watched her stand and walk away, he felt himself stiffen. Her beautiful, bodacious bottom jiggling ever so slightly with each step. The white lace teddy with the white lace garters fastened to sheer white stockings popped on her soft brown skin. Very retro. Slightly trashy. Ultra-sexy.

At that moment he thought how gorgeous his wife was and what a fool he was to ever betray her trust. Brenda was an amazing woman. Beautiful, inside and out. Funny, smart and witty. A perfect housewife. A perfect wife. He'd be happy to spend the rest of his life with her.

It was time for a change. Time that he and Meredith had a little talk. The game was over.

*****

"What the hell do you mean *over*?!"

"Could you scream any louder?"

"Yes, actually I could! Where is this coming from David?"

Dave sat behind his desk as Meredith loomed over him. Pissed. "Meredith. Look, I just changed my mind, ok. I don't want to do this anymore. I shouldn't have been involved in this in the first place."

"Are you fucking kidding me? We've been cultivating this for almost three years now. Three years! The deal is almost done." She squinted and raised a suspicious brow. "And all of a sudden you don't want to *do it* anymore? What the fuck is that?!"

"It's not all of a sudden! All right!"

Meredith's eyes welled. She paused for a moment. Then she looked him in the eyes. "You love her."

Dave sat silently. He didn't want to hurt her. But the answer was an unequivocal yes. He'd fallen for Brenda hard. Long ago. Shortly after he and Meredith hatched their scheme, but he never let on. Meredith was too dangerous. She knew way too much. And then there was that saying…hell hath no fury. If she knew his true feelings, she would blow everything up and not only would he not have Brenda, he wouldn't have the money and he'd probably end up in jail. Meredith was so vindictive that she'd do every day of her jail time just to see him do his.

He'd stopped sleeping with her. As much. They still had the occasional encounter, but for him it was nothing more than an obligatory placation, until he could figure out how to unwind everything he'd done. He ignored her question. "Mer, this just isn't right."

She wiped a tear and laughed. "Ok. So then it's over."

He stopped in his tracks. Hoping to God she'd said what he thought he heard. "What? It's over?"

"Yes. If that's what you really want. Tank the deal. We have enough money. We still have the firm. You can get a quickie divorce. Then we can be together. Right?" She looked intently into his eyes.

He sighed. Frustrated…and disappointed. She was painting him into a corner. "What do you expect me to do? Just go home tonight and tell her it's over? Tell her I'm in love with you? And walk out? You think it's gonna be that easy? Besides she'd probably kill us both."

Meredith walked over to him and stroked his face. "I'm gonna give you some time."

"Really?"

"Yes, time come to your senses. I rented a nice little beach house in Rehoboth for the weekend. We'll go there. We'll talk. It'll be nice. Romantic." She kissed him softly on the lips. "Just like old times. I think we need to just…we just need to recharge. This woman has gotten way too far under your skin." She unbuttoned her cardigan exposing her lace bra. Then she reached for his belt.

He grabbed her hand, thinking fast on how to get out of another obligatory encounter. "Hey." He smiled. "Let's save it for the weekend."

She smiled and gave him a quick peck on the lips. "Yes. The weekend."

Meredith left the office beaming, as she thought of all of the naughty things they'd get into on the beach. Meanwhile Dave was panicking inside. It was clear that Meredith wasn't gonna just let it go. He had to figure a way out. Before the weekend. Before it all blew up in his face. Because if it did, losing Brenda would be the least of his worries.

Under Control

Carmen was called into a boardroom and cautioned, strongly, by the studio execs to fall short of inciting another incident that could make the network liable. She assured them that she had everything under control before heading back to the set to resume the show.

Missy was perched on her throne, being powdered and retouched by makeup and re-coifed by hair.

On the advice of legal counsel, Kevin would do the rest of his segment from backstage. There would be a monitor with a live feed from his dressing room. For everyone's safety.

Chucky had barely composed himself before Carmen introduced him to the world as the official winner of Season 3 of Black Love: The Ex Factor.

He put on his game face and walked out on the stage to thunderous applause. The fellas barked and the ladies hollered, as he hammed it up for the cameras. GQ posing and dancing across the set. Missy stood to receive him and they kissed, prompting another screaming ovation from the crowd. He took her hand in his when they sat and they both smiled wide for the camera.

With a bit of a devilish smirk, Carmen congratulated the "happy couple." "So Chucky. How does it feel to finally get to see your lady? I know it had to be hard this last month. Having to stay away from each other until the reunion."

"Honestly, it was hard." He smirked. "*Real* hard. But we talked on the phone a lot. Every day and every night. The separation only built the excitement." He glanced over at Missy and squeezed her hand. Que the *awwwws* from the audience.

"Umm hmm. I'll bet it did." Carmen winked. The audience

laughed. "So Missy, how does it feel to finally have your man?"

She smiled at Chucky and gave his hand a squeeze. "It's peace." More *awwwws* from the audience.

Carmen grinned. "So sweet. You two are like the perfect couple. Aren't they perfect ladies and gentlemen?"

The audience applauded. Chucky and Missy turned to each other and grinned. Carmen signaled for a stage hand to come over. She whispered something in his ear. He handed her something, and she sent him on his way. Then she cleared her throat.

"So I'm holding here in my hands a stack of questions from our viewers. Trust me when I tell you we got many. But I'll read a few." She shuffled through the cards a moment and pulled one from the top of the stack. "Ok. the first question is from Antoinette from Detroit, Michigan. Antoinette wants to know if wedding bells are in your future. That's a great question."

Missy interjected, unintentionally interrupting Chucky before he answered. "No. Carmen, no, we're not there." She looked over at him. "We're just taking it easy. Enjoying each other. Getting to know each other again."

Her words stung. Chucky swallowed hard and feigned a smile. "Yeah. We're not there yet, Carmen."

"Okay. Well. Time will tell now, won't it? Next question is from Jerome, here in DC. Jerome wants to know from you Missy, did America get it right?"

Missy gushed and looked at Chucky again. "Of course they did. There was never any question."

Carmen zeroed in on Chucky. He was so disappointed in Missy's response to the first question it was hard for him to go on. "Chucky, you look like you have something to say."

"No, not at all. I'm just...taking it easy."

Missy got the hint. He was pissed. She didn't mean anything by what she said. They weren't ready for marriage. He was trippin. But she'd straighten it out later, she thought, at home.

"Next question is from Omar in Chicago. Omar wants to know, from you Chucky, did you hit?" Carmen laughed. "Oh *my*. I think we all know what he meant by that. Can you answer that,

Chucky?"

"Chucky leaned forward, "Listen..."

Missy interjected, intentionally, "Come on Carmen. We're not about to do that. The answer is no. Next question please."

Chucky leaned back and crossed his legs. Turning his body away from her. Carmen acknowledged his slight shade. "Is that true, Chucky?"

"You heard what the lady said."

"Umm hmm." Carmen shuffled her cards. "OK, we'll do one more question. This question is from Queenie in Brooklyn, New York. Queenie wants to know, from you Missy, did you sleep with Kevin during the show?" Carmen winced. "Ooh. They're really going in with these questions. Can you answer that?"

Missy scowled at her. "Yes I certainly can. The answer is no. I did not sleep with Kevin. That's ridiculous."

"Ok, well, I guess we'll have to take your word for it. But Missy, I can see why she'd ask. I can see why people might come to that conclusion. You two have a pretty amazing chemistry. I mean you could see that the moment he walked in. And that last date was pretty hot and heavy. You two looked pretty cozy....I'm just saying."

"And *I'm* saying. Nothing happened. Case closed."

"Well...let's not close it just yet. We happen to have some footage from Kevin's first night at the mansion. Footage that didn't quite make it to the show. Let's take a look."

Carmen turned toward a large television monitor that was slowly lowered from the ceiling, playing the drunken flirtation from Missy and Kevin's night in the parlor. Zeroing in on Missy's constant and unmistakable blushing at everything that came from Kevin's mouth.

As the video went on, Carmen tried to conceal her smile. Missy sat uncomfortably, trying to avoid the occasional glares from Chucky at her left. She just wished it would stop. Everything.

Carmen clicked a remote to pause the tape. "Now it definitely appears that *something* is cooking there. Wouldn't you agree?"

The audience agreed. She pressed play and Missy watched in horror as Kevin leaned over to her for a kiss and she returned it with mounds of hot tongue. She cringed as she watched herself grabbing the back of Kevin's neck and plunging her tongue into his mouth, before she seductively bit his lip and pulled away. A familiar tease that made Chucky's ears turn hot. Missy could feel his breathing getting heavier and heavier as he sat and watched beside her.

Shortly after the kiss at the bar they showed them walking back toward their suites. Then the goodnight kiss. More passionate than the one before. Carmen paused the tape.

She turned to Missy. "So from this footage, at least, you can see why one would deduce that there was more going on there than just a goodnight kiss. At what point *did* you two say goodnight?"

Missy stammered. "Just…just because I…"

Chucky interrupted. "Look, we all know how y'all edit this shit. So they kissed. So what? If she said nuthin happened, then nuthin happened." He grabbed her hand and clasped his fingers through. "Now just move on."

Carmen raised her hand. "Well, wait a minute. We have a few more seconds on the reel." Again, she pressed play.

The video picked up the tail end of the kiss. Missy pulled away, then she opened the door to her suite and went inside. Kevin followed. The door closed behind them. A couple seconds passed, then the door opened. Kevin stepped out and affixed the Do Not Disturb sign on the knob before he stepped back and closed the door shut. The screen went blank.

There were ooohs from the audience. Missy sat still; stunned, staring at the blank screen. Afraid to speak or to move. Chucky squeezed her hand, a little too tightly as he laughed nervously and shook his head.

Carmen went straight in. "Now Chucky, you seem pretty confident in your lady. And that's what a relationship is supposed to be based on. Trust. But I would be remiss if I didn't allow the other party to respond. So ladies and gentleman, once again we have Kevin Clark, live from backstage."

Kevin appeared on the screen. A slight bruise under his eye was still visible through the heavy TV makeup.

"Kevin."

"Carmen."

"Welcome back."

"Thank you."

"So, we were just discussing you. If I may recap for those who may have just tuned in. We just took a question from one of our viewers. The question was for Missy. The viewer asked if you two slept together during the show. We played some of the footage from your first night. Well…the footage from the *outside* of her suite. I'm sure you saw that backstage. Now Missy has emphatically denied that you two were intimate…beyond the kissing. So I'm asking you…?"

"Carmen!" Missy snapped. "It didn't happen."

The truth was Missy didn't know what happened that night. She only vaguely remembered the kiss at the bar. But everything after that was a blur. She certainly didn't feel like she'd had sex the morning after. Then again Kevin was so small. Maybe she wouldn't have. She couldn't believe she'd drank that much. It was so unlike her. And she couldn't wait to see Carmen after the show. She thought, *this bitch is really asking for it.*

Carmen turned back to Kevin. "Kevin. Do you care to comment?"

"As I've said before. I'm a gentleman. And if the lady doesn't want to discuss what happened that night…" He shrugged. "…who am I to divulge? You all saw the tape. You do the math."

Carmen turned back to the camera. "And on that note, we'll be right back."

The director yelled. "Clear!"

Chucky yelled at the screen. "Hey! Little dick! You gon stop fakin like you been with my girl."

Kevin hollered back from the comfort and the safety of his dressing room. "Come on man, don't blame me if the lady chose me. What is it they say? Don't hate the playa?"

A resounding *Ooohh* came from the instigating audience.

Chucky frowned. "Playa? Are you serious? Nigga, you know what she call you? A Gherkin. You know what that shit is? Go head and put your fuckin fancy degree to work. You baby dick *bastard.*"

The crowd went crazy with *oohs, ahhs* and *oh em gees,* getting more excited with each insult the guys hurled at each other. According to Kevin, Chucky was a washed up comic looking for a comeback on reality TV. According to Chucky, Kevin was a bitch hiding behind a TV screen, and as soon as he found out what room he was hiding in he was coming for his ass.

As the men continued to take shots at each other, Missy sat back, completely dumfounded and disgusted. Thanks to Carmen, she was looking exactly what she worked so hard to avoid. Crazy. For all her fighting and negotiating, the show turned out to be just what she dreaded. Ratchet. She felt set up.

She surveyed the room. On one side, Chucky stood cursing at the top of his lungs, hurling threats and nasty insults at a television monitor. In front of her a rowdy studio audience stood at their feet, cheering the foolishness on. Hyping Chucky even more. Her exes were seated off to the side immersed in their own melodrama, and Carmen sat at the center of it all. The orchestrator. The conductor. Missy wanted to slap the stupid smirk from her face. But she'd probably enjoy it. More drama for the cameras.

Missy watched as long as she could before she sprang from her seat and grabbed Carmen by the arm. "I need to talk to you. In private!"

Carmen snatched away. "Ok, ok. Easy on the Chanel, girl. We can go to the back." She stepped aside to allow Missy to walk in front then turned around to the cameraman and mouthed, "Keep rolling."

Second Thoughts

Brenda stood over the range fishing a fresh piece of fried catfish out of the pan when her cell phone rang.

"Hey Aunt Pat. What's happenin?"

"Hey baby girl. I was callin to let you know my man finally got back to me on that thing you were asking about. You got some time to talk?"

"Oh, no. You didn't get my message? Forget about that. I'm over it now..."

"I'm on my way."

"Wait..."

Aunt Pat hung up the phone. Brenda called her back to tell her never to mind, but she didn't answer. She called again. No answer.

Things between her and David had never been better. The shift was a real thing. Something she couldn't explain, but was extraordinarily pleased with. So she didn't question it. They were dating. Actually talking to each other. And he was finally listening. Ignorance was bliss.

Aunt Pat pulled into the driveway. Her pickup was unusually loud. Brenda could hear the muffler from the kitchen. She went to the door and as soon as she opened it Aunt Pat shoved an envelope into her hand. "Take this! Read it. Call me as soon as you're done. You hear me?"

"Aunt Pat–"

"Brenda!"

"Okay."

Aunt Pat walked back to her truck and took off down the driveway, leaving a puddle and a trail of dark liquid behind her.

Brenda closed the door and walked back into the kitchen.

She laid the envelope on the counter and went back to fixing Dave's meal. He walked in the door and she greeted him with a long passionate kiss.

He smiled. "Smells good in here. Fried chicken?"

Brenda grinned. "Fish. Here, let me take your coat. You go in and make yourself comfortable, and I'll make you a drink. Martini?"

Dave stood over the stove uncovering pots and pans. "Yeah, dirty babe."

Brenda walked back into the kitchen with two martinis and they toasted before they kissed and sipped. Dave picked up the unmarked manila envelope from the counter. "What's this?"

She grabbed the envelope. "Oh. Nothing. Just some stuff Aunt Pat brought over about my mom's house." She walked it over to the junk drawer and threw it in. Dave stood behind her watching her body parts jiggling in her leggings and tank top. He took her right there on the floor and they made love, passionately, ignoring the smell of the burning fish grease and the sound of Brenda's ringing cell phone.

The next morning, Brenda kissed her handsome husband and saw him off with a huge smile on her face. She was the happiest she'd ever been, looking forward to their future. Still smiling, she loaded the dishwasher and ignored Aunt Pat's call. She didn't want to hear anything from anyone that would undermine her newfound happiness. That went for Aunt Pat, Evelyn, Meredith, whoever.

She sat at the island sipping a hot cup of tea and watching the phone vibrate across the counter. She'd turned the ringer off somewhere around the fifth call. Somewhere around the eleventh, she'd had enough. Brenda walked over and picked up the phone from the table. She was going to put a stop to all of the interference. Whatever was in that fucking envelope could stay there. In fact, she was going to just destroy it and tell Aunt Pat to mind her business and leave her be. Politely, though.

She pressed the answer button. "Hello."

"Brenda! Girl! I been callin you. You ok in there? Where Dave at?"

"Dave is gone to work."

"Work! Did you open that envelope?"

"No."

"No?! Are you fuckin–"

Brenda hit the red button, hanging up the phone. Then she powered it down and took another sip of tea. Hot cup in hand, she walked out onto the patio. Away from the kitchen. As far away from the envelope as she could get.

Chamomile tea was supposed to soothe. At least that's what it said on the side of the box. But it would take a lot more than herbs and lemon zest to calm her increasingly shaky nerves.

She sat on the edge of the pool with both feet immersed in warm chlorinated water, sipping and asking herself why the universe was so intent on ruining her happiness. All the questions. The innuendo. Aunt Pat, Missy. Then there was overbearing Evelyn hovering around, trying to cause problems. Attitudy Lucy scowling every time they crossed paths. Why couldn't they all just leave her alone. She was fine. They were fine. Perfectly fine.

Several hours, two more cups of chamomile, and a cat nap later, Brenda's curiosity had gotten the very best of her. The catnap brought on daymares, a couple of which included the opening of a manila envelope and a subsequent gasping for air.

The first revealed several marriage certificates with the names of several women that her loving husband was currently married to. The last of which, was a redheaded paralegal that closely resembled Lucille Ball. So he was a bigamist. A liar. And she was right about Lucy all along. She opened her watery eyes, hurt and angry but soon fell back to sleep, relieved.

Moments later, she jerked herself awake. Seconds before that, she stood in her dining room flipping through a stack of eight by ten color photos of her loving husband in various compromising positions with a beautiful Brazilian bombshell with Dolly's rack, J-Lo's glutes and Dirk Diggler's bulge in her panties. She shuddered at the thought.

As much as she dreaded knowing the unknown, she knew that the envelope would control her every thought until she opened it. So it was time to just rip the fuckin seal and get it over with. She peeled herself off the lounger, walked back into the kitchen and over to the credenza. She took a deep breath and snatched open the drawer. The envelope was gone.

Gettin Played

"Before I get into anything else, how the *hell* would Chucky know I call Kevin a gherkin?!

Carmen looked puzzled. "What? Girl ion know. Maybe you talk in your sleep…or wrote it in your diary or something. What would I look like telling him some shit like that? Missy, come on now."

"Come on?"

"Yes. What are you tryna say?"

"I'm saying you *fucked* me, Carmen. You have been lying to me from day one. The exes? Kevin? The videotape? Why would you do that to me? Carmen, WHY would you DO that to me?!"

"Do what?! Get you paid!"

"FUCK that money! You know damn well it's not about that!"

"Oh really? So if you didn't do it for the money then what…the fame?"

"Carmen…"

"No, Carmen my ass. Like I made you do all that shit on tape. I didn't force you to drink or make you kiss Kevin in the mouth or call him to your bedroom. Missy, you knew what you signed up for. You watched reality TV before. You knew there were cameras all around, and now you mad because the producers had the *nerve* to show the world what you did? That shit was bought and paid for when you cashed that check so you not gon keep makin me out to be the bad guy. How bout you take some responsibility for what *you* did!"

Missy rolled her eyes and turned away. "Bottom line is I don't trust you. You're shady. This whole thing has been shady from day one."

"What shady?" Carmen slapped the top of the table. "It's a

fuckin reality show! This is my job, Missy! Look, I came to you with a mutually beneficial opportunity that you accepted. An opportunity that you got paid for. Paid well. You asked for more money, and I got it for you. Everything you asked for, I gave it to you. I fought for that. Because YOU ARE MY FRIEND! But this is also my JOB! I don't write the damned scripts! I don't own a network! I don't have the final say, Missy! What do you want from me?!"

Missy sat quietly for a moment. Nothing Carmen said was a lie. But still... "I don't know. I just don't like feeling like I've been used. Or...or played. That's how I feel. I mean...this whole Kevin situation? Carmen, if you..."

Gun shots rang out, echoing loud into the hall, outside their door. The girls hit the floor and crawled under a table. There were screams from down the hall. A stampede right past their door. Then there was quiet. An eerie quiet that scared them almost as much as the gunfire.

They huddled closely together. Trembling. Terrified. With tears in her eyes, Carmen mumbled, "Oh God. What just happened. What have I done?"

There were several minutes of silence before the footsteps. Slow and heavy. They stopped in front of their door. The handle jiggled. The door swung open. They gasped...

When the Shit Hits the Fan

Brenda walked around the house checking every corner and crevice for the envelope. In the drawers, behind the credenza, under the fridge. Downstairs, upstairs, even outside on the patio. *What the hell could have happened to it?* It was weird. Finally, she went into the bedroom. Still, no luck.

She thought, *Was Dave acting strange this morning?* It was the first morning in quite a while that they didn't have sex. Then again they'd had a marathon session the night before. But that usually didn't matter. Dave was insatiable. He always wanted it. *Whatever*, she thought. *It'll turn up.*

She dressed and primped and readied herself for the day. Her best girlfriend Tina was in town for the weekend, and they were heading out to the Leesburg Premium Outlets in Virginia to get some power discount shopping in. Not that Brenda needed to shop for discounts anymore, but Tina was a fanatic for a sale so she indulged her bestie.

Brenda drove into the city. Past the Ridgewood housing project she grew up in, past her mother's old row house, the one where Aunt Pat currently resided. She definitely didn't want to run into her. Tina was waiting outside on her mother's front porch, dressed in a fitted designer jogging suit and sneakers, the total opposite of Brenda's conservative pantsuit and stilettos.

Tina hopped in the car. "*Girlll.* Look at *you.* Why you so dressed up?"

"It's just a pant suit."

Tina looked over the seat. "And heels? When you start dressin up to go to the mall? You too fancy for me now."

Brenda laughed. "Shut up."

Tina reached for her seatbelt. "This is a nice ass BMW. Ion

think I seen this one before."

Brenda smiled, "You haven't. It's the new 8 series."

"Okay…okay. Somebody ballin."

"Girl please. We ain't hardly ballin. We do ok though."

"Chile." Tina reached over and lifted Brenda's left hand from the steering. "Look at that fuckin ring. You rollin up on $80,000 wheels and livin on Crest Lane in McLean. Youz a rich bitch. But I ain't mad at you. You know you treatin today, right?"

Brenda giggled. "Tina…let's go.

Tina laughed. "Imma go head and take that as a yes."

Brenda dropped more than a few thousand that day. Both her and Tina's arms were full from wrist to elbow with shopping bags. They loaded up in Michael Kors, True Religion and Burberry. Brenda copped a few pairs of high end boots from the Barney's outlet. A few neckties from Armani for her husband.

After the spree they headed over to the waterfront at the National Harbor for some seafood and some good girlfriend conversation.

Tina cracked her lobster open and poured hot butter over it. She took a bite of the succulent shellfish and a sip of white wine. "My God, this is good."

Brenda closed her eyes and hummed, after taking a bite of the same. "It is, right? I've always loved this place. I should order one for Dave."

"You know I was just joking when I said you was treatin right. I didn't expect for you to pay for everything. But I appreciate it tho. For real. Thank you."

"I know you appreciate it, and I'm happy to do it. What's the good in having all this money if you can't share a little of it?"

"Oh so you admittin you got money now."

She held up her thumb and forefinger, pinched them together and laughed, "A lil bit."

"Um hmm. Well I wanna know how ya'll doin it. Last you told me he was a criminal defense attorney with no clients. So how ya'll livin in a $4.4-million-dollar house with a half million dollars' worth of mobiles in your garage? Yes, I told you I looked it up. I'm just sayin. I need the secret cause me and Tony must be doin something real wrong. We need to come holla at y'all."

Brenda's smile faded. She took a sip of her wine, and a moment to collect her thoughts before responding. She was really tired of people insinuating there was something sketchy about how her husband made his money. Tired of defending her life. First there was Missy, then Aunt Pat, and now her best friend. Haters. All of them. Why couldn't they just let her live?

"Tina. My husband is Jewish, he's an attorney, and he comes from money. He's also a very savvy investor. He takes care of the business, I take care of home and it works for us. No secrets. We're just blessed."

Tina scowled. "Um hmm."

Brenda signaled the waiter. "Can we get the check please?"

Tina called out. "Yeah and can you bring me a box for this? Girl, this lobster is the bomb. I shoulda ordered two."

Brenda was about ready to take her lowkey hatin, lightweight moochin BFF the hell on home. *Sitting there talking shit and not spending a damn dime. Tryna judge somebody.* Tina packed her leftovers and they headed back to the car, back to the 295 interstate toward DC, fast. Brenda popped in a cd and cranked the volume so she wouldn't have to talk. Tina felt the slight shade. She turned the volume down.

"Ok, look. I didn't mean to insult you, or overstep my *boundaries* or whatever. I just wanna make sure you ok, Brenda. That's all. I mean, you always have a way of like...lookin the other way. Like if you don't admit the shit is goin on, then maybe it ain't true. You my girl. I just wanna make sure you good."

"Tina, I'm good. I was married to a hustla for twenty years, and I'm done with that life. If it was something else goin on I would just tell you. I promise you everything's legit. I'm ok. All right?"

"All right then. If you say you ok, then you ok. So wassup? Can a sistah get a invite or somethin? Come over, lay out by your pool."

"Hmm. Not today you can't."

Tina laughed. "You petty."

"Nah, I'll come and get you tomorrow so we can hang. I

gotta get home and get dinner started."

"Umm hmm. Ole happy homemaker ass."

"Whateva. Don't hate."

*****

There was heavy afternoon traffic on the George Washington Parkway, but Brenda made it home in just enough time to get dinner started. She dropped her shopping bags into the bedroom closet and changed into her lounging attire, leggings and a tank top.

Halfway down the stairs she realized she was still wearing her ring. Dave had been nagging her lately about wearing it while she cooked and cleaned the house. "Brenda, that's one of the most expensive things we own, please stop covering it with flour and putting it in detergent," he would say. So she agreed to put it back in the safe at night.

She ran upstairs into the bedroom and pulled back the hinged picture frame on the wall above their bed. 07-14-01-15-76. His and her birthday. The safe wouldn't open. 07-14-01-15-76. Nothing. She picked up her cell.

"Hey babe."

"Hey beautiful lady. What's up?"

"I was trying to open the safe to put my ring back in *like you asked me,* and it wouldn't open. Did you change the combination?"

"What. Change the combination? Why would I change the combination? What reason would I have to change the combination?"

"Well...for some reason it won't open."

"Well....did you put the numbers in right? 07-14-01-15-76?"

"Yes. I know the combination. I tried it several times, and I still can't turn the latch."

"Well maybe there's a glitch with the code or something. I'll check it when I get home. It's 07-14-01-15-76."

"Yes Dave you said that. I know what it is. Our birthdays. But it doesn't work."

"Yeah…well maybe there's glitch. I'll try it when I get home. But I'm glad you called. I was just about to call you actually."

"Why?"

"I have some really great news to share with you. Something you've been waiting for, so don't worry about dinner tonight. I want you to go into that closet, pull out your best outfit, and get yourself all dolled up for me. I'm taking you out to celebrate."

"Ooh, there's something to celebrate?"

"Yeah I'm taking you out to celebrate."

"You just said that."

"Right. You are going to *love* me."

"I already love you."

"I know you do. Now hurry up and get yourself right. I really need you to be ready when I get there. I'm on my way. Right now. So hurry up babe."

"Ok, ok. I'll be ready. I love you."

"I love you, too. Hurry and get dressed babe. Bye."

Dave grabbed his briefcase and tore out of the office at top speed. He ran down to the garage. There was no attendant in sight so he grabbed his keys from the booth and ran around looking for his car. So frantically he didn't realize that he'd passed it twice already. When he finally spotted it he hopped in and ripped around every bend to the top level.

There was a line of traffic at the exit. He was starting to sweat so he removed his jacket, loosened his tie. He sat on his horn. "Go! What the fuck!"

Singh, the parking attendant walked over to him. "Everything all right, Mr. Cohen?"

"Why isn't anyone moving?!"

"It is rush hour, Mr. Cohen. It is always like this. The traffic light is red at the street. And it is a long light."

Dave hit the steering wheel. "Fuuuck!" Singh looked on, slightly puzzled but not sure what he could do. The traffic would move soon enough. But the question was, would he make it home before Brenda got into that safe?

It's a Wrap

"Chucky?!" Missy looked out from under the table.

"Yeah, come on let's get the fuck outta here."

She breathed a sigh of relief and crawled out from underneath the table. "What happened?"

"*Yo* muthafuckin crazy ass ex-boyfriend. Dre. That's what happened. That nigga came back on set blastin. He got Ian's ass, too. Dead in the chest."

Carmen gripped both sides of her face and whispered. "Oh my God. He's…"

"Dead? No. Well not yet. The paramedics were workin on him when they wheeled him out. He lost a gang of blood tho."

"So, where's Dre?"

"Out there on the ground. Shakin and droolin and shit."

"What?"

"Big Mike tazed the shit out his ass. In the neck. Snatched the gun right out his hand. The police got him handcuffed and the paramedics checkin him out."

"Whaaat?"

"Yeah. That shit was crazy. I bet they got it all on camera, too. Oh Carmen, I think your boss out there lookin for you. You might wanna go handle that. Come on Missy, let's go."

"Y'all leaving?" Carmen fretted.

Chucky took Missy by the hand and threw up a two finger peace sign. "We out."

Unpleasant Surprises

Brenda sat at her vanity table, smiling to herself and thinking what a wonderful husband she had in David Cohen. He was so funny. And so predictable. He couldn't keep a secret or tell a lie to save his life. He'd always get nervous and start stuttering or repeating himself. Outside of a courtroom, the guy really was terrible under pressure. She reflected on the conversation. *Repeating himself.*

She stroked her right cheek with the soft mink blush brush, giving her brown skin a peachy glow. She looked over at the picture above the bed. The one covering the safe. *Hmm.*

She traced the rim of her eyelid with a felt liner creating the perfect winged affect then she twirled the rotating mascara brush over her lashes. As she glided creamy lipstick over her lips, careful to stay inside the liner, a strange feeling came over her. She paused for a moment. But it passed.

When her face was sufficiently "beat," she stood and stepped into her beautiful new Giuseppe sandals— silver, stilleto, part of the bounty from Barney's clearance rack. She stood tall in the mirror and checked herself out from every angle. The nagging feeling was back. Stronger than before. *Somethin ain't right.*

Brenda walked over the bed and swung back the picture frame, exposing the safe. She tried the combination one last time 07-14-01-15-76. Still nothing. *What could he have changed it to.*

Dave had a tendency to use the same numbers often, like most. So she tried multiple combinations of significant dates. Their wedding date. The day they met. Their ages and birthdates. That latch just refused to turn.

She picked up her cell. "Hi Evelyn. It's Brenda."

"Yes, I know the number, dear. What can I do for you?"

"I'm working on Dave's calendar. Trying to put together some exciting things for vacations next year and I want to make sure I'm not stepping on anyone's toes. Can you tell me, when is your birthday? I know the next one is a *big one*."

"Well that's very considerate of you, dear, and smart. It's January 2nd."

"Oh ok so we have a New Year celebration. Perfect. And when is Mr. Cohen's birthday?"

"Why would you need my husband's birthday?"

Brenda had to think fast. Why *would* she need a dead man's birthday? "Well Dave mentioned that he wanted to do something special to celebrate it next year. I just wanted to get it on the calendar."

"Well, he needn't wait a year; Joshua's birthday is next month. On the 16th. But David never mentioned he—"

"Thank you so much, Evelyn. I really appreciate your help. I'll get in touch with you about Dave's plans for next month. Talk to you soon."

Evelyn was in mid-sentence when Brenda hung up the phone. She went back to the safe and bit down hard on her lip when she entered his and his parent's birthdates. There was a click and then the latch pulled down with ease. *Mu-tha-fucka.* There amongst the jewels and the cash and their wills was the manila envelope she'd been searching for.

Her eyes welled, and soon tears streamed down her freshly painted face. Somehow she knew that the contents of that envelope would change her whole life. The wonderful life that she'd built with a man that she loved. A man that loved her…or so she thought. What was he hiding?

She sat at the edge of her bed holding the envelope in her hand and weeping. As badly as she wanted to rip it into a thousand tiny pieces and throw it into a burning fireplace, she knew she had to open it. Aunt Pat already knew what was in it so she couldn't avoid it. No matter how much she wanted to.

She wiped tears from her burning eyes with the back of her hand, smearing the carefully blended shadows and mascara along the side of her face. Then she tore into the envelope. A half hour later, Brenda lay on the bedroom floor screaming. As far as she was concerned, Dave was a dead man.

The Quiet Storm

The ride home was uncomfortable, to say the least. Neither wanted to be the one to break silence, though the question burned at the tip of both their tongues. The question that overshadowed all else. The one that Missy couldn't confidently answer and Chucky was too afraid to ask.

He'd imagined the night of the reunion show about a million times in the month that they'd been apart. He prepared well for it. In the trunk of his SUV was a wicker basket with a vintage bottle of wine and some of Missy favorite bougie treats on ice. An '85 Montrachet. Siberian caviar on brioche, filet mignon canapes and Avocrab Cocktail. For dessert, the infamous and ridiculously expensive 24 karat gold Kristal Ube donut. One hundred dollars for one damned donut. He knew she'd get a kick out of that. He ditched the red cups for lead crystal wine goblets. The fancy ones she liked.

In his pocket was a tiny velvet box. In that box was the five carat vintage diamond she'd posted several times on her social media. Each time she captioned the photo, *Ev-er-y-thing*. He took the hint, and the long drive up to New York to meet the jeweler.

When he laid eyes on that ring, he knew he had to get it for her. The pictures didn't do it justice. It was so much more exquisite than it was shown and he'd been beside himself for the last few days thinking about her reaction when she opened the box.

He'd planned to propose to her on the show. A hopelessly clichéd down on one knee display that would melt the hearts of many and solidify his commitment in front of all them ex bammas from her past. She would shed many tears at the sight of the diamond she'd pined over. The diamond that he'd spent nearly his entire reality show paycheck for. She'd throw her arms around him and kiss him like she never had. For the cameras. For the haters. For the Vine. Then they'd picnic in the park and make sweet love under the stars.

But none of that happened. The Black Love reunion show had come and gone. With a bang even. And instead of a sappy proposal, he got to witness his beloved slam her tongue down another man's throat and invite him into her bed. All on camera. In front of a live studio audience. It was easily the most painful, most humiliating thing he'd ever endured.

The more he played back the reunion in his mind the angrier he became. He sat quietly on the drive, seething, trying desperately to calm the storm raging inside of him. As much as he loved Missy he couldn't even look at her. He didn't speak because he was too afraid of what he might say, and that burning question seemed moot after the watching the video. Still he needed to hear the words from her lips. Either way.

"I didn't sleep with Kevin."

Lies. He thought.

Chucky didn't respond, instead he stayed silent, pretending to be too focused on the road for her distraction.

"Did you hear me? I said I didn't have sex with Kevin."

"I heard what you said."

"But do you believe what I said?"

"Missy." He sighed. "I really don't want to do this right now."

She turned back toward the window. "Fine."

He pulled into her driveway, and she jumped out slamming the door behind her. He never even waited for her to get inside. Her key was barely in the door when she heard the screech of his tires. He sped down the driveway and off the block without looking back.

Brenda's Wrath

Over an hour in rush hour traffic and Dave was in full panic mode. His shirt was wet with sweat. He'd never honked his horn so much in his life. When he reached the house, his car was barely in park before he hopped out. He ran up to the door with his briefcase in one hand and a dozen purple tulips that he'd purchased at a long red light in the other. As soon as he stepped through the front door he heard Brenda upstairs, screaming. *FUCK! She got into the safe.*

He stood at the bottom of the stairs for what seemed like forever, listening to her gut-wrenching sobs. Her heart breaking into pieces. His heart ached for her, too, and he wanted to rush to her side, but he was way too scared to trek those stairs.

Dave never had the misfortune of witnessing Brenda's wrath, but he'd heard a few stories. And after what he and Meredith had done to her, he wouldn't have blamed her if she was sitting up there waiting for him with a shotgun in her lap.

He swallowed hard and dropped the briefcase at the bottom of the stairs. He walked up, slowly with the tulips in hand, thinking on how to approach the situation. Should he address it head on or just wait to see what she says? Or does? He thought, *Oh God.* He was scared all over again.

When he reached the top of the stairs, the crying stopped. The sudden silence was unnerving. "Babe," he called out. There was no response. He walked slowly and carefully to the bedroom. Then he peered in. Brenda sat on the side of the bed. The envelope beside her. Papers spread out in front of her.

"Sweetheart. Please, let me explain this."

She spoke just above a whisper. Never lifting her head. "You stole my life."

"I'm sorry, baby...what?"

She turned to him. Her words were, louder, clearer, succinct. "You. Stole. My Life."

"Ok, I understand why you would think that. Babe, but it's not what it seems. Just please give me a chance to explain."

She began to cry again. "My husband loved me. Melvin loved me. He did exactly what he said he was gonna do. And you took it." She pulled herself to her feet.

Dave was scared stiff. He didn't move a muscle. Too afraid he'd provoke her. "Brenda please." His eyes welled and voice began to crack. "I love you. I swear I do. Can you just give me a chance to explain this?"

"Explain what, Dave? How you and little girlfriend forged my signature on these deeds? You signed them. She notarized them. It's all right here in black and white."

"Yes I know. But listen..."

"And here I was thinking that you were the best thing that ever happened to me. A rich successful lawyer, with class and a pedigree. Wanted *me*. *Me*. Little ghetto Brenda from Ridgewood Terrace. A drug dealers widow. High school dropout. Ex-convict. Can't even hold on to my children. What the hell was I thinkin?"

"Baby, it's—"

"You're a good liar, Dave. A really good actor. Playing my ass from day one. Until I opened that envelope today...no one, and I mean NO ONE could have ever made me believe that you didn't love me. That you weren't *in* love with me. Was any of it real?"

"Yes! Yes, Brenda I do love you. Baby I love you. I am IN LOVE with you."

"Really."

"Can we just sit and – "

"Talk? You wanna talk? Tell me how you and your little girlfriend set me up? Took everything. Sold everything."

Dave pleaded. "I'll fix it. I mean...I'm fixin it. Brenda just let me – "

"So, tell me. What was I to you? Huh? A mark?"

"No!"

"I mean really. Was I like yourrrr...your fuckin little Hottentot Venus fantasy. You love my ass so much. You love my big black ass right?"

"Come on. Brenda—"

"Am I your fetish? Jungle fever. Big black girl fetish. BBW. You like your girls BBW?"

"No! I mean...yeah..."

"No, wait. I'm probably your little slave girl fantasy? Huh?"

"Brenda!"

She stood, kicked off her shoes, then unzipped her dress and stepped out of it. She unfastened her bra and threw it on the bed, pushed her panties to the floor and stepped out of them, revealing her naked body. Then she turned around slowly. "Good enough? No wait..."

"Baby, what are you doing?"

She pulled a footstool from the corner and dragged it over to the bed. "This how they used to do it, right?" She stepped up onto the stool and held her arms out. "You can see her real good now, Mas'r. She got good arms. She'a do a heap a work for ya. She'a cook for you. She clean, and she a purdy nigga, too..."

Tears streamed her face again as she continued her rant, spitting venom. Making the most insulting, demeaning and dehumanizing slave references, Dave cringed. But he knew better than to interrupt her. "She'a do whatever you want her to do. She'a suck ya. She'a fuck ya. And this one don't talk back neither. You just make sure she stays up in the big house, an you can do whateva you want." She dropped the Southern accent, and she spoke slowly in her normal tone. "How much is she worth to you?"

He stood there, sad...embarrassed, and a little terrified. The muscle in her right eye twitched. She inhaled deeply, exhaled slowly. The breaths grew shorter... and shorter. Her eyes were suddenly bright and wild. She looked directly into his. "I loved you, Dave. I really loved you." She wiped her face again, smearing more of her makeup. "I gave you all of me. And your *cracker ass* was just plottin on me. The whole *FUCKIN time.*"

Hearing her say the words out loud, watching her heart breaking in front of him, knowing he was the reason. It was too much. Dave broke down. His voice shaky, he said, "I'm sorry. Jesus God I'm so sorry Brenda. I love you so much and I know what I did was unforgivable but if you'd just listen to – "

Brenda's nostrils flared. "…stealing from my children. From my *husband*. You stole my life. I should FUCKIN KILL YOU!"

She leaped off of the stool, ran over to him and unleashed. Brenda unloaded blow after devastating blow to his head, neck and his face. Backing him up, out of the room and into the hall. He tried to brace himself and take what he deserved, but she was so strong. *Crazy* strong. After a while, he attempted to block her punches, but they were coming too fast. Dave would never dream of hitting her, but she was really hurting him.

Blood poured from his nose and trickled from his lip. He could feel his left eye beginning to close. When she hit the other eye with a powerful closed fist punch, his reflex kicked in, and he pushed her back into the wall. "Brenda please!" She came right back at him charging with the force of a wild bull. When she hit him the force was so strong, he nearly broke through the bannister.

He grabbed the post at the top of the stairs and slipped, reaching out for her. He managed to grab her by the arm, just trying to grip something – anything to stop his fall, but it was no use. They both went tumbling, three stories down, only Brenda caught one of the slats in the railing to stop her fall.

Dave wasn't so lucky.

Love Sick

Her headaches were getting worse everyday. The resident physician at the free clinic referred her to a specialist, but doctors weren't exactly her thing. The one was enough, and if he couldn't fix it then fuck it, she thought. Cognac didn't make the pain go away, but it numbed her to all the other shit going on. Bills piling up. Streets drying up. The residual effects of her heart being snatched directly out of her chest and trampled on live television.

After all they'd been through together, Connie hadn't called her once since the show. No apology. She just hightailed it with the Spaniard and blew town. Back to her old life. And she didn't look back. Aunt Pat wasn't really one to show emotion. But the loss cut deep. Not even the most nubile of the young things in her stable could cure her ills. But that didn't stop her from trying them all.

As she sat at the edge of her bed, gently rubbing her chest, she couldn't help thinking, was love sickness really a thing? She felt perfectly fine…perfectly normal before that show. Before Connie left. Now she was hurting. Not just the headaches, but every time she thought of Connie…every time she thought she'd never see her again…about the baby growing inside her…about her waking up every morning and going to bed every night with someone else…she felt ill. Seriously, physically ill. Her heart was hurting. It was heavy. And there wasn't an antacid known to man that could ease that pain.

Dead Wrong

When PJ walked through the front door, Dave was still lying at the bottom of the staircase, sprawled out, his body contorted, pointing in three different directions at once. His eyes were opened wide and vacant. Dave was indeed a dead man. And Brenda was nowhere in sight.

He walked around whispering her name. "Brenda? Brenda, girl, where you at?"

Moments later, she walked out of the kitchen, stark naked, and gripping a lowball half full of brown liquor. He winced. "Oh God! Brenda! Put some clothes on."

She mumbled, "He stole my life."

"He what?" PJ looked around the room. He ran over and grabbed a throw from the living room sofa and wrapped her in it. Then he walked her over to the sofa and sat her down.

She kept repeating herself. "He stole from us, PJ. He stole. I was rich. You know that? I'm rich right now. This is really all my shit."

"Brenda. Please, hunny tell me what happened. What did you do?"

She sat on the edge of the large sofa, rocking back and forth. "He stole it…Yeah he stole it all. He stole, PJ."

"Stole what?! Brenda…"

She rocked harder and her voice became louder. "He took it all! He stole everything we had. Everything. He stole my life…"

"What are you talking—"

"He stole it!" She screamed. "He STOLE it! HE STOLE IT FROM ME!"

Brenda!" He slapped her hard across the face.

She quickly returned the slap with one of her own. She yelled, "What?! The fuck you hit me for!"

PJ grabbed his cheek. It stung like someone had lit it afire. "Shit, girl, I was trying to snap you out of it! What the hell happened in here?!"

"He's dead."

"I fuckin see that! What HAPPENED?!"

She clenched the blanket to her chest and curled up in the corner of the sofa. She swallowed down the last in her glass and handed it to PJ. "Can you get me some more of this?"

"Yeah." He took the glass from her hand and rushed into the kitchen to refresh it. When he returned, she was crying. Her head laid on the arm of the sofa. He handed her the glass and she swallowed most of it down.

"Stupid. How could I be so fuckin stupid?"

"You're not stupid. Hunny what happened?"

She nursed the rest of her drink while she explained, starting with the contents of the envelope. Four quitclaim deeds. One for a small retail shopping center that was located just around the corner from the Ridgewood projects; another to a restaurant property located near the Howard University Hospital, a three-bedroom condominium near the Southwest waterfront and the last to a 6,500 square foot single family home in southern Maryland.

Melvin purchased the properties out of foreclosure, and they closed the day before he died. It was everything they'd been planning for their family. A new business venture for Melvin, a restaurant for Brenda, a luxury condo in the city and a country home with a spacious backyard and a pool for the children. Something outside the city, away from the drama. Businesses. Real estate. Wealth to pass down to their children, and their children's children, and so on. A legacy.

A title search revealed that the deeds were purchased by Melvin Johnson, just one day before he died. They were then transferred to his wife, Brenda Elaine James-Johnson, on or about the date that she was sentenced to prison. Finally, the deeds were transferred from Brenda Cohen to Cohen and Doyle

LLC. The founding partners of that LLC were David L. Cohen and Meredith P. Doyle. The date of transfer was her wedding date.

In addition to the incriminating documents, there were several photos of Dave with Meredith, in somewhat compromising positions, the most recent of which was taken just a few days earlier. A photograph of them walking arm in arm at the park, across the street from his office.

"So let me get this straight. Melvin bought you a house, a condo, a restaurant, and a fucking shopping mall? The day before he died?"

"Strip mall. Yeah."

"Then Dave forged his name and transferred the titles from Melvin to you...on the day you went to prison..."

"Umm hmm."

"Then he transferred everything to a company that he owns with the redhead, who he's been messing with the whole damn time."

"Uh huh."

"Now he's sold everything off and there's nothing left."

"Nothing."

"*Damn* Brenda. I don't even know what to say. So he's been playing you this whole time?"

"Apparently." Brenda pulled the blanket over her face and sobbed.

PJ rubbed her back and tried to comfort her. He looked across the room at Dave's lifeless body and rolled his eyes. If he wasn't scared of waking the dead, he would have walked over and kicked him in his ass.

"PJ, I feel so fuckin stupid. All this time we been livin off the money from the businesses. Businesses Melvin paid for. So it's like...it's like Melvin's been taking care of me all along. Fuck! *And* Dave!"

"Wow."

"Yeah. So this is Melvin's house. Melvin's cars out there in the driveway. Shit, that's Melvin's law firm. Dave couldn't afford that high-ass rent on K street on his own. And what hurts me so bad…" She sniffled. "…what's hurts me so FUCKIN bad, is that…I remember the night before Melvin died. I was so mad at him for coming home late. It was the first time he missed Mandy's bath time. I called him a couple times, and he didn't answer his phone. When he finally got home, I asked him where he was and he said…he said he was out handling business so he could take care of his family. He tried to touch me that night, and I pushed him away."

"Brenda, baby don't beat yourself up about it. You didn't know."

"I know, but PJ, I should have."

"I'm just confused. Like…how did this shit even get started. Did he know Melvin before?"

"His father was Melvin's lawyer for years. Melvin must have used their law firm to handle the sale. Then once I got in my trouble and called him…I guess he just saw an opportunity and took it."

"Yeah him *and* his bitch. This just seems so crazy to me, Brenda. It's been like three years. How do you fake it like that for three whole years? I've seen y'all together. It doesn't make sense."

"It's not crazy, PJ. People do anything for money. You know that. What would you do for $30,000 a month?"

"That's how much he was gettin?!"

"Check the bank statements. Between the shopping center and the restaurant. And that was just his share. Remember, Lucy got a cut, too."

"Awww that's right. Damn! That nigga got some balls. Well…had some balls."

Brenda sat up on the sofa. She took a deep breath. "We might as well get this over with. Hand me the phone."

"Who you callin?"

"The police, PJ, who else?"

"This was an accident."

"I know, and that's just what imma tell em."

"You think that's a good idea? Look at his face Brenda. You fucked him up. Real bad."

"Well...once I tell em the whole story, I'm sure they'll understand."

"Bitch, are you high?"

"PJ..."

"Girl you are a convicted felon."

"The conviction was over-turned."

"And this is a white man –"

"Who is my *husband*–"

"Who's DEAD!" PJ stood and reached for her glass. "Are you fuckin serious right now?"

She handed him her glass. "Where you goin?"

"To get us a refill and to make your phone call."

Man Down

She picked up on the fourth ring of the second call. Just before the voicemail. "Wassup boy? I'm in the middle of somethin."

"Yeah, well pull up your pants up, Ma. We need you out here. I'm in Mclean."

"Shit." She pushed the girl away and pulled up her pants. "What happened?"

"Well…ummmm…we got us a man down situation."

"For real?

"Yeah, I think you gon need to bring Manny."

"Manny?"

"Manny."

Aunt Pat knew exactly what that meant. Manuelo Fuentes was hired to make things disappear. For good. He wasn't cheap, but he was good. And reliable. To make an uptown Jew lawyer disappear without a trace, you needed good and reliable.

She borrowed Rocky's car and drove across town to Mount Pleasant Street. Manny was sitting at an old wooden table in back of his restaurant, gutting a fish. When he looked up and saw her he already knew what it was. He walked back inside and after a few short minutes he walked back out, carrying a large black duffle.

Manny spoke little English, and he wasn't much for small talk anyway so they rode most of the way to McLean in silence. A few blocks away from the house, they pulled to the side of the road to let several speeding police cruisers go by. When they turned onto Crest Lane, those same cars were parked at Brenda's gate, overhead lights flashing so brightly they lit the whole block.

Both Pat and Manny were armed, so she drove past the gate, slowly and carefully, peering in. Officers were leading Brenda and PJ out of the house in handcuffs. She made a U-turn at the end of the long block and came back down. When she reached Brenda's gate again, she saw a gurney being pushed out of the house, the body covered with a white sheet.

She left the block, frustrated, fighting back tears. Not just because she didn't want Manny to see her weakness, but once again the family was handing her some impossible shit to deal with. Her money was low, and her resources were drying up by the day. Friends were walking away. The bar was on the verge of closing, and she was doing everything she could think of to just stay afloat. There was more than enough on her plate. But there was no time for wallowing. She needed to shift gears and do it fast. It was time to go to work.

Breaking News

The crime section of the Washington Post detailed everything from the mundane jaywalking ticket on the streets of Chinatown to the bloody murders that were still happening in the east quadrants of the city. Today's headline read:

DC trial lawyer killed in McLean home

The article went on to name Brenda the number one suspect. It detailed Brenda's first murder charge and conviction, no mention that the conviction was overturned. It mentioned her alleged sordid past as the wife of a drug kingpin and her various assault charges dating back to her teens. The officers on scene were quoted saying she was "curiously calm" during her arrest – a psychopathic tendency that a DA could play up at trial.

When the police walked her into the station, the redneck posse was in full effect. Waiting on her. Some angry. Some of them laughing. One removed her cuffs and shoved her into her cell so hard she hit a wall.

He smirked. "When will these yuppie boys learn? You can't take niggers…I'm sorry…*niggaz* outta the ghetto."

Under normal circumstances, Brenda would have fired off a snappy retort, but she thought better of it. Though they were in one of the wealthiest, most sophisticated commonwealths in the country, and they were husband and wife, at the end of the day there was still a white man dead at the hands of a black. She had no interest in becoming the next hashtag for Al Sharpton to march to.

PJ was taken in a different car that went in a different direction. She was afraid for him. She yelled through the bars of her cell. "Hey! Excuse me! Officer! Where's my cousin? The guy you picked up with me?"

"Oh you mean that there sissy boy with the women's high heels and all that eye makeup?"

"Yes, him."

He walked over to the bars where she stood and gave her a wicked smirk. "I don't know who you talkin bout."

A chill went up her spine, and a tear escaped her eye. She prayed they hadn't hurt PJ.

The officer sat on the edge of his desk, shelling peanuts and throwing them into his mouth. "You know y'all in a whole heap a trouble for what y'all done to that man. Nice upstanding white lawyer. Y'all beat him and killed him. What, he didn't wanna give up his money or sumpim?"

Brenda put on her best wife-of-a-prominent-Jewish attorney posture. Standing up right with her head held high and using the most proper diction. Hitting all the *er*'s and the *i n g's* at the end of her words. "Sir, I've told you repeatedly, I did not kill my husband. We had a fight. Unfortunately, things went terribly left, and it got physical. We went from the bedroom out into the hallway, toward the stairs where we fell. We both fell. You can see the bruises on my arms from the fall. I would never hurt him and I have nothing to hide here."

"Well, you can save that speech for a jury, ma'am."

"It's no speech. It's what happened."

"Come on y'all beat the hell outta that man. I saw his face. You can say what you want, little lady. You and that little girly boy is goin ta jail for a mighty long time."

She couldn't help her scowl. "I thought you didn't know who I was talkin bout."

The officer smiled. "I don't.

"Officer, he's my cousin, his name is Patrick. He came over after everything had already happened. He had absolutely nothing to do with it. He's completely innocent and shouldn't even be here."

"Look here, lady. I ain't the one you need to be talkin to."

"Well who should I be talking to?"

"I'd say your lawyer. Now sit tight. You gon be here a while."

He walked out of the room and slammed the heavy steel door behind him. The sound was all too familiar. The cell was suddenly small. She felt queasy. And a little faint. She banged on the bars.

"Hey! Guard! I think I...I need some help."

Mama's Baby

Nearly three months had passed since Missy had heard from Chucky. She'd seen him though. On TV. Thanks to the exposure from *Black Love*, he finally got an offer to do a stand-up special. BET wanted to strike while the iron was still hot from the reality show, so they gave him a sixty-minute set. It wasn't exactly his "Eddie Murphy Raw" moment, but all things considered it was a pretty damned decent segue back into the business.

She'd always heard the first trimester was the hardest. Her morning sickness was next level. She'd been on saltine crackers and ginger ale for weeks. Trying to hide her anguish. Putting on a little extra make up every morning to hide her unusually pale skin and the dark circles under her eyes. She wondered how someone could be so happy and so miserable at the same time.

Missy defied the odds. A thirty percent chance at conception. That's what they told her. *Bullshit* she thought. She had a tiny little miracle inside her and she intended to savor every second of it. Morning sickness and all.

It had only been a week since the white stick turned blue, and a day since she got her confirmation from her doctor. Her emotions were on high. All of them. The joy of being with child when she thought she never would. The guilt of her silence. The shame of not knowing for certain who the father was.

Kevin was adamant that they'd slept together, and although she would never fess up, she knew it was at least a possibility. He'd never been known to be a liar, but how could she not remember a thing. Not feel a thing. Nothing.

She wrestled with the thought of telling Chucky. But clearly he was done. Not one phone call, text or even an email since the night he dropped her off after the reunion. And he seemed happy enough with what he had going on in his life. Just that morning he was featured on the local Fox morning news show to promote his comedy show that night at the DC Improv.

The television was kind to him. Or maybe he'd been working out. Whatever the case he seemed good. And she could live with that. But the question was, could he? If he had all of the information, could he? Probably not, she thought. But she definitely didn't want *this* to be the reason he came back. She didn't want to be *that* woman. So she decided, no. For now. She'd tell him. When the time was right. Later.

Meanwhile she took her vitamins and drank her water and ate her saltines with the widest silliest grin on her pale face. Despite the odds and despite the messy circumstance, Missy James was having a BABY! And no one could take that away from her.

As the days passed, she couldn't seem to get Chucky off of her mind. Maybe it's just the hormones, she thought. But the longing was so strong. Unyielding. She missed him with every ounce of her being. She craved his smell. A strange mix of essential oils he bought from a kiosk at Union Station mall.

She thought of what a wonderful father he was to his daughter, Deja, and how happy he would be if he knew he was going to be a father again. The thought of giving him a son. A boy that looked like him with a wide toothy smile and one deep dimple on the right side of his face. That brought a smile to her face.

She picked up the phone and dialed his number. Then she hung up after the second ring. A few minutes passed, and nothing. He usually called back when she did that. An hour later she sat at the edge of her bed with her cell phone in hand. She dialed again. He picked up on the second ring.

He didn't speak but she knew he was there. He knew she was there. But no words were spoken. Finally, she mustered the nerve.

"Chucky." She took a long deep breath and then she exhaled. "I'm pregnant."

Three beeps and the call was disconnected. She looked at

the telephone screen. *Did he just hang up on me?* She dialed him again. The call was sent to voice mail. Then the second call. The third. The thirteenth call was sent to voice mail and she was beside herself. She laid the phone down on the bed. *It's Kevin. He's upset.* She understood.

She picked up the phone and began writing a text so long it broke off into ten different messages on his phone.

11:17 a.m.

...and I understand that you're upset. I get that. But you have to know that I haven't been with Kevin. I meant everything I said to you that night at the house, and I would never betray you that way.... After all these years and everything we've been through I would think you'd know me better than that...You can believe me or not, I don't really care at this point. What I care about is our child. I'm here when you're ready to talk.

Over an hour later no response. Several more of her calls went straight to voice mail. She text him again.

12:36 p.m.

Ok, I'm a little confused. I tell you I'm pregnant, and you don't even have the decency to respond to me? You won't answer your phone?

Two more hours passed with no response. She was hurt...and bewildered. He'd never done her this way.

2:53 p.m.

I have always thought so much more of you as a person and as a man than what I am seeing right now. We really need to talk about this. This is not something that will just go away. No matter how you feel about me right now. I need to talk to you. We have to figure this out.

Most of the day had gone and she'd done nothing but call and text and think about Chucky. The tears were flowing. She felt defeated. What was next? The money was nearly gone and nothing was coming in. She had no support. Brenda was gone. She hadn't had any real contact with the rest of the family in years and now the father of her child had all but abandoned her. She texted him again.

4:12 p.m.

Really? Wow.

Missy pulled herself out of bed and went down to the kitchen to make dinner. Brandy would be walking through the door any minute with Misa who'd be fresh off her afternoon nap and begging for attention. As she stood at the island chopping fresh bell pepper and onions for stir fry her eyes began to water again. It wasn't the onion. She was angry. Incredibly so. *Who the hell does he think he is? Like I need his ass.* She picked up her cell again.

4:57 p.m.

You Chucky Wilson are a coward, a heartless bastard and a despicable human being. You wanna use Kevin as an excuse to walk away from me? Walk away from your responsibility like your deadbeat daddy did to you? That's perfectly fine because I don't want SHIT from you. After the DNA test proves 99.99999% that you ARE this child's father, all I want from YOUR SORRY ASS is for you to sign over your rights to this child and you don't EVER have to worry about us again. I'm done with you. Have a nice life. - Missy

Chucky finally responded at 5:23 p.m.

First of all my phone has been down all day today and you know I don't like texting, but here you go. When you told me that you were pregnant this morning I was so shocked I accidentally dropped my phone in the sink. By the time I grabbed it I was too late. I'm just opening these text messages on my new phone. My apologies for all of the stress that this has obviously caused YOU today but I too have been stressed. ALL day. At first I thought you were joking, but you don't really joke. Then I thought maybe you were lying. But then I was like Missy is not a liar. Then I thought, wow, she's pregnant. I cried for the first time I have since my deadbeat daddy didn't come home for Christmas. Thank you for reminding me of that. Missy you DO know me. I curse too much. I play too much and I say nigga a lot, even though you ask me not to. I don't know why I guess I can't help it. But I am not a coward. I have a good heart and I am a decent human being. I also had a vasectomy 2 years ago Missy. So if you are not joking or lying and you are in fact pregnant, there is no need for a DNA test because I could not be your child's father and apparently I DON'T know you because you

HAVE betrayed me and now I am DONE with you. You take care of yourself. —Chucky

Missy sat the phone back down. She felt like she had just been kicked in the gut. *Is he serious?* But she already knew the answer. Chucky was a great many things but a liar he was not. In fact, he was the total opposite. Unfiltered and brutally honest about everything, which always bothered her.

She took a deep breath after reading the text again. And then another. *Fucking Kevin.* Another deep breath. She grabbed her purse from the counter and fished around for her pills. *Shit.* She couldn't take them anymore. She grabbed a glass from the cabinet and ran a little water from the faucet. Her breathing was labored and she felt light headed. She drank the water down and leaned on the island for support as she tried desperately to catch her next breath. The panic was setting in.

Her phone dinged again and she reached across the counter to pick it up.

5:37 p.m.

P.S. Tell Kevin, or whoever, I said congratulations.

Missy broke down completely. She threw her phone across the room and sat on the kitchen floor balling. She never even heard the front door open. When she looked up Misa stood in front of her. "Mommy why you cry?"

Recidivisms

A week after his arrest PJ was finally freed. The bruises had almost healed by then, but he'd sweated out his perm something awful. He couldn't wait to get back to the shop. The creamy crack was calling him by name. But first he had to get to Ridgewood, to find out what mom's plan was. He knew she had somethin up her sleeve. She always did.

The day before his release, Brenda gave a full account of what happened, and the charges against him were dismissed. So there she was, back in jail. A different jail, where there were no family connections and no support. No one there to have her back. Brenda wasn't scary, but at the present, she was scared. Something told her, this time wouldn't go by so easy.

The Fairfax County Jail system was different from DC. You had to fill out an application online and wait to receive an approval for visits, so it would be at least a couple days before Brenda could be seen. The only person that had been there thus far was a public defender that she turned away.

Aunt Pat showed up the next day. They led Brenda into a room full of monitors. No contact visits. You got to see your loved ones on a screen. Fearing it was being recorded, the women chose their words carefully.

"Hey."

"Hey baby. How you doin."

"I'm in jail."

Aunt Pat cracked a half smile. "I gotta come up with some new questions, huh."

"Did you get my lawyer yet?"

"Yeah, she'll be here tomorrow."

"A woman? Where'd you find her?"

"She's from Missy's stepmothers firm."

"Why? I thought you were using your guy?"

"My guy ain't lawyerin no more."

"Why not?"

"Let's just say…he got into some trouble."

"Well is she expensive?"

"It's pro bono."

"Pro bono? No. I ain't tryna take no hand-outs from Missy's stepmother."

"Well you ain't got no choice. You ain't got no money."

"What? That's crazy…"

"It's not. Dave's name is on all your accounts and them accounts is frozen."

"Frozen?! They can't do that."

"Yeah they can…and they did."

"But that's my fuckin money."

"Well your mother in law is involved now, so that's dead. Any account that he is named on is frozen. Until you're acquitted, you're not beneficiary to anything he has. Bank accounts, life insurance, nothing. She been on the news twice talking about she wasn't surprised you *finally* killed him. Whatever the fuck that mean. The second time she had that redheaded girl with her."

"I know I shoulda called you after I saw – "

Aunt Pat raised her hand. "Don't even worry bout it. Besides, this ain't your fault anyway. It was an accident. We'll prove it soon enough and get you up outta here."

"Is PJ ok?"

"He still a lil bruised up, but he good. How they treatin you in here?"

"Like I killed a white man."

"Bad like that?"

"I mean…it's mostly just people talkin shit. I threw my food away this morning. Looked like somebody spit in it or somethin."

"Shit. Ion really know nobody up in here, but if they transfer you over to the Correctional Center or back to Fluvanna, you'll be straight. I'm on it."

"My girls?"

"Brandy know what's goin on. She ain't said nothing to me yet though. Just give her some time. She'll come around."

"How's Missy?"

"She aight. Still fuckin with Carmen and that reality show bullshit. She said she'll be down here this week to check on you, though."

A banner scrolled across the monitor. *5 minutes remaining.* Aunt Pat stood. "Aight baby. Look like they puttin us out. I'll be back here soon as I can, but I'll holla at you through your lawyer, too, aaight."

"Ok. I love you."

"I love you, too. You keep your head up hear? You ain't gon be here long."

Aunt Pat immediately regretted making that promise. She didn't have a single idea how to get Brenda out of jail. Brenda beat the shit out of that white man. He deserved it for sure. He deserved worse. But proving his death was an accident after beatin em half to death wasn't gon be no easy feat. No matter how good the lawyer was. They needed an alternate plan. Something out of the box, because the truth probably wasn't gon set Brenda's black ass free. But then again, you never knew.

A Whole New World

The time had come. Missy had done all she could do and had gotten as far behind as she could get before everything would crumble and her private anguish would become her public shame. She'd endured repossessions and foreclosures once before, and that was one time too many. She was not about to go through that shit again.

She drove the cars back to the dealership and completed the necessary paperwork for the voluntary repossessions. She put the house on the market, and the movers were scheduled. It was time to go.

Brandy was away with her friends for the weekend, so she thought it best to just move everything while she was gone. She'd explain it all to her when she picked her up from the airport on Monday. Maybe, by then, she could figure out how to break the news to her without completely breaking down. Maybe by then she'd be all dried out because tears of sorrow, regret and hormonal changes had been flowing all week as she secretly packed their lives, little by little, into large cardboard boxes and stashed them in the basement.

The ride back to DC was a hard one. She blasted Mary J on the dinky little radio in the U-Haul truck as it bounced up and down, over and through the deep potholes on the city streets, no doubt destroying half the fragile cargo she packed.

They pulled onto Champlain St. near dusk. The narrow street wasn't wide enough to allow any other cars to pass so she was forced to park it in an alleyway about a half block down the street from her building, which meant she and the movers had to walk a half block up the street with her things.

Misa whined for McDonald's. The movers grumbled about

the uphill climb, and Missy tried her level best not to completely spazz out on everybody, as she fished around in her purse for the keys. It wasn't long before she realized that she'd left the keys. On the kitchen counter. Back in Great Falls. Some thirty-seven miles away. She screamed "Fuck!" to which Misa replied, "Awwwww, you say bad word."

Though sympathetic to her dilemma, and her tears, the foreman politely informed her that they had another job and simply could not wait for her to take a round trip drive in rush hour traffic. They had to get started unloading her things somewhere.

With no leverage and no money to pay them for the overtime it would take to finish the job, they settled on moving everything to the storage unit in the basement of the building. Missy called her neighbor, Mrs. Gomez, and asked her to come out and unlock the front door of the building.

An hour-and-a-half later, she sat frustrated in the truck, locked out of her new home with a screaming child and all of her exquisite belongings sitting three stories below in a damp musky dungeon.

She took Misa for her Happy Meal but didn't have the stomach for the greasy food. They drove back to Virginia for the keys, and by the time they got back to Adams Morgan, it was almost midnight. Misa was asleep in the passenger seat. The U-Haul store was closed, so she was forced to keep the truck overnight. She was dead tired, but their beds were in the dungeon, and she'd maxed out her last credit card paying the movers so there was no money for a hotel. She just sat there and cried.

With nowhere else to turn and no one else to call, she made the first step, reluctantly. A half ring and she quickly ended the call thinking, *No! I won't do it.* Minutes later her phone rang back.

"It's about time you called me, girl."

"It was an accident."

"No, it wasn't, and I'm not about to play this game with you. I been thinkin about you. A lot. I miss you."

She felt the lump forming in her throat. She missed him so

badly. "Me too."

He was quiet for a moment. "How you doin?"

That was such a loaded question. She didn't have the energy to divulge it all. "I'm ok."

"That's good. Where are you?"

She sighed. "On Champlain."

"This time of night? Why?"

"Because I live here now."

"Since when?"

"Since today."

"I need to see you."

"No. Chucky. We don't–"

"Look I just wanna see your face. That's all. I won't stay long I promise. Please?"

"Chucky–"

"I'm on my way."

"Chucky…"

He hung up the phone. Seventeen minutes later she heard the roar of his Porsche as it turned the corner at the end of the block. He drove up to her window.

"Why you sittin out here?"

"I don't know. Just park."

He found a space at the corner and walked back uphill. He looked inside the truck "Why do you have Misa sittin out here sleep in this truck? It's after midnight, Missy."

She started crying.

He was confused. He walked over to the passenger side and eased Misa out of her seat. "Come on, let's go inside and get her to bed."

Missy wiped her face and sniffled. "Ok. But I have to tell you somethin…"

"Shhh, we'll talk about it inside."

They walked up the street and into the building. Misa started to whine and wiggle. Chucky rubbed her back and hushed her back to sleep. When Missy opened the door he looked around the completely empty apartment, confused. "Where's your shit?!"

"It's down in the basement."

"The basement? Why?"

"It's a long story, Chucky. Can we just go down and grab a few things?"

"Yeah, yeah. Hold on to her for a second. Is the basement door unlocked?"

"Yeah."

He re-emerged with Misa's crib mattress and bedding, then he arranged a comfortable space in the far corner of the room. He took Misa from Missy's arms, laid her down and tucked her in. She squirmed and he rubbed her back until she settled in peacefully.

Missy watched him tend to her baby, and it made her heart warm. Chucky was such a good man. Why did everything have to get so messed up, she thought. Why couldn't they just get it together. That's really all she wanted. But no one ever asked what she wanted. Things were what they were and too much had happened to go back. Still, she was happy that he was there for her. If only for a little while.

He took Missy's hand and walked her into the kitchen. "So, what's going on?"

She sighed. "Everything."

"Well, you look beautiful."

"Liar. I look terrible. You can say it. It's ok."

"Yeah, you *are* a little pale. Got bags all under your eyes and shit. But you still look good to me."

She laughed. For the first time in a long while. "Shut up."

"Can I see it?"

"See what?"

He looked down. She grabbed his hand, lifted her shirt and gently placed it on her small rounding belly. She couldn't quite decipher the look on his face. He pulled his hand away and walked to the other side of the room, near the window. She gave him a short moment before she walked over and stood next to him. They stood quietly together for a couple minutes before he spoke, in a low tone. Almost a whisper. "So, how's Kevin?"

She shrugged. "I wouldn't know. I haven't spoken to him.

Not since the show."

He turned and looked her in the eye and then back toward the window. "Why?"

"Because this is not his baby. It's *my* baby. And when I decide – *if* I decide – he'll know. Until then…look I have enough on my plate to deal with right now."

She walked back to the kitchen. He followed. "Well I guess you know what you're doin. So what else is going on with you. What are you doing here?"

"Can we go down and grab some more stuff from the basement? Do you mind?"

As they brought up the boxes of essentials from the basement Missy explained her situation. The whole situation and she was relieved to finally get it all off her chest. The burdens had just become too hard to carry alone.

Chucky excused himself and went down to his car. He re-emerged holding his emergency bottle of Hennessy in one hand and a pack of plastic cups in the other. "Oh yeahhhh."

"Now you know I can't have that."

"Yeah I know." He poured himself a healthy cup and waved it under her nose. "Smell good don't it?"

She hit him on the arm and laughed. "That's so mean. I swear I'd give anything for a little buzz."

They sat next to each other on the kitchen floor and talked for hours. Chucky nearly emptied the fifth size bottle. She put her arm through his and leaned on his shoulder. "I'm so tired."

"You ready for me to leave?"

"No. You're fine. I mean *emotionally* tired. Tired and drained. Tired of pretending everything's ok all the time. Tired of pretending I can handle everything on my own. I just don't wanna live like this anymore."

"Well you never had to. You wanted to."

"What?"

"You heard what I said. You so busy walkin around acting like you got shit together. On your Olivia Pope shit. Like you got everything handled. So nobody bothers with you. You broke, and you won't ask for help. You pregnant, and you won't tell the daddy. Baby, you gotta learn to let people be there for you sometimes."

She rolled her eyes. "Please. People like who?"

He glared at her. "Really? I've always been here. Always. And I ain't goin nowhere. That's why you called me. Cause you know dat shit. You pregnant with another man's child and you see I still rushed my black ass right over here."

"Your yellow ass."

He rubbed his face. "Yeah I am kinda light skinded. But I'm tough though."

She giggled.

"Oh...wait." He leaned into her. "Is that a smile I see?"

"She pushed his hand away and stood up. "No. Stop it."

"Seriously girl. I feel like that nigga on Brokeback Mountain. I don't know *why* I can't quit you."

Missy burst out laughing so hard it caused a stomach pang.

He smiled. "It's good to see you smile again girl."

"It's good to be smiling. You always make me smile."

They leaned in to each other and kissed. Soft, tender pecks with open eyes. Silent confirmations of an understanding that only they understood. He wrapped his arms around her and held her tight. "Damn. I have missed you Melissa James."

The warmth of his arms was all the comfort she needed. "I've missed you, too. So much." She released the pent-up emotion, and he hugged her tighter, nudging her to let it all go. The tears flowed heavy. She tried desperately to control her sobs so as not to awaken the baby. Chucky went right into protector mode. "Shh. That's right baby. Just let it go. It's ok. I'm here. And I'll fix it...if you let me."

Missy couldn't have been more thankful to have him there, in that moment. Plus, she was majorly, unbelievably...horny. A symptom that her internet research assured her was perfectly normal for a healthy pregnant woman.

She pulled away from his embrace, pushed him slowly to the floor and kissed him again. Deeply and passionately this time. With closed eyes, beckoning for his tongue which he gave freely and enthusiastically. She straddled him and he responded through his pants.

"Wait, Missy." He glanced down at her stomach. "Is this ok?"

She responded, excitedly. "Oh yes. Yes, baby. It's perfect."

Just as she pulled at the drawstring to free him from his sweatpants they heard Misa rustling in her bed. "Mommy."

"Shit." She pulled her shirt down and raced over to Misa's bed. "Mommy's here. Come on. Come on baby, Let's go back to sleep." She pulled Misa close to her bosom and started to sing her favorite lullaby. Chucky watched adoringly. Thinking what a wonderful mother Missy would be to his children. He felt suddenly guilty. Regretful. He poured himself the last of the Hennessy.

She walked back over to him. "Hey you. Why are you looking so blue when I'm the one with all the problems?"

He took the last swallow of his drink and put the cup down. Then he pulled her close to him. "I love you. You know that?" He laid her head on his chest and held her tight.

"I love you, too, babe. I'm just so sorry things are so messed up. I'd give anything to fix it."

"There's nothing to fix."

"I love you for saying that." She laid there with her head on his chest as they rocked slowly from side to side. Both of them feeling completely at home in each other's arms. "Can I ask you something?"

"You can ask me anything."

"You only have one child. Why did you have a vasectomy?"

"I didn't."

*****

"WHY THE FUCK WOULD YOU TELL ME THAT?!?!?!" Missy shoved Chucky hard into the refrigerator.

He nearly fell down but quickly regained his balance. "Shhh! Will you lower your voice before you wake her back up?"

Missy lowered it, to an angry whisper. "I don't care! Chucky why would you say that to me? Why would you do me like that?

Don't you realize..."

"Because I wanted to get the truth!" he shouted.

"What?"

"You never responded. Did you? All that shit I wrote and you never responded. So I got my answer."

Missy stood silent.

Chucky scowled. "Exactly. So you fucked him. It is what it is. I just needed to know."

"It's not even like that." She teared up. "I mean...you don't understand."

"Understand what? That you lied? That you had sex with your ex two days after being with me? Two days after telling me I'm the only man for you and that you wanted to be my wife? And all that other bullshit you said?"

"It wasn't bullshit."

"Really."

"Chucky, I don't remember what happened. I honestly don't remember having sex with him."

He looked up at the ceiling and then back at her. "Get the fuck outta here with that bullshit, Missy. I saw the video. Everybody saw the video. I mean, just admit it. And then we can just move on."

"I love how you don't even give me the benefit of the doubt. When have I ever lied to you?"

"Besides right now?"

"YOU let me think that this couldn't be your baby. You have no idea what that did to me. All that time I spent..."

"It's been THREE WEEKS!"

She shushed him as Misa turned over on her bed. Missy whispered. "Let's just go in the bedroom." She ushered him inside and closed the door behind them.

He turned to her. "You really wanna come at me crazy about three damn weeks? Don't you think I deserve a little bit of time to fuckin digest the maybe factor here?"

"What?"

"Yeah maybe. The fact that *maybe* that's not my baby. That *maybe* I am your baby daddy. Or I maybe fuckin not. Or that I'm totally and completely in love with a woman that cheated on me and now *maybe* she's carrying another man's child. So I need a minute! Is that ok with you?"

She leaned against the wall and wiped a tear. "I'm sorry."

"You're sorry."

"YES! Yes, Chucky, I'm sorry! I'm sorry! I'm fucking sorry, ok! I'm sorry I got you into this mess. I'm sorry I ever did the stupid fuckin show! I'm sorry I drank too much! I'm sorry I had unprotected sex that I don't even FUCKIN remember! I'm sorry. Ok?! I'm sorry…"

At about the tenth sorry, she was crying and hyperventilating. She held the wall to keep herself steady and Chucky, who was standing on the other side of the room, rushed over to her side. "Babe! You ok?"

She breathed in and out heavily. "Yeah, I just…I just need a drink of water, please."

"Ok." He ran out to the kitchen and came back with a cold bottle of water and Missy's sable coat. He handed her the water and laid the coat on the floor to make a comfortable space. He motioned to her. "Come here. Come over here and sit down for a second."

She crawled over to him and nestled in between his legs, her back leaning against his chest. He held her close and her breathing gradually slowed to normal. They sat quietly for some time. "I'm sorry."

"Missy if you say that one more time…"

"But I am."

"I know." He kissed her cheek. "I know you are. I've been thinking about it for three weeks. Thinking about you…" He reached under her arms and clasped his hands together as they rest on her small belly. "Thinking about Jr."

She laughed. "Chucky…stop playing with me."

"I'm serious. I love you, Missy. And I ain't goin nowhere. I ain't gon lie. I thought about it. But at the end of the day, this baby is probably mine. I mean I pumped a mean hot load in you that night in the park, and the way my sperm is set up…"

"Chucky!"

"Ok. Seriously. As mad as I was...well I still am mad at you for what you did. But I don't wanna lose you. Bottom line. If I gotta live with this to live with you...then that's what it is."

"But what about..."

"We'll cross that bridge when we need to. For now, I just want my girl back." He pulled her hair to the side and kissed her gently on the nape of her neck. Then up and over to her sensitive spot.

She moaned with delight. "I don't deserve you."

He trailed her neck with his warm tongue. Up to her ear and breathed. "No...you don't."

Missy felt a stirring inside her. Her body was twice as sensitive to touch now so the hairs on her neck and every nerve was standing on end. She turned around, just enough to reach his lips. He kissed her lovingly and she leaned back into his arms, letting him take control. He laid her down on the soft fur and kissed her from head to toe, spending a considerable amount of time at her belly which made them both emotional. It was the best love they'd ever made.

*****

The sun shone brightly though the bare windows, waking Missy from her sleep. She was still so spent that she could barely lift her head from the makeshift pillow. She turned over and noticed the velvet box just next to her head. She smiled as the tears formed in her eyes. Chucky was still fast asleep. When she opened the box the tears began to flow. She slid the precious vintage diamond on her ring finger and smiled through happy tears. Then she proceeded to wake Chucky in a manner he always appreciated.

He moaned with his eyes still closed. Appreciating. When he reached down to grab her hand, he felt the ring. He looked down at her, and they both smiled before he pulled her on top of him. Once again they made love, silently consummating a promise of all things new and good to come.

Just as Chucky was nearing his peak the alarm on Missy's

phone sounded. She stopped in mid motion. "Oh, baby I gotta get Misa up for school."

"Wait, no. Baby don't stop," he whined. "Two minutes...I just need two more minutes please..."

She pecked him on the lips and dismounted. "Come on. Hurry up and get dressed so we can grab a few more boxes from the basement." She jumped up, wriggled herself back into her jeans and threw on her T-shirt. "I gotta get Misa to school on time. And I need to get this U-Haul back."

He grumbled. "Just let her stay hooomme. I'll pay for the U-Haul. Come back here." He reached for her legs. "Lay back down with me. Five minutes."

She pulled away. "See, you just said two minutes. Now it's five, and five will turn into twenty. Come on baby, I have a lot to do today, and I can't get it done with Misa hanging off my hip all day."

He rolled over, shielding his eyes from the blinding sun with his forearm. "Okaaay. Okaaay."

She threw him his sweatpants. "Hurry up and get dressed. I'll make us some coffee for the road."

Chucky smiled, as he pulled on his pants. He watched his soon-to-be-wife scurry out of the room, and at that moment felt more grateful than he ever had. Finally, he was getting everything he wanted. Business opportunities were flooding in. His finances were back on track. He was about to become a father again, and he was more than ready to begin building a life with the only woman he'd ever loved. Yes, there was drama. But there's always drama, he thought. *Love will see us through it all.* He laughed to himself, thinking how corny he was becoming. So not gangsta.

He stuck a foot into his timberland boot and nearly fell over, startled at the sound of the piercing scream.

A Handsome Ransom

"Chucky! Chucky she's gone! Misa's gone!"

He ran out of the room, half dressed. "What?!"

"She's gone!" Missy ran barefoot out into the hall, downstairs and into the street. "Misa! Misa baby! Where are you?!"

Chucky was right at her heels, trying to run after her in heavy construction boots that were still untied. His shirt hung off on one arm. His head was still groggy from all the Hennessy. "Missy wait! Calm down! What happened?"

She walked steadily but quickly, going in no particular direction. Crying and stopping anyone who would listen. "Excuse me, ma'am, have you seen a little girl out here? Walking out here, by herself? Sir, excuse me have you seen a little girl waking around?"

They were a block away, running now. Chucky tripped on his shoe laces. "Wait Missy! Slow down. Did you check in the building? The basement?"

"Shit! No. Come on!"

She took off racing back to the building with Chucky close behind. They got back to the building and the security door was locked. She screamed, "God dammit!" They banged mercilessly on the glass. Her elderly tenant, Mrs. Rivera came out of her apartment and opened the door."

"Thank you! Thank you. Mrs. Rivera, right?"

"Si."

Chucky ran down the stairs shouting, "I'll check the basement! You look upstairs!"

Mrs. Rivera have you seen a little girl in the building? In the hallway or out on the porch?"

Mrs. Rivera looked a bit puzzled. Missy realized she didn't speak English. *Fuck!* "Uhhhh...has...has visto a una nina?"

"Oh si! Si vi a una nina con un hombre ella estaba llorando!"

"When? I mean...um...Cuando fue esto?"

"Hace tan solo unos minutos."

"Ummm...um...Como se veia!"

"Un hombre negro..grande? Todo esta bien?"

"Oh my God."

Chucky ran back up the stairs. Out of breath. "I...I checked everywhere down there. Every room. Every corner. She's not down there."

Missy ran back up the stairs to the apartment and Chucky followed. Mrs. Rivera yelled after them. "Senora! Todo esta bien?!"

Missy raced through the house looking for her keys. Chucky grabbed her shoes and threw them at her. "Babe slow down for a second! We gon find her. We gon find her! Just tell me what happened when you came out here."

"Somebody took her! Mrs. Rivera said she saw Misa getting into a car with a man. A black man. A tall black man." Missy screamed. "WHERE THE FUCK ARE MY KEYS?"

"Wait, when?!"

"Like...an hour ago. We gotta call the police. Where's my PHONE?!!"

He reached in his pants pocket. "Here take mine. An hour ago?"

"YES an hour ago! While we were in here fuckin somebody came in here and took my damn child! Your phone's dying. Where's your charger? Oh my God." Missy clutched her chest and dropped the phone, shattering the screen to pieces. She leaned on the counter. Her breathing was labored and her chest heaved up and down.

Chucky grabbed her shoulder and tried to turn her toward him. "Babe! You ok?!

She ran over to the kitchen sink and threw up. Then she cried. "No! No I'm not ok, Chucky! We gotta find my baby. Please. Please help me find my baby."

"We gon find her baby just calm down." He picked up his phone from the floor. The screen was blank. He reached in her purse and grabbed her phone for her. "I'll call the police." He dialed the phone and walked to the refrigerator. There were several bottles of water. He handed her one. "Just sit down for a second. Drink some of this water and calm down. Don't worry, I got this."

Missy paced the living room floor, still crying. Chucky was trying to maintain his calm but he had a bad feeling. The operator picked up.

"Police, what's your emergency."

"Yes I'd like to report a missing child…"

Missy yelled out. "A kidnapping. You're reporting a kidnapping!" She ran over and snatched the phone from his hand.

"Yes this is the mother of the child. We think she may have been kidnapped…"

Missy went on to detail the morning's events, describe what Misa was wearing, and what Mrs. Rivera told her. Chucky was now pacing the floor. Trying to figure out what to do next. Hoping for the best, because at that point it was all he could do.

He walked over to Misa's bed and pulled the covers back. "Missy! Come here?! What the fuck is this?!"

She hung up the phone.

*****

She stood there holding Misa's doll and crying. The noose was tied tightly around the dolls neck with a note that read:

Let's try this again. One payment. One million dollars. One week. I'll be in touch.

She handed it back to Chucky and grabbed him, holding him tight and sobbing desperately.

"Missy, what the hell is this about? Who wrote this?"

He sat on the floor beside her and held her hand while she explained it all. From the day she found Ray's body dangling from their second story railing, to the day Little Gi started extorting her. Showing up at her house and handing her photos of her girls. Making the most heinous threats anyone could ever dream against innocent children. She had no idea if he was really capable of going through with them, but by not making her last several payments she'd put herself and her family in just the position to find out.

"...I just didn't have the money. I'd already given him everything I had, Chucky. There's nothing left. All I have now is the income from this building, and that's coming in slow. My savings, gone. My retirement, all of it, gone." She laid on his chest and balled. "I don't know what to do."

He rubbed her hair. "Damn baby. Why didn't you come to me?"

She sniffled and wiped her wet face with her hands. "You have a million dollars to give me?"

"Well. No I don't, but I could have helped you figure something out. He shook his head. "DAMN!" She jumped at the sound of his booming voice. "This nigga dead, and he STILL fuckin up your life!"

There was a hard knock at the door. "Police."

Missy and Chucky looked at each other. He got up and helped her to her feet. "So what you gon do? You gon tell em or what?"

"No. At least not yet."

She stuffed the note and the doll in her purse, then opened the door to two concerned patrol officers. The woman pulled a pad from her shirt pocket and started firing off questions. Missy repeated everything that she'd already relayed to the operator over the phone and with no way to dial it back, they set off on the business of finding her missing child.

Within the hour, Amber alerts flashed across every television screen, radio program, and every smart phone over the greater DMV area. Posters were being printed to hang on trees and search parties were being assembled.

Chucky stood silent listening to Missy. She was racked with guilt for putting the community through the wild goose chase but had no choice. She couldn't tell the police where Misa really was. It could very well mean her life. So she played it out, the role of the distraught mother with a missing child. At least that much was still true.

As soon as the police left, Missy called Mandy's boarding school to make sure she was safe. Then she called her Uncle Edward and asked him to pick Mandy up and keep her for a while.

Between her attempts to reach Brandy, Missy's phone rang and vibrated with constant messages. She only answered the one call.

"Hey Aunt Pat."

"'Hey?' What the fuck is going on? I just looked at my phone. Somebody snatched Misa?! Where you at?!"

"I'm on Champlain right now."

"Aaight I'm on my way…"

"No! Wait! Aunt Pat. Don't come."

"What?"

"Don't come here. I'll come to you. Can you do me a favor and get everyone together at your house?"

"Ok, yeah. You talked to Brandy yet?"

"No. I've been calling, but she's not answering her phone."

"Where's Mandy?"

"She's fine, she's at school. I asked Uncle Edward to pick her up and keep her for a while."

"OK, I'll give him a call and make sure she's straight. You sure you don't want me to come and get you?"

"No, Chucky's here with me. He'll drive me over there. We'll be there in a few minutes."

Missy kept trying Brandy's cell, but there was no answer.

"Chucky, can you use your phone to call her? I'm worried. She always answers her phone."

He pulled the phone from his pocket. "I can try. The screen's broken, remember?" He slid a careful forefinger over the shattered glass to unlock it. Then he dialed Brandy's number and hit the speaker. The phone rang twice before the call was picked up. There was a pause before she spoke.

"Hello."

Missy grabbed the phone and yelled. "Brandy! Where are you? Brandy. Hel..hello!"

The call was disconnected. She dialed again. And again. The calls went straight to the voicemail. "That didn't sound like her voice, Chucky. Oh God. Chucky, what if..."

"Missy don't. Don't do that to yourself. Brandy is fine."

"Yeah, or maybe he fuckin took her, too! Missy banged her hands on the dashboard. "Oh God. Oh my God! This is too MUCH."

Missy cried the entire way to Aunt Pat's house. Chucky held her hand and concentrated on navigating through the busy morning traffic. By the time they drove up to the house, half the neighborhood was already assembled in the front yard. Chucky ushered a very shaken Missy through the crowd and into the house where Aunt Pat sat in her recliner, barking orders to some of her minions, "Imma need y'all to get your mommas, your daddies, your kids, anybody that can walk a city block to get these flyers up. Monte, you take your boys and get to the south side. Lorraine, I need you uptown and Calvin, you take everybody out there on that porch and get these up on every tree and every lamppost in Ridgewood–"

"Aunt Pat," Missy interrupted. "Can I talk to you? Alone?"

"Yeah." Aunt Pat waved everyone off. "Aaight y'all go head out there and get those posters up. Meet me back here at three o'clock."

One by one, the concerned friends filed out of the house. Missy grabbed Rocky's hand. "No, I think we need you to stay."

Aunt Pat sat at the edge of her chair. "Ok, baby start from the beginning. Wait, where's Brandy?"

Missy began to cry again. "I...I don't know."

"Fuck you mean you don't know?"

Missy went through the entire story. "...and now I can't find Brandy. She's not answering her phone. For all I know, he has her, too."

Aunt Pat sat quiet. Unusually quiet. Uncharacteristically silent after being told that her family had been taken for ransom. She took a sip of her tea, closed her eyes and leaned back into her chair.

Missy waited what she thought was an appropriate amount of time. "So you're just gonna sit there and drink your tea?! What are we gonna do!"

Aunt Pat paused for a moment, before she threw her cup against the wall and screamed. "Who da fuck you think you talkin to?!"

Startled, Missy backed down. "I'm...I'm sorry. I just...I don't know what to do. I don't know what to do." She cried. "I need my baby back, Aunt Pat. Please help me. I need your help."

Aunt Pat grumbled. "Yeah. You need my help. Brenda need my help. Everybody need my muthafuckin help but don't NOBODY come to ask me what to do before they do it. Y'all go out here and do shit on your own and expect me to fix the shit when you fuck it up." She sat back in her chair, fuming. "Missy, why you ain't come to me before now? Huh? You done gone and started playing the game with this nigga, gave him all your fuckin money. Got this baby taken and *now* you need some help?" She stood and walked over to a closet. She reached far in the back and pulled out a gorgeous shiny gold Mark I Desert Eagle pistol. A gift from Consuela's father, who just happened to be one of the most notorious cocaine dealers in all of Mexico. She grabbed her jacket, tucked the heavy gun in her waistband and headed for the front door.

Brandy walked in the door with a bewildered look on her face. "What's going on?"

Missy ran over to her and wrapped her in a bear hug. Kissing her all over her face. "Oh Brandy. Baby. You're ok. You're ok."

"Aunt Missy, stahhhp." Brandy backed her off. She looked around the room and noted the serious looks on everyone's faces. "What's wrong with y'all?"

Aunt Pat grabbed her keys from the table. "I'll be back in an hour. And don't NOBODY leave here until I get back. Hear? Come on Rocky, let's go."

Missy called out to her as she walked out the front door. "Where are you going?"

Aunt Pat ignored the question. She wasn't intentionally

being flip. Just in deep thought. Missy had no idea what she had gotten them into. Gi's reputation preceded him from Vegas to VA to NY. He was a motherfucker. Nothing like his father. No scruples. No code of honor. A sadistic bastard that would have no issue with hacking off a kid's body parts and leaving them on your doorstep. And for much less than a million dollars.

She hit the highway in a race. She needed answers…and reinforcement.

*****

"Brandy, how'd you get here?

Tay walked in behind Brandy. "Hello everybody."

Missy scowled. "Why is he here?"

Brandy snapped. "*He's* here because he picked me up from the airport. You didn't answer your phone when I called you. I thought you said you were picking me up this morning?"

"I was. I've been calling you all morning! Why weren't you answering your phone?"

"Oh…dang. I forgot to give you my new number. I had to get a new phone."

"Why?"

Brandy glared back at Tay. "A *crackhead* stole it."

Missy frowned. "What?"

"Nevermind. What's going on? Why are all those people out in the yard?"

Missy looked at Tay. "It's family business."

Tay got the hint. "I'm leaving. Brandy, I'll bring your bag in."

"OK, thank you for picking me up, Tay."

"You know it's no problem. Y'all have a good day."

Tay passed PJ coming in the front door. PJ sat his purse on the sofa, "So what's goin on? Ma said it was an emergency." He looked around the room at the long faces. "What's wrong with y'all?"

Missy composed herself and instructed everyone to have a seat. Once again, she explained the situation. At the end Brandy was inconsolable. PJ held her in his arms, trying to calm her down. "Brandy. Come on baby it's gon be ok." He looked over at Missy. "Where'd my mother go?"

Missy threw her hands in the air. "I don't know. She just said she'll be back."

PJ shook his head. "Damn. A million dollars? Do you have that?"

"If I had it, I'd have my daughter now wouldn't I?"

"You ain't gotta get snappy with me. I'm just askin. Girl, why you ain't say somethin before?"

"For what? Do you have a million dollars?"

"You *know* what I mean. We could've figured something out before it got to this!"

Aunt Pat walked in the door, alone. She took her gun from her waist and replaced it in the top of her closet. Then she shooed Brandy out of her recliner and sat down. There was a long awkward silence as everyone stood staring at her. Waiting for her to speak. Her eyes were closed as she rocked slowly, back and forth in the chair.

A few minutes later she spoke, her eyes still closed. "OK this is the deal. Misa's on her way to New York. Probably to a house on Staten Island. I'm not sure yet. I'll know by tonight. Gi wants a million in cash and we got five days to get *it* or to get *her*.

Brandy murmured, "Aunt Pat. Do you really think he would..."

"I don't know, baby. Honestly, I really don't know. But we ain't gon let it get to that."

"Oh God." Missy buckled and Chucky ran to catch her before she hit the floor.

Brandy looked over at Missy. "Look what you did? This is all your fault."

Missy looked up at her. "What?"

"THIS IS ALL YOUR FAULT! That's my baby! You took my baby and now you let him take her and..."

"Brandy!" Aunt Pat yelled. "Knock that shit off. She didn't ask for nobody to take that child. Now we gon get her back, and everything gon be fine. But it ain't shit you can do, so I want you to get yourself together and get outta here. PJ, you let Brandy stay with you."

"Yeah, of course." He agreed.

"Good. Y'all don't say nothin to nobody about what's goin on. As far as the police and everybody else is concerned, that baby still missin and we don't have no idea where she is. Now go head."

Brandy walked out slamming the door so hard it rattled the glass pane. PJ grabbed his purse. "Don't worry about it. I got her." He walked over and hugged Aunt Pat. "Ma, you need anything from me?"

"Not right now, but I'll let you know. I'll call you later."

"Ok." He shook his head at Missy and walked out the door.

"So yeah," Aunt Pat continued. "Like I said. As far as the public is concerned she's just missin. We gotta play that kidnappin shit down. We don't need Gi thinkin we workin with the police. So we'll say the old lady ain't know what she as talkin bout. Missy you can stay here or go home but I want you inside. Don't come out. Don't talk to the news, to the neighbors, nobody. Not until I get back to you and let you know what's what. You hear me?"

Missy nodded.

"I'm serious, hear? That goes for you, too, Chucky. Don't talk to nobody about this."

"I gotchu. I'm takin her with me."

"Aaight, well ya'll go'on get outta here. I got shit to do."

Missy ran over to her aunt and hugged her tight. "Thank you. Thank you. Thank you. You don't know how much I appreciate you."

"I know you do. Now get outta my face, please."

Missy managed a smile. She snuck in a kiss on Aunt Pat's cheek before being pushed away.

"Stop it, Missy. Go head now. Chucky, you make sure she's all right."

He dapped up the big boss lady. "I gotchu." And they left. Both of them feeling a little more at ease than they were before they came.

When the front door was securely locked, the blinds were closed shut, and the heavy drapes were drawn, Aunt Pat sank back down into her chair. Her eyes welled. She tried hard but couldn't stop the tears from falling. So she laid back and let them fall free. No one was watching. No one would ever know.

Life on the outside was taking a toll. Bad finances aside, she had Brenda sitting in jail, and she hadn't figured out how to get her out. Now they added a kidnap and ransom to her plate of already impossible shit to handle. And she'd just lied to everyone's faces. Bold faced lied. Little Giovanni Scarsi was as dangerous as they came, and if they didn't come up with his cash, or some kinda plan, Misa would die. For sure. She thought, *the James Girls is too much motherfuckin trouble. For real.*

Once she got it all out, and pulled herself back together, she went back to the closet and grabbed her gun, some duct tape, a few bottles from under the kitchen sink, and a few articles from the junk drawer. Rocky was waiting. It was time to put in some work.

Pain for Pain

PJ rode around the neighborhood for almost an hour when he spotted Brandy sitting on the ground in an alley a few blocks from the house. He drove up beside her and unlocked his door.

"Girl, if you don't get your ass up off that ground and get in this car!"

She didn't move.

"Brandy. Brandy!"

Still she didn't move.

He threw the truck in park and hopped out. When he walked over to her she jumped, which made him jump. "Girl! What the hell is wrong with you?!"

She said nothing. He stood there for a minute. "Brandy." Her eyes were vacant. He grabbed her hand and tugged. "Brandy!" Still, nothing. When he let go she fell limp back onto the concrete wall. Her eyes watered and a tear fell. She whispered.

"Seventeen minutes."

PJ didn't understand. "What?"

"Seventeen minutes. That's how long I was in labor. The nurse said it was the quickest labor she'd ever had. She said, *Girl your baby couldn't wait to get outta you.* That made me sad. Then…then Aunt Missy came and took her away. I barely even got to hold her."

"Why don't we get in the car so we can talk?"

She ignored him. "You know I didn't breast feed. They say that's the best way to bond with your baby. But I never got to do that. I tried a few times. But she wouldn't have it. She just wouldn't latch on to me. Aunt Missy said we should just give her formula. But I wanted to try again. I really did. Sometimes when

Aunt Missy was asleep. I would go into Misa's room and try again. I would pick her up and kiss her until she was awake. Then I'd pull out my breast and position my nipple at her little mouth. Even squeeze out a little of the milk. But she never took it. Misa acted like my milk was poisonous." She laughed. "You know, like it was...venom or something. That made me so...sad. She never wanted me. Only Aunt Missy. I don't know why. She just didn't."

PJ knelt down in front of her, resting on the balls of his stilettos. "Brandy, baby. Let's get outta this dirty alley. Come on. Let's just go for a ride and talk." He reached for her hand again.

She pulled away. "She was like...I wanna say...six months old when she said *mama* for the first time. I was like, wow is she supposed to be talking yet? I looked it up online, and everything I read said it was too early for her to know what she was actually saying. But she did. She knew. I knew that she knew. Because she never said it to me. Only to Aunt Missy. I would say it to her, over and over and over. Everyday. And she would never repeat it. Not once did she repeat it for me. I handed her to Aunt Missy...and guess what? *Mama, mama, mama.* Not once. Not twice. She wouldn't stop saying it."

"Brandy I'm sure it was..."

"You know she walked to Aunt Missy first. Her first steps. Straight over to her. Like I wasn't even there. Like she knew I gave her away..."

Listening to her pain reminded him of his own. Way back when. Which didn't seem that long ago. He thought, if only he would have had someone to talk to back then. Someone who actually cared, and wasn't in it for their own selfish reasons. Maybe things would have been different for him. Or maybe not.

Without regard for his delicate leather boots or his three hundred dollar dungarees, he sat down on the ground next to her. And just listened.

"I didn't wanna do it. I didn't wanna give up my baby Uncle PJ. But she said it would ruin my future. She said it was the best thing for everybody. She said Misa didn't need to know she was a child of rape. It would ruin her life. So I let her take my baby from me. And then I had nothing. And I felt like nothing. And I decided...I decided that's what I wanted to be. Nothing."

Though no tears fell, PJ recognized the inflection in her voice. The desperation. Despair. Almost instinctively, he reached for her hand and turned her wrist. He turned to look her in the eye. Hers were watered. He knew. He unbuttoned his sleeve at the wrist and pushed it up his elbow. Then he held his arm out next to hers.

Scare Tactics

Aunt Pat walked down into the dark basement of her bar. She'd made many changes since the last captive managed to squeeze his way out of a narrow window to freedom. The windows were barred now, the walls soundproofed and the doors, reinforced steel. The room boasted state-of-the-art security systems with a ten-digit pin and digital cameras mounted in every corner. No one was getting in, out or around in the joint without her seein it.

Rocky had worked him over pretty good. Genovese "Geno" Scarsi, the great uncle of one Little Gi Scarsi, "The Terror," was a pretty tough old geeze, staring defiantly into her eyes as Rocky landed blow after devastating blow to his face and body.

"Where's Gi?"

He spat blood on the floor. "Fucka you!"

She laughed. *Whap!* "Fuck me?" *Whap! Whap!*

Aunt Pat stood in the doorway watching in amusement as Rocky became more and more frustrated with the old man. She snickered. "Gettin tired."

Rocky panted. "Nah I'm good. I'm just gettin started." She rolled her head around and hopped from side to side, then landed in a boxer's stance. *Whap, whap!* She hit him with a hard overhand left and an uppercut to the chin." His head snapped backward, and his eyes rolled around.

Aunt Pat laughed. "What you tryna do, knock him out?"

"He ain't talkin anyway." *Whap! Whap!* "Maybe if I knock his bitch ass out, he might wake up wit a different attitude."

Aunt Pat waved her off. "Aight, enough a dat. I got somethin for him. He'll talk."

Aunt Pat walked over to Geno and smacked him lightly on

the face to get his attention. "Hey! You still wit us OG?"

He pulled his head forward and slurred. "My family will kill your family."

She shrugged. "Maybe." Then she walked over to a table by the bar, about 10 feet in front of him. She dropped her duffle bag on the table and began to unpack it, slowly, for effect.

"So. Geno. You don't mind if I call you Geno?" she asked, facetiously. "I was really hoping that you would have given my partner some answers by now. So I wouldn't have to bother with all...*this*." She removed her wares from the bag. A large syringe. A large Ziplock storage bag half full with a white powdery substance. A bottle of Clorox. A large spool of double barbed wire. An electric saw zaw and an array knives folded in a sheath. She arranged everything neatly on the table, in what seemed to be least to deadliest order.

She put on a rubber butcher's apron. Then she tore off a piece of thick gray duct tape and affixed it to Geno's mouth. "So no one can hear us." She unsheathed her tactical knife. "You see this?" She held it up so that her captive could get a good look. "This here, is a Gerber Mark II. It's a fighting knife. One of the deadliest ever made. So deadly they actually stopped production for a while. The military deemed it too *ferocious*. Imagine that."

She ran a careful forefinger across the razor sharp, serrated edges. "Twelve inches long with six point seven five inches of blade. Pretty ain't it? I don't do much fightin no more. Gettin too old. But you never forget how, you know. My husband taught me how to use this. He was military. I say *was*, because he's no longer with us. I killed him."

Geno rolled his eyes. Unimpressed.

"I was a young girl. Just outta high school. Racked my momma's shotgun and left his brains on our livin room wall. And I loved that man. I really did. But that shit was easy. It was a him or me typa thing. So you know. Had to be him."

She reared back in the desk chair.

"So I did my first bid for the state of North Carolina. Murder two. Ten years. Well not quite ten. I got out just shy of ten. But it might as well have been ten. And that shit was tough.

I ain't gon even lie. It was my first time in. I was young. A little scared. People tryin me left and right. Constantly fightin off some old, hard, country, shit kickin, nuttin to lose ass, murderous bitches. I had to learn quick, too. I had to kill inside. A couple times. I'm telling you…you never know how strong you are until you gotta get a big bitch up off your throat. But you do what you gotta do, you know. That day, I used my bare hands."

She set the knife down in her lap and held out her hands.

"These hands." She reached out toward his neck. "I squeezed and I squeezed and squeeeeezzzzed the life from her eyes. Just took the breath from her body. Man, I ain't never gon forget that shit."

She leaned back in her chair and picked up the knife. "I don't dream about her as much as I used to. But I ain't never gon forget. Over the years, I've mostly used my gun. Gutted a few with this here. But feeling the life drain out a muthafucka…in your bare hands. Yeah that's some shit you gotta do to really know about. You know what I'm sayin?"

She laughed.

"Damn. I done got way off subject. What was I getting at?"

She paused and looked up into the ceiling for a moment.

"Oh yeah. So we used to raise up hogs right. Well…he raised em. My husband. I just cooked em up after slaughter. And I wuddn't too happy bout it neither. The meat was too fresh. It just didn't…didn't seem right. All that fresh blood. But then we fell on some tough times. I mean real tough. Both of us got laid off from the mill. No money. Down to a piglet. We called him Hubert, so Willie Earl – that was my husband, Willie Earl – he had gone lookin for work, a couple towns over. He didn't come home that night. Bad cloud came up that night. Outta nowhere, too. Skies just went dark and then the wind came. Strong ass wind had the trees leanin almost down to the ground. Knockin up against the windows. I could hear the whistle from the tornado comin. I went out there and grabbed Hu from the pen. I brought him inside with me. Didn't want him to get blown away. So I picked his fat ass up and I put him in the tub wit me. He laid in my lap gruntin and snortin and shit. We sat in that bathtub til mornin. He slept good, too. Right at the bottom, at my feet. He kept lookin up at me with them eyes. Them beady ass lil black eyes. I felt like I got to know him a lil bit. So anyway, I got up and went outside to see what was left of our little farm, and it was pretty much gone. Everything. The Barn. The chicken coup. Everything was gone. Wuddn't nuttin left but some old rotten wood and some loose fence wire. All that was left was me and ole Hu."

"I went for *days* without seeing anybody. I tried to head to town, but the bridges was washed out. It was too dangerous. So I went back home. We ate everything we had in the cupboard. Me and Hu. Down to the last grit. Until the only thing left to eat…was Hu. I spent bout half a day thinkin bout it, long enough for them hunger pangs to start feelin like gut punches. Long enough for that bad acid to creep up to my throat. Ion know if you know what that feel like. But it ain't nuttin good. Bein hungry. So I went in the kitchen and grabbed Willie Earl's butcher knife and the hacksaw from the closet. I took Hu out back and went for what I knew. Well…what I thought I knew. Turns out I wuddn't dat good at butcherin. What I did to that poor little pig would definitely be considered…what's the word…inhumane. By today's standards anyway."

Geno shifted in his chair.

Aunt Pat smiled. "You startin to look bored. You want me to get to the point right? Ok. Well the reason I'm tellin you this, old man…it's cause I want you to know I'm not really a killer. I mean…I've killed. Many times. But not without good, GOOD reason. It was always to save somethin…or somebody. To save myself from hurt…or hunger. To save my friends or my family from some typa danger. Always…somebody needin savin. And today ain't no different. Your family has my family. Your nephew has my niece. My beautiful, innocent baby grand-niece that ain't got shit to do with no business y'all had with Ray Coleman's punk ass when he was alive. And now she need savin. And now I'm forced right back in that position where I gotta take a life or two to make that shit right. I don't *like* it. But make no mistake about it, Geno, if it means savin that baby's life…bringin her back home to her mama…"

She leaned down and stared him directly in the eyes. Then she touched the tip of his nose with the point of her knife. "…I will take this knife…and I will gut your motherfuckin ass like a farm animal. Slow. But first, I will take that bleach over there…mix it with that dope in that bag, fill that syringe and pump your muthafuckin veins full, my nigga. Do you know what that poison will do to you once it's in your blood stream? No? Well me either…but if you don't tell me what the fuck I wanna hear old man, we both gon learn ta-day."

She pulled the knife back, leaving the tiniest prick and the tiniest spec of blood on the tip of his nose.

"Now Imma take off this tape. And you gon tell me what I need to hear, right?" She snatched the tape off. "Now where. The fuck. Is Gi?"

Geno looked her square in the eyes. He spat blood on the floor before he spoke. "I am an old man now. I have lived my life. I have done things that you could not even imagine. You think I'm afraid of you? Weak. Pathetic. *Woman.*" He spat at her feet. "Cazzo Negro! Fucka you."

Aunt Pat rose from her chair. "Okay then." She waved a hand, and Rocky left the room. Then she replaced the tape over Geno's mouth and walked back over to the table. She pulled on a pair of thick rubber gloves and pulled a respirator mask over her face. Then she took a small measuring cup and reached into the plastic Zip lock storage bag, sifting out about a quarter cup of the powder and dumping it into a glass bowl. She opened the Clorox bottle and poured about a half cup of the liquid into another measuring cup and then slowly poured it in with the powder. You could hear the concoction, as it crackled and fizzed. When it settled, she pulled the gaseous liquid mixture into a syringe and placed the syringe back on the table.

She spoke with her back turned to him. "So Geno. I was thinkin. How old are you…around 70…75 maybe? I know you a old G. Tough old dude. I knew it wuddn't gon be easy to get you to talk. So I thought I'd get a little reinforcement. Some back-up…just in case you needed a little more persuasion."

In walked Rocky pushing a desk chair on rollers. In that chair, half-beaten with her mouth taped tightly, was Geno's seventeen-year-old great granddaughter, Sophia.

Geno's eyes bulged, and he jerked around so violently in his chair that he fell over on the floor. The duct tape, loosened from the moisture and barely muffled his screams. He watched in horror while Rocky held her still, and Aunt Pat pierced the side of her neck with the needle. Slowly, she pushed the syringe down to the end, injecting the entire chemical into his baby girl's veins.

"Sophiiiieee!!!!!!"

Thinkin of a Master Plan

"Pat."

"Yeah?"

"I thought you told me you killed your husband before he was supposed to go off to war."

"I did."

They laughed.

"The knives?"

"Manny's. He left em in my trunk when we went out McLean to fix that Brenda shit."

Rocky shook her head. "And the pig?"

Aunt Pat snickered. "More bullshit."

Rocky laughed. "Where the fuck do you come up with these stories? You damn near had *me* convinced."

"What can I say? I spent a lot of time inside. I read."

"I swear I thought he wuddn't gon never talk. I damn near broke my fist on his old ass face. He can take some punishment. That's for damned sure."

"Yeah he a tough old dude. They say he was a mean muufucka back in the day tho. He definitely got some battle scars. I was tryna think of somethin that would scare em some. But it didn't matter what I said. He ain't care bout none a that shit. Only thing Geno was gon respond to was his damsels in distress."

"We fucked him up when we stuck Sophia's ass but you see his face when we wheeled his wife out? When you put that needle up to her neck? Man I thought that nigga was gon have a heart attack right then and there."

"Yeah I knew that shit was gon do it. But you ain't have to beat up that old lady like that Rocky."

"Sheeit. If you woulda heard some of dat slick shit she was talking to me upstairs. You ain't hear it so you'on know."

"You ain't even hear it! The bitch don't even speak English."

"I know what nigga is in Italian."

"What is it?"

"What's this a fuckin quiz. Nero. She kept sayin Nero."

"That just means black."

"Yeah, well she was sayin it too strong. I told her to stop and she kept doin that shit. So…"

Aunt Pat shook her head. "You got em back over the bridge?"

"Yeah I put the blindfolds back on em and dropped em off at the back door. I still don't get why we let em go."

"Cause we don't need em."

"Well I think we could –"

"Rocky. I didn't ask you what you thought."

"Ok, ok. You got it boss. So what you stick her with anyway?"

"What?"

"The syringe. What you put in it?"

"Oh, bakin soda and white vinegar."

Rocky laughed. "I thought I smelled vinegar. I was wonderin what all that fizzin shit was. What made you use that?"

"High school science project."

"What?"

"We made volcanos for my science project and that's what we used to make the lava bubble up and come down the mountain."

Rocky laughed. "Is she good?"

"Yeah, she'll be aight. Probably gon run her fuckin blood pressure up. But she'll live."

"Pat you crazy as hell. You think they gon come back for us?"

"Well they gotta figure out who *us* is first. By that time we'll have Misa back. Either way we'll be waitin on em. Your boys on point?"

"They good. You think Geno told you the truth?"

"Hell yeah. He was too scared not to, plus I already had Imelda's people to check it out. They got Misa at Gi's father's house out on Staten Island. I just needed confirmation."

"Ok, so when we goin up?"

"I don't know yet. I gotta figure this shit out."

"Well you better think fast man. We got less than a week now. We need to get on this shit like asap."

Aunt Pat snapped back. "Don't you think I fuckin know dat?! Damn. Y'all muthafuckas act like I'm James Bond. Newsflash! Ion fuckin know everything."

"Aight, I'm jus tryna help Pat."

She sighed and leaned back in her chair. "I know. I know you are. And I appreciate it."

"Umm hmm."

"Nah I'm serious. You always got my back. And I appreciate it, for real. You know that."

"I know."

"I'm just tired Rock. I mean *TIRED*. You know how much shit I been in since I been home. How much shit I done had to handle. And it ain't even been none of *my* shit! Not once have I had to handle my own shit! Always somebody else's shit."

"Sounds shitty."

Pat smiled. "Don't mock me. Seriously, sometimes I'm like what is this shit all about?"

"What shit, life?"

"Yeah, man. I mean…hustlin ain't the same. You remember. We only started doin this shit cause niggas said we couldn't. Remember Suga Pops?"

"Of course I remember Suga Pops. Who don't remember Suga Pops."

"That muthafucka tried to prophesy my demise. When I first got in the game. Said wuddn't no bitches gon run no game in DC. Then I took every bitch that nigga had from the top to the bottom. Tammy. Janet. Raynell. Remember Lee Ann?"

"That was his wife right?"

"Yeah his first wife. Bottom bitch. I took the second one,

too. The country one. Alabama. I made more money with Alabama then all the rest a them hoes put together."

"I can't lie, that bitch was fine."

"And she was nice, too. Sweet. That's what them tricks loved about her. All that sweet country talk. She knew how to make a muthafucka think she really cared about em, you know. That's all they be wantin for real."

"True."

"Somebody to act like they give a fuck."

"You liked her though."

"Nah I loved her. Real talk. She was my first bitch on the outside. Fucked my marriage up, too. She da one that made me say fuck it. I am what I am you know."

"Sunshine?"

They laughed at the *Harlem Nights* reference to good, magical pussy.

"Yeah man. Ole Alabama. She put me on, too. Hooked me up with Suga Pops' connect, and that nigga was done. I had his girls, that good dope, and the whole northeast locked down. And I ain't even have to kill nobody."

"Yeah, you was definitely doin it big. I saw how you was movin. Snow white Cadillacs and jet black minks on your back. Aaahhhhh! I wanted in on that shit. For real."

Aunt Pat took a pull on her cigar and a swig of her cognac. "Um hmm. I had to teach your young ass a lesson, too." She pointed at Rocky's face. "You lucky I ain't kill your muthafuckin ass."

"Yeah I know, I know. I was wrong. But I gave your money back."

Aunt Pat blew a ring of smoke. "You muufuckin right you did."

"Pat, how many times I gotta apologize for that?"

"Ion know. I'll tell you when you get there."

"Whatever man. Seriously tho. You really thinkin bout givin this up?"

"Hell yeah. Well…maybe not the bar but the game? Definitely. It's just too fucked up out here. These youngin's just don't give a fuck. Ain't no love. Ain't no loyalty. They ain't got no respect for us no more. I gotta damn near kill a nigga to make em understand. And we gettin old, Rock. How long we gon be able to do this?"

"Shiiit. *You* getting old. You better speak for yo-self."

"Bitch, you was bout to have a asthma attack tryna fight that old man. And he was tied up. Fuck outta here."

"Aight...so I'm gettin old. But it ain't nuttin old bout this muufuckin fo-five tho. They raised their guns. Pats a shiny gold and Rocky's a matte black with a pearl handle. *Clink.*

Pat laughed. "Rocky, you crazy."

"You better know it."

"On the real, I need a fuckin break. From all this shit. The game. The bar. All this rescue shit. I'm like, is the James Girls the only muufuckas with these problems? Cause ion hear these stories from nobody else. The shit is crazy. Fuckin tabloids...reality TV. Kidnappin and suicide. I still don't know what the fuck umma do about Brenda's situation. And now I'm tangled up with some muthafuckin mobsters." She laughed loud. "Where they do this at Rocky?"

"For real. Y'all muufuckas need to write a book...or sumthin"

"I'm sayin." Aunt Pat threw back the last of her drink and got up.

"Where you goin?"

"Upstairs to close the bar. Then imma grab a bottle a yack, and sit my ass back down here until I figure all this shit out. You down?"

"You already know."

Three hours and a bottle of Remy XO later, the plan was game tight. Operation Spring Misa was underway and in 72 hours they'd be seated on the Staten Island Ferry. Headed to Gi's daddy's house. Armed. Amped. Ready.

My Baby's Keeper

Chucky sat at the opposite end of his sofa and watched her as she slept, feeling more helpless than he ever had. He thought, *Damn, this woman has the most problems.* But he would have done anything to make her world right again.

Missy was a mess. She couldn't eat, couldn't sleep. The panic attacks were coming with no warning and she was becoming increasingly agitated with every single thing he did or said. After an entire day of nervous, cranky, bitchy alertness, Chucky had finally convinced her to take a sleeping pill.

He wanted to sleep too. But he couldn't. He worried for her. Worried for Misa and what she was probably going through at that very moment. Laying somewhere in someone's dark basement. Cold, hungry and probably hurting. Alone and afraid. His mind wandered to the same horrible places he thought Missy must have been dreaming of, as she jerked around in her sleep.

He looked over at her hand. Petite and in need of a manicure. In all the melee they hadn't once addressed their engagement. They were finally together. Actually *engaged* and had barely acknowledged it. Technically, he didn't even ask for her hand, so technically she never gave it. He felt like he cheated himself of his big moment. Especially after all he went through to get the ring. He wanted a do over.

His pouting only lasted a moment as guilt quickly settled in. Here he was worried about not getting a big enough pat on his back while Missy lay there suffering unimaginable pain and grief; tears seeped from the corners of her eyes as she slept. Misa was gone. Taken, kicking and screaming by some gangsters that promised her death by the end of the week if Missy didn't come up with ridiculous sums of money.

Though Chucky still knew his way around a pistol, sort of, this was a situation he knew he needed to stay away from. He had too much to lose now. He was barely back in the game after his dumb ex-wife's restraining order was thrown out, so getting involved in some gangsta shit with Ms. Pat would be so much less than smart. But then again, Missy needed him. But then again...what was he really gonna do?

He still had a few friends in the game. Some old heads from back in Ridgewood that would love to be down with a good "mission". Dudes that would jump at the chance to be a part of one of them stories people always told about Ms. Pat. But...no. That was stupid. Plus, half of them stories probably weren't even true. But then again...

Chucky sat in the quiet living room sipping Scotch. Contemplating. Allowing his mind to wander off into the most outlandish rescue scenarios he could think of. Crazier than anything he'd seen on TV. He imagined himself climbing up the side of a building and crashing into a window. Firing away with a gun in each hand. Reloading with extra clips stuffed in his jacket. Walking toward his target in slow motion as bullets flew overhead and all around him. And he dodged every one of those motherfuckers like Neo from the Matrix. He was bulletproof. Invincible. He laughed. It was stupid. But then again...

He grabbed his phone from the coffee table and dialed. She answered on the first ring. "Hello."

"Ms. Pat."

"Yeah. Who dis?"

"It's Chucky."

"Hey Chucky. How Missy doin?"

"Not too good. Tryna be strong but...you know. I finally got her to take that sleeping pill so she could get some rest. She's out right now."

"Good. We on our way up state now. We gon take care of everything. Just tell her I said hold tight. I got her."

"Where ya'll at now?"

"Jersey Turnpike. We'll be there in a few. Set up shop tonight, hit the Island and handle business tomorrow."

"Hmm. I was just thinkin."

"Thinkin what?"

"Thinkin…maybe I should come up."

"Up where?"

"Up there. With y'all."

"What?"

"Yeah, you know. I can grab a couple of my go hard men. Meet ya'll up there later on tonight. I got a couple niggas that ain't gon have no problem with…"

"What niggas Chucky?"

"From Ridgewood."

"Who?"

"Uh…Black Tony…"

"No. Black Tony is stupid."

"Stupid? Ok, Big Shawn…"

"Stupid *and* scary."

"Scary? Aight, then what about Ev? You *know* he go hard."

"Yeah but Ev just got home. He ain't gon help you do shit."

"Nah Ev owe me. Much money as I sent him while he was in. He'll get wit it."

"Look, you don't need to get involved in this. We got it. You just make sure Missy is taken care of. That's all I want you to do. That's your job."

"Ms. Pat, I can't just sit here and do nothin. I wanna help."

"You already are."

Three beeps and the call was disconnected. He hung up the phone just as Missy beckoned. "Chuckyyyyy!"

Shit. "I'm comin baby!"

Uncle PJ

Brandy sat opposite PJ on his plush sofa. Her mouth still agape from all that she'd heard. "I'm so sad for you, Uncle PJ. I thought I had problems."

PJ swirled his red wine around in his goblet, sniffed the rim and took a dainty sip. "You ain't hardly gotta be sad for me, chile. I'm fine. You go through it, you get through it, you move on. I live a good life now. Trust me."

Brandy surveyed the spacious living room with modern luxury décor. Plush alpaca carpeting beneath Italian leather furniture, stacked with high end designer throws and pillows. "Well I can *see that*."

"I don't mean all this. Well kinda, but what I really mean is…I'm comfortable with me now. And I wasn't before. Not like I am now."

"Are you kidding me? *You* not comfortable with yourself?"

"Yes *me*. I'm human. An utterly fabulous human, yes that is true, but human nonetheless."

Brandy laughed. "See, that's exactly what I'm talking about."

"Child. Learning to love me was a process. Believe me. It wasn't always this way. But you didn't know me then. During my wonder years."

"Wonder years?"

"Yes, all the years I wondered who I was. What and why I was. Why I had been through *so damned much*. I wondered if God hated me."

"Do you still?"

"Still what?"

"Wonder if God hates you?"

"No. I mean…not really. I'm not like religious or anything,

but I do believe in God. A higher power that created us. And if I go by what Uncle Edward says about us all being created in His image and perfect and all that, then no, God doesn't hate me. He made me and how could you hate something you made?"

"I think people hate their kids all the time."

"Brandy—"

"Well."

"Well whatever. I'm just saying. I took the long route from shame to pride. And I'm not just talkin about gay pride. That's a part of it. Of course. But I mean pride in who I am as a person. I don't have to steal and scam and hustle for it no more. I don't have to depend on anybody else for anything, anymore. I earn a good livin doin exactly what I want to be doing now. Slaying heads and just bein me. It don't get no better than that baby girl." He kicked off his stilettos and rested his feet on top of the coffee table. "It don't get no better."

"How did you like…get over it. You know…get past it all?"

"I really haven't. To be honest. I haven't forgotten anything. I still think about the bad, from time to time, but I don't dwell. You can't stop shit from poppin up in your head but as long as you don't dwell…you know."

"Yeah. I guess that's my problem. The dwelling."

"My mother helped me a lot. Just talking to her. Actually if it wasn't for *your* mother, I wouldn't even be where I am right now."

"How's that?"

"She convinced me to reach out to my mother. To take the first step. After my mother came home, we didn't talk much at all. And when we did it was, borderline hostile. At that time, I honestly didn't care if I ever talked to her. She wasn't there for me when I needed her. So I was like, fuck her. For real."

"Well, I guess we got something else in common."

"No, it's not the same thing. Suga you gotta let that go."

Brandy rolled her eyes as she turned her head. "Hmm."

"No, I'm so serious right now. Your mother loves you Brandy. She loves all of her children. More than anything. Please don't be fooled by anything Missy says to you."

"Aunt Missy hasn't said anything bad about my mother. Ever."

"Then why do you hate her so much? I don't understand it. I know you don't wanna hear it, and maybe it doesn't matter to you, but your mother went into that man's house that night, guns blazin for *you*. No regard for her own life or her own safety. She took that murder charge for MJ. Without the slightest hesitation. She signed over custody to Missy so that y'all could be taken care of. So y'all would have a better life until she came home. *That's* what a mother does."

Brandy pursed her lips and sighed. "Um hmm."

"So, that don't make sense to you? That don't move you at all, huh? Well *my* mother *killed* my father. Murdered him. But not before she built herself an enterprise financed by hookers and heroin and then managed to get herself hooked on the shit she was sellin. And I got to see it all. Every bit of it. The pimps, the hoes, people shootin up in our living room. Needles everywhere. I was young but I still remember a lot of it. Then she went to jail and left me to be raised by an abuser and a rapist. So tell me again why you mad at *your* mother."

"She left us! She left us and didn't look back! She didn't call or…or let us visit. Not one letter. Uncle PJ I needed my mother! I needed her. I had a fuckin baby!"

"You don't understand."

"I don't understand what?! That she didn't care about us?"

"She couldn't face you! I talked to her so many times about bringin you to see her. She didn't want you there. At a jail! She didn't want you to hear the announcement that a call was coming from a prison. She didn't want you to see that stamped on a letter. She thought that would only hurt you more. Scar you or something. I tried to convince her otherwise. I did. But she wouldn't hear it and I swear to you Brandy she felt like she was doing it for your own good. Plus she was dealing with her own guilt.."

"What *guilt?*"

"About how y'all lived. Growing up how you did. With Melvin in the streets. All the shit she went through because of it.

She almost lost you once and…"

"Lost me? Lost me how?"

"Well…I'll let her tell you that herself but the thought that she…well her choices in life were the reason you all were hurting was a lot to handle. She had a lot of regrets and she just felt like she'd hurt you all enough. So she withdrew. But not before she made sure Missy would take care of you. Baby I promise you, everything she did, good or bad, was for you. You and MJ and Brandy. It all came from a very loving place. Trust me. You need to talk to her. Seriously. Y'all need to put this bullshit behind you once and for all. I'll take you down there myself."

"So *now* it's ok for me to go to a jail?"

"No. I'm sure she'll say no. But we ain't askin her permission. We just gon show up. Will you at least think about it?"

"I'll think about it."

"For real?"

"Yes. I said I'll think about it. Can you take me home?"

"Why? You don't wanna stay here with me?"

"No it's not like that. I just had a really long night and a long day and I really just wanna sleep in my own bed."

"You sure."

Yes, Uncle PJ, please. Take me home."

"Girl, my mother is probably gonna to kill me, but ok. Just let me finish my wine."

No Place Like Home

Sitting atop the kitchen counter in hysteria, she frantically dialed them all. Over and again her calls went to voice mail. Aunt Missy, Aunt Pat. PJ. Even Tay. No answer. Finally, someone picked up.

"Hello."

She yelled into the receiver, "Hello?! Chucky let me speak to my aunt please!"

"She's asleep. What's wrong?"

"What's wrong?! What's wrong is I am standing in, I guess, what *used* to be my damned house? My clothes are gone. The furniture. What is going on?"

"Hold on a second." He attempted to shake Missy awake. She rolled over and went back to sleep. He whispered, "Missy. Missy!"

She rolled back over, still groggy from the medication, "Whaaat?"

"Brandy's on the phone. She said she's standin in what *used* to be her house? She didn't know you moved?"

"Shit. It's too much goin on. Just tell her to come here."

"Here?"

"Yes, here."

He put the receiver back to his ear. "Your aunt says to just come here."

"Come where? I got dropped off I'm not driving! Can I speak to her please?!"

"Ok, hold on." He shook Missy again. "Missy, she wants to talk to you."

"What!" Missy started crying again. "Chucky I don't feel like this. It's too much! Just tell her to go to Uncle Edward's! I'll pick her up later."

"But she said…" Missy closed her eyes. "…never mind."

He picked up the receiver again. "She said, can you go to your Uncle Edward's house?"

"I JUST SAID I'M NOT DRIVING! Why can't she just come to the phone?!"

"I gave her a sleeping pill so she could rest. She's been through a lot and…"

"And I haven't! What about me?! She took my baby from me! She lost my baby! Now I'm stuck out here without a pillow to lay my fuckin head on!" Chucky could hear her breaking down. The call was dropped.

He shook Missy again. "Missy! What's your address? Imma go and pick Brandy up. Missy!"

She didn't move. He went into her purse and pulled her driver's license from her wallet. Then he set off for Great Falls.

About forty minutes later he pulled into Missy's driveway. Brandy was sitting on the porch. Smoking a joint. When she saw him she tried to put it down to her side. He waved it off.

"Nah you good. Don't put it away for me."

She picked it back up and took a pull. Then she blew the smoke in his direction. "She sent you to get me?"

"Let me hit that." He took a pull and blew his smoke right back at her." Nah, I came on my own. She's still out."

"Oh." He passed her the joint and she took a long pull. "Do you know what's goin on?"

"I think. She moved yesterday. Over to Champlain."

"Champlain? Why? Why wouldn't she just tell me that. What's with all the secrecy? Who *does* that? Moves out in a day. Like somebody chasin her. Is that what this is? This stuff with Misa?"

"Kinda, I think. Has she talked to you about her money issues. At all?"

"No. What money issues?"

Chucky relayed everything he knew. He didn't think of it as overstepping. He really just wanted to relieve that burden from Missy. Obviously, it was too difficult for her to articulate that she was broke. She'd kept it hidden for too long and now everything was blowing up in her face. She needed to come clean and she needed some help.

Brandy was completely taken aback by the news.

"So we're broke?"

"I mean...yeah. Pretty much."

"Like *broke*, broke?"

"Yeah Brandy. She turned in the cars, and the house is already on the market. Champlain was the only real option, you know. That's all she has left, and thank God for that. I'm here now, and I'll help wherever I can, but you know how she is. She'll never ask me."

"I know. She's stubborn. I wish I would have known this before."

"You think you could have helped?"

"Not really help, but I definitely could have like, changed what I was doing. Spending. Bugging her about getting me a new car."

"Well, baby gal...there's nothing we can do about yesterday. We can only start from now. First thing, we gon get Misa back. Your Aunt Pat is already on it. After that, we can start fresh. It's a lot goin on and comin up. But I'll let your aunt tell you all that stuff herself."

"What stuff?"

He smiled. "Just...stuff."

"Come on now Chucky. You already told me mostly everything. Might as well give me the rest."

He took the last pull off the joint. "Nah. She already gon curse my ass out for telling you she broke...but you needed to know it. She got the rest." He put the joint out on the ground. "This weed some shit, too."

"I can't tell. You smoked the whole J."

"I was just being social. I got somethin for you in the car though. You ready to go?"

"Yeah I'm ready."

"Chucky."

"Yeah?"

"I'm glad you're back."

"Yeah. Ion know how long imma stay tho. Y'all muthafuckas got too many problems!"

*****

When Chucky got back to his house, Missy was in the kitchen trying to open a bottle of wine with a butter knife.

"Hey babe. You up." He took the bottle from her hands and put it back in the refrigerator. "Now you *know* you can't have that."

"I just wanted a sip. One sip won't hurt anything. "

"You don't know that. I'll make you some tea."

"Thank you. And where've you been?"

"I went to pick Brandy up."

"From where? Where is she?"

"I dropped her off at your uncle's house. Missy why didn't you tell that girl what was going on? You know she had PJ drop her off at the old house, only to get in there and see that you moved. She was stranded out there. That ain't right."

"Damn. Is she mad?"

"You think?"

"Yeah well it's not like I haven't been dealing with some things these last couple of days."

"I'm talking about before now, Missy."

"What did she say? What did you tell her?"

"Huh?"

"Yeah…huh! WHAT did you say to her?"

"I mean…I told her what was happenin. She needed to know."

"That wasn't your place, Chucky."

"Well you was actin like it wasn't yours either. She's grown, Missy. She's not a little girl. She can handle it."

"Well? How did she handle it?"

"Oh, she was pissed! Rollin round on the ground screamin and hollerin and cryin. She was like *I hate that bitch! I hope she die!*"

"Chucky!"

"Nah, I'm playin. She was cool. She just said she wished you would have told her before. That's all."

"I just didn't wanna disappoint her."

"That's what I told her. She gets it."

"Is that all you told her?"

"Yeah. Well I told her there was more to tell. But I told her you needed to tell her."

"Good."

"But now I have a question for you."

"Hmm?"

"When were you planning to tell me about Misa?"

Missy nearly choked on her tea. "What?"

"Huh...what...yeah. When?"

"I can't even believe she would tell you that."

"Well she did. And never mind that. How come you didn't feel like you could trust me with it? You notice I never asked you who Misa's father was. I never asked any details about her. I was just waitin for you to talk to me about it."

"It's not really something we discuss. For all intents and purposes Misa James is my daughter. It's legal. It's final. It's what it is. And Brandy didn't need to deal with all that. You know what happened to her."

"Yes I remember what happened, but I didn't know she had a baby."

"Exactly. Only family knew. And not all of the family. Just the people who needed to know. And it all worked out."

"Brandy said you made her sign over her baby, and she never wanted that."

Missy scowled at him. Chucky knew he'd said a little too much. She pointed at his face. "I'm not doing this with *you*. It's not your business."

"Babe. I'm just—"

She walked off. "I'll talk to Brandy myself."

"No, don't go off on her please. The girl was just being honest. Missy, where you goin?"

"I am going to find out if my aunt has an update on my child. And then I'm going back to bed. Alone. Goodnight Chucky."

She stomped up the stairs and slammed the bedroom door. Chucky called out, "Goodnight."

He didn't mind being bid an early goodnight. He had some phone calls to make anyway. Things to do. Places to be. She'd thank him later.

In or Out?

After a half hour of circling the block, they finally found a parking space on the street, near Imelda's bistro. They sat in the car for some time. Contemplating all the ifs. If they asked for Imelda's help, would she do it? If she helped them what would it cost them? Could they trust her? You could never really tell with her.

There wasn't much time to ponder. Aunt Pat had it on good authority that Gi was still in DC. But for how long? No one knew. Misa was with his elderly grandfather and a housekeeper, but the house was also heavily guarded with state of the art security systems and seven bodyguards that were stationed in and outside the house 24/7.

There were still four days until the deadline, but the deadline didn't matter. They didn't have the money and didn't even try to raise the money. Aunt Pat's plan was to go in Kamikaze style, take the guards down and snatch Misa. Simple as that. With a couple of more bodies lent to her from Imelda's crew, they could definitely get it done.

"Pat?"

"Yeah."

"We gon get out the car?"

"Yeah."

"Today?'

"Rocky I'm tryna think."

"Well, I can probably help you with that."

"I know." She sighed. "I don't know if I wanna fuck wit Imelda."

"What? Then what we doin here?"

"We need her."

"Ok then. Let's just go in there and get this over with. She gon say yes or she gon say no. It's gon get done either way. But it'll be easier with her help. Come on. Let's go."

Aunt Pat reluctantly let go of the steering wheel and took a deep breath. "Aaight, let's go."

Peta greeted them at the front. "Buenos Dias Ms. Patricia."

"How you doin Peta?"

Peta sneered. "*Rocky.*"

Rocky's nostril flared. "You better get her, Pat. Before I hurt her lil ass."

"Rocky, leave that little girl alone."

Peta giggled. "Mami's in the back. Follow me."

She walked them back to the storeroom. Imelda was seated at a table having her dinner and reading the paper. She stood when they entered, wiped her mouth and hands with the cloth napkin from her lap. "Ladies. What brings you here? In the middle of the week? Please, have a seat."

Aunt Pat pulled out a chair. "I need your help with somethin."

Imelda returned to her seat. And placed her napkin back in her lap. She took a bite of her spicy chorizo and sat silently chewing for a moment. "You hungry?"

"Nah, not really. We just…"

"Nonsense. Peta. Peta!"

Peta stuck her head in "Yes mami?"

"Bring our guests the special, and some Chica." She looked over at Aunt Pat and Rocky. "Bandeja…it's fresh…you'll like it. Now what can I do for you ladies?"

Aunt Pat gave her the run down. The background, the kidnapping, the extortion. The plan. Imelda listened attentively, as she sipped the cloudy, pungent alcohol mix. Aunt Pat and Rocky sat wondering the exact same thing. What the fuck was she drinking? But neither inquired.

Imelda took the last swallow of her drink and sat the mason jar on the table. "One hundred thousand."

Aunt Pat squinted. "What?"

"If you would like my help. If you would like me to dispatch my men. Young Giovanni is not one that I like. But I do not have problems with him, or his family. So. One hundred thousand."

"Imelda. I don't have that right now."

"Don't worry." She smiled. "I'm sure we can...work some things out."

Peta walked in with two healthy plates and a pitcher of whatever it was Imelda was drinking. She poured two glasses about half full before Aunt Pat declined hers.

Imelda chimed in, "Drink up Patricia."

"No, thank you. I need to have a clear head for tomorrow."

"Nothing is happening tomorrow."

Aunt Pat frowned. "What you mean?"

Imelda smiled. "I mean...your plan. It's not smart. You're gonna get yourself, Rocky here, and your little grandniece killed. Look...I'll help you. But I need another day or two, at least, to figure out a plan that actually *works*."

In that moment, Aunt Pat regretted ever walking into the grubby little restaurant. It was all she could do not to slap the smug look off Imelda's fat round face and walk the fuck out. But she digressed and took another deep breath before responding. "We don't have another day or two, Imelda. Gi gave us a week. That's four more days. We need to go in when he's not expecting us and I know for fact that he's still in DC. We have to do it now. It's our best shot."

"Patricia, you came here because you knew you needed help. And you do. If you don't want my help–"

Rocky chimed in. "Pat. Come on. We need her."

Aunt Pat glared at Rocky, rose from her seat and extended her hand. "Thank you for the meal and the wine."

Imelda took her hand and held it for a moment. "All right. Good luck to you."

"Thanks. Let's go, Rock."

Peta leaned against the doorway and grinned. "*Adios Rocky.*"

Rocky scowled and sucked her teeth at Peta before following Aunt Pat out of the restaurant. When they got to the car Rocky didn't waste any time voicing her concerns. "I think you makin a mistake."

"Really."

"We need to go back in there and work this out."

"Rocky. If you scared just say you scared. Cause you can head back to DC and I'll do this shit on my own."

"That's not what I mean Pat, and you know I ain't never been scared. I'm witchu a hunnid percent. I just don't think we ready, man. A couple more guns ain't gon hurt."

"This shit ain't no different than when we hit Suga Pops. Or...or Black Tom or the Southside Boys. The B Squad. A hit is a fuckin hit..."

"Yeah but this ain't DC. This ain't our town man. The shits a lil different don't you think? We don't even know where the fuck we at!"

"Look I ain't got time for this. All this doubtin and back and forth. We know everything we need to know. So either you in or out?"

Rocky sighed. "Hey..."

"IN or OUT Rocky!"

"Aight....I'm in."

"Good. Now let's go."

Rocky started the car. "Where we headed?"

"Downtown. To the docks to check everything out. We gon do a quick dry run, then come back uptown to Sylvia's."

"The soul food spot?"

"Yeah. I need some *real* food."

"Oh hell yeah. I hope they still make that cornmeal catfish."

"Look up the menu online. We might as well eat good tonight. Cause tomorrow..."

"We gon knock some blocks off?"

They slapped hands and laughed. "Muufuckin right."

Sweet Brandywine

Brenda walked down to the visiting hall. She'd had a rough week. And she needed an update on Misa. She saw the news. Fox 5 reported that Misa was still missing after three days of searching every corner of the city. There were no new leads.

She sat at the table waiting for PJ to appear on the screen. Somehow he was always the last one to come online, and there was always some commotion going on behind him. Whether it was him pushing up on an unwilling security guard or some animated exchange with one of the other visitors, he managed to capture the attention of everyone in the room. Brenda looked forward to his shenanigans every week.

As per the usual, there was a ruckus when he finally appeared on screen. PJ screamed. "You better watch your fuckin mouth. That's my niece you talkin to."

Brenda swallowed down hard when she saw Brandy sit down beside him. PJ squinted as his face came closer to the screen. "Brenda. What happened to your face?"

"Never mind what happened to my face. What is Brandy doing here? Are you crazy, PJ! You GET HER OUTTA HERE!" Brenda screamed so loud it brought the entire visiting hall to attention. She motioned to the guard. "Take me back to my cell please."

"Ma! Please!" Brandy pleaded through watery eyes. "Don't go."

Brenda stood for moment. She knew walking away wasn't an option. The guard stepped away. PJ excused himself. And she fought back her tears as she sat back down in front of the camera to face what she'd been dreading since the first time she was taken away.

Brenda didn't know what to say, sitting in her bright orange prison garb, one side of her face still swollen from a scuffle she'd gotten into earlier that day.

Brandy's tears fell in the tiniest puddle on the counter below her. "Are you ok?"

Brenda cleared her throat. "Stop crying, baby. I'm fine. Just had a little accident today. But I'm fine."

Brandy could always tell when Brenda was lying. She wiped her face. "I miss you, ma." She broke down.

Brenda swallowed down hard, trying desperately to hold it together. She was on the verge of a breakdown herself, but knew it wouldn't help Brandy. "I miss you, too, *Brandywine*"

Brandy smiled. "You haven't called me that in a long time."

"I know. Come on, stop crying. Tell me what's been goin on with you?"

Forty minutes later the tears had dried and the mood was much lighter. Brenda kept the conversation light. On Brandy and all of her adventures. School. Travel. Boys.

Brenda laughed. "So you finally ran into Keisha."

Brandy smiled. "Yeah."

"You wanted to beat on her didn't you?"

"Beat her fuckin ass. Oh! I'm sorry for cussin."

Brenda raised a hand. And giggled "That's ok. Trust me, I get it. So what's going on with you and Tay?"

"Nothing. We're just friends."

"Really?"

"Yeah, we're just friends."

"Child if it's one thing I know about that boy, it's that he don't wanna just be your friend."

"Well...it doesn't really matter what he wants."

"No? Well what do *you* want?"

"Ma..."

"Baby listen. I'm not tryna to tell you to go to this boy and get all tangled up in no baby mama drama. I don't want that for you. But I won't tell you *not to* either. You are my beautiful baby girl, and I love you to death. I want you to do well. I want you to live a good life and be happy. What I'm tryna say is...if Tay makes you happy. If he's what you want. Don't let nobody stand in the way of that. Not me. Not Keisha. Not the past. Life is too short and Lord knows tomorrow ain't promised. So if you got a chance at happiness you need to grab it while you can and ride that muthafucka til the wheels fall off."

"Really ma?"

"Sorry for cussin. But you know what I mean."

"I know."

The guard gave the five-minute warning. "Baby, let me talk to PJ before y'all go."

"Ok."

"I love you, hear?"

"I love you too, ma."

"Brandy, you remember what I said."

"I remember."

Brandy handed PJ the receiver and walked over to the door. PJ beamed. "Okaaayy. Look at yall. Just makin up and shit."

"Yeah, but I'm still mad at you for bringing her."

"No, you're not. You're happy to be back in your daughter's good graces. Besides, I just did what you woulda done. And now that everything's good again…"

"Not everything. What's the word on Misa?"

"Oh. Ma and Rocky already went upstate. They'll be bringing her back soon."

"Upstate?"

"Yeah they said the nigga took her to New York to hide her while he waited for the money."

"They gon pay him?"

PJ pursed his lips and raised a brow. "What *you* think?"

"Yeah, I guess that's a stupid question. I know this is hard on Missy. How is she?"

He shrugged. "Upset, I guess."

"You guess?"

"She's upset. But ma got it covered. Misa'll be home like tomorrow. Ain't really nuttin to worry about."

"Well I'll send up a prayer anyway."

"If you must chile. What's happening with your case?"

"The trial date's set. It's in six weeks. I still don't know about taking this to trial. Aunt Pat's insisting we ride it out but the shit don't look good for me at all. They offered me manslaughter. I feel like I should take it P."

"If ma said ride it out, you ride it out. She must have a plan, so stop worryin. "

"I don't think it's that simple."

"Well...has she ever let us down?"

"No...but..."

"Ain't no but. And girl what happened to your face?"

Brenda touched the strawberry on her cheek. "Bitch tried to steal from my package. I caught her in my cell and she bucked on me like *I* was wrong for sayin somethin. She hit me in the face with her shoe."

"Did you get her?"

"Fucked that bitch *up*. For real. People been tryin me a lot lately. The inmates. The guards. This the third fight I been in."

"For real? Where ma people at?"

"Ion know. Somebody was supposed to be comin to see me, but I ain't heard from nobody since I been in here. I ain't wanna bother her with it though. She got enough on her plate."

"Nah, I'll talk to her when she gets back. Dem bitches need to know who dey fuckin wit. Trust me, we gon straighten that shit out. Just hold tight for a minute."

"Yeah, I'm holdin."

The guard called out "All right people. Visiting hours are now over... "

PJ stood. "Well that's our time, baby girl. We'll be back next week, same time aight? Call me when you can."

"Aight I will. Love you P."

"I love you, too. And don't worry. We got you babes."

The car ride home was pretty quiet. PJ decided to leave Brandy with her thoughts, so he opened the sunroof and pumped the satellite radio. He took a couple business calls.

Brandy stared out of her window, occasionally smiling. Feeling a strange mix of angst and relief. It was the first time she'd connected with her mother in three years. And it felt good.

She only wished she could have had more time with her. More time to really talk. The truth was on the tip of her tongue. But every time she thought to tell it, she clammed up. MJ's voice rang in her head. *Brandy, some things mama don't need to know. It ain't gon fix nuttin and it don't matter now anyway. So just let it go.*

Brandy thought, maybe it wouldn't fix anything and maybe it didn't really matter. But she had the right to know the truth. And the next time she saw her, she would tell it. She'd carried the weight for too long. And it was time to let it go. Come what may.

The Mission

Rocky stood in line for two ferry tickets while Aunt Pat surveyed the dock one last time. They boarded the Staten Island Ferry, armed to the hilt. Security had already been supremely compensated for turning off the bells and whistles that would inevitably be triggered by the heavy artillery stuffed in their backpacks and in various sealed pockets of oversized cargo pants.

They blended into the mass of people waiting to get a good seat on the ferry. There would be no talking on the way over. The plan was etched in their memories and the ladies were well prepared for every carefully calculated step of the rescue plan.

Neither would ever admit it but both were nervous as all hell. Sweaty palms and slight butterflies. Perfectly normal feelings when the potential of staring death in the face was particularly high.

Rocky whispered. "Pat."

Aunt Pat glared at her. Slightly annoyed that Rocky was already breaking the no talking rule. Rocky nodded to her left. They boarded the ferry. Rocky smiled as Aunt Pat seethed. You could almost see the steam coming from her ears. The passengers scrambled for the best spots to catch a view of the city as the ferry sailed off, across the Hudson River. The ladies took a walk.

He was standing on the top deck taking a selfie, dressed entirely in camouflage and carrying a small duffle bag.

Aunt Pat whispered through clenched teeth. "What the *fuck* are you doing here, Chucky?"

Startled, he dropped his phone overboard, and he would have fallen over after it if Rocky hadn't snatched him back over the railing by the back of his shirt. "Shit! My phone!"

"Fuck that phone. Boy didn't I tell you to stay yo ass home. How'd you know where we was at?"

"PJ. I told him I was gone help y'all out. Me and my man."

"Your man?"

"Ev."

"She looked around. Where he at?"

"Oh he gon meet us over there. His bus was late."

"Nigga, is you crazy! Call him right now and tell him don't bring his ass over here."

"Can't."

"Why?"

"Dropped my phone."

She pulled out her phone and shoved it in his face. "Call him."

He smiled and shoved it back at her. "Can't."

"What? Why?!"

"The number's in my phone."

Aunt Pat snarled. "You tryna fuck with me, boy? Look, when they stop this muthafuckin boat, you gon carry your stupid ass over to the other side and catch the ferry back. You hear me?"

"Come on, Ms. Pat. I know ya'll can use me for *somethin*. Don't make me go back. Please."

"Use you? For what?"

"For whatever. Trust me, I'm ready for *whateva*." He unzipped his duffle and pulled it half open. At first glance you could see a police issued taser, a billy club, a Glock 9 and a badge.

Rocky tugged the bag open a little further and reached in. "Pat. This nigga bought a grappling hook?!" She burst out laughing.

That pissed Aunt Pat off all the more. She whispered, "Nigga. You think this a fuckin video game?!"

Rocky laughed so hard she could hardly breathe. She had to hold on to the railing to keep herself up.

Chucky raised a brow at her. Slightly embarrassed by her clowning. "I mean you ain't gotta laugh. I ain't know what y'all was gon need. So I just brought everything I could think of."

Aunt Pat moved closer to him. "What the fuck you was gon do with that? Huh?" She put her hands over her face for a moment and breathed a heavy sigh. Frustrated. Trying to calm herself. Trying to find some Zen.

The rest of the ferry ride was made in the most uncomfortable silence, as Chucky sat between Aunt Pat and Rocky like a scolded child with his bag in his lap. It was the longest twenty minutes of his life.

The ferry jerked to a halt when it pulled into the dock. The ladies stood and pulled their backpacks over their shoulders. When Chucky attempted to rise, Aunt Pat nudged him back down into his seat. She bent down to face him. "Chucky." She popped him on the cheek. "Look at me."

He looked up at her. "Huh?"

"I want you to get up, walk slowly and calmly off this boat, get on the return ferry and ion wanna see yo ass again until I get back to DC. You hear me?"

He looked away. "Aight."

"If I see you before then, I swear for God umma put a hot one in you, boy."

His eyes bucked wide. *A hot one?*

"Do you hear me, Chucky?"

"I hear you."

She grit her teeth. "DO YOU HEAR ME?"

"Ms. Pat, I hear you."

The passengers piled up at the exit and started filing off the boat. Aunt Pat pointed toward them, glared at Chucky and commanded, "You. Go *THAT* way."

Sulking but without further protest, Chucky picked up his duffle and walked to the exit. Rocky smiled and shook her head. Aunt Pat tried to stifle a giggle but couldn't hold it in. She laughed. "*This* nigga. Let's get the fuck off this boat."

*****

Parked in the middle of a crowded lot just off the dock was

a blue cargo van with dark tinted windows and the keys in the glove box. The ladies jumped in the back of the van and assembled their weapons. Once everything was secure and in place, their watches synched, it was time to roll.

Aunt Pat started the engine and sat for a moment. Her hands trembled atop the steering wheel. She pulled them away before Rocky could notce and sat them in her lap.

Rocky was busy fiddling with her gun, she hadn't noticed they were still sitting. She looked up and checked her watch. "What's up Pat?"

Aunt Pat turned off the engine. She cracked her knuckles to sooth her nerves, took a sip from her water bottle and pulled the plans from her jacket pocket. "One more time."

The foolishness with Chucky had thrown her off, so she needed to make sure they were still on the exact same page. Timing was everything and the smallest miscalculation, the tiniest mistep could cost lives. Misa's most importantly and come hell or highwater, she was bringing that baby back home.

She unfolded the diagram of the house and spread it out on the dash. "...now the guards switch out at nine o'clock so at nine-o-two, imma need you right here. I'll be..."

Rocky drew her gun and pointed it at her head. Actually a couple inches to the right of her head. Aimed at the driver's window. Aunt Pat jumped when Chucky screamed, "Wait! It's me!"

She fumed. "I THOUGHT I TOLD YOU TO GET THE FUCK OUTTA HERE, CHUCKY!"

"Shhhh. I know, and I was. But I missed the ferry. Come on Ms. Pat, let me go. Please?"

Rocky smiled and re-holstered her pistol. "Pat let the nigga come. He can sit in the van and keep it runnin. In case we gotta come out hot or somethin. I mean...you never know."

Chucky chimed in. "Yeah, yeah I can definitely do dat."

Aunt Pat rolled her eyes. It wasn't a bad idea to have him keep the van running. But she was pissed that nobody was listening to her. She grunted. "Get yo ass in the back."

Chucky smiled wide. Ready to get in the mix. He ran to the

passenger side and threw his duffle bag in. Then climbed over Rocky to the back, accidentally elbowing Aunt Pat in the eye. Her reflex kicked in and she pushed him hard to the back, causing him to fall on his chest.

"I'm sorry. I'm sorry," he said.

The ladies ran through the plan for the last time. Chucky was amped. He couldn't resist chiming in. "Yeah and then I can take this taser right…"

Aunt Pat snapped. "Zip that muthafuckin bag up! Ain't nobody usin nothin outta that bag, boy."

Rocky couldn't get herself together. Her stomach was starting to ache from the laughter.

Aunt Pat huffed. She was growing more frustrated by the minute, with both of them. "Y'all act like this shit a joke. This ain't play time. Stop *fuckin* around!"

Rocky composed herself. "Aaight, aight Pat calm down. We good."

She yelled. "Shit!"

They went over the security system once more. Then the floor plan. Chucky looked over their shoulders at the drawings. "Umh."

Aunt Pat turned to him and glared. He held his hands up. "Sorry."

They went through plans A, B and C. Then the contingency plan. All of which had to be tweaked slightly to include the get away driver.

Chucky grunted again. "Umh."

"Got dammit! Rocky, if he say one more word, I want you to climb back there, open that door and push his ass out the back."

Chucky whined. "But Ms. Pat, I ain't even say nuthin."

She slammed on the brakes, turned around and looked at him. He got the silent message loud and clear and he sat silently for the rest of the ride.

*****

Gi's home was a lavish, 12,000-square-foot mansion located in the Grymes Hill neighborhood of Staten Island. It was well protected by electric fencing, bulletproof glass windows and over a dozen infrared security cameras all controlled by one remote. The entryway gate was vast. Twelve feet in height, wrought iron.

A total of seven armed bodyguards were stationed both in and outside the home – one at the exterior gate, one at the front door, and one at the back of the property. Four men were inside. Though not impossible, this mission would certainly not be an easy one.

They pulled the van over, about a half block from the house and turned off the lights. Aunt Pat and Rocky screwed the suppressors onto their weapons, grabbed their packs and put them on their backs.

Rocky looked back at Chucky. Beads of sweat had formed on his forehead. He inhaled deeply and exhaled through his mouth. Rocky laughed. "You aight back there chief?"

Aunt Pat looked back and noticed his nerves. "Chucky!"

He jumped. "Yeah I'm good. I'm good."

"Boy…don't make me regret this. You get up here, sit your ass in this seat and keep this car runnin. Don't say shit, don't do shit…don't even think shit. Just be ready to mash this muthafacka when we come out. You think you can you handle that?"

"Most definitely. All you gotta say is…"

"Chucky…"

"Yeah, yeah I got it, Ms. Pat. Be ready to drive. I got it."

"Good."

They ladies hopped out of the van and set off toward the house. On the opposite side of the street. Aunt pat pulled a pair of binoculars and peered into the compound to confirm positions. Then she opened the security app on her phone. She disabled the electric fencing and they jogged quickly over to the wall on the side of the front gate. Next, she opened up the dating app and started typing.

Anthony. I don't know what it is about you...but I can't stop thinking about you.

The guard picked up his cell phone and smiled wide before typing his reply.

Oh, really? What are you thinking?

As Aunt Pat went into full Girl 6 mode, detailing the many wondrous things she could do to him with her pierced tongue, Rocky used her considerable biceps to pull herself up on the security wall. She aimed the rifle and adjusted the scope. The guard fell to the ground with a *thud* before she could even get to the trigger. She looked behind her. Perched on a branch of a massive cedar tree was Peta with a crossbow aimed at the guard's tower. She smiled and waved.

Rocky hopped down off the wall and ran over to the gate to let Aunt Pat inside. Peta leaped from the tree, onto the gate and into the yard. She darted off and disappeared behind the house.

Rocky whispered. "Fuck is she doin here?"

Aunt Pat shrugged and waved Rocky over to the front door where another guard lay gasping for air as his lungs were pierced by the serrated edges of a Peta's hunting arrow. Rocky quickly grabbed the fallen guard and pulled him into the shrubbery, out of site.

The front door swung open and they both drew their weapons. Peta stood smiling then took off, leaping up the main staircase two by two with her crossbow slung over her shoulder, a micro uzi with a suppressor in her hands and a Ruger .45 holstered at her side.

Rocky turned to Aunt Pat again, puzzled. "What is she doin?"

A succession of bullets and a loud scream could be heard upstairs. "Look like she gettin niggas out the way. Clear the kitchen, I'm goin to the basement for Misa."

"Bet."

With her pretty gold gat raised and at the ready, Aunt Pat eased down the hall. Slowly. Everything was quiet. Behind her, two shots and a thud. She hoped Rocky got one.

She kept moving. A large potted vase beside her shattered

as gun shots rang out. She backed against the wall, positioning herself to return fire in the direction of the shots. She fired several rounds up at the second floor landing, hitting a guard in the chest and the stomach, but it was the shot to the back of his head that brought him over the railing, falling directly in front of her.

Peta stood looking down from the railing, smiling and holding her gun. She ran off again. Aunt Pat shook her head and made a mental note. *That was four. There should be three more guards in the house.*

She could hear gunshots overhead and behind her, as she ran down the stairs to the basement. With no way to tell if it was friendly fire, she kept going. The sooner they found Misa, the better. The basement ran the length and width of the house, and the diagram showed at least six rooms. She saw a shadow at the bottom of the stairs and fired just as a guard rounded the corner into her sightline. *Five.*

In the kitchen, Rocky put one down. Two to the chest and the guard fell hard to the ground. *Six.* With her gun raised, she tip-toed out of the kitchen, back out into the foyer headed toward the basement. She noticed the front door was wide open, darted over to close it. Just as she kicked the door closed, a slightly pudgy Cilician reached out and grabbed her by the neck. He squeezed tight with one hand choking the air from her, as he landed a heavy fist to her face and then another. Half dazed, Rocky swung back but before she could connect, she screamed. The Sicilian loosened his grip and fell to the floor. After taking a considerable chunk of flesh from Rocky's right arm, the spear pierced him through his collar bone and deep into his chest. Rocky laid on the floor gasping for air, as Peta leapt the stairs to her aid. She fired three bullets into the guard, as he attempted to lift his head from the floor. *Seven.*

Rocky groaned, as Peta knelt and quickly examined her wound. "It's fine." She pulled Rocky to her feet. "Go!" They rushed toward the basement. As soon as they opened the door, Rocky was hit twice in the chest, throwing her backward to the floor. Peta drew down and returned fire, hitting the guard once in the forehead and sending him tumbling backward down the stairs.

Peta ran over to Rocky and pulled the Velcro back on her vest to see if the bullet penetrated through. It hadn't. So she helped a slow moving Rocky back to her feet and handed her her gun.

They hurried down the stairs as Aunt Pat rounded the corner, running with Misa cradled in her arms. "Let's go!" The ladies turned and dashed for the door when shots were fired. Aunt Pat fell forward to her knees as a bullet hit her in the back. Rocky caught Misa and Peta returned fire taking down the guard and the end of the staircase. *Eight?*

Peta helped Aunt Pat back to her feet. She grimaced and stood tall. "I'm good! Go!"

Rocky led the way out with the ladies running as fast as their battered bodies would let them.

Papas Maybe

Missy lifted her head from the pillow, feeing groggy with the slightest throb at her temple. Melatonin was the safest method for bringing slumber, but it also brought about the most vivid dreams since she could remember.

The last one that woke her up was a melee. A replay of the reality show reunion that ended with Chucky being hauled away in handcuffs and Kevin pulled away on a gurney with a blood-soaked sheet covering his body. The crowd cheered, and Carmen yelled for the cameras to keep rolling as Missy knelt on the ground holding her stomach, screaming in pain and bleeding. The blood pooled beneath her, and she begged for help, but no one listened.

She felt wetness between her legs and beneath her. Sure enough, there was blood rolling down her inner thigh and staining the sheets. She sprang out of bed and ran to the bathroom. There were no stomach cramps but more blood than seemed safe for a pregnant woman, so after she cleaned herself and the bed, she thought it best to head to the emergency room.

Sitting in the waiting room of the George Washington Hospital's Emergency ward, waiting to be triaged, Missy was pissed. Chucky wasn't answering his cell. She decided not to leave a message. No sense in alarming him until she knew what was what, but she was still pissed at him for not cancelling his gig. He'd explained that it had been booked months earlier and that if he backed out at the last minute he'd probably be sued. He argued that it was just for one night and he'd be back in a day.

A $20,000 gig wasn't exactly easy to come by after all of his personal drama. She understood that, but still, she wished he would have stayed with her until everything was resolved.

Aunt Pat hadn't answered her phone since she took off for New York the day before. Missy desperately needed an update but she also needed to believe that, as per usual, Aunt Pat had every single thing under control. That being the case, Misa would be back home very soon. Safe and sound. And she'd have her family back again. Her new family. She smiled at the thought.

The bleeding had stopped since the second time she checked but she was starting to get a little crampy. She walked over to the counter and asked how much longer it would be before she could be seen. The triage nurse told her that she would be next and it would only be a few more minutes. So Missy walked back to her seat.

After clearing it with security and the other patrons who were patiently waiting in the waiting area, she changed the TV channel to Fox 5 to see the ten o'clock news broadcast. The sound wasn't very clear with all of the commotion in the waiting room but she didn't really need to hear it to decipher what was going down. The usual foolishness. A shooting on the southside that left one dead and several wounded. A woman accosted in Prince Georges County while standing alone at a bus stop. A strong arm robbery of a cell phone in the Chinatown subway station.

The registrar called Missy's name just as the headline flashed across the television screen. *Breaking News. Former DC Mayor Kevin Clark Arrested for Multiple Sexual Assaults.* Kevin's picture flashed in the upper right hand corner of the screen while the anchor, Tony Perkins, mouthed the story. The room was still too noisy to hear anything, so she walked over and turned up the volume.

First, Tony went through Kevin's political history in DC. From his days as an ancillary neighborhood commissioner to having a seat on the school board, then the city council and finally the mayor of the nation's great capitol. Next there was a photo of his cover of Black Enterprise and details of his current position as a top entertainment lawyer at one of the wealthiest law firms in the country. Born and bred in DC, a product of the

DC public school system, Kevin Clark was one of the most admired men in DC. An inspiration to young brothers everywhere.

When the praise piece concluded, the camera panned to a room full of women whose faces were blurred and voices were digitally disguised. Each woman recounted details of an encounter in which they had a drink with Kevin and the next thing they remember was waking up in his bed in various stages of undress.

The allegations went back more than ten years, and two of the women claimed that the rapes produced children, for which they were receiving support. Several of the women were violating terms of settlement agreements by speaking, but they said they didn't care. They wanted justice.

There were several women he dated in college. Interns, aides and colleagues. Multiple women from dating sites and ads on Craigslist. All told, the number of accusers were at 19, but that number would eventually climb.

The story ended with footage from earlier that day of Kevin being led out of his downtown law office into a squad car. Cameras flashed as reporters shouted a barrage of questions at him. His ex-wife was caught on camera leaving her office. The media swarmed around her, barely allowing her access to her car. Tony Perkins promised to provide an update as soon as new information was received.

Missy stood in front of the television. Oblivious to the tears streaming down her cheeks and the streaming down her legs, soaking her pants.

A patient called out to her. "Ma'am. Excuse me. Ma'am! I think you're bleeding."

The Getaway

The van wasn't running. Chucky wasn't ready. Peta jumped in the driver's seat as Aunt Pat and Rocky ran to the back of the van. Aunt Pat jumped in back with Misa. Rocky pulled Chucky from the ground.

"Nigga what the fuck you doin?! Let's go!"

"Wait! We can't just…"

Aunt Pat charged out of the van and punch him hard in the jaw. "Muthafucka!" The ladies snatched him up by the collar of his jacket and threw him in head first. The doors were barely closed shut when Peta mashed the gas, screeching away from the curb.

Aunt Pat buckled Misa in tight as Peta drove wildly through the streets trying to make it back to the docks to get the last ferry back to the city. She banged on the cab. "Come on Peta, we gotta make it. I need you to drive this thing!"

Rocky ripped the bloody sleeve from her shoulder. She winced. "Shit."

Aunt Pat inquired. "You hit bad?"

"I'm aight. Prolly just need some stitches." She ripped a strip off her shirt and tied it tightly around her arm to slow the bleeding.

"I think you gon need more than some stiches. That's deep." Aunt Pat took off her jacket and handed it to her. "Here put this on before we get to that ferry."

Chucky sat in the corner quietly, trying to avoid Aunt Pat's glare. He held tight to a safety strap, trying not to slide too close to her.

Peta yelled, "Hijo de Puta!"

Aunt Pat hollered up. "What's up Peta? We close?"

"Tenemose compania!"

"English Peta!"

"We ave company!"

Peta spotted the two black SUVs three or four cars behind. They'd been weaving in and out of traffic, around cars for at least two blocks. One behind the other. Peta slowed down at an intersection as a city ambulance with lights flashing and sirens wailing crossed in front of her. The cars behind her slowed to a halt, trapping the SUVs between them in the heavy traffic. Two firetrucks followed the ambulance. The first truck crossed the intersection. Peta hit the gas, weaving between them, through the intersection, just making it in front of the second truck, just making it through the yellow light and leaving every other car behind her on the red with the last fire truck blocking the intersection as its driver slammed the brakes.

Peta drove furiously through traffic, running every red light and stop sign in her path. Several miles down the road she looked back and still didn't see the SUV's. So there was time. She took a sharp right into an alleyway, behind a warehouse and through another alleyway leading to the parking lot by the dock. It was 11:26pm. Just four minutes until the last departure. Missing the ferry was not an option. With no time to park she drove straight to the edge of the dock.

The van screeched to a halt. Aunt Pat unbuckled Misa and everyone jumped out of the van. They ran top speed through the terminal toward the boat ramp. Moments later the SUV's pulled next to the van. Gi, Rob and their crew took off running into the terminal. Hands in their jackets. Prepared to draw and fire, given a clean shot.

Peta lead the way. The terminal was packed. They fought their way through the crowd toward the front of the line, trying not to draw any attention, trying not to be spotted. Chucky kept looking back. So much that he could barely keep up. He spotted Gi and his crew. They were hard to miss, as they were the only other ones running through the terminal, darting through the crowd at top speed.

He tugged on Rocky's shirt to let her know. She whispered

to Aunt Pat who clued Peta in and they picked up the pace.

Onto the ferry, to the front then down the stairs to the bottom deck. Peta untied a rope ladder and dropped it, then she took Misa from Aunt Pat's arms. They climbed one by one down the ladder and onto an idling speedboat with Imelda at the helm. As they sped away they could see Gi and his crew in the distance, on the bottom deck with guns drawn.

Several rounds were fired. They crouched down as low as they could, as Imelda swung the boat in front of the ferry to get them out of the line of fire. Chucky never felt the bullet when it hit him.

Easy to Go

Her cramps worsened by the second. She'd thrown up twice. Nurses cut the heavily soiled pants from her body and took her straight to the O.R. Several hours later, Missy laid in recovery listening to a surgeon explain that one of her fallopian tubes ruptured as a result of an ectopic pregnancy. The pregnancy would never have made it to term and could have killed her if she hadn't been standing in the emergency room when the rupture occurred.

She braced herself as she inquired about her chances of ever conceiving again. The news was grim, but not surprising. First the damage from the botched abortion, now one less fallopian tube. The doctor said they could do further testing for a more accurate prognosis, but given the current factors, which also included her age, there was a less than a ten percent chance of conception. Fertility drugs were too risky and in vitro would be too costly under her new circumstances. So that was it.

When he left, she cried. Silent tears, because there was no one around who'd care if they heard. Chucky, Aunt Pat, Brenda. Everyone was away. PJ couldn't stand her and at the moment neither could Brandy. So she handled it the only way she could. Alone.

And so it was official. Kevin drugged her. There was no other explanation for what happened that night at the mansion. She'd never passed out drunk before, not even in college, and she knew that she hadn't had enough alcohol to cause her to blank out. She called for her nurse.

"Excuse me..." She looked over at the name on the dry erase board. "Laura?

"Yes Ms. James? I'm Laura your nurse. What can I do for

you?"

"I think I was the victim of a sexual assault."

Nurse Laura paused for just a moment before responding, "I'm sorry, what?"

"I was raped. It didn't happen tonight, or even recently. I think it happened a few months ago and I think there's a chance that this pregnancy was a result of that assault."

The nurse took a deep breath. "Ok. Can you tell me what happened, exactly? And start from the beginning?"

After hearing the details Nurse Laura informed Missy that there was a simple test that could be done to detect if she had any of the common date rape drugs in her system, but unfortunately for her those tests would have needed to be administered within 12 hours of ingesting them. She did, however explain that a blood test could be done on the fetus to determine paternity. They could preserve the remains for later testing. Missy declined. The thought sickened her actually. She asked that the remains be disposed of in accordance with hospital procedure. She'd just have to be ok with not knowing.

She giggled. Then laughed. Nurse Laura stood next to her with a most confused look on her face. "Ms. James? Are you ok?"

The sheer ridiculousness of the nurse's inquiry made her laugh all the more. Harder and louder in fact. "Yes Laura, I am laughing. And I know it seems out of place. Inappropriate. But I swear I have to laugh to keep from crying. My life. Ahhhhh, my life my life my life. Nurse Laura. In the last few years, my life went from a grand, magical, mystical fairytale to a colossal, catastrophic fuck-ing night-mare."

"Ms. James…"

"Foolery!" she yelled. "The fuckery. All the lies. My husband beat me. On our wedding night actually. That was the first time. But there were many, many others. Then he fell in love with a tranny. A beauuutiful transvestite named Carlita who, strangely enough, I really liked. Then I fell back in love with my ex. Then there was a suicide. My husband. Wait, no. A homicide. He didn't actually kill himself, we just thought he killed himself.

They made it look like he killed himself. The mob. Then they came after me for the money my husband still owed them when he died. A million dollars. Of course I didn't have it. They put me on a payment plan. And then I missed a payment. One damned payment! Or was it two? No, it was definitely two. Anyway, I got the ransom note…oh but we have to back up. So I can tell you how I got roofied. Roofies! Who gets roofied?!"

She laughed hysterically and Laura listened intently.

"You know Laura…I have been trying to get pregnant for *years*. YEARS!" She yelled, startling the nurse a little. "I finally settle with the man I want to spend the rest of my life with, after so many years of drama, and a roofie comes between us. This is the ex I was talking about. Did I mention he was a comedian? Yeah, really successful for a while, but he had some domestic issues with his ex-wife and she got a restraining order against him and all this crazy stuff happened. So then he got divorced, came back to me. On a reality tv show. Wait, I already said that right? Oh, no. We reconnected on a reality show on BET. Do you watch BET?"

"No, ma'am I sure don't." Laura answered.

"Well neither did I. Not really. But with the whole ransom thing, I was so broke, I had no choice but to go on tv. And that's where the roofie comes in. He roofied me, my ex, who's the former Mayor of DC by the way. Crazy right? He drugged me, had sex with me and it was pretty much exposed on tv. The sex part, not the roofies. I just found that out today…"

Nurse Laura excused herself as Missy's rambling went on and on about reality tv and ransom notes and her gangster aunt traveling to New York on a rescue mission to get her niece/daughter back from the mob. G6 airplanes and meeting President Obama at a party. Missy never even noticed her leaving. She just kept talking. Ten minutes later, Nurse Laura reappeared with a doctor. A different one.

He interrupted her, now tear-filled rant. He spoke clearly but softly as he sat on the end of her hospital bed and flipped through Missy's chart. "Ms. James. Hi, I'm Doctor Ballentine. I just have a few questions for you. Is that all right?"

Missy looked around the room at the serious faces. "Uhh...yeah."

"Great. Ok, first, can you give me your full name?"

"Sure, Melissa James."

He jotted onto a notepad. "Good, That's very good Ms. James. Now can you tell me what year this is?"

"Wait, what?"

*****

After the barrage of inane questions and the not so subtle suggestion that she take a walk up to the psychiatric ward, Missy swiftly signed herself out of the George Washington Hospital. She pulled into Chucky's little garage and sat there for a while, reflecting on everything that happened that day. From the disturbing news report to the crazy rant that nearly got her locked away. She laughed thinking, *why in the hell did I do that?* Every word she spoke was the truth but so unbelievable that she didn't blame that nurse for going to get help.

She felt pressure in her pelvis, as she soiled the heavy hospital padding. It was as if life was still seeping from inside her. The gravity of the situation set in. Her eyes welled again. Her baby was gone. Her one chance to experience bringing life into the world was forever gone, and she'd likely never have another chance. No more morning sickness. No more cravings. No more Parenthood magazines and expectant mother literature. No need. Little Farrah or Ethan existed only in her imagination, and her memory.

Both of her babies had left her. One cradled in the arms of the Almighty, and the other held hostage, God only knew where. God and Aunt Pat. She could only hope and pray for Misa's safe return. She tried Aunt Pat's cell again. Straight to voice mail. She tried Chucky's phone. The same.

As she showered the tragic events of the day away, she heard the doorbell ringing. She grabbed Chucky's robe from the back of the bathroom door and ran downstairs. She peeked out of the window. PJ stood waiting impatiently, frowning, tapping his heel on the pavement.

She opened the door. "What are you doing here?"

"Hello to you too Missy." PJ looked up and around. "I didn't know Chucky had a house in Georgetown. I thought he was out of work."

"No, actually he's not out of work. And if you *must* know, this house was willed to him by his grandfather."

"Grandfather?"

"Yeah it's the father that fathers the mother or the father."

"Don't get smart. I'm just saying. I know this house has gotta be worth a couple million, at least. I thought Chucky's people were from Ridgewood."

"Some of them, yes. His grandfather was one of the original blacks that lived in Georgetown before it was gentrified. Most were forced out. A few of them fought and stayed. He stayed."

PJ smiled with pride. The kinda communal pride black folks feel when other black folks score a point for their people. "Ok den. That's what's up Grandpa. I wish somebody left me a house in Georgetown."

"So what brings you here?"

"Oh. I need you to get dressed."

"Dressed? For what?"

"Cause we gotta go."

"Go where?"

"New York."

Caution to the Wind

Brandy picked up her phone and rolled her eyes. She sent the call to voice mail. Missy was the last person she felt like talking to. A text came through: *Brandy I need you to go back over to Uncle Edwards and check on Mandy for me. I'll call you in the morning.*

She threw the phone back on the bed. *Whatever.*

She laid across her new full-size mattress, a downgrade from the queen poster bed in her old room, and stared at the ceiling. She felt suffocated. And it wasn't just the new small space. It wasn't just the fact they'd left a beautiful six thousand square foot home in a gated suburban community and moved into a tiny two-bedroom apartment on a tiny crowded street in a tiny crowded neighborhood in the city. Her life just felt so small. So complicated. So...lacking.

There was chaos all around. All of the time. And she knew that wouldn't change anytime soon. Her sister/daughter who was taken from her at birth, against her will, had been kidnapped. Actually kidnapped, and her family was probably involved in some unspeakable criminal shit trying to bring her home. Because *that* shit was normal. Her mother was in prison, for the second time. For killing someone. For the second time. Her car, her purse and likely her identity were currently at large, in the possession of her exes drug addicted baby mama who was also her ex best friend. She'd quietly withdrawn from Georgetown University. No way she was going back there after what they'd done to Tay. And it was only a matter of time before Aunt Missy found out about that.

Brandy couldn't help thinking what was it what she was doing wrong. What had she done to deserve to have every single thing in her life go so incredibly wrong. More importantly, what in the world could she do to make things better.

She couldn't remember the last time she felt happy. Probably the last time she'd felt the warmth of her father's arms, and that had been ions ago. The closest since then had to be the time she'd spent with Tay and little TJ. But that was the part that was complicated. God knew she loved him and wanted more than anything to be back with him again. But it just wasn't that simple. She wished it was.

Hours passed as she sat on the edge of her bed. Mulling over her life. Trying to figure out what part of the crazy was in her power to fix. What did she actually have control of. Not much. Not her mom's situation. Nothing with Misa. But what she could do, was confront her feelings for Tay, once and for all and she could decide, for herself, where her life was going from there.

In the midst of fantasizing about how wonderful her life could be if she'd only followed her heart, her phone rang. She reached over and picked it up, Aunt Pat. She knew better than to send her to voice mail, so she just let it ring and do its thing. Two calls later she got the voice mail alert. Then a text: *Brandy, I don't want you to panic, but if you're home, I need you to get out of the house. Right now. Go to the place where your sister is and call me as soon as you get there, hear? Go right now.*

Brandy threw the phone back down on the bed and screamed, "Fuck!" She was tired of getting ordered around every single second of her life. But it didn't take long for her to come to her senses. No telling what was going on and ignoring Aunt Pat was never a good idea. So she packed a bag and dressed in a hurry. *Lord, please let this be over soon.*

Clearing the Air

The conversation was tense at first, then it went dark. It lightened up somewhere around Delaware, and by the time they reached the Holland Tunnel, leading into New York, they were laughing like old Judy's. They'd even tackled the infamous misunderstanding from Missy's engagement party, the root of PJ's long held contempt for her. He squealed.

"Biiiitch. I was *so over* your ass. You was cute and everything. Your party was real nice, but the way you carried it, hunny. I was like ooop! Did she just send me to her assistant? Did this bitch just dismiss Miss P? Oh no!"

Missy laughed. "Noooo, Brenda told me you were mad about that. I really didn't dismiss you. It's just that the team owners wanted to speak with Ray, and they'd already been waiting for a while. Ray gave me that look...and you know. I had to go."

"That *look*? So you mean to tell me he was already beatin yo ass?"

"No, PJ. He wasn't. Ray was just really demanding. He knew he was coming to end of his career and there was talk of a trade. He was panicky. I was just trying to do my wifely duties. I really didn't mean to put you off...or make you feel dismissed. There was just a lot going on that night."

"Um hmm."

"I'm serious. Now. For the record. I. Am. Sorry. Can we please be friends now?"

PJ gave a side eye and a smirk. "Yeah bitch, we friends."

Missy wrapped her arms around him and kissed him on the cheek. "Good. I still can't believe you were that mad at me over a party."

"Oh don't get it twisted. I was mad about how you treated me. Damn right. I don't play that fake shit. But I was mostly mad at how you treated *us*. The family. Your mom and Brenda. That's the shit I couldn't understand. All that actin like you too good to come around us."

"It wasn't even..."

"Nope." He interrupted. "Please. Don't even try. We good now. Let's just leave it there."

She laughed. "Ok. But that's another conversation for another time."

"Fair enough."

After their issue was settled, the new besties shared hearty laughs and juicy gossip. Missy had no idea PJ was so well connected. And so smart. Up until then she'd shamefully pegged him as a loudmouth label whore with no education and no class. She couldn't have been happier to be wrong. PJ's perception of her hadn't changed a bit. He didn't believe a word of that bullshit about the party. But why hold a grudge. The bitch was family.

When they pulled up to the hospital, reality set in again. PJ let Missy out in front while he looked for a parking space. She ran inside. The front desk clerk was on the rude side, but eventually she found the waiting area outside the operating room. When she walked up Aunt Pat was sitting in a chair with Misa asleep in her lap, an intense look on her face, whispering something in Rocky's ear.

Missy ran over to her and pulled Misa out of her lap. "Misa! Oh my God! Baby!" The tears flowed. Missy sobbed uncontrollably as Misa whined, irritable after being awaken so abruptly from her sleep. "Why didn't you call me?! Oh God." She pulled Misa's jacket off and started examining her for any obvious signs of abuse...or whatever.

Aunt Pat calmed her. "Missy, she fine. She ain't hurt. I already had the doctor check her out. She's good. How'd you get here?"

"Oh my God. Oh my God." Missy kissed her sweet baby repeatedly, all over her face and neck. "Mommy's so happy to see you! Oh God."

PJ walked up. "Hey."

"What are y'all doing here? How'd you find out where we was at?" Aunt Pat asked.

"Chucky called. How is he?"

Aunt Pat made a mental note to punch him in the throat when they got home. "He's good. It was just a flesh wound. They took the bullet out, and he's in recovery. They'll probably let him go tomorrow."

"Ma, what happened?"

"You know I'm not about to talk about that with you. And why the hell would you tell Chucky where we were, boy? I told you my whereabouts in case something happened to ME. Not for you to go and run your mouth to somebody else! You realize what position you put me in? You know you the reason he got shot."

"Well...in my defense...."

"Yeah I can't wait to hear this..."

"In my DEFENSE, I really thought I was doing somethin right. Chucky came to me, he was upset, he said he wanted to help and he couldn't just sit back and do nothing. He said that he wanted to help you all out and I thought–"

"You thought I needed help?"

"No that's not what I'm saying at all. I just thought–"

"You didn't think!"

Aunt Pat grabbed PJ's arm and walked him into a small conference room. "You know he brought Ev with him."

"Ev? Everett Smalls?"

"Yeah. Ev."

"Whaaaat? Oh, I know he acted a fool."

"Actually he didn't. He never got a chance to."

"What? Why?"

"Long story short, he missed his bus, got to the spot late, walked up on Chucky's scary ass in the van and got tazed."

PJ broke out laughing. "Oh no!"

"It ain't funny, boy. You always laughin at the wrong shit."

He took a breath and composed himself. "Whoo! Ok. Ok, I'm sorry ma. But that shit is funny. Where is he now?"

"He's dead."

PJ's jaw dropped and before he could ask the next obvious question Rocky walked in. "Hey Pat, we gotta go."

Aunt Pat turned to PJ. "Don't say nothin to Chucky. He don't know yet, and I don't want him to freak out."

"Well where does he think he is?"

"In a hospital on Staten Island. Which is true. He just…in the morgue."

"Damn."

"Yeah, I'll tell him when we get back home. I want him to hear it from me…"

Rocky yelled, "Pat! We gotta go! Now!"

"Aaight I'm comin! Look PJ I need you to make sure they all get home tomorrow. Y'all can stay at your cousin Myrna's house out in Queens tonight. I'll text you the number and address in a minute. Then I'll meet you tomorrow night back at the bar so we can talk." She yelled as she ran out behind Rocky. "Make sure you call me when y'all get back!"

PJ stood, dumbfounded. Dyyyiiing to get some answers. "Ok."

Re-Candling the Flame

Ignoring Aunt Pat's direction to go to her Uncle Edwards house, she knocked.

He answered. "Hey! What are you doin here?"

"I need an invitation now?"

Tay smiled. "No, of course you don't."

Brandy smiled. "Ok, so I'm here."

"You changed your hair."

"Yeah, I was getting bored with the red. And I'll be job hunting soon, so I thought I should tone it down a little. You like it?"

"I love it. It's beautiful."

"Aww, thanks babes." She pecked him on the lips.

Tay placed a gentle hand on her cheek and leaned into her for a longer, more passionate kiss. He looked into her eyes. "Thank you."

She smiled. "What are you thanking me for?"

"For just…for coming here. After I got that text…"

"Forget about that text."

"It's forgotten."

"Ok. Are you gonna invite me in?"

Just then he realized they were still standing in the doorway. Drawing a few curious glances from the neighborhood. "Oh shoot, yeah. I'm sorry. Come in."

He stepped aside and ushered her in by the small of her back, resisting the strong urge to allow that hand to travel south of her tiny waist, down to a place that was much fatter and rounder than he ever remembered. Tay was a gentleman. But that urge was strong.

Lil Brandy wasn't so little anymore. Her pink glossy lips

were now ruby red, and her teenage hips had amply spread. She was all woman now. Images began to flood his mind. Images of things he hadn't seen but had often imagined. Especially since the day he'd popped up at her house. Seeing her in her bra and panties. Trying to play it cool as she toyed with him. His imagination had gone wild. It was all he could do not to push her up against the wall and put his tongue in her mouth again. But that would have been creepy, he thought. So he chilled.

It had been a while since he'd felt a woman's warmth. He wasn't abstaining, necessarily. Just tired of the same old same. The young girls were just too young. The older ones were too...old. Although they'd taught him a lot, he was hardly looking for another mother figure. But now, by some divine miracle, Brandy was back in his life. In his home. Standing in front of him, more beautiful than he'd ever seen her.

When she turned to speak, he could barely hear her words. Too busy drinking her in. Every inch of her. From the highlights in her hair to her delicate hands and manicured feet. Shiny red polish popped off of her smooth caramel skin. The sweet citrusy scent of her perfume awakened something in him...so he adjusted his shorts. "Uhh...why don't we have a seat? So we can talk."

They sat for a while. Just talking. He could barely keep up with the conversation with all the distractions. The batting lashes, the flipping of the hair. The graceful way she shifted from one cross legged position to the other. Brandy was a shameless flirt. And he loved every single second of it.

The conversation was good. Comfortable. Much different than he remembered. In the two and a half years since he'd been without her she'd grown so much. Not just outwardly. There was a calm about her now. An elegance that only a woman with some real life experience could carry. Obviously, she'd been through some things.

He knew about the heartache. At least some of it. But he wondered what really lay behind her soulful eyes and her coy smile. Where had she been and what had she done? What did she dream of? Did any of those dreams include him? He desperately wanted them to.

But then again, they'd been through so much. His betrayal. All of her family drama. His brother violating her in the worst possible way. He couldn't have blamed her for not coming back. For moving on without looking back. But she did. Despite all if it. She came back, so there had to be something there. Something that was worth salvaging to her.

"Tay? Are you listening to me? Is it ok if I stay?"

"Huh? Yeah, girl. Stay forever."

She laughed. "No, not forever. Just tonight."

"Yes, of course. Whatever you need."

"Good, thanks. So where's my boy?"

"TJ?"

"No, your other secret lovechild. Of course TJ."

"One of his schoolmates had a sleepover."

"Awww." She pouted. "I wanted to see him."

"You can go with me to pick him up in the morning if you want." The timer on the oven sounded. He stood and walked into the kitchen. "You hungry?"

"A little." She followed him into the kitchen. "What are you cooking? It smells really good in here."

"Just a lil sumthin sumthin." He uncovered a couple pots. "We got some baked fish, fried cabbage, macaroni and cheese, cornbread."

"Whaaaat. All that? Were you expecting company?"

"No, I like to cook a full meal at least a couple times a week so I'll have leftovers for work."

"Such a responsible young man you are."

"I try to be." He fed her a forkful of the mac and cheese.

"Um, that's good. Who taught you how to cook like this?"

"My mom taught me a little, but mostly I just look up different stuff online and follow the recipes. I follow a few different chefs. G. Garvin, Bobby Flay. I just got hip to this new cat named Darius Williams. He does soul food and his stuff always looks good. And if I wanna get a lil fancy, I pull up my man Chef Roble. He's dope."

"So, you get fancy?"

"Yeah I get a lil fancy from time to time."

"Um hmmm. Well. I can't cook a lick. My mother would be so ashamed."

"It ain't nothin to it girl. I'll teach you what I know. Then we can learn the rest, together."

She smiled. "Together, huh?"

He blushed. "Oh, was that too much? I'm sorry. I just..."

She laughed. "No, it's fine." Then she leaned in for a smooch. "Together is good."

There was nothing he could do to conceal his excitement at *together is good*. She may as well have said, *I do*. Grinning like a Cheshire cat and trying to will away another unwelcomed hard on, he gave her a soft peck on the lips. "You ready to eat?"

"Absolutely."

"Just let me set the table first."

"Ok, I'll help."

"No, I got this. You just go over there and have a seat on the couch."

"Well all right. I think I can get used to this."

Brandy sat back down on the sofa and watched, gushing as he spread out a white linen cloth over the small square table and set it with real plates and real silverware. Real water goblets. He lit two votive candles in the center of the table and dimmed the lights.

He pulled out her chair and held out his hand. "My lady." When she was seated he laid a napkin across her lap.

She was quite impressed.

After they were seated, he took her hands in his and prayed over the meal. Just like he used to. Then they ate and talked about life. Just like they used to. Only now there was so much more to talk about.

During the course of the meal, Tay asked all of the things he'd wondered about. Where she'd been. What she'd done. Who she'd loved. What'd happened in her life to give her the calm beautiful spirit that illuminated the room when she walked in.

After hearing her stories of grand parties in Paris, skiing the Swiss Alps and backpacking across Spain with her college roomies, he could easily see where the newfound wisdom and maturity had come. She was stunningly beautiful, inside and out. But there was also a depth to her, one that he hadn't yet experienced, despite having dated mostly older women since they parted.

He reached to the center of the table and helped himself to a little more fish. "So who was the last guy you dated?"

Brandy gushed. "Ooh...Ambrogio."

"Am *what*?"

She laughed. "Don't be like that. His name is Ambrogio. I met him when I was in Milan. We dated for a few months but I broke it off."

"Why?"

"Well...I was coming back to the states...and he couldn't...and I didn't really want to do the long distance thing."

"Hmm. How'd he take it?"

"Really hard. And I felt bad. So I didn't talk to him after I left. I really didn't see the point. It just made things easier."

"So, you're just breaking hearts, huh?"

She laughed. "No. It wasn't like that."

"Um hmm. Who else?"

"You sure you wanna hear about this?"

"Yeah, I'm asking."

"OK, well...before him there was Stephen. He was an exchange student from Nice and Eduardo. He was from Columbia. He looked kinda like that guy from the Desperado movies. Antoniooo..."

"Banderas."

"Yeah Banderas. We dated the longest. Like...six months or so."

"And what happened to him?"

"Too clingy. And possessive. The Spanish guys are *always* like that."

"Is that right."

"Yes! Seriously. It's really bad. So Julio..."

"I thought you said Eduardo."

"Eduardo was Columbian. Julio was Puerto Rican. But he

looked more Caucasian if you ask me. They tend to have more Caucasian features than other Hispanics."

"They?"

"Puerto Ricans. They tend to have lighter skin, thinner noses. Stuff like that. But this guy. Oh my God. The calling, the texting, the showing up at my door unannounced. It was really crazy. My roommates used to screen for me all the time. Oh, oh, but the funniest experience was with Tai. Chinese guy in my human studies class. "

"A Chinese guy named Ty?"

"Yes, spelled T.A.I. not like Tyrone. This guy is really smart. Like build you a freakin computer from scratch smart. But he was so goofy. I actually liked him a lot. But not like *that*. He's just really cool. We still hang out sometimes."

Brandy picked at her plate as she went on and on, regaling dating stories at home and abroad. She looked up and noticed the uneasy look on Tay's face.

"What's wrong?"

"What?"

"With your face?"

"Nothing's wrong with my face."

"Well you look like you have something to say."

"Nah, I don't."

"Yes, you do. Just say it."

He paused for a second. Searching for his words. "You just a regular United Nations of love ain't you."

Brandy frowned. "Ex-*cuse* me?"

"Never mind."

"No, not never mind. It sounds like you just called me an international hoe."

"You know I would never call you that."

"Then what's your problem?"

"I mean…it's not really a problem. But you just sat here and rattled off a pretty long list of dudes. Black man, white man, Chinese man. It ain't been that damn long since we broke up Brandy."

"First of all, I said *dated*, not slept with. Dated does not necessarily mean sexed."

"Necessarily?"

She shook her head at him. "Um mm. Don't judge me."

"No judgment."

She snatched her napkin from her lap and threw it on the table. "You know what? I think I'm just gonna go to my uncles…"

He grabbed her hand. "No. No I'm sorry. Brandy. Don't go. Please. Let's just change the subject? Ok?"

"No, how about we *not* change the subject. You just sat here and rattled off your list of dried up old–"

"Mature–"

"D-RIED UP OLD ladies and young thots. And I bet you slept with every single one of them. Right? Including Ke-isha. Remember her? Your baby mama?"

"Brandy…"

"Don't say my name."

"I'm sorry. Just…please sit back down."

He stood to get her chair and she waved him off. She sat back down and replaced her napkin in her lap. "I swear, I get so sick and tired of this double standard bull from guys. A girl sleeps with a couple of guys in a couple of years, and automatically she's a ho. But ya'll can triple that list, sleep with the whole hood. With best friends and cousins, mamas and daughters, and you a playa." She sucked her teeth. "Please."

"Ok, you're right. You're right and I'm sorry. I didn't mean to offend you."

She rolled her eyes. "Well, you did."

"And I am so-rry. Ok? I'm sorry babe. But you have to understand…"

"Understand what?! That you–"

"I am a man! A man that loves you. Do you think it's easy for me to sit here and listen to you talk about being with ten different men?"

"Who says that I–"

"Brandy, please stop interrupting. Let me finish. It's not just the sex. Whether you slept with some or with none of them.

That's not the point."

Brandy pursed her lips. "It's not?"

"No. It's not. You just don't get it."

"Tay…"

"I love you, Brandy. You are the only woman I have ever loved. Period. I messed it up. I own that. And I've had to live with that for years now. Missing you every day. Every single day for so long. Not knowing where you were…or how you were. That shit killed me. I asked around and looked around. But nobody would give me any answers. Eventually I had to let it go. Loving TJ is the only thing that kept me going. The one good thing that came out of that madness. And now you're back here. In my home. In my space. You see the smile on my face right now? This is what happy looks like. So when you sit here and you start talking to me about one guy after another guy after another guy…sharing pieces of you that I've never known. And *I'm* the one who loves you."

She teased. "Well how do you know they didn't love me?"

"Because they couldn't. They couldn't even know you. Not like I do. Not in two or three months." He threw his napkin on the table. "Come on now."

She sensed his aggravation. "It was a joke. Tay. How about we just stop with the talking about the exes?"

Disappointed with her nonresponse to his profession of love, he dryly answered, "Fine."

They finished the meal in near silence, which only caused tension to build as their minds raced. All of the unanswered questions about his relationship with her former bestie Keisha were on the tip of her tongue but she couldn't bring herself to ask them. No way that would end well. So she finished her soul food and kept her thoughts and emotions at bay.

Meanwhile Tay was tempering a mild aggravation about her list. *Chinese?* Despite his insistence that sex wasn't the issue, he couldn't help wondering just how *experienced* she really was.

When the silence reached its most uncomfortable point he decided to inject some humor.

"Hey, you wanna hear sumthin funny?"

"Huh?"

"Something funny. You wanna hear it?"

"Uh, yeah. Why not."

"Ok. What do you call an Asian in a drive by?

"What?"

"Cap a chino."

Brandy smiled and shook her head. "No."

"Ok, then. What do you call a Chinese secretary?"

"What?"

"Tai Ping."

She laughed. "That is so corny. Just stop it."

"Ok, one more. One more. But don't get mad at me."

"I don't wanna hear it."

"No, for real. Just one more. I promise."

She smiled. "Go ahead Tay."

"What did the Chinese couple name their retarded baby."

"Oh my God. Tay don't..."

"Sum Ting Wong."

She threw her napkin at his face and laughed. "That was SO not funny."

"But you laughed."

"Seriously. Don't make fun of Asian people. It's just...*Wong*."

Gone Too Far

Aunt Pat and Rocky rushed out of the hospital and over to Imelda's. Peta sent for them. When they pulled up the restaurant was dark. In the middle of the day. The front door was locked with a closed for business sign hanging from the top lock. They walked around to the back. Peta let them in. She was not smiling this time. She led them quietly to the store room where Imelda sat with three very large Columbian men and several high powered automatic weapons lying on the table in front of her.

Rocky salivated at the sight of an HK MG4 machine gun sitting on its bipod. "Daaammmm! Imelda is that a HK?"

Imelda didn't answer her right away. "Hey, guys, can you give us a minute?"

The men walked out of the room and Peta close the door behind them. Rocky picked the gun up, folded the bipod back and aimed it at the wall. "This a bad muuufucka right here. ConTINuous rounds! It ain't even heavy. A bitch could do some damage with this."

Imelda picked up the ammunition belt and handed it off. She proceeded loading bullets into a magazine. "You know that old man you all killed?"

Rocky snapped. "Who killed? *We* ain't kill shit! Peta did that!"

"Ok well, the old man that *was* killed. That was Gi's grandfather."

The room was quiet a moment. Rocky's face was tight. She stared directly at Peta who was staring at the floor.

Aunt Pat shifted in her chair. Impatient. "We know that Imelda. So what now?"

Imelda snapped a magazine into her handgun and pulled

back the slide to chamber a round. "Gi has to go."

"That ain't no mufuckin revelation Imelda. He was already goin."

"Well he has to go *now*. Right now. Before one of us goes first. Clearly he knows who you are. He may know we're involved now. So it's gotta happen. Immediately. Before he can mobilize. He'll find your families. Here in New York. Back in DC. He knows my family. Many people will die for this."

Rocky shouted. "This some bullshit! Fuckin Peta shoot a got damn elderly man in the neck, and now we all gotta die?"

Peta shrugged and exclaimed in her heavy Columbian accent, "I was just only trying to help you out."

"Bullshit! You walked around stabbing people with that dumb ass crossbow like you in the fuckin hunger games! Dumb ass bitch! I got kids!"

Rocky leaped over the table toward Peta but she moved out of the way too quickly, raised her right hand and slapped Rocky hard across the face sending her down hard to the floor. Then she leapt to the other side of the table. "You move very slow Rocky."

"Peta!" Imelda yelled. "DEJALO!"

Rocky picked herself up from the floor and lunged at her again.

Aunt Pat snapped. "Rocky! Leave her alone! We ain't got time for this shit!"

*****

Imelda insisted that everyone stay at her house under heavy guard until they could devise a plan to eliminate the problem. Her guys loaded their trucks with the weaponry hidden beneath the floor boards in the store room. Then they locked the restaurant down and set off for North Jersey.

Aunt Pat and Rocky followed Imelda in their car. Rocky sat silently in the passenger seat with a twitch in her eye and her right leg shaking so fiercely that Aunt Pat could feel the car moving when they stopped at a traffic light. "You aight Rock?"

"Fuck no I ain't aight."

"Look this dumb shit between you and Peta got to stop. Y'all need to fight, or fuck or do something to dead this shit cause you need to get your mind right."

"I woulda deaded it but you stopped me from puttin my hands on her."

"No *she* stopped you from puttin your hands on her." Aunt Pat chuckled. "She was right. You too slow. Rocky I keep tellin you, you ain't as spry as you used to be. That little girl is fast and strong and quick on her toes. You keep it up and she gon whoop your old lanky ass."

"Stop playin wit me Pat."

"I ain't playin. Your best bet is to just squash this shit so we can go'on handle our business and get the fuck back home."

"Squash...Pat I got thirty-two stitches in my arm right now cause this bitch accidentally on purpose hit me wit that goddam dumb ass crossbow. And you want me to apologize."

"I didn't *say* apologize. I said squash. At least until we do what we gotta do. Come on now this stupid shit got you distracted. You gon get yourself killed. Or worse. *Me.*"

Rocky managed a giggle. "Yeah and we wouldn't want that now would we."

"No, so get it together. Y'all can fight when this shit is over with."

"How long you think we gon be here?"

"No tellin. Imelda likes to do all this elaborate schemin and plottin and plannin. I ain't tryna be up here too long, but you know. She know the land better than I do, and she got all the resources so...I guess we rollin with her."

"I just wanna get my hands on that HK."

"I'll bet you do. Just keep your hands off Peta. For me. Aight?"

"Yeah, well you just keep her ass away from me."

"Rocky."

"Aaight. I ain't gon touch that girl."

Aunt Pat twisted her lip. "Yeah aight." She looked around. "We shoulda been to Jersey by now. Where the hell she takin us?"

Candy Strippers

Sitting in the far corner of the hospital room Missy noticed Chucky staring slyly out into the hall. He turned away when he noticed her noticing him. Seconds later, a bodacious, buxom blonde bombshell, with more body than either of them had ever seen on a white woman walked in. She smiled cheerily. "Good afternoon, Mr. Wilson, my name is Sarah, and I'll be your nurse for this evening."

"Hey Sarah."

She moved over to is bed and sat at the edge, flipped her hair and smiled. "You now I am a huge fan of your work. You are so *awesome*! I've been watching you since you were on Comic Watch."

Chucky gushed, "Really? That was a while back."

"Yes, I know. I've been following your career. That last comedy special you did on BET…"

Missy snatched the curtain back making herself visible. "Oh, you watch BET?"

Sarah turned around, startled. "Uh…yes I do actually." She moved away from the bed. "I'm sorry and you are?"

Missy shifted Misa to her right shoulder so she could extend her hand, and annunciate. "His fi-a-ncé. Melissa. And this is our daughter, Misa."

Chucky looked over at Missy, his brow slightly raised, but his mouth firmly shut.

Sarah smiled. "Pleasure to meet you Melissa."

Missy sneered. "Yes, I'm sure."

Chucky interrupted the catty exchange. "So Sarah, when you think they gon let me up out this piece?"

Sarah giggled a little too loudly. Effectively pissing Missy off. Then she picked up Chucky's chart from the end of his bed and thumbed through it. "It looks like you can go home today, actually. The doctor hasn't been in yet?"

Missy spoke for her fi-an-cé. "No, actually he hasn't."

"Ok well it says here that the bullet was removed successfully. All of your scans were fine. Looks like you just need to get your prescriptions and you can be discharged."

Missy squealed. "*Awesome!*"

Sarah scowled at the obvious mocking. "Yes, it is." She turned back to Chucky. "I'll go see if the doctor is on the floor. I'll be back shortly Mr. Wilson."

As soon as she stepped out of the door, Chucky pursed his lips and shook his head at Missy. "You petty."

Missy looked at him, astonished, "Me? Petty?"

"Pet-ty."

"No, I'm not. I just know a THOT when I see one."

He laughed. "Why she gotta be a THOT."

"Don't play with me. If I hadn't pulled this curtain back she would still be sittin there grinning at you and pointin her big ass, hard ass nipples in your face."

"You saw that shit too?! I was wondering if it was just me. It ain't even chilly in here. Them joints was like comin at me through her shirt."

"Umm hmm. THOT."

"Ooh *Missy James*…ion think I ever seen you jealous."

"I'm not."

"Then what you call it?"

"Alert. I saw you staring at her ass too. Don't think I didn't see that."

"No I wasn't. And that lady ain't thinkin bout me. She just doin her job. Stop trippin."

"Whatever Chucky."

Sarah walked back in the room. Chucky took care to divert his eyes everywhere but the nurse's nipplage. "Here you are, Mr. Wilson. Your prescriptions. Your discharge papers. All you have to do is sign where marked and unless you have more questions for the doctor, you're free to go."

Chucky responded, with his eyes directly on his fiancé. "No I think I'm good. Thank you Sarah."

"All right then." She looked over at Missy and smiled. "It was a pleasure meeting you both. Good luck Mr. Wilson."

Sarah walked out of the room, as PJ walked in. "Ew. She need to turn down her damn high beams. You see her nipples?"

Missy rolled her eyes. "We saw them."

"Chile. I wonder if them thangs real. Anyway, so what the doctor say?"

Chucky threw his good arm in the air. "They said I can go shawty. Got my discharge papers. We can be out."

"Good. And if y'all don't mind, I'm tryna hit the highway right now so we can get back to DC. I'm definitely not tryna stay with no cousins out in *Queens*. Cousin's I don't even know. No thank you."

"That's cool with me. I'd rather be in my bed tonight anyway. You ok with that Missy?"

She shrugged. "I guess. But, maybe we should call Aunt Pat first."

PJ agreed. "Yeah, I'll call her from the car."

*****

PJ pushed the charger into the port. "Does anybody have a charger? For some reason mine ain't workin."

"It was working on the way up?"

He snarled. "Yes Missy it was. But it ain't workin now. Chucky, you got your charger on you?"

"Nah, ion even have a phone."

Missy turned to the back seat. "What happened to your phone?"

"I can't tell you."

"What? Why?"

"Ms. Pat said not to tell *nobody* about what went down. So I can't tell y'all."

Missy smiled. "You wanna tell us don't you?"

Chucky yelled. "Like shit!"

They all burst out laughing.

PJ's phone chimed and illuminated. He shouted. "Ooh! I think it's chargin." He picked it up and it went dark again. "Never mind. Ugh! I HATE these damn smartphones. They cost an arm and a leg and the accessories don't last but a month before you gotta spend another $30 on another charger just to get the shit workin again. It's a conspiracy if you ask me."

Chucky joked. "Whatever big money. You got it."

"Well I don't wanna keep spendin it on no damn phone chargers. And speaking of *having it*...I didn't know you lived in Georgetown. Missy told me your grandfather left you that house?"

"Yeah about six years ago when he passed."

"That's wassup. How'd the rest of the family feel about it?"

"Oh you know them niggas was mad. Kept tellin me it wasn't fair and I should sell it and break the money down and all that bullshit. They actually tried to sue me."

"What?"

"Yeah, they tried to say I coerced my grandfather into signing it over. I didn't even know he was leaving it to me. We went to court and everything."

"Well what happened?"

"You see who got the house."

"Hmm."

"That shit fucked the family up for a minute. Nobody was speaking. Everybody was mad. People picking sides. It cost a grip in lawyer fees and court costs. They spent half of the money he left them trying to take the house from me. Dumb shit."

"So y'all ok now."

"Yeah...pretty much. Some of them still talking shit now that they money gone. But you know. They'll get over it. Or not. Whatever.'"

"Ion know. I probably would have sued your ass, too. I know that house is worth a couple mil at least."

Chucky smiled. "Two point six to be exact. But I ain't really countin."

Missy shook her head and snapped. "I don't know why

people think you're automatically rich because you own real estate. Property taxes in DC are ridiculous, so even if you don't have a mortgage there are still things to be paid. The rent that I get barely pays the mortgage on Champlain, now that I've moved in and the place needs work. Trust me, things are not always as they seem."

Chucky nodded. "True but after you pack that ass up and come live wit ya boy, we gon fix all lat. We bout to be ballin baby!"

PJ danced in his seat. "Oh that's right! That's right! So when's the wedding y'all?! You know I gotta get my schedule together."

Chucky beamed. "Ion know. Missy might wanna drop that load first so she can fit into that weddin gown. What we got now, six-months baby?"

PJ shrieked. "Uh! Uh! Bitch you pregnant?!"

Missy glared at Chucky and yelled. "Really Chucky!"

He shrugged.

PJ pursed his lips. "Bitch, we was in this car for five hours and you ain't tell me you was pregnant." He sucked his teeth. "A mess. I ain't mad at you though. It's early. How far along?"

Missy tried to think of a clever way to redirect the conversation. She looked up the road. "Oh my God. The Delaware bridge. I really hate going over bridges."

"Since when?" Chucky challenged. "You just asked me if we could go on a helicopter ride over the Grand Canyon, but you scared to ride over a bridge? Girl bye."

"Chucky shut – "

The truck plunged forward and skidded to the right, nearly side swiping another car. PJ screamed. "What the fuck?!" He looked behind him and there was a black van riding his rear bumper. "Who is that?!"

Chucky's eyes bulged. "Oh shit! That look like that nigga from the ferry!"

PJ yelled, "Who?!"

Missy shouted, "What ferry?!"

The engine roared and again the truck was hit hard from

behind. Missy screamed. "Oh my God! Chucky get Misa!

"No! You think it's safe to take her out of her car seat?!"

PJ hollered, "Shut up! Shut up!" The van pulled to the left and sped up to PJ's window. A man yelled out of the passenger window. "Pull the fuckin car over! Now!"

PJ hit the gas and sped up, toward the bridge. He didn't want to enter it, but there were cars on either side, and behind him, so he couldn't stop safely. Not that he wanted to. The van sped up on the side of them, and this time the man held a gun. He pointed it directly at PJ. Before he could get a clean shot, PJ floored it, hitting the car in front of him, causing it to veer off the road and just miss the entrance to the bridge. He could only hope the little old man in the little green Honda was ok. The van moved behind them, sped up, and hit them again from behind.

Misa wailed, "Mommyyyyyy!"

Missy cried, "Chucky, get my baby!"

"No!" He reached over Misa for his duffle bag. "PJ imma need you to drive this muthafucka!"

PJ screamed. "What the fuck you think I'm doin?!"

"No I mean get out in front of em. That's a cargo van. It can't keep up with this Range Rover. I need you to get like a car length in from of em, at least. Maybe two."

"For what!"

"Just do it!"

PJ sped up and around a taxi that was just ahead of him, leaving the van a couple car lengths behind. The van swung over to the right to pass the taxi. Chucky pulled the grappling hook from his bag and fastened it to the end of a long linked chain. "PJ drive!"

PJ hit the gas again, passing another car on his right as the van sped up and around two cars trying to catch up. Shots rang out, shattering the rear window of the SUV. Everyone ducked down. Missy screamed, Misa screamed, Chucky hollered "Motherfucker!"

The van was gaining. A little more than a car length behind on their left. Chucky hurled the grappling hook out of the window, as far across the two lanes toward the median as he could get it. When the driver of the van noticed the spikes it was too late. The front tires exploded, and the van skidded out of control. It crossed the median, nearly hitting a semi head on. The driver swerved as hard and as far back over to the right as he could, and he'd almost made it but the semi caught his tail, spinning the van around. It hit another car and tumbled five times before it flipped over the side railing and into the murky depths of the Delaware River.

Missy screamed in horror. "Ohh!!! Oh God! Stop! PJ stop the car!"

PJ's SUV made sparks as it grazed the sides of the toll booth and bounced over the speed bump at the end of the bridge. "What?! FUCK no!"

Best Laid Plan

When they passed the second exit for the Jersey turnpike, Aunt Pat dialed Imelda's cell. "Hey. Imelda. Where we headed?"

"My house."

"I thought you lived in Jersey?"

"I do."

"Then why—"

"Just stay behind us." She hung up.

Imelda's driver and sometime companion, Raul, took an exit off of the interstate and followed a narrow pathway through a wooded area. Aunt Pat wasn't sure her pint-sized rented SUV would make it through as it bounced up and down over large branches and through divots in the soft ground. Imelda's Humvee and the Suburban that followed had little trouble navigating the rough terrain while Rocky had a tough time just holding on to the dash.

She yelled as her head hit the window, "Damn! Where the fuck is she takin us!"

Aunt Pat had to speed up to keep up. "Just hold on, Rocky."

The convoy was really moving. The path lead them down a hill then below an underpass.

Rocky cried, "Hold up. I know they ain't bout to go through that water."

The Humvee forged ahead, plowing through a stretch of shallow swamp water to get to the other side of a ravine, back onto dry land. The trucks stopped abruptly. Aunt Pat screeched to a halt behind them, just missing the bumper on the Suburban as she veered a little to the right of it. "The fuck they doin now?"

Raul stepped out of the car and climbed on top of the hood. He stood looking through a pair of high powered binoculars for a moment then hopped back down and stuck his head back in his car window. Seconds later he raised a fist. Imelda and every one of her men hopped out of their cars and started pulling weapons from their trunks and pulling on their body armor. Aunt Pat and Rocky followed suit.

Imelda walked back to their truck.

Aunt Pat peeped her serious expression. "So what's happenin?"

"Giovanni and his men are already at the house waiting."

"Oh, for real?" Rocky raised her gun and smiled. "Aaight let's do it."

"No. The men will go ahead."

"What? Why?!"

"Because, the men will go ahead. Patricia are you all right?"

"Yeah I'm fine."

"You don't seem well. You look tired. We can—"

"Imelda, I'm good. Let's do it."

Rocky smiled. "You heard her. Let's do it."

Imelda shot her a fierce glare. "We will do it, when I say we do it, *Racquel.*"

Peta snickered.

Rocky huffed.

The men stood wait patiently.

Imelda rounded everyone up for one last word. They huddled. She spoke with a stern expression on her face. "...este es nuestro mejor y sólo tiro para conseguir este tipo. Se inteligente. Ten cuidado. Ser perfecto. Y no destruir *mi casa.*"

Aunt Pat rolled her eyes. "Imelda. *English?*"

Imelda chuckled. "I said, try not to fuck up my house."

****

Armed with a variable arsenal of high powered assault rifles, among other highly illegal weaponry and explosives, Aunt Pat, Rocky, Peta, Raul, Imelda and five of Imelda's men scaled a short hill into a wooded area behind Imelda's house.

There were at least ten of Gi's men milling about on the

outside. No telling how many more were inside the house but there were four trucks tucked away near the high shrubbery on the side of the house – a side that would render them undetectable to those who entered the estate through the front gates. They were, however, easily detectable from the wooded area behind the house.

Quietly, Imelda led them through the woods to a spot nearer the front of the house. A spot dense with trees.

Peta and Marco, another wiry, member of the crew, scaled an oak and perched themselves upon a limb sufficient to support their weight and their weapons. The rest positioned themselves with a sightline of at least one target and beside trees thick enough to provide good cover from return fire.

They stood still and silent, waiting for a signal. After a while, Peta's leg began to go numb. Aunt Pat's gun was getting heavier by the minute, but Rocky was most excitable, as she'd finally gotten her hands on Imelda's HK. Her trigger finger burned.

Imelda held her posture, stiff as a statue, barely blinking as she kept her site squarely on the front door. Gi was surely inside, and she knew if she could take him first the rest would be easy.

The front door opened. Rob stood in the doorway, looking out into the courtyard. She knew Gi wasn't far behind. She raised her hand high and everyone hit the safety's on their weapons. Rob stepped down onto the porch. Gi stepped into the doorway. He stood for a moment, and then walked out into the sun. Imelda dropped her hand down to her side.

One by one, the bodies began to fall.

The Chase

About fifty miles from the scene of the accident, PJ took an exit off the highway. They were running low on gas, and Misa had to "pee-pee." Missy was still crying. Chucky was shaken up from having sent someone spiraling to certain death, but he tried to rationalize it. In his head and out loud, he argued, *Those muthafuckas tried to kill me. Not once but twice. Now they puttin my family in harm's way? They deserved that shit. Fuck em.*

Missy didn't want to hear anything anybody had to say. She just wanted to get back home. Somewhere safe.

PJ was surprisingly calm. He unbuckled himself. "Y'all need anything from inside the store?"

Nobody spoke. PJ's phone rang. He picked up the call.

Aunt Pat screamed into the receiver. "PJ! Boy, why you not answering your goddamn phone?!"

"Ma! Something was wrong with my charger. My phone just charged up."

"Where y'all at?"

"We on the road. On the way back home."

"What happened to going to QUEENS?!"

"Everybody just wanted to go home."

"But what did I say? I'm gettin tired of y'all with this shit. Don't nobody listen and when—"

"Ma!"

"What?"

"Somethin happened."

PJ walked away from the car. Away from Misa who'd just calmed down enough to eat her popsicle. He gave Aunt Pat the run down. She cursed.

"Damn! Ok, Where y'all at right now? Exactly."

"We at a gas station off I-95. Bout fifty miles from DC."

"Ok, we bout to get on the road now. Just keep movin. Call me when you get there."

"Aight."

"PJ!"

"Ok!"

"AS SOON as you get there!"

"Ma ok!"

PJ buckled himself back in. Chucky popped the lid on a can of beer. The only thing alcoholic in the little general store. Missy climbed in the back and fiddled with Misa's car seat. "So, what did Aunt Pat say?"

"She said for us to keep movin cause Gi might be right behind us."

"So you didn't tell her Gi was in the river?"

"No, cause he ain't. He wasn't in that van. She said he's in a black Suburban with two other men, probably on the way to DC. So she said we can't go home."

Chucky gulped the beer. "Then where we goin?"

"To Ahmed's, in Accokeek."

Missy replied. "I thought you weren't talking to him?"

"I wasn't. But I am today."

"You don't have to. I have someplace for us to go."

Ready or Not

Tay's eyes rolled to the very back of his head as Brandy set out to show him just how much she'd grown up. After much protest, he allowed her to unbuckle him, pull his pants to his ankles and fall, submissively to her knees. He'd attempted to pull her back up. "Babe...no you don't have to do that."

She pushed his hands away and shoved him down on the sofa. "Tay. Stop it. I want to."

The first minute or so was awkward. He could barely look at her. She'd never really seen his manhood, never really touched it full on, and there she was on her knees bringing it to the very back of her throat, swallowing it whole, stroking it with her full lips, and teasing it with the tip of her tongue. He was afraid to relax. Too afraid he'd lose it.

She could feel that he was tense and she wanted him to relax. So she stopped for a moment. Rubbed and kissed his thighs. "Baby. Relax."

That only made him more tense. "Wait...Brandy.... baby."

"Tay...relaxxxx." She parted his leg with a gentle nudge at his inner thighs and delved down further filling her mouth at the bottom and placing both hands on top. As she stroked and licked and sucked using the tension of her lips and the palms of her hands at random, Tay was barely able to keep still. His eyes closed tightly. She looked up at him and grinned. "Look at me."

"Huh?" He moaned. "Ummmm."

"Open your eyes and look at me."

He opened one eye.

"No. Open your eyes Tay. Look. At. Me."

He opened both eyes and looked down at his girl. With her lips stained rouge, dripping with her wetness. She penetrated him with her stare, as she reached down and cupped him with one hand, reached up and gently gripped him with the other, stroking and massaging the wetness over him. His manhood pulsated strong between her fingers. She could tell he was nearing climax, so she intensified the movements of her wrist and the tips of her fingers to bring him all the way home. He moaned loudly and turned to look away. "Oh God, baby. Baby!"

She commanded. "No...look at me."

"I'm about to cum! I'm bout to cum!" He looked down at her. "Baby! I'm—"

She took him in her mouth and allowed him to release in its warmth. He squealed with delight. Brandy smirked satisfaction at a job well done, then they both jumped at the loud rapping on the window. They looked up.

"Yeah, take the dick out ya mouf, *bitch*! And open da muthafuckin door."

*****

Brandy ran to the bathroom while Tay stepped into the hall to quietly call the police. Keisha banged again. "Open tha door!" After he hung up the phone, he opened the door and invited her in. He planned to make sure she stayed there until the police came.

She walked inside. Looking far worse than Tay had ever seen her and smelling of musk and spice...or something. She yelled at Brandy through the bathroom door. "Yeah that's right. Go'on spit that shit out. Witcho nasty ass."

Tay stood at the window practically willing the police to come. Keisha was very obviously high, and she smelled. "Keisha what are you doing here? Where is Brandy's car and her purse?"

"That raggedy ass car outside. I think it might need a starter or somethin."

"What? Where's her purse?"

"I didn't touch her purse. It's in the car."

He asked, rhetorically, "If you didn't touch it then how did it get from the kitchen counter to the car?"

Brandy walked out of the bathroom. "Where's my purse?"

"Like I just told *him*, your raggedy ass car is outside, and I ain't touch yo purse. It's out there. Go get it."

Brandy shot her an icy glare. It was all she could do not to snatch her. But she didn't even want to touch her filthy ass. "Why? Why would you do this?"

"Do what? Borrow your car? Girl bye."

"What have I done to you?"

"Look, I ain't even come here for all at. I just came here to get my money."

"What?"

"The fifty dollaz Tay s'posed to give me for my medicine."

Tay frowned. "What are you *talking* about?"

"Money for my meds? Remember?"

"What meds!"

"Can I just get my money? Please! If you give it to me, I'll leave."

Tay snarled at her and walked back over to the window. The police were taking way too long. They needed to hurry up and get Keisha's ass outta there so he could finish his night. He hoped she hadn't fucked it up for him.

Keisha walked in circles around Brandy. Looking her up and down. "So, I guess you think you won."

"Excuse me?"

"You think you won. I'm outside lookin in. Yah in here all laid up. *Makin love* and shit. Where my son at? What yah put him out? So yah could fuck? Turble."

Brandy huffed and shook her head. "Girrrlllll."

"Girl what? Where yo baby at?"

For a moment, Brandy wondered if she *knew*. But she couldn't. No one knew.

Keisha looked her up and down. "You up in here playin mommy and shit. Where your muufuckin baby at?"

"Tay...you better get her," Brandy warned.

Keisha smirked. "Tay ain't gotta get shit ova here."

Tay yelled, "Keisha! What did you come here for?"

"I already told you." She held out her hand and slapped her

palm repeatedly. "Fiddy. Fiddy I need fiddy dollas. How many times I gotta say it."

Just then two police cars pulled in front of the house. Blue lights flashed brightly through the window.

"Oh...uh uh...no yah didn't." She looked at Brandy. "Bitch, you called the police on me?"

Brandy pursed her lips and didn't get a full roll of her eye before Keisha connected one. The white light from the sucker punch stunned her for a split second, but she recovered quickly enough. She swung hard from behind her back, hitting Keisha in the side of her head with a powerful closed fist. Keisha stumbled but not before Brandy grabbed a handful of her loose ponytail and landed two more blows.

Keisha, already high, was completely disoriented, but she still pawed away as Brandy connected a couple more to her face and to Tay's arm. He was in the way.

The police banged hard on the door. Tay was torn between breaking up the fight and opening the door to let them in. He dashed over to the door, snatched it open, and ran back over to catch Brandy in mid swing.

As soon as Keisha saw the police she screamed bloody murder. "Owww. You're hurting me! Please stop hitting me! Somebody make her stop hitting me!"

The female officer grabbed Brandy and pulled out her cuffs.

Tay yelled, "Wait a minute. Not *her*. She's not the one that started it."

The officer shrugged. "All we saw was *her* throwing punches. So we gotta take her in. Step back, sir."

The other officer helped Keisha to her feet "Ma'am, do you want to press charges?"

"You got damn muthafuckin right I wanna press charges. Lock that bitch up! Ole dick suckin ass ho. You know I caught her in here suckin his dick?"

The officer raised her brow, tried not to laugh. "Ma'am—"

"This bitch came up in my house with *my* muthafuckin man and..."

"Your what!" Tay yelled.

"That's right. I said it. You my man. You gon always be my muthafuckin man cause we got babies."

Tay raised his hands. "Ok, wait. Wait wait. Just listen."

About a half hour later, the stories were told, and the air was cleared. Both ladies agreed not to press charges against the other and to go their respective ways. They checked the car for Brandy's purse. Since everything was intact the car theft was summarily forgotten. Keisha was warned to heed the restraining order. She left the scene walking fast. But still talking shit.

The neighborhood weed man Calvin sat on his car across the street with his entourage. He yelled over. "Tay. Aye. Tay! You good?!"

Tay hollered back, "Yeah I'm good man."

"Aight."

And so, everything was good. The police drove away. Tay led Brandy back inside and locked the door, leaving the noise, and the confusion and Keisha on the outside.

He started, "Babe…I don't even know what to say. I'm so sorry about all this. Keisha is just gone. Gone. I don't know what to do about her."

Brandy plopped down on the sofa, leaned back and closed her eyes. She rubbed the top of her right hand. Tay quickly went to the freezer to grab something cold. He kissed her hand gently and placed the bag of frozen peas on top, to soothe her. When she opened her eyes and looked at him he was looking intently at her. His face washed with worry and regret. Then she burst into a fit of laugher. "What. Was. That?"

Taking her queue, he joined in the laughter. "I don't *even* know. But you beat that ass, though."

"Oh yeah I beat that ass."

"You feel better?"

"Not really. But she shouldn'ta put her hands on me."

"Yeah. I ain't think she would do that. I'm sorry about your shirt."

Brandy looked down at it. Keisha had all but torn the expensive designer tee off her body. The cleavage bearing slits that were so meticulously cut by Versace were now gaping holes that completely bared her lacy satin bra. "It's ok."

"I'll buy you another one. How much was it?"

"You don't even wanna know. But don't worry about it."

"Well...can I get you a T-shirt or somethin? Cover you up?"

She looked him in the eye and smiled, coyly. "No."

Mama Linda

PJ rolled onto the cobblestone driveway of a very substantial Georgian style home on a quiet street in Bethesda, Maryland.

"Who's place is this, Missy?"

"My stepmother Linda's."

Chucky barked. "Damn! Stepmom's ballin'!"

Before Missy could knock, Linda flung open the front door looking like a modern day Alexis Carrington in a floor-sweeping silk robe and kitten-heeled slippers. The robe was half open revealing her exquisite lace undergarments. She quickly tied it closed.

"Melissa, darling it's so good to see you. What brings you here? During the middle of the day..." She smiled nervously. "unannounced."

"I know Linda, and I'm so sorry about this. I'm having some issues at my place right now and I...we need to stay here a couple days if that's ok. Just a couple days. At the most."

"Yes, yes of course. Come in. Everyone come in. Is everything all right? Anything I can help with?"

"No, everything's fine. I was entertaining my houseguests for the week and the electricity shut down on us."

"Oh no!"

"Yes, the entire house. My electrician says it'll be a couple days before everything's restored. We were actually going to get a suite at the Plaza but..."

"Oh, nonsense." Linda shushed. "This is your home."

"Thanks Linda."

"Can I get you something to eat? Is anyone hungry?"

They all declined. Linda protested. "Nonsense. Esther's gone for the day, but I'll whip up something. She bent down in front of Misa. "And who do we have here?"

Missy smiled. "This is my daughter, Misa."

"Your daughter?" Linda put her hand over her mouth. Her eyes welled. "Ohhh. Missy she's gorgeous. Can I?"

"Sure."

Linda picked Misa up and hugged her tight.

"And Linda, this is my cousin PJ and my fiancé, Charles."

Chucky glared at Missy before extending his hand. "Pleasure to meet you. Everyone calls me Chucky by the way."

Linda smiled wide. "Likewise." She turned to Missy. "Fiancé. Hmm. I see we have a lot to catch up on. But first…" She took Misa by the hand. "…let's see what goodies Nana Linda has in the kitchen."

When she walked off, there was a soft knock at the door. Missy looked at Chucky. "Nobody knows we're here," she said.

Chucky cleared his throat and took his voice down about a level and a half, a strong baritone. "No. I got it. I'm the man, I'll get the door." He walked over slowly and carefully, peeked out of the glass pane. He looked back and whispered, "It's the police."

*****

At the third knock. Missy sprang up from the couch, "This is stupid."

Chucky caught her by the arm. "Wait, what are you doing?"

"I'm opening the door."

"No, wait…I got it." He placed his hand on the nob and stood for a moment.

Missy shouted, "Will you just open it!"

He raised a hand. "Ok, ok."

The officer had a puzzled look on his face. He peeked in and then he pulled a notepad from his shirt pocket. "I'm sorry, I'm looking for a…Linda Chambers?"

"Oh yes, come in," Chucky said, and Missy called for Linda.

The exceptionally well-built officer looked up and around the house. "Nice house." He looked over at PJ, who smiled sheepishly and stared very obviously below the officer's waistline. "Is this a party or somethin? I was under the impression that I was just here for Ms. Chambers."

Now, Missy was puzzled. Linda walked out holding Misa's hand. "Oh my God! Jake." She handed Misa over to Missy, took Jake's hand and ushered him toward the front door. Then she grabbed her purse from the table and walked him outside. While they talked on the porch, PJ stared at them out of the window. "Ummm. He is *tasty,* chile."

Chucky whispered, "Damn. I wonder what's up. You think she in trouble?"

PJ laughed. "Trouble? Chile, you know that wasn't no police. Not with that tight ass uniform. He's driving an unmarked pickup. Ooh look, she goin in her purse. Um hmm. Chile, that's the *help.*"

Chucky frowned. "Help?"

"You ain't too bright is you?"

Missy snapped. "Shut up you two. She's coming back."

Linda walked back inside, smiling nervously. Jake's truck roared off in the distance. "He's a friend."

PJ grinned. "I'll bet he is, Mama Linda. Tasty too. Yessss hunny." He held up his hand.

She giggled and slapped PJ a high five. "Come on in the kitchen. Mama Linda needs a cocktail."

"Um hmm. I'll bet you do." PJ followed close behind her. "So Mama Linda, your friend got a friend?"

Missing in Action

Aunt Pat and Rocky pulled onto the cobblestone driveway of the Chambers estate. Chucky answered the door. Rocky shook her head and smiled as Aunt Pat stepped directly in front of him and gave him a death glare. There was so much she wanted to say to the fool, but it wasn't the time or place. *Later*, she thought. *Definitely later.*

Missy walked up and gave her a warm, tight hug. "Thank you. I really don't even know what to say."

"You ain't gotta say nothin. It's fine. How is she?"

"She's good. Seems normal. We asked her what happened and she said they played lots of games, and she watched TV. She's in the kitchen with Linda."

"Good. We ain't stayin. We just came to check on y'all. Imma need y'all to stay here until I call you and let you know it's ok to leave. Aight?"

"Yeah, of course. We'll be here."

"Where's PJ?"

"He went to get some clothes. He said he'd be right back though."

Aunt Pat stood silently for a second before speaking. "Why didn't you call me?"

"Huh?"

"Why. Didn't. You. Call. Me?"

"I…I'm sorry. I mean…I don't know he said he'd be right back. You know how he is."

Chucky chimed in, "Ms. Pat, I tried to tell him not to go, but he wouldn't listen."

She shot him a don't-say-shit-to-me look and pulled her cell from her jacket pocket. She spoke calmly, though she was seething inside. On the third ring of the second call, PJ picked up.

"This is PJ."

"I'm so sick and tired of you motherfuckers not listening to me. Like I'm talkin just to hear myself talk. I'm tired of this. I'm tired of all a y'all. For real."

"Ma, I just needed some clothes. I'm coming right, right back, I promise."

"GET THE FUCK OUTTA THERE, PJ!"

"OK, OK! I'm leaving right now."

"I mean NOW, boy, and call me soon as you get back here."

"Ok, yes I'll call you. I promise."

"How long you gon be?"

"Like 45 minutes. I'm leaving out the door right now!"

"Bye."

Aunt Pat turned back to Missy and Chucky. She spoke with one finger pointed in their general direction. "Y'all muthafuckas keep thinkin this shit a joke if you want. You think this nigga Gi playin? People gettin shot up, stabbed up, fucked up behind this bullshit, and y'all still actin like you don't get it! I can't keep doin this shit." She felt a lump forming in her throat. So she walked out before the emotions had a chance to surface. "I can't keep DOIN THIS!"

She stormed out of the house, knocking over Linda's vintage porcelain umbrella stand. Chucky closed the door behind her. Once he was out of earshot he turned to Missy and snickered. "She mad or nah?"

*****

PJ hung up the phone and set it back on the dock. He untied his bathrobe and stepped into the luxuriousness of his lavender scented bubble bath thinking, *she worries too much.*

The eerie sound of a creaking bathroom door was drowned by the sweet sounds of Angela Winbush singing of sunrises, sunsets and no regrets. He took a deep breath and immersed himself fully into his bath, sliding underwater, beneath the thick layer of suds.

Underwater he exhaled, releasing the stresses of the day with every air bubble that burst at its surface. Finally, it was quiet. There was peace. And he never heard them coming.

That's The Other Thing

"Babe."

"Huh?"

"All this excitement got me feelin some typa way." Chucky looked down at the hard on that was stretching his sweatpants.

Missy giggled. "No."

"Why no?"

"Because. It's not time for that."

"Why ain't it?!"

"Because! Chucky are you crazy? Do you realize what we've just been through?"

He nodded at his shoulder. "Uhhh…yeah."

"Exactly. Look at your arm. I just got my daughter back." She kissed Misa on the forehead and pulled her blankie up over her shoulders. "Let's just be grateful everyone is home safe. In one piece. Ok?"

Chucky couldn't help thinking, not everyone was home safe. Aunt Pat told him she'd let him know about Ev as soon as she had more information. But the way she was looking at him when he opened that door he wasn't about to ask her any questions. He was probably fine. He had to be fine. It was just a taze. He tried to put it out of his mind. "Please Missy. Just give me five minutes. I'll be quick."

"And that's your selling point?"

"You know what I mean, girl. Just come here a second." He tugged at the belt loop on her jeans.

"Chucky, stop it. My stepmother is right upstairs."

Linda walked downstairs dressed sexily in a red mini dress with a small piece of designer luggage in tow. "Darling, I'm leaving for the night. There's a spare key in the drawer of the credenza if you need to go out, but everything you need is here. Esther will be back in the morning. Don't wait up." She winked in their direction and sauntered out the door.

Chucky smiled wide. "Bye Mama Linda." He turned back to Missy. "Aight, now where were we?" He pulled her close and caught her at her neck. Her spot. Kissing and sucking it with such fervor she had to squeeze her legs together to temper the tingles.

She jumped up from the couch. Away from him. Smiling. "You're gonna wake the baby."

He whispered, "No. I won't. I promise." He walked up behind her and reached into her mane, grabbing a handful of hair and pulling her neck back to his lips. Then he reached under her shirt, expertly undoing the clasp on her bra and sliding one hand underneath. With his tongue on her neck and his thumb and forefinger tweaking her right nipple he walked her slowly into the kitchen and bent her over the table.

Missy was completely immersed in his passion, the warmth of his tongue, his heavy panting. Nothing turned her on more than being devoured by a man that wanted nothing more in a moment than to have her. To be inside her. He flipped her over and pulled her shirt overhead. She looked down at him as he pushed his pants down, then pushed down his underwear to free his hardness. The sight of it when it sprang up sent a surge through her body that caused a release and quickly reminded her that she wasn't in a way for intercourse. In fact, not 24 hours earlier, the emergency room doctor warned against sex for at least a month.

Chucky was way past ready and she hated like hell to disturb his groove, but she had no choice. "Baby."

He pushed her breasts together and put both nipples in his mouth.

She gasped and moaned, silently and unintentionally encouraging him to suck a little harder. "Ooooh. Wait, wait…wait. Baby stop. We gotta talk."

"Ok." He pulled her down to the edge of the table, swiftly unbuttoned her pants and reached inside as he continued to nibble and suck at her right nipple.

"Wait…wait, wait, wait. Ummmmm. Chucky. Stop!"

He lifted his head from her chest. "Whaaat?!"

Ten minutes later, his pants were up, his erection was gone, and his throat burned from trying to hold back his tears. He pulled her close. "Are you ok?"

"No." She broke down. It was the first time she was able to really release since she left the hospital. Chucky tried his best to stay strong for her but he couldn't stop the tears from falling. Not just for her, or the baby he'd lost but for the last few days in general.

He held Missy tightly, until she was calm and seated. Then he pulled a bottle from the wine chiller and popped the cork. He grabbed two glasses from the cabinet and some orange juice from the fridge. Missy waved a hand. "None for me. I'm taking medication for a while."

"Oh, right. You mind if I…"

"No, go ahead. Knock yourself out."

"Yeah, I wish I could knock myself out. I need a King Kong or Long Island or something; I wonder if she got some brown liquor around here."

"There's a bar downstairs."

Chucky went down and walked back upstairs holding a bottle of Remy Martin. He grinned. "Oh yeahhhhh."

"Chucky, don't drink up all her liquor."

"I'm not. I just need to take the edge off, and that champagne ain't gon cut it. Plus, she got like a hundred bottles down there." He dropped a couple of cubes of ice in a rocks glass and poured it half full with champagne, half full with the cognac. He took a sip. "Ooohweee! That right there. That's good."

Missy slid off her stool, walked over and took the glass from his hands.

"What you doin?"

"I'm making it better."

She took a shaker from the cabinet and poured his drink into it. Then she added a little sugar and a splash of lemon juice.

She shook the shaker and strained the liquid into a crystal champagne flute. "Voila."

Chucky took a sip and sucked his tongue. "Umm, that's good girl. What is it?'

"A French 75."

"Where you learn to make that?"

"France."

He laughed. "Yeahhh. I like your French."

"I'll bet you do." She winked.

"I'm serious. I remember the first time you talked that talk to me. In that hotel room. At the W. The night I got that ass back. That fishnet bodysuit. All that baby oil in your ass. Them cherry red lips and that long, sexy black wig. Girrrrlllll...." He grabbed his crotch. "I *slaughtered* the pussy that night."

She laughed hard. "You, sir, are common and crass."

"Yes I'm that. And more. But you love it."

"Yeah I do. *Sometimes.*"

"You a fine muthafucka, Missy James. And you know it, too. You know exactly what to do to turn a nigga on. Turn a nigga OUT!"

"Shh. Please don't wake Misa up."

"I'm not. You know, we haven't talked much about that ring on your finger."

"We never really got a chance to."

"I know, right. I'm glad you wearin it."

"Of course I'm wearing it."

"I'm glad you mine."

She smiled. "Me too."

"You make me very, very happy Missy James." He reached across the table and touched her left hand. "You know it ain't nuttin I wouldn't do for you." He kissed her on the hand. "You know that right?"

"I know."

"You sure we can't...do a lil sumthin?"

"Chucky! I said no. Finish your drink."

He swallowed the last of the glass and she poured him another. The potent mix had him feeling relaxed. Chatty. "So, I don't know if this is allowed…or appropriate right now, but imma ask anyway."

"Go ahead."

"Have you talked to Kevin yet?"

The question caught her off guard. In all of the madness, she'd actually forgotten about the scandal. Her thoughts ran away with her for just a moment. She imagined him dropping something in her drink and then getting on top of her. She took a deep breath. Tears welled in her eyes. "Yeah. Well…that's the other thing…"

F.A.G.

An hour had passed. PJ's phone went straight to voice mail, frustrating her even more. She looked over at Rocky. "Now he ain't answerin his fuckin phone."

"Stop trippin, Pat. He prolly just need to charge his phone or somethin. He aight. You wanna stop and get a drink somewhere?

"Yeah, after I talk to him."

"Come on, you need something to take your mind off this shit. For just a little while. Let's go to the Stadium."

"What? No."

"Why not?"

"Are you crazy? You sittin up here, tryna see some ass and titties and I'm tryna make sure my family safe." She pulled to the side of the road. "I mean…is everybody fuckin crazy around me? Rocky, we don't know even know where Gi is right now. That nigga could be in New York or he could be sittin right in front of my house right now. We don't know what's what and who's where and you wanna see some ass. Obviously I'm the only one that think this shit is serious? Bullets been flyin over your head for two days, your arm in a sling full of staples and you wanna go to the strip club? Seriously?"

"You damn right."

Aunt Pat rolled her eyes. "Pshh."

"Look, life is short Pat. You know dat. Tomorrow ain't promised to nobody. We could go any day any time. Specially with this shit we dealin with right now. Sheeit. What we need is a night off. The kids good. Everybody is accounted for and who's to say Gi even down here. Shit, who's to say that nigga even still alive. Many shots we put through that car? I know somebody got hit."

"Come on Rocky, think. Who you think sent them niggas at PJ on the highway? He's here. And if he ain't here he on his way."

Rocky sighed. "I still don't know how Imelda missed that fuckin shot. We had his ass. Right there. The bitch had sights on him and missed! What the fuck man."

"It happens."

"Shiit. Not to us."

"They ain't us."

Rocky laughed. "You got that right. So what's next?"

"Next we make sure PJ gets to safety. Gi don't know nuttin bout Linda's place. They can lay low there for a couple days. Then we figure out where this nigga at and go do what we gotta do."

"Aight. So we go get PJ, drop his ass off at Linda's and *then* we can take a break. Just a lil break. Hit the pause button. Just for tonight. It's all gon be there tomorrow."

"Rocky..."

"I'm serious, Pat. You know I always ride with you. I'm down a hunnid percent. Always. But I need a second man. For real. Matter fact, I don't wanna hear nuttin else bout no plots, and no plans, no Italian Mafia, none a dat shit. We can go check on PJ and make sure he good, but I'm tellin you now, I ain't firin anuthu muthafuckin bullet til I get me some titties in my face. For real. So you can either drop me off to my car, or bring your bad ass on here and get you a good lap dance before we handle business. Tomorrow, we can go after Gi, hard, but *tonight*..." Rocky turned up the volume on the radio and bobbed her head to the old school go-go."...we gettin it iinnnnnnn."

Aunt Pat laughed, "Aight, aight. You ain't gotta keep sellin it. We can go to the club. *After* I check on PJ."

Rocky danced a little harder. "Now THAT's what I'm talm bout baby!" She cranked the radio a little louder, as the old school go-go mix put her in the right groove. She threw her hands up. "Yeahhhh. I'm bout to call up there right now. Make sure we get us a table at the front. What's that the kids be sayin now? *TURN UP!*"

*****

Aunt Pat pulled into the driveway, where PJ's Range Rover was parked. She looked at Rocky. "See. I knew his ass was still here."

They walked over to his truck. Dings, dents and scratches all over. Bullet holes, shattered glass. The rear bumper hanging on by a thread. Rocky squealed. "Dammmmn. That shit is totaled."

They walked up to the front door. Aunt Pat pulled her keys from her pocket. "Imma surprise his ass."

"Wait, Pat it's open."

They both looked around to make sure no one was watching before they drew their guns and walked slowly inside. The ladies had long since had their signals down. No need for words. Not really. A simple nod of the head or pointing of a finger had preceded many a quiet ambush on an unsuspecting rival.

After clearing the first floor, Aunt Pat nodded toward the basement and pointed up. She scaled the basement stairs while Rocky tiptoed up to the second level.

The basement was quiet and dimly lit by the sunlight that crept in through partially opened mini blinds. She checked the bathroom first and then the bedroom, quietly swinging the doors open and aiming her weapon. Both were clear. So she headed back upstairs.

Rocky reached the top of the stairs. Four rooms, four doors. All closed. The first two bedrooms were empty as was the bathroom. She swung open the double doors to the master bedroom and raised her weapon. Nothing in the sitting room to her right. The walk in closet off to her left. Clear. Ahead of her were two smaller double doors.

She flung open the doors to the master bath, and again raised her weapon high. Her elbows locked with her finger grazing a hair trigger. Straight ahead of her was a vintage claw footed soaking bathtub filled with water, colored crimson. The water was still. Much of it had spilled over the side of the tub and onto the white bath rug. A mound of cascading hair floated at the top. *Shit.* She lowered her gun and leaned against the doorway, afraid to move any closer, afraid to freely see what she knew was there.

Her heart sank, as she heard Aunt Pat climbing the creaky stairs. She could hear her walking down the hall and then into the bedroom. "Aye, Rock." Aunt Pat whispered. Rocky stood frozen, waiting for her best friend to come inside and confront her worst fears. A shiver went down her spine when she felt Pat's breath at her neck. "Aye, downstairs is clear. Did you see…"

Aunt Pat stopped at the doorway. Her view was crystal clear. She gasped before dropping her gun to the floor and running over to the tub to see what Rocky couldn't bring herself to.

PJ lay floating with his eyes wide open and a tiny hole still seeping blood from his frontal lobe. She jumped into the tub and pulled her baby boy up from the bloody bath. She held him tightly in her arms. Several deep breaths and then a scream escaped her lungs. From the diaphragm. From the depths of her wounded soul.

Rocky sobbed. "Pat. Oh God, Pat I'm so sorry. I'm sorry. I'm so sorry." She punched the door, hard, "Fuck!" Then punched it again. "Shit! This shit is fucked up. Fucked UP! This shit is fucked UP! Pat…oh God…Pat."

Aunt Pat sat on the edge of the tub with PJ in her arms. Tears rolled down her cheeks. Her screams were muffled. She just sat and hummed for a while then she kissed him on the head. It was time. "Rock. Rocky. Rocky!" She broke Rocky from her hysteria. Rocky had nearly punched the door off its hinges. "Come on over here. Help me get him to the bed. Please."

Rocky laid her gun down on the sink and wiped the tears. She walked over to them, slowly, still sobbing. She grabbed PJ's lifeless legs as Aunt Pat lifted him from under his arms. They pulled his long thin frame out of the bathtub and both had to gasp for air at the sight of the grotesqueness that Gi left them. With tears streaming steadily Aunt Pat summoned the strength to keep moving as they carried him into the bedroom and laid him on his bed. Rocky hurriedly grabbed the blanket from the foot of the bed and covered him up.

The monsters had removed PJ's pride and joys. Flaps of skin were left hanging where his perfect D cups used to be, a small mound of flesh where his manhood once was. Three letters carved into his torso. F.A.G.

Aunt Pat felt numb. She took a seat on the bed next to him and placed his head in her lap. She stroked his face and hair. Told him that she loved him more than anything. That he was the best thing she'd ever done. The only good thing she'd ever done. She apologized. For everything.

Rocky stood next to her. Unsure of what to do. What to say. What could she? Though there was a burning question on her lips she didn't speak. No need to ask what was next. She already knew. She pulled herself together.

"Hey, Pat. Imma go on downstairs. Make the call."

"No."

"No?"

"No.

Bitch Assness

"On my LIFE! Imma kill his bitch ass," Chucky seethed.

Missy stood silently and let him vent.

"Bitch ass nigga walkin round with muufuckin roofies in his pocket. Can't get no pussy no other way. Needle dick nigga! Imma kill his muufuckin ass. You can believe that shit."

"He's already in jail."

"What the fuck that mean? You think a nigga can't get at him in jail? Sheeit. Now I know where he at and where the fuck he gon be. Killin his muufuckin ass."

Missy sighed. "Chucky. Please."

"Please what? How you calm?"

"What should I be? Jumping up and down in this kitchen won't help the situation. He's already in jail. He'll stand trial. He'll pay for what he did."

"Nah FUCK THAT!" Chucky leapt off his stool and threw it to the ground. He paced the floor. "Killin his muufuckin ass. You hear me? Dead."

Missy pursed her lips and rolled her eyes. "So you spend two days with my aunt and now you're a killer?"

"Don't mock me, girl."

"I'm not mocking you at all. I'm saying Kevin will get what's coming to him. Sooner than later he'll get what's coming."

"How you sound? Sooner or later. Missy, you just lost a child. Because of his bitch ass, you lost a fuckin child. He fuckin violated you! And you just sittin here like…"

Missy jumped up and screamed. "You don't think I know that?! Huh?! You don't think I feel disgusted at the thought of him drugging me and entering my BODY?! You don't think I understand that *life* was taken from me?! I am fucking

BLEEDING right now." She cried. "They put a goddamned vacuum inside my body and sucked a life out of me! So don't fucking TELL ME how to feel!"

He grabbed her and hugged her tight. "Ok. You're right, I'm sorry. Missy I'm sorry. Come here."

They sat on the kitchen floor. Her head in his chest, she sobbed and tears streamed his face. "Baby I'm so sorry this happened to you. I'm so, so sorry. I should have protected you. I shouldn'ta left you alone with his ass."

She sniffled. "No, Chucky, this isn't your fault."

"It's my fault."

"It's not. Please don't say that."

He sighed. "If I could just get my hands on that muufucka. I swear, Just ONE muufuckin time..."

'Well you can't. So just stop this. Please promise me you won't do anything stupid. Kevin is going to jail for a very long time. He didn't just do this to me. There's a line of women that stretches down the block. I'm not the only one. He'll get his. Right now, I just want to focus on us. Focus on our family. Chucky we've been through enough. Haven't we? I just...I just need it to be about us right now."

Chucky kissed her on the forehead. "Ok."

"I'm serious. I just wanna get away. When all this is over I want to get as far away from the DMV as we can possibly get. Just for a little while."

"Ok."

She looked up at him. "Really?"

"Really. If that's what my baby wants....that's what she gets. We can take your little woosah vacation if you want."

"Don't tease me."

"No teasin. We out."

Worth the Wait

Brandy pulled off what was left of her torn T-shirt, peeled away her cutoffs, and stepped out of them. Then she unfastened her bra and dropped it in his lap. Tay's heart pounded as she turned her back to him, exposing her red thong. She peered seductively over her shoulder. "You wanna help me with these?

He swallowed hard. "Yeah."

Her nakedness was unexpected. Her forwardness, intimidating. He reached out and touched a cheek with each hand. Taking a moment to revel in the softness of her skin. Not a dimple or a blemish. Just as he imagined a thousand times, she was perfect. He slipped his fingers under the elastic at the sides of her panties and pulled them down, slowly to the floor. She stepped out of them and turned to face him. The view was just as wonderful from the front.

Brandy pushed him back onto the sofa and climbed on top. She straddled him, and they kissed, slowly, passionately as she gyrated her hips in a slow grinding motion. She pulled his shirt overhead and gently ran her hands over his muscular chest. Her touch sent a wave of intense pleasure through him. He grew harder, grabbed a handful of her ample bottom and began to move in her rhythm. She took his face in her hands and gave him more of her tongue. The bulge in his pants was growing more uncomfortable in his tight boxer briefs, but he didn't want her to stop. She stopped.

"Babe, what's wrong?"

"How about we take this into your bedroom? You got Peeping Toms."

She stood and walked seductively in front of him, toward the bedroom, beckoning him to follow. He waited, for just a moment. To catch the view from behind. And to adjust the part of him that grew through the opening in his shorts.

There was no way to keep his cool when he walked into the room and saw Brandy sprawled across his bed in all her naked glory. He hurriedly undressed down to his socks and crawled over to her. "You sure you want to do this?"

"I am absolutely sure."

He climbed over her and leaned down for a kiss. She stopped him. Just before their lips touched.

"Tay."

"Yeah?"

"I love you too."

Tay kissed her lips with all the passion he'd been holding for only her. He couldn't help but moan when their bodies touched for the first time. The warmth and softness of her skin felt like home. His excitement pressed against her inner thigh.

She squirmed, as his tongue entered her ear, moaned as he kissed and sucked her neck. He propped himself up enough to take a look down at her naked body. Her breasts more perfect than any he'd seen. Her tiny waist accentuated with a thin belly chain attached to a diamond piercing. He whispered, "You, are *sexy*."

He lightly traced her body with the tips of his fingers. From her lips, over her collarbone, down into her cleavage and over her nipples. He pulled one to his lips and gently sucked as he continued to trace her body with his free hand. Over the flatness of her belly and then down into her nether region. She was soft and smooth, except for the small strip of hair just above her opening.

He rubbed her just right. Just enough to hear her wetness and then he slid his third finger inside her, gently penetrating her while massaging her clit with his thumb. She whimpered softly, and her hips began to move again. He kept her rhythm as he moved his hand inside of her, while suckling gently on her right nipple.

When he pulled away from her breast and removed his finger, she quietly protested. He hushed her and slid down to position, his head between her legs. To show her what the D-RIED UP old ladies had taught him. Tay fancied himself a young connoisseur of the cunnilingus. She'd be thanking those old ladies later.

He pulled a blanket over his head and went to work, using both hands, all fingers and the entire lower half of his face from the tip of his nose, to his lips, to the whole of his tongue and the tip of his chin. Brandy had never seen or felt anything remotely close to it, not even from the nice white gentleman she met in Wales who'd been rumored to be the best in the village. He'd gifted her with her very first orgasm. Until that day, she thought there could be no better. She released and tried to squirm away, but Tay wouldn't let her. He kissed and softly rubbed her legs and thighs until the post-orgasmic sensitivity passed, and then he went back to his business. She released again. And once more before he pulled himself up and out from under the blanket, parted her legs and started working his way inside her. She gasped as soon as he entered her. "Wait, we need to..."

"I already have it on."

She looked down at his beautiful brown skin, his muscular torso with the smooth hair leading down to his manhood. She watched, mouth gaped wide open as he entered her slowly inch by inch. When he was completely inside her, he laid on top of her and held her tightly in his arms. "Oh." He winced. "Ohhhh. Brandy. Brandy baby." He penetrated her with slow strokes, in and out of her, over and over again. "You feel so good. It's so tight. Ahhh. Baby. So tight."

The words echoed in her head. "It's so *tight*." *Tight. Tight.* Her body became stiff. Numb. Suddenly everything around her was in stereo. His heavy breathing. The squeaking mattress. The beeping of the smoke detector in the next room.

"Get off me!"

*****

Brandy pushed Tay off of her hard and jumped off of the bed. She ran out into the living room and grabbed her shorts from the floor. As she tried to wriggle them back over her hips, Tay pleaded with her.

"Babe! Wait! What's wrong? What did I do?"

She fastened her bra. "Nothing! Nothing, ok! Where's my shirt?!" She slid into her sandals and attempted to put her arms through the tattered tee again.

"Wait." He went back into the bedroom and grabbed a tee shirt from his dresser. "Here. Put this on."

She snatched it from his hand and pulled it over her head. "I have to go."

"Go where? Babe!" He grabbed her hand as she turned to walk away. "Brandy please. Can we just sit and talk...for just a second? Don't leave like this."

She snatched her hand away. "I can't be here! It's...this house! I can't...I have to go!"

"Brandy...babe let's just sit down for a second. Let's just talk. Ok? Come here." She took his hand and walked with him back over to the sofa. He wiped the tears from her face. "Don't cry."

Her eyes blurred with tears. Her throat burned. She leaned into him and kissed him softly on the lips. "Goodbye Tay."

The goodbye made his heart sink. The way she said it with such finality, and the look in her eye...he could almost feel his heart breaking in his chest. "*Goodbye?*"

He watched, powerlessly as she picked up her purse from the table and walked toward the door. "Brandy."

The sound of his voice just made her sad. Why'd she ever come back there.

He pleaded through teary eyes. "Brandy!"

Ignoring his call, she took her keys from her purse, pulled the strap over her shoulder and opened the front door.

Tay's eyes bulged wide before he yelled. "BRANDY!"

She walked straight into the barrel of Gi's gun.

*****

Gi backed her inside. Tay stood behind her, stark naked,

eyes bucked. He went immediately into protective mode, stepping in front of her and putting an arm across her chest. "What the fuck man?"

Gi snapped. "Put some fucking clothes on."

Rob raised his gun to Tay's head. "Come on man. Pants."

Rob walked him into the bedroom.

Tay jumped into his shorts and hurried back out into the living room. He grabbed Brandy's hand and stood tall, in a show of defiance. One that she appreciated. "Look I don't have any money…"

Gi snapped. "Patricia James. Where is she?"

Tay looked at Brandy and back at Gi. "Who? We don't know."

Gi raised his gun to Brandy's head and cocked it. "I will not ask you again."

Gun shots rang out, so loud it seemed they were right in front of the door. Rob ran over to the window just in time to see their SUV peel away from the curb, with two men firing shots through its back window.

"Fuck! G! They shootin at Silvio! The trucks gone!"

Rob's eyes bucked as the shooters turned and walked toward the house. He didn't wait for them to reach the door. Tay and Brandy ran for cover as Rob and Gi stood at each other's side and shot straight through the front door.

Got Eem!

Rocky sat in the car outside the Bodega. Pat insisted on going in alone. Her cell phone rang from an unknown number. She didn't normally answer those calls, but it was good news, better than anything they could have hoped for. She was almost giddy.

Aunt Pat pulled off her gloves and stuffed them into her pocket, as she walked back to the truck, where Rocky was engrossed in a call. She opened the door to the back seat and climbed in. The seats and the floors were covered in plastic. She began removing her blood soaked clothes as Rocky wrapped up her conversation. "Is she ok? Good take her over to Pat's house and make sure somebody stays with her til we get there. No, don't do that. Don't do nothin. Just take them niggas to the spot. We on our way right now."

"Take who to my house? What's going on?"

Rocky turned to face her in the back seat. She smiled wide. "You ain't gon believe dis shit, Pat."

She answered as she pulled a wet wipe from the container and wiped the spattered blood from her face. "Believe what?"

"We got em."

*****

When the smoke cleared, Rob lay dead on the living room floor. Gi laid on the floor behind the sofa. He'd taken a bullet to his right shoulder and his left thigh. He'd run out of ammunition so he was completely defenseless by the time Calvin and three of his men kicked in the front door.

Tay was under the dining room table, sprawled on top of Brandy.

Calvin walked over to them. "Y'all good? Anybody hit?"

Tay crawled from under the table and helped Brandy to her feet. "Yeah we good."

"Aaight let's go."

"Go where?"

"Don't ask questions, nigga let's go."

Tay grabbed a shirt and jumped into his boots. He and Brandy ran out behind Calvin, who was leading Gi out of the house with a shotgun in his back. They stepped over Rob who laid on the floor, near the door, seeping blood into the carpet.

They sped away from the scene, in the opposite direction of the police sirens wailing in the distance. Two of Calvin's crew stayed behind to make sure no one talked to the police. No one did.

The ride was short but tense. Calvin's man, Keith drove with Brandy sitting next to him in the front seat, tapping her foot nervously and gnawing at her finger nails. Tay sat in the middle row of the truck, beside Wayne who was pointing a loaded glock nine millimeter pistol at Gi's face. Gi sat in the third row beside Calvin, who was mean muggin him as he pierced him in the side with the barrel of his shotgun.

Calvin snarled. "So you thought you was just gon rough these peoples off like dat? And get off the block? Don't nobody here give a fuck about that fake ass mob shit. We mob, nigga! You'n get off this block unless we *let* you off this muufucka. You herrrd me."

Gi grunted and shifted in his seat. Tay cowered as Wayne cocked his pistol and Calvin pressed the shotgun deeper into Gi's side. "Move one more mufuckin time. *Please* move. Blow yo shit all over dis seat, nigga."

Calvin pulled his cell phone from his pocket and tossed it up front to Keith. "Call Rocky."

Per Rocky's instruction, they stopped at Aunt Pat's house first. They let the kids and Wayne out.

Calvin called out to Wayne, "You got em?"

Wayne nodded. "Yeah they good."

Then Keith headed over to the bar. They drove around to the back and walked Gi down the stairs to the basement entrance. Calvin punched in the alarm code. When they walked in they immediately spotted a table with a myriad of weaponry laid out. The knives and paraphernalia left from the last captive.

"One hundred thousand dollars," Gi said.

Calvin frowned. "What? Fuck you talkin bout?"

"To let me go. Right now. One hundred thousand."

Calvin hit him in the mouth. "Shut the fuck up."

Gi grinned through the blood. "Five hundred thousand."

"Aye Keith, hand me that tape over there." He pointed the shotgun and Gi's face. "Say one more word, and I swear to God imma take that knife, and imma take that tongue. Now take your clothes off."

"What?"

"Your clothes, mufucka. We need your clothes."

"For what?"

Calvin raised the shotgun with one hand and pressed the barrel up against Gi's forehead, pushing it slightly back. "Now I was told not to kill you. And I said I wouldn't. Don't make me go back on my word, man. Just take ya clothes off."

Gi stepped out of his pants. "One million. Cash."

Calvin pursed his lips. "You got a million dollars?"

"It's in a safe. In Virginia. You let me go, I'll take you to it right now."

"So it's close by?" He frowned. "Wait, stop. Keep ya draws on man. Ain't nobody tryna see all dat."

Keith burst out laughing as Gi pulled his boxers back up around his waist. "It's close enough. In Old Towne. Thirty minutes. I'll make you a very rich man."

Calvin stood for a moment. In thought. He lowered his gun to his side. Then He threw Keith the shotgun, shoved Gi down on a chair and snatched his hands behind him. "Sound like some bullshit to me." He wound duct tape around G's wrists and ankles, then ripped off a smaller piece and slapped it over his mouth. "And even if it ain't, you ain't mine to let go, playa." He pulled another chair up in front of Gi and sat down. Then he looked down at his watch and leaned back in the chair. "She'll be here in a minute. Aye Keith?"

Keith was behind the bar pouring himself a drink. "Wassup C?"

"I wonder what Ms. Pat got planned for the nigga that killed her only son."

"Ion know young. But it ain't gon be nuttin nice. You want a drink?"

"Yeah pour me one. "Calvin leaned over, resting his elbows on his knees. He looked Gi in the eye and shook his head. "Damn. I hate to be yo muthafuckin ass right now." He laughed. "Cause she gon fuck yo shit UP my nigga. *And* your family. Your kids. You got kids?"

Gi rolled his eyes.

"Oh you ain't trippin huh? Tough guy. Wise guy. You'n even look scared. Aye Keith?"

"Wassup?"

"He ain't scared."

"Oh yeah? Not *yet*."

Calvin smirked and took a sip of cognac. "Look at this nigga, Keith. Over here all brave and shit. That's good though. Ain't no sense in gettin yourself all worked up now. Gettin ya blood pressure all up before it's time. It's still early. So you doin right. Keepin it on the calm down." He laughed. "But let me tell you somethin. I done heard the stories. My uncle ran with her back in the day. Man. That bitch mean. Mean. Like the villain in a super hero movie type mean. Diabolical and shit."

Keith chuckled from behind the bar. "Diabolical man? Really?"

"Yeah. I'm serious Keith. Ms. Pat been slayin niggas for like thirty years. And when it come to her family? Pshhhhh. She goes *in*. Trust me. And then Rocky big, tall, strong, freak ass, wit dem big ass hands. She be itchin to break a nigga down. Wit her hands though shawty. I done watched her Kimbo Slice niggas in the street. I mean, don't get me wrong, she'll pull that pistol out in a minute, but she like to fight."

"Oh, yeah, Rocky ain't no joke," Keith agreed.

"No joke at all. But Ms. Pat. She like…ion even know what to call her. But man, this one time I heard she took a carving knife right, and…"

For the next twenty minutes, Calvin went on rattling off stories his parents told him. Stuff he'd heard in the streets. Gunfights, kidnappings and torture. Bodies weighted down in Potomac River, disposed of at the Blue Plains sewage plant and the swamps under the little bridges on the BW Parkway. He could barely contain his excitement. "…and all that shit? That shit was just about money. I can't even imagine what she gon do to *yo ass*."

Calvin looked up and around the dark basement. "And they say she got this joint soundproofed. So nobody can hear the screams. They'll leave a nigga down here screamin and dying while they upstairs servin drinks and partyin like ain't nuttin even happenin down here. They cold blooded, slim. And you done went and killed Ms. Pat son? Her son?!" He laughed hard. "Sheeit. Nigga, you gon die a extra special slow death for that shit." He held out his glass. "Here, you want some of this?" He pulled the tape off and put the glass up to Gi's lips. Gi turned away. He pressed the tape on. "Aaight. Suit yourself nigga."

The security alarm beeped and the deadbolt clicked behind the reinforced steel door. Calvin stood from his chair and smiled. "Whelp, looks like it's about that time."

Rocky pushed the heavy door open. Her expression was stern. She looked over at Gi then at Calvin. "He hurt?"

Calvin gulped the last of his drink and sat the glass down on the bar, "Nah, not really. Bullet to the shoulder but it look like it went through. One in the leg. I had to hit him in the mouth one time, but that's it. Oh he tried to bribe me to let him go. He said he had a million in a safe somewhere in Virginia. Old Towne."

Rocky looked at Gi. "Nah he ain't got a million. Not no more."

"What, y'all got it?"

She smirked. "There's a backpack in the back of my truck. It's a hundred g's in there. I want you to take fifty over to Ev's wife and kids and you can split the rest with your men however you want. Cool?"

They dapped. "I gotchu. Aight Rocky."

Keith walked out behind Calvin. "Later Rock." He looked back and laughed. "Aight Gi. Be easy."

Once the guys were off, Rocky locked the door behind them, both deadbolts and the barricade. She locked the interior door to the upstairs. Then she walked over to the corner and flipped on the stereo. Gi sat still. Wondering what she had planned. Not particularly afraid. But curious.

She started packing up the items from the kill table. She sheathed the knives, corked the bottles, and capped the syringes, moving at a snail's pace, attempting to draw fear, or at least unnerve her captive. But Gi would not be moved so easily. He sat silently, expressionless and emotionless, trying to prepare mentally for whatever fuckery they had planned for him.

Having been held for ransom several times in his life, kidnap and torture wasn't foreign to him. Cuts, bruises, broken bones. They'd always heal, eventually. But you stand strong, no matter what. And if it was his time tonight then hey…it was his time. Everybody had to go sometime. But what he wasn't going to do was show these black bitches weakness. No matter what.

Behind the bar, Rocky poured from the bottle of cognac Keith had opened. Two glasses, one on the rocks. She stood and drank hers down, slowly as she stared into Gi's eyes. He kept her gaze, just to let her know he would not be moved. She picked up the other glass and walked over to him. She pulled the tape from his mouth. "Drink."

He spat at her feet. "Fuck you."

She laughed. "Y'all Italians like that spittin shit, don't you? Your uncle pulled that shit last week. You know how nasty it is to spit on a motherfucker?" *Whap!* A sharp overhand right landed at his jaw and loosened a tooth. "Now. I'm just tryna help you relax a little. We got a long night ahead of us, Gi. So you might as well go ahead and get faded. But…if you don't want the drink, don't drink the drink."

She swallowed what was in his glass and replaced the tape over his mouth. His eyes trailed her, as she walked across the room and dialed down the dimmer on the recessed lighting. She walked back across the room, over to the stereo and cranked up the volume. Marvin Gaye wailed about getting it on, as she sang loudly and off key.

She walked back over to the bar where she opened an overhead cabinet and removed a small cardboard box. She reached inside and one by one she lined up her goods on top of the counter. She crooned to the music blasting on the stereo. *Aaaahhhh baby, lets get it awwwwn. Sugaaa...*

Gi's eyes bucked wide and he inhaled deeply. She smiled as she undressed, slowly, down to her boxers and a white tank top. Then she suited up, buckled up and headed in his direction.

A wave of panic came over Gi like he'd never felt. He screamed behind the duct tape. Screams muffled by the sounds of classic mood music playing loudly on overhead speakers. She came closer to him. He jerked around in his chair. Jumped up and down until he fell over onto the floor.

Rocky smiled as she watched him squirm around on the floor. Gi was in for a wild night. And she intended to enjoy every second of it. For PJ.

*****

The next morning when Aunt Pat walked through the basement door, Rocky and Gi lay spooning half naked on a blanket on the hard basement floor. Rocky's long arms and legs stretched out a foot past Gi's in either direction. Aunt Pat slammed the door shut, startling them both. "I'm sorry. Am I interrupting?"

Rocky stretched her arms and yawned. Then she kissed Gi on his neck. He flinched. "Nah I think we done." She looked at Gi. "Unless you want some more." Gi's eyes were red and swollen from all the crying...and the effects of the quick dissolving ecstasy tab Rocky slipped into his mouth while he was talking shit. It was the love drug that made him love it even when he didn't want to.

Aunt Pat shook her head. "Get him up."

Rocky pulled him up to his feet. "Come on. Let's go love muffin."

"How long is it gon take for that shit to wear off Rock?"

"The ex or the afterglow?" She laughed. "It should've worn off already. But hit em with some smellin salts, and he'll be alert for you."

"Cool."

Rocky sat him back in the chair and pulled his pants over his feet. "So where we takin em? The park?"

"Nah. The site. It's empty today right?"

"Yeah. I gave my boys the day off. They ain't gon be back til Monday."

"Ok mix the stuff. I'll meet you over there around three o'clock."

"You sure you don't need my help here?"

"No. Looks like you helped yourself enough last night." Aunt Pat nodded to the king size strap on Rocky left sitting on the bar. "Pack that shit up and take it with you. And wipe my bar off please."

Rocky laughed as she cleared the bar of her wares. Toys, lubes a giant pink feather and a leather strap. She walked over to Gi and whispered in his ear. "I hope it was as good for you as it was for me. *Little G.*" Then she kissed him on the cheek. The tape had fallen off, but they didn't need it. Gi was effectively muted, still in shock from the night's events and still on the groggy side from the ex.

Aunt Pat looked around. "Where's my stuff?"

"Over in the drawer behind the bar."

"Aight, be careful. Call me when everything's ready."

"Aight." Rocky pushed her gun down in her waist band and headed out.

Aunt Pat locked the door behind her and walked over to the bar where her wares were tucked away. She removed them from the drawer and lined them back up on the bar. Then she pulled her gun from her waistband. A Smith and Wesson .38 with laser sights. She snapped in the magazine and aimed in a particularly painful place. "Aye Gi." She let one go, completely shattering his right ankle.

Gi screamed. "God dammit! You fuckin cunt bitch!"

"So," she smirked, "the dead has arisen." She aimed and let another one go to his right knee cap.

"Ahhhhh! Fuck!" Gi's breathing was heavy. The pain was unbearable. "You want money."

"You know better than that, Gi, I already have your money. I already have your family. What I want now is your *soul*. I want to watch it leave your body. Slow."

She aimed the laser up and down his body, toying with him for a while. She went back and forth from one eye to the other as he jerked his head around. Another round. *Pop!* His right elbow. He cried out, as saliva dripped from his mouth. "You killed first! You killed first, you fuckin bitch. You killed my grandfather. If you hadn't, your faggot son would still be alive."

"My faggot son."

"Yes fuckin faggot. You fuckin dike. Queers! All a yous is fucked up. All a yous is goin to hell." He spat at the floor in front of her.

"Well...you'll beat me there."

She raised the gun, pointing the laser at his frontal lobe. It took every ounce of reserve she had to hold that trigger. She wanted to plant one between his eyes in worst way, but a head shot was too easy. Too good for him. He needed to suffer. He had to.

She stood and walked back to the table. She put the gun down on the table and poured another drink. Her back was turned to him. She couldn't let him see the tears in her eyes. PJ's face was before her. Streaming like a movie reel. Her baby boy in the little blue suit, crying after her in a courtroom. The divo walking down the aisle of the church in a million worth of diamonds and sequins, throwing his pashmina over his shoulder and sashaying out the front door of her bar. His vacant eyes half clouded with blood that seeped from the bullet hole in his forehead. She sobbed. Then she screamed. Then she calmed herself and replaced the gun with her fighting knife. She didn't even bother with her butcher's apron and surgical gloves or the plastic sheeting she was supposed to drape his space with.

Gi was still breathing heavily trying to temper the pain from the small caliber bullets left in his joints. She snatched him back by his hair, took the tip of the knife and as he screamed for mercy carved into his chest a closed circle around his right breast. Then she dug into the flesh and pulled the circle of skin cleanly off of his chest, nipple and all. She doused the open flesh lightly with rubbing alcohol and laughed while Gi seemed to convulse. "Did you cut my son Gi?"

"Nooo!"

"Gi! Did you CUT MY SON?!"

He shook violently in his chair. "Oh God nooooo!"

She dug into his flesh and carved another circle on the left side. Then she snatched the skin away. This one didn't peel off so easily, so she carved a little more. When she doused him with the alcohol Gi's eyes rolled back into his head. He kicked out, so much so that his chair toppled over and hit the ground. Aunt Pat picked the chair back up with ease and pushed it up against the wall. Gi passed out. She grabbed bandages from her bag and wrapped his chest up tight to stop the bleeding. Then she cracked the smelling salt under his nose to wake him.

"Get up muthufucka. You'n get to sleep. We got business to discuss."

He cried, "What fuckin business? What do you want?!"

"I'll tell you in a minute." She walked to the table and replaced the carving knife with a small circular sawzall. Then she walked back to Gi and reached into his underwear.

"Oh God. Oh God. Wait!"

She pulled out his penis and cut it at the head, slowly letting the blade saw through the layers of flesh. She threw it on the pile of flesh lying on the floor beside him. Gi was shaking so violently at this point his chair was jumping up and down, off the floor. His screams were primal, as were her laughs.

He groaned in pain. She walked back to the table and replaced the sawzall with a syringe. Filled it with enough morphine to take the pain but keep him on the coherent side. "Lift your fuckin legs." She pulled an adult diaper over his feet and up to his waist. Then she sat and watched him until the morphine kicked in, and he was calm again.

"Listen. I understand why you killed my son. I understand, it's part of the game. Just like your grandfather. But you ain't have to torture him like that Gi. Humiliate him like you did. That shit wuddn't called for. No matter what you think about who he was." She wiped the tears from her eye. "He was mine. That boy was all I had. All I had, Gi. And I just got him back. I spent most of his life in prison. I took his father from him. I wasn't there to protect him when he…when he needed me." She cried. "But we got back. We got it back. He was even callin me *ma* again. Now, because of you, I ain't got shit, you know. I'm just out here. Streets ain't the same. Game ain't the same. I ain't got shit to live for out here. And I can't be out here like this. Cause right now, I ain't got no more fucks to give. And that shit is no good. It's no good. I can't be out here like this, Gi. I can't."

Saliva dripped from his mouth as he talked. "What the f…f…fuck are you talking about?"

When Gi passed out again, she left him and went to clean herself up. After she tidied the room, from the store room she grabbed a dolly. She untied him from the chair, dressed him, and taped him upright to the dolly. Then she backed her moving truck up to the dock and loaded him in. Halfway to the spot her phone rang.

"Pat, it's almost one o'clock. I'm here. Where you at?"

"On my way. I'll be there in about twenty minutes. You mix the stuff yet?

"Yeah we good."

"Aight, go ahead and back the truck up to the spot. I'll see you in a few."

*****

The construction site was deserted. Aunt Pat parked as close to the spot as she could. She lifted the door on the back of the truck and wheeled the dolly down the ramp.

Gi was beginning to come to. He opened his eyes and squinted. "Where am I?"

She pushed the dolly down into the hollow ground and

stood him upright. Then she pulled a syringe from her jacket pocket, popped the cap and injected the needle into Gi's arm. Aunt Pat slapped him lightly on the cheek. "You good? You up?"

He was up. Suddenly alert. Painfully aware that he was standing in the middle of a gaping hole in the ground. The morphine had taken away his pain but the adrenaline shot she'd just given seemed to bring it all back. Along with some very intense heart palpitations. He looked up and panicked at the sight of the truck, spinning fast in a counterclockwise motion, churning wet cement. It beeped loudly, as it backed up near the hole. "Wait, what are you doing? Where the fuck are you going?" He yelled as Aunt Pat climbed back out of the hole, leaving him to his impending doom.

She yelled, "Aight Rock. Let it go."

Rocky pulled a lever and cement began to pour into the hole. It quickly covered Gi's feet and rose slowly but steadily. He jerked himself back and forth. His breathing was heavy. His chest heaved up and down. Faster by the second.

Aunt Pat yelled down at him, over the noise. "You need to calm down before you give yourself a heart attack."

He started to breath in and out, slowly.

"Good. Now Gi I won't lie to you. You gon die today. There's no question about that. The question is, how. And how many will you take with you."

Gi screamed, "What the fuck do you want from me?"

She smirked as the cement rose above his ankles, nearing his shins." What I want is your money. The rest of your money. I know you got more than we took, and where you goin, you ain't gon need it."

Gi laughed at the sheer ridiculousness of what was going on around him. He knew he was going to die. That was pretty evident. And after the humiliation and the mutilation he'd already been subjected to, he didn't really fuckin care. But what he wasn't doing was turning his money over to these two wicked black bitches as a parting gift. The cement reached his knees. It was moving slowly. "Patricia James! You will die. Soon. My people will kill you. I can promise you that."

She laughed. "You know somethin, Gi…that is exactly what I thought. And I ain't ashamed to say, I was kinda worried about that. Cause I'm getting old. These old legs ain't what they used to be. They ain't meant for all that runnin and duckin and shit no more. I'm done with that. The good news is, I ain't got to. I ain't gotta go lookin for nobody. And ain't nobody comin lookin for me. Not no more."

"What the fuck are you talking about?"

"I'm talkin about you…and all *your* talkin. You see, I know a few people in a few places. You can't survive in this game for all these years and not know people. Not build friendships and relationships and earn a few favors. Nowadays they call it building your brand. I just call it the game. And the game is simple. If you wanna stay out on these streets, you gotta make your word your bond. Don't make idle threats. Do a nigga a favor every now and again and know when to shut the fuck up. That's somethin you young bucks don't know nothin bout."

Gi looked down at the cement. It was up to his thighs and starting to burn his skin.

"That cement startin to burn a little bit, huh? Well let me get to the point. To make a long story short, one of them people that owe me one of them favors let me know that you got caught bringing quite a bit of narcotic into the city, by way of a cargo ship coming across the Potomac. Why the fuck you was on that ship with all those drugs and that dead body and a laptop with the names of everybody in your organization, I don't hardly know, but as far as the DEA is concerned, it's all on you. Now, you facin life in prison on drug, murder *and* federal racketeerin charges. But because you a filthy fuckin *rat*, that ain't built to do no hard jail time, you givin up all your peoples to the feds. Your Uncle Tony, your cousin Viggo, Angelo. Basically the whole Scarsi family. You takin everybody down to save your own pathetic little grease ball ass."

"You lie! You a fuckin liar!" Gi hocked up a load and spat…onto the rising cement.

She laughed. "Yeah I'm lyin. But that's the story I told them. And that's the story they believe. I spent all night and all mornin workin this shit out. I got the paper trail and everything. Arrest warrants, arrest records, mug shots, witness statements, etc., etc., etc. They say that Photoshop thing is a beast. I wouldn't know cause I can't even work a computer. But fortunately for me, some of them people that owe me some of them favors do. So *Paizon*." She mocked. "I get to have *your* lil punk ass free and clear. But what I gotta pay for is your granddaddy. The Scarsi family not lettin that shit go. And I get it. I wouldn't let it go either. So that million dollars you was waitin to get from us…they still want it. In the next 24 hours. And that's where you come in."

"You're crazy enough to think I will give you my money before you kill me? I'll see you bitches in hell!"

"Yeah, you probably will. But right now…" She looked over at Rocky, who shut off the valve. The cement settled around his waist. "…but right now in my hand I have three pictures. Pictures of people I wouldn't normally fuck with. But like I mentioned to you earlier, I ain't got nothin else out here to live for. So…you know…fuck it."

She flung the pictures in front of him one by one. "Marie, your sweet old grandmother. Eighty-six years old. Her only contribution to society was raising a bunch of wise guys. A gang of thieves and thugs. Robbers and killers. The world wouldn't miss her. I got a couple young essays with no papers that love old lady pussy. And *you know* they like it rough. Then there's Adrianna, your baby sister. A whore and a dope fiend. We'd probably be doin her a favor. Cause she ain't gon last out here on these streets anyway. You did a good thing puttin her back in that rehab. I know you love her. So we won't kill her right away. We'll pull her out. String her out. Turn her out and after I make a few dollars off her, I'll fill that bitch up with a needle full of shit so hot itta burn her ass up from the inside out. Last but not least, there is your daughter. Gabriella. The one out in Montgomery County that you think no one knows about. The beautiful and smart half-black half-Italian beauty with a head full of curly black hair and deep dimples. She would probably make something good outta her life if it wasn't for you. *Her* I won't touch. Cause ion hurt kids. But Rocky would. She don't give a fuck. She'll sell little Gabby's ass to the highest bidder, and your baby would most likely end up turning tricks in a rundown tenement somewhere in the Ukraine. I don't know how much she worth to them foreigners. Cause that ain't my thing, but I'm sure she'll be worth a lot to somebody. Now I got my people stationed right outside of each of their houses, and they ready to ride with a phone call."

"You're bluffing. If you kill them, you know you will go to war."

She shrugged. "Hey, if we don't give them the money in the next 24, we go to war anyway. What's a few more bodies? So, we got a crane over there that can pull you up outta there if you tell me what I wanna hear. I'll pull you out, give you two to the head. It'll be quick and painless, and your family will go on for generations. *Or* you can sit there and let that cement harden up on you, pull all the water from your body and break your organs down slow till your heart or your bladder pops. Then I'll hit this group text and end the lives of the people you love the most in the world. It's up to you. So what you gon do? And don't think too long, Gi. When that shit starts hardening up, it ain't nothin nobody can do.

She nodded and Rocky hit the lever again. The cement poured in slowly, climbing up steadily. There was no time to ponder. Soon he would be drowning, suffocating as the thick wet substance plugged his nostrils. It reached his chest. He began to panic at the thought. "Ok. Ok, yes. I want out. I'll tell you where everything is. Just get me out of this."

Aunt Pat yelled to Rocky. "Aye Rock! Chill."

Rocky hit the lever and the barrel began to turn faster, cement gushed out at twice the speed. She pushed the lever back up and then down. The barrel kept turning. "Pat! I can't stop this thing!"

"Fuck you mean you can't stop it?!" She ran over to the truck and poked her head in. "What you doin? Turn it off!"

"I'm tryin!"

"Tryin? Ain't this your truck?!"

"Yeah but ion really know how to work it. This ain't my job."

"Got dammit, Rocky! Aunt Pat got in and began pushing and pulling levers, banging on buttons until the barrel stopped turning. She jumped out and looked over at Gi. He was covered up to his chin, trying to hold his head back far enough so that the cement wouldn't get to his mouth. "Gi, we good. We can still pull you out, man. We got you. Just tell us where the money is. Which house? We'll pull you out as soon as they have it in hand. Nobody will touch your family. I give you my word."

"The cement was weighing heavy on him. He could barely breathe but managed to get out the words. "It's at my mother's in Stone Harbor. Buried in the ground under her garage. Now please. Pull me out! Get me outta this!"

Aunt Pat turned to Rocky. "You know how to lower that crane?

Rocky smiled. "Nope."

Aunt Pat shook her head. "Rocky."

"Well. You ain't say nothin bout no crane. You asked me if I could work the cement truck. I'm workin the truck. Stop adibbin and shit."

She laughed. "So yo gon make me break my word?"

Rocky frowned. "What? Your word? Fuck outta here. You ain't say shit about lettin this nigga outta here."

"Yeah I know but…"

"Man FUCK him. Don't nobody know you gave him your word but him. And he gon die any fuckin way. What difference do it make now? Fuck is you a mercenary now? *He* deserve *your* mercy?"

"That's ain't what that mean Rocky."

"Well, whatever. That nigga lucky I ain't fuck his ass to death. You shouldn't'a gave his ass that morphine. That was mercy enough."

They sat for a moment. Long enough for Aunt Pat to wander off in her thoughts. Rocky was growing impatient.

"Pat!"

"Yeah."

"Wassup?!"

"What you mean wassup?"

"I mean we can't stay out here all day. You really got people sittin outside his people house? Waitin on your call?"

"Nah."

They both laughed. Rocky took the key from the ignition and put it back in her pocket. "Fuck this shit man, I'm hungry. You eat yet?"

Aunt Pat looked over at Gi, up to his chin in concrete, taking long deep breaths, exhaling out of his mouth. Waiting for the merciful two bullet reprieve she promised him. She thought, *fuck it* then she turned back to Rocky. "Pancake house?"

A Royal Homegoing

The funeral for Patrick James, also known as PJ, better known as Miss P, rivaled that of Hollywood royalty. There was standing room only in the rented cathedral and with Missy's help, Aunt Pat sent him home in the exact fashion that he would have wanted. Fancy.

A mirrored casket with solid gold hardware and plush designer bedding from Versace. A crown of white roses placed on his head. A complement to the white Valentino pantsuit and his signature red bottom stilettos, which were clearly visible as Missy had the funeral directors open the entire casket for his viewing. As he would have wanted.

His transportation was a white horse drawn carriage with a rainbow flag affixed to the front. There were three Rolls Royces for family cars, and a funeral procession that looked like half the lot at Elite Luxury Motors.

The VIP section took up at least a quarter of the church. His new friends. Reality stars and other C-list celebrities, laden with diamonds and heavy furs despite the unseasonably warm fall weather. Missy arranged for his favorite gospel singer to bless the congregation with his favorite song about falling down and getting back up again. Brandy composed herself long enough to stand and sing a tribute to her favorite uncle a capella. Uncle Edward held her hand to help her through it. She didn't get through it.

Despite the reverend's repeated warning about time, the tributes went on for well over an hour. Family and friends, old and new. Dozens of stories Aunt Pat had never heard. Going way back to grade school. She appreciated every kind word, though the pangs of guilt from her absence pierced her heavy heart. The reverend eulogized him superbly, capturing the very best of who he was, no doubt following Missy's explicit direction. He preached the love of God and invited all to partake in the magnificence that is God's undying love.

When the call was made to close the casket Aunt Pat rose slowly from the pew. She walked over to the casket. "Let me." She took the crank from the undertaker then kissed her son lightly on his forehead and whispered her last loving words to him before lowering him down into the casket. The church was quiet, save the muffled cries of the ones who were especially touched by her grief.

She stepped back into the aisle and watched as the funeral director closed the bottom half of the casket and secured it. He moved up to the top half. He reached for the lid and she yelled, "Wait!"

Aunt Pat stood on shaky legs, trying desperately to fight back her tears. She walked slowly back over to the casket and stood in front of it. Then she gave her boy one last kiss. The funeral director reached out to console her. He touched her shoulder. She pushed him away. "Stop."

Rocky rose from her seat and whispered. "Pat."

Aunt Pat breathed in deeply. Then she backed up a few steps. "Close it."

Unsure, the undertaker looked back at Rocky. Rocky nodded yes, so he walked back over to the head of the casket and pulled the lid down. Slowly he closed the lid and fastened it tightly. Then he reached over and pulled the elaborate floral arrangement, a blanket of white roses over the top of the casket. He motioned to the pall bearers. They stood. That made it all too real.

Every being in the church jumped to attention as Aunt Pat bellowed a gut wrenching scream. She fell to her knees, buried her face in her hands and cried. "My baby. They took my boy!" Her sobs shook her entire body. Rocky and Missy rushed to her side. The entire room was brought to tears.

The undertaker gave her a moment to calm before signaling the pallbearers to move. Rocky and Uncle Edward took her by the arms and helped her back to her feet. Weak with grief, she had to be held up as she followed the casket out of the church. Though it was understandable, it was a sight that no one could claim to have seen. A sight that awed all who knew her. Ms. Pat was broken.

*****

The stories had already started circulating – the who's, why's and how it happened, especially after some kids found Gi's head sitting atop a concrete slab on the construction site. It had hit the national news as soon as Gi was positively identified. One of the nation's most notorious mobsters murdered and buried gangster style as an example to his crew. Rocky smirked at the story.

After the service, Aunt Pat took a long valium-induced nap. She asked Missy to take care of the repast because she wasn't gonna make it. Everyone understood. She woke up, grabbed an energy drink, and hit the road without a word to anyone.

Rocky had lent her her bike. Aunt Pat hadn't hopped on a hog in a while, but she never forgot. The roar of the engine beneath her. The open road. The fresh air. The freedom to be and to think without any distraction. There was no feeling like it.

She hit the interstate, riding at a steady pace, enjoying the warm breeze blowing through her moto jacket. I95 North. Over the Delaware Bridge and through the Lincoln Tunnel. Over the Brooklyn Bridge. She sat outside for nearly an hour before she would summon the courage to walk up and knock on the door.

She barely knocked before the door was opened.

"Hey. I'm sorry to be comin to your place like this, unannounced. But I had to see you. One last time."

*****

"I hear about PJ. I'm so sawdy, mami. I want to call but–"
"Yeah. We buried him today."

Consuela took Aunt Pat in her arms and held her close as she cried. Consuela had been the only person up to that point that ever saw Aunt Pat shed a tear. The only one that really knew her in that way. *Patricia.* The vulnerable side.

Aunt Pat wiped the tears from her face and tried to compose herself. "I can't stay long. I just had to see you. One last time. I'm gon be going away for a while. And I just couldn't go without coming here to...without asking you."

"Of course. You can ask me anything, mami."

"Why?"

That one word brought so many emotions. Consuela felt a lump forming in her throat. Her eyes welled. One word, three little letters with no easy answer. It took a while for her to come up with something that made sense. "It just...I don't know, Patreesha...it just got so hard."

Aunt Pat kissed her hand, stood and walked toward the door.

Consuela and her overgrown belly beat her to the door. "Wait. Patreesha. I'm so sawdy. I know...I owe joo mor'd then that. I do. Please, sit?"

Aunt Pat walked back over to the sofa and listened halfheartedly to Consuela's apology.

"Eet's so hard to living this life. You know thees. My children want to have their familee back together. My family leave me because of you. My mother was no speaking to me anymore. And you had no time for me. You were gone all of the time in the day and in the night. I was lonely. So veddy lonely, Patreesha. And I knew about you other girls. At the bar. I never say notheen. But I knew. Then when the lady call and they offer me the more money to do the tweest for the show. I know it was wrong. I know it hurt you. I wanted to hurt you. Like you hurt me. But I don't want to anymore. Carlos is gone now. I ask him to leave. Three months ago. I no love him. I never love him. I only love you. I only want you."

Aunt Pat wasn't really sure what she expected by going there. An apology? A door slammed in her face? A fight with Carlos? Consuela's words were completely unexpected, and they hurt so much more than they helped. Knowing now that she was the one that pushed Consuela away. Knowing that Carlos was gone and Consuela wanted her back; that they could just be together. But too much had happened to even think about starting over. Too much pain. And that shit hurt. She stood once again, kissed Consuela on the forehead. "Thank you." She headed for the door. "Take care of yourself Connie."

Consuela watched in tears as Aunt Pat climbed back onto her bike and drove away. Over the Brooklyn Bridge. Through Jersey. Back over the Delaware Bridge and onto the 95 interstate. She made it back in record time.

The next morning was her weekly visit. She pushed her way through the line and to the front. The guards checked her ID and let her through.

Brenda walked out to the visiting hall in her bright orange jumpsuit and loose French braids with too many fly-aways. Her eyes were red and puffy. As soon as Aunt Pat's face appeared on the monitor, she broke down again. "I still can't believe this. Aunt Pat. I'm so sorry."

Aunt Pat tried desperately to keep herself together. She'd cried enough in public already. "I know, baby. I'm sorry I wasn't able to get them to let you come to the funeral. I know you wanted to be there."

"I did. I can't believe he's gone. I can't believe this." She sobbed uncontrollably for some time. Until a guard came over to check on her.

Aunt Pat addressed the guard. "She aight. Let her be." She let Brenda get it all out before she started in on her about her case. "So what's the latest on your case?"

"Ion know. Same shit. My lawyer said Petty is offering murder two, seventeen years and I should take it. Ion even give a fuck no more Aunt Pat. What's the fuckin point."

"Brenda. Listen I might just have a way out."

"Aunt Pat don't even—"

"Look! Just hang tight all right. Just hang tight. I gotta go. I love you."

"I love you too." Brenda cried all the way back to her cell.

Aunt Pat knew now more than before that she had to do what she planned.

*****

She parked her pickup on the meter outside the D.C. Superior Courthouse. She dropped in her change and adjusted her pantyhose. As she stood on line to enter the building she garnered a few curious stares.

"Ms. Pat? Is that you?"

"Rich?! My muufuckin man! When you get out?!" Her outburst caused more stares from the curious onlookers.

"I got out last month. Up here to see my P.O."

"And you ain't come around the way?"

"Nah, a nigga tryna stay outta trouble. For real."

"I can respect that. Well you know if you need anything. *Anything.* Come over to the bar and holla at me."

"Aight. I definitely will. Aye what's up with your hair though?"

For a minute she'd forgotten she was wearing a wig. It was sliding to the back of her head. "Oh." She pulled it down. "Just a lil sumthin I'm tryin. It ain't nuttin."

He smiled, trying hard not to laugh. "Aaight then Ms. Pat. I'll holla at you later."

"Aight Rich." Just then she felt a breeze and noticed her dress was tucked into her hose. Way in. Clearly showing her bunched up boxer shorts to all who stood behind her. She turned around. "Oh so nobody wuddn't gon tell me I had my shit tucked in?"

She slid through the metal detectors and up the escalators to the ADA's office. Adjusting her drawers the whole way. When she reached the reception desk she felt a bit uneasy. But she wasn't sure why. "I'm here to see Tyrone Petty. I called earlier."

The sour faced old secretary looked her up and own. "*You* Ms. Carter?"

She frowned. "That's right." She knew this woman from *somewhere. Where, where, where?*

"Um hmm. You can go in."

Aunt Pat scowled at her before moving on to see the ADA. Halfway down the hall she looked back and the lady was still watching. Face still sour. *Fuck wrong with her.* His door was half open. She knocked lightly before walking in.

Assistant District Attorney Tyrone Petty, was a reverse racist. Modern day Uncle Tom. The inmates nicknamed him Petty Ty while many of his colleagues joked that he was Uncle Ruckus from the Boondocks cartoon fame. Hardly a compliment. Petty was an ultra conservative, highly unsympathetic, and highly effective tool of the establishment. A black man who had nothing but contempt for black people. Contempt for his own black skin. He prosecuted Brenda's first murder case and was all too happy to see her name back on the docket after the embarrassment of having her conviction overturned.

He noticed the crooked wig, messy eye makeup and the uncomfortable walk. *This lady is a weirdo.* He shook Aunt Pat's hand. "Ms. Carter. What can I do for you today?"

She adjusted her dress once more and gave him an unusually strong shake for a lady. "It's about what I can do for you Mr. Petty."

Petty raised a quizzical brow. "Really. Have a seat."

Aunt Pat made a passionate appeal for Brenda. Beginning with a picture that she laid on Petty's desk in front of him. A professional portrait taken at Sears Department store. Brenda was three years old with two twisted pig tails, a tear in her eye and a seemingly forced snaggletoothed smile. She sat cross-legged on a color blocked rug holding a teddy bear. Aunt Pat pointed at the picture.

"You see this little girl? This missing tooth? This tear in her eye? This little girl was abused for the first thirteen years of her life. Physically, mentally, emotionally. Her mother was a junky, and her father took her innocence. Her only way out was running away. And she ran right into the arms of a young dumb drug dealer who continued to abuse her until his death. Made her his property. Then she met a man that she thought loved her and had her back. Eventually he raised his hand to her. And she snapped. She got the best of him. And then he fell. It's as simple and as complicated as that. She's not who you think she is."

"She's not?"

"No. She's not."

"And who is she to you?"

"I was best friends with her mother. She's like…my niece, so to speak."

Petty picked up the photo, scanned it once more and tossed it back at her. In that moment, Aunt Pat wanted to break his hand but somehow managed to maintain her resolve as she made her proposal, strongly emphasizing the likelihood of an acquittal if he decided to go for murder two.

"…and ain't no way you gon get murder two. You can't prove that, and Brenda will most likely walk free. Same as she did before. And where would that leave you?"

Petty leaned back in his chair and sighed. "Ms. James. You're asking a lot."

"But I'm giving you much more, Ty."

"Mr. Petty."

"Whatever. Think about it." She pulled his Mont Blanc pen from its holder and grabbed a post it from his desk. Then she scribbled down a number. "You can reach me here. But I need to hear from you by the end of the week. That's three days. You have a good day Mr. Petty." She walked out without looking back. Past the old sour face. Tugging at her pantyhose.

Petty bit down on his pen and rested his feet upon his desk. It was an interesting proposition. He wanted Brenda James. Bad. There was no doubt about that. No way that black bitch was supposed to just keep killing men and walking away. No matter how bad some of them were.

He'd had Brenda all figured out, in his mind. She'd tricked some young boy into selling drugs to take care of her, probably had him killed for the money, killed another drug dealer after he had sex with her slut daughter and now she'd tricked this good *wholesome* white man into marrying her so she could kill him for his insurance money.

Now this crazy-looking woman walks in thinking she could change his mind with a sob story and a baby photo. He was just supposed to ignore facts. Fact was Brenda James murdered two men. The world wouldn't miss the nigger at all, but that white man didn't deserve to die at her hands. She was a cold-blooded killer and deserved much more than the twenty years he planned on giving her, no matter what the hell happened to her when she was a little girl. He picked up the picture from his desk and tossed it in the trash. *Scum bitch.*

Aunt Pat's words still rang in his ear, though: "It'll be the biggest story this city has ever seen…You'll get all the shine…I can make you famous."

What this woman was offering was newsworthy. Career-making. And she was handing it all to him on a silver platter. It just seemed too good to be true. He stared at the number on the paper for a while, then he picked up the phone. "Kristoff. I need you to look up a name for me. Yeah. Patricia Carter."

Bumps N' Bruises

Brenda walked out into the conference room and took a seat at the table. "Aunt Pat, how'd you get in here? Where's my lawyer?"

Aunt Pat adjusted her wig. "I'm your lawyer today. I needed to talk to you about somethin. Face to face. "Wait…" She squinted, then reached over the table and took Brenda by the chin. She nudged Brenda's head back a bit. "What happened to your eye?"

Brenda had done her level best to conceal it with a homemade concealer. A black eye from a fight the night before. "It's nothing. I just fell into the…"

"Don't play with me girl. Who hit you in yo eye? A CO?"

"It's not even that serious, Aunt Pat."

"Brenda."

"I just got into it with this girl last night—"

"A inmate?!"

"Yeah."

"WHO?!"

"Her name is Deirdre."

"Deirdre? Who she with?"

"Deirdre Braxton."

Aunt Pat pondered a moment. "She kin to Karen Braxton?"

"Yeah. That's her aunt. It's a few of em in here. They got a lil crew goin."

"What she come at you for?"

"My canteen. All my toiletries and personal stuff you sent me last week. Food."

"This happen before?"

"A couple times. But not her. A different girl." Brenda raised her hand, examining her bruised knuckle. "I can handle it though. I'm aaight."

Aunt Pat smiled. "You get her?"

Brenda smiled back. "Oh, you already know. I worked out on her."

They laughed. "My girl. Did you go to Irene about this?"

"Irene got transferred to Fluvanna. Like a month ago. She got her time."

"What about Mikki? She still in here right?"

"Yeah she around. She don't really say nuthin to me though. It's funny. They act like they scared to talk to me or somethin. So I just stay to myself. Work, write, read books. But I'm good."

"Naw baby, you ain't good. You got more to worry about than just you now. You been eatin? Gettin some exercise? Ion want you to end up like I did. Gainin fifty pounds up in here."

"I'm takin good care of myself. And I can handle myself. Stop worrying."

"I know you can Brenda, but these bitches ain't s'posed to be comin at you like that, though. Especially not now. They s'posed to know better. This shit is crazy."

"Some people just don't care."

"Yeah, well they will. They gon care. Just give me a couple days to work some shit out and you'll be good. Meanwhile, if this nigga Petty call you out to talk to you, I need you to play a role."

"A role? What kinda role?"

"Well…you remember that picture you sent me? The baby picture of you with the little pony tail. You was sittin on the floor with that teddy bear?"

"Yeah."

"I gave it to him."

"For what?"

"I just wanted him to look at you different. He got this idea that you this man eatin, murderin hustler's wife and I need him to see you in a different way. Not that he gon believe it, but if I can just plant a lil doubt. I mean, it's reachin, but you know…whatever works."

"What you tell him?"

"Basically that you was molested and abused by your father.

Your mother was a junky. You ran away and ended up with Melvin. Oh yeah…and he beat you."

"Who Melvin?"

"Yeah."

"What?! Aunt Pat. Come on. Why would you tell him that?"

"Cause I aint fuckin Florida Evans and this ain't *Good Times*. We gon do whateva we gotta do to get your ass up outta here. Who gives a fuck what he think?"

"So you think tellin him all them lies is gon get me outta here?"

"Maybe, I don't know. Look I just need him to get murder two off his mind in case shit don't work out."

"Which means you think it won't work out."

Aunt Pat let out a heavy frustrated sigh. "No. I'm not sayin that. I'm just tryna cover all the bases here Brenda. I'm tryna work some stuff out. Will you just work with me, please? Just do what I ask you? For once?"

"Okay. whatever you say."

"Good." She smiled. "You know your mother would kick my ass for telling people *she* was the junky."

"Yeah I know. She prolly rollin all around her grave right now."

"For real." She laughed. "Ahhhh, I really miss that girl."

Brenda sighed. "Yeah. Me too Aunt Pat. Everyday. I been dreamin about her a lot lately."

"That's crazy, cause I been dreamin bout her to. Maybe she tryna tell us somethin."

"Maybe. Have you seen Brandy? I was hoping she'd come today. She said she was gon write me but I haven't gotten anything from her yet."

"Honestly I haven't seen her since the funeral. I been kinda busy."

"I'm sure you have. How you doin? You ok?"

"No. But…" She shrugged. "…you know."

"Yeah I know."

"Brandy's at home. Over on Champlain. She's safe. That's what's most important. She'll reach out to you when she ready."

"Yeah, I guess. Hey, I been meaning to ask you something."

"What?"

"Well. I been thinkin about this for a while. Years actually. But I know how private you are about your business. And then after all the stuff with the reality show and…"

"Brenda. What is it?"

"I wanna write a book. About your life."

"My what?" Aunt Pat frowned. "Hell nah…"

"No, hear me out Aunt Pat. I started on it the last time I was in. I got like sixty pages so far, and it's good. Real good. And that's mainly just from the stuff that mama told me."

"Girl. No. What I need people knowin all in my business for?"

"People already know your business. It's public record."

"People know what I want em to know. Aight."

Brenda pleaded. "But it's a good stoooory."

"Maybe. But it's my story and I said no. Don't write nothin bout me."

"Just listen, I let the librarian read what I wrote. Kinda critique my writing. And she loved it. She said it had the makings of a best seller if I did it right. She actually wrote the words 'captivating' on the top page. I'm telling you Aunt Pat.."

"Brenda! What part of NO don't you understand?"

The guard tapped on the window. "Time's up counselor."

Aunt Pat stood. "Aight, I gotta get outta here. Imma handle all this stuff on the inside. Don't worry about it. Just sit tight."

"Ok."

"And remember what I said about Petty. If he call you out you *gotta* play that role. This is important."

"Aight."

"I'm serious."

"I got it."

"And Brenda."

"Yeah."

"I'm not playin wit you about that book. The answer is no. And ion wanna talk about it no more, hear?

"Yeah."

You hear me?"

Yeeeeesssss."

"Aight, I'll see you in a few days. I love you."

"Love you too."

At the end of the visit both ladies left the visiting hall on a mission. Aunt Pat left the facility, steam coming from every hole in her head. *Braxton bitches musta lost they muthafuckin mind. But they gon find it today.*

Brenda went right back to the library. Back to her desktop. Back to her captivating manuscript. Working title, *The Notorious P.A.T.: The Story of Patricia James.* She pecked at the keyboard and smiled thinking, *Ion care wat she say. This shit is good. She gon thank me later.*

Diva Las Vegas

Finally, it was all over. The games, the lies, the misunderstandings. The *danger*. And they could just be. After a night of purging, and heavy drinks, they'd made a pact to never discuss the pregnancy again. Or Kevin. Or the reality show. The kidnapping. It was all behind them, and it was time to start living the lives they both dreamed of. Together.

Missy pulled on her garter then her edible lace panties in his favorite flavor. A nice surprise for after the ceremony. Yellow. Pineapple. To match her yellow diamond and the Something Yellow Manolo Blahnik pumps she wore for her wedding day.

The day before, Chucky surprised her with a series of plane tickets and a confirmed itinerary for the wonderfully extravagant week-long West Coast woosah vacation she told him that she'd always wanted to take.

The trip would start with power shopping at the Wynn and the Venetian in Vegas, followed by a romantic helicopter ride over the Grand Canyon, followed by an equally romantic dinner down inside it. The next morning they'd rent a shiny red convertible and drive through the desert with the top down, headed to L.A. for more power shopping on Rodeo Drive. They'd have lunch in The Grove, dinner at Mr. Chow and dancing with the stars in the VIP section at Club AV. They'd spend the night at the luxurious Beverly Wilshire and take an early morning drive to San Diego to visit the zoo, SeaWorld, and walk barefoot along Coronado Beach. They'd end the trip with a glorious weekend of pampering at the famous Mii Amo spa in Sedona, Arizona.

Chucky had just received a fat advance for his role in a new DC-based Rom-Com starring opposite his old schoolmate,

Taraji Henson. The working title for the film was *Dem Bammas Be Trippin*. He even had some writing credits. Chucky Baby was back! So the first-class flights were booked, the hotels were prepaid, and a beautiful red convertible Mercedes was reserved. Missy thanked him *good* that night and the next morning they were taxiing down the runway to forever.

Chucky knocked on the bedroom door. "Hey babe. You ready?" He jiggled the handle.

"No! Chucky don't come in here! I don't want you to see me before the ceremony. It's bad luck."

"Girl, stop trippin. That's some old dumb superstitious bullshit white people made up. You think the slaves did that shit? And they marriages lasted through the underground railroad."

"I don't care what the slaves did. Don't bring your butt in this room. I have to put on my finishing touches. Go ahead to the chapel and I'll meet you down there."

"You're not going with me?"

"No I'll take a taxi. Now go, so we don't miss our appointment time."

"Aight. I'll take the taxi. You can drive the car."

"Ok, well have the valet pull it around for me please. I'll see you in a few."

"Ok. And Missy."

"Yes?"

"I love you, gurrrl."

She giggled. "I know you do."

"I mean, you got me all shook up."

"Really?"

"Yeah, like I can't help falling in love with you?"

"Is that right?"

"That's right. And imma give you summa dis hound dog later on."

She laughed. "Will you go ahead Chucky!"

"Aight. But for real. I love you Missy."

"I love you too...fool."

She spritzed her beautiful wavy blonde coif within an inch of its life, lined her lips to perfection and painted them a glossy red. Then she perfected the faux beauty mark on her right upper lip. She smoothed down the skirt on her sexy white halter dress and stepped into her Manolo's. "Perfect."

In typical Missy fashion she attracted considerable attention, as she sauntered through the hotel lobby and casino. The men gawked, some whistled and some stared. Most of the women glared. She smiled, she winked, and she even blew a few kisses. Very dramatic like.

The valet joked that she made the real Marilyn Monroe look like Marilyn Manson. To that compliment, she planted her ruby red lips on his cheek and kicked up her heel. Then she slid into the driver's seat and set off for her date with destiny.

She pulled into the crowded parking lot of the infamous Graceland Chapel. Missy walked into the lobby and wondered what the *hell* she had let Chucky talk her into. Elvis impersonators were everywhere. Of every nationality. Black Elvis. Indian Elvis. A little Chinese Elvis Presley with a little electric guitar. Several couples in full wedding attire were standing in line waiting to take their walk down the aisle. *This is nuts*, she thought.

Just when she started to have second thoughts, Chucky appeared in the doorway. She looked at his side-burned wig, white bellbottomed jumpsuit covered in rhinestones and mirrored aviator shades, and she completely lost it. Laughing herself to tears. "Chucky what the HELL are we doin?"

We havin fun, girl. Stop trippin." Then he tripped on his too long pant leg and fell down the steps of the short landing.

Several costumed patrons rushed to his aide. "Sir! Sir, are you ok?"

Embarrassed, he sprang right back up and got into character "Yeah! That wuddn't nuttin but a hound dog baby."

Missy screamed out laughing. "Oh gawd! No!"

Chucky slow pimped over to Missy and stood next to her in line. He murmured. "*Shit.*"

Missy was still laughing. "Are you ok?"

He grabbed his leg. "No. I think I knocked my damn knee cap loose. Shit. Come on, we next."

She couldn't stop laughing. "No wait. Chucky, you got me cryin. My eyelashes are coming off."

"Then just take em off."

"No, wait." She pulled herself together, pinched them back on tightly, and they grabbed hands before walking into the sanctuary.

Exactly twelve minutes later the quickie wedding was in the books and they were dancing back down the aisle to Elvis' *Can't Help Falling in Love*; hand in hand, smiling ear to ear, husband and wife. It was the happiest either of them had ever been, and long overdue.

Missy was cheesin and Chucky was hyped, hollerin "This is my WIFE! *My* wife yawl!" to anyone who would listen. They hopped in the convertible and hit the gas, ready to paint Sin City red.

Planned to a tee, the rest of the excursion went off without a hitch. They spent the rest of the day in costume. Blowing money at the crap tables in the Mirage. Sipping champagne while soaring over the Grand Canyon; feeding on frijoles and Prickly Pear margaritas as they gazed up at the stars from the inside it.

Missy allowed her hair to blow freely in the wind as they drove top speed on winding roads through the Nevada desert. Back to the hotel. Chucky had been waiting all day to eat her out of those pineapple draws. And he didn't disappoint. He put in all of the work and Missy was grateful for the absolute bestest, stickiest, most delicious good time they'd had to date.

The next morning, they were both spent and virtually stuck together but excited to hit the highway to continue the fun.

Beverly Hills was as fabulous as it ever was. Armed with Chucky's black card, and plenty bougie black girl magic, Missy pranced through the mannequins at Prada, perused case after display case of exquisite baubles at Chanel's Fine Jewelry Boutique and sipped champagne in the private suite at Louis Vuitton as she waited for her newly monogrammed satchels to be presented to her for examination. She sashayed down Rodeo toting thousands in spoils; living out her Pretty Woman fantasy to the fullest. She'd almost forgotten the feeling of a good carefree shopping spree. It was good to be back.

San Diego was a wonderfully romantic adventure starting with breakfast cocktails at the Fairmont, a guided city tour, a hot air balloon ride and a torch lit picnic dinner on the secluded beach under a bright full moon; the only intrusion to their love making were the sounds of a low tide coming into shore.

Lastly and most decadently, the Hozhooji treatment at the Mii Amo spa was every bit the life altering experience she was told that it would be. As she sat immersed up to her neck in a bath of organic milk and honey, Missy could not have been happier. Their honeymoon week was an absolutely unforgettable whirlwind of pleasures that she couldn't begin to thank him for.

Though she wasn't able to sway Chucky's alpha male ego into a rejuvenating spa treatment, he most definitely appreciated the residual effects that it had on her. Missy came back from the spa, relaxed and centered, regenerated and reinvigorated. Appreciative and ready.

He laid naked, waiting on the bed with a massive erection and come-hither-y expression. She untied the terry robe and opened it wide, revealing her nakedness. He motioned for her to come over to the bed. She smiled and shook her head *no*. Then she closed and retied her robe. He shrugged and pulled the thin bed sheet over his body, his erection creating a little tent that seemed to turn her on. She stared at it, biting her bottom lip, wanting to climb underneath. But she resisted the urge.

She untied her robe and walked toward the bed. Then she sat down in an arm chair beside it and lifted a leg over the arm, exposing her fresh Brazilian. She placed her middle finger inside her mouth and pulled it out slow, then she reached down and touched herself. Chucky's eyes were aglow. He smirked. Two could definitely play that game because she didn't like to be teased any more than he.

He reached below the sheet and grabbed hold of his manhood. The sheet began to move. Missy tried to focus on his eyes, but her mind wandered to the scene under that sheet. Chucky tried to keep her gaze and ignore her pretty pink manicure exploring south of her navel, covered in her wetness, making the sweetest sounds.

Neither of them lasted long. The teasing soon became unbearable, as they both yearned deeply for the other's touch. Chucky reached out and grabbed her by the bottom of her robe, forcefully pulling her over to the bed, down onto his face just as she snatched the sheet from his waist and took him in her mouth. They moaned as each struck the other's nerve, both getting closer to a climax but neither wanting to be the first to give.

Missy gave first. Hard and loud. She tried to pull away, but Chucky buried his face deeper into her flesh, intensifying his tongue thrusts as she squirmed and he held her firmly at her thighs so she couldn't get away. She pleaded for him to stop. He didn't. Instead he threw her onto her side and lifted her leg high. The tingles hadn't yet subsided so when he entered her it sent a wave through her body causing her to gasp and yell out for him.

"Ahhh! Chucky!"

"That's right. What's my muthufuckin name?" He thrust himself completely inside her. She hollered.

"Oh God."

"No, not God. What's my name?"

"Chucky. "He thrust again, and she squealed. "Oh!"

"Say it again."

"Shiiit!"

Chucky continued to thrust hard, long and strong, searching for that spot he always seemed to find. He whispered his commands in her ear and she responded in kind. Missy went from moaning to shouting as he stirred up every good feeling inside her. He turned her over onto her back and mounted her missionary so he could look her into her eyes and tell her how much he loved her as he gave her every inch of him. Before long, he found that spot and he relished in every second of the most intensely emotional climax he'd ever seen her have.

Missy wiped the tears from her eyes and laid her head on his chest. He held her close sand kissed her on the forehead.

"Thought you was gon come up in here and fuck me to sleep didn't you?"

She lifted her head. "What?"

"I'm hip to your game now, girl. That's why I had to fuck the tears up out that ass."

She slapped him on the chest and blushed. "I swear I can't stand you!"

"Yes you can. And you gon be standing me for a long, looong time, Mrs. Charles Wade Wilson the Third."

She kissed him softly on the lips and slid her hand under the covers, bringing him to attention in an instant.

He sighed. "What you doin, girl?"

She whispered, "Redeeming myself." And she slipped under the covers.

Thirteen minutes and one earth-shattering, toe-curling, profanity-laced orgasm later, Chucky was fast asleep, snoring loudly and Missy smirked satisfaction. She kissed him softy on the lips and snuggled back up onto his chest.

She laid there, just listening to him breathe for a while. Feeling the pulsating rhythm of a man's heart that she knew, beat just for her. There was no feeling that could compare. None that she'd experienced. It was overwhelming.

Tears rolled from the corner of her eyes onto his chest. Never had she been loved so wholly and so completely as she had with Chucky Wilson. And from the very beginning. His love was always there and it was always true. She thanked God for that. She thanked God for him and she thanked Him for giving them yet another chance at love.

Lord. I know I don't talk to you very much. But I just want to thank you. Thank you for blessing me and keeping me. Thank you for keeping my family and thank you for sending me love. I ask that you bless my husband and bless my marriage. Continue to bless and protect us all. Amen.

Missy laid long enough to realize sleep wasn't coming that night. There was just too much running through her mind. She climbed out of bed, walked over to the bar and poured the last of the champagne. Missy stood in the picture window, sipping bubbles and gazing out into the beautiful Southwestern landscape of Sedona. The sun rose over red rock mountains as far as her eye could see. Mii Amo was every bit as magnificent as the pictures in the brochures.

Missy wished they could stay there in the confines of the beautiful resort for a while longer. To escape the very real issues that were waiting for them at home. The aftermath. The residual effects of all the tragic events that had taken place over the course of yet another gut wrenching, catastrophic, drama filled year in the lives of the James Girls. Complete and utter, extreme ridiculousness. Always.

She swallowed the last of her champagne and slid back under the covers. Back into her husband's loving arms for a little rest. For in just a few short hours they were to rise and board a jet plane. Two first class one-way tickets back to the DMV. Back to reality.

Identity Crisis

Kristoff Sanderson, young private investigator for the district government, stepped into Petty's office with a manila envelope and a perplexed look on his face. "Mr. Petty I didn't find anything on a middle-aged black woman named Patricia Carter. I put the picture from the security camera through and didn't get any hits at all. Nothing."

"You sure you checked everything?"

"Every database I had access to. The ones that mattered. Police, FBI, CIA. Nothing."

Petty's sour-faced secretary set his coffee on his desk, glanced at the eight by ten pic of Aunt Pat walking into the building and mumbled, "That ain't no Patricia Carter."

Petty looked up at her. "I'm sorry, did you say something, Mable?"

"Yeah I did. That ain't no Patricia Carter."

"You know her?"

"That's Patricia James. One of them James Girls from over at the Ridgewood projects. She came in here yesterday with that Carter business. But I knew who she was."

"How do *you* know her?"

"Just look her up. I know what I'm talkin bout. You'll see." She walked out of the office, back to her desk, back to her iPad, streaming the Dr. Oz show with the volume down low.

Petty turned back to Kristoff. "Ok, Patricia James. Go look her up."

Kristoff headed for the door. "You got it boss."

An hour later, Kristoff walked back into Petty's office with a large brown accordion file folder, filled to capacity with smaller manila folders. Each of the smaller manila folders held mug shots, paperwork, case files. The State of North Carolina vs. Patricia Ann James. Manslaughter. Plea deal taken. The State of Virginia vs. Patricia Ann James. The District of Columbia vs. Patricia Ann James. There were multiple arrests for pandering, drug possession and drug trafficking. Various assaults. Several with a deadly weapon. She'd been charged with kidnapping, extortion, making terroristic threats, intimidating a witness and conspiracy to commit murder. There were nearly three dozen cases brought against her, most of which she'd beaten or taken pleas for unusually short sentences. There were mugshots dating back thirty years. You could tell by the hair. From afros to cornrows to Jheri curls and crewcuts. Same smug fuck-the-establishment expression every time.

Petty spent the rest of the day pouring through the files, feeling a little played. He reached in the desk drawer for the Post-it and dialed. The voice mail picked up.

"This message is for Ms. Patricia Carter. It's Assistant District Attorney Tyrone Petty. I just received some very interesting information. I'd like to continue our discussion. Please meet me in my office tomorrow morning, first thing. I look forward to speaking with you."

*****

The next morning, Aunt Pat walked into Petty's office. She reached for his hand. "Mr. Petty."

He obliged. "Ms. James."

She smiled, then pulled her wig off, revealing a fresh Caesar cut with an immaculately shaped up hairline. "So I guess we can cut right through the bullshit."

"Yes, let's. I looked you up—"

"I figured you might."

He picked up the stack of files from the floor and sat it on the desk in front of her. "I found some very interesting things in here."

She pushed it back in his direction. "I'm sure you did. And now that you know who *I* am, like I said, we can cut through the bullshit. So what's your answer?"

"Now why on *earth* would I want to do business with you? You're a murderer." He began to count off the felony charges on his fingers. "...a murderer, a drug dealer, pimp–"

She reared back in her chair and interrupted. "Oh yeah. I'm *all that*. And a whole lot more. But we ain't here to talk about me. We here to talk about my niece. And she ain't none-a that. So I need you to let her go. Let her go and be a mother to her children. Have a life. And I'll give you back yours. For your troubles."

"Excuse me?"

"I did my homework too. Heard you just got busted down to ADA last year for your *conduct*. And right now, you needin something to put you back in that top spot. I got that for you. Like I said before, this shit gon make you a celebrity. That's if you handle it right. It's up to you. That's if you want it."

"Ms. James, I appreciate the *concern*, but in case you haven't heard, I've been cleared of all wrongdoing. Looks like you didn't finish your homework, ma'am. Or sir or whatever you are. I'll have my spot back soon enough."

Aunt Pat bit down on her bottom lip. It was all she could do not to reach over that desk and grab the nigga by his throat. But she kept it cool. "Negro *please*. You know well as I do that white girl done took yo spot and ran wit it. She ain't lost a case yet. That's that new affirmative action. Might as well stick a fork in your career here, cause that shit is done son."

"I think I'll be just fine."

She pulled herself to the edge of her chair, rested her elbows on his desk and looked him intently in the eye. 'Will you?"

Petty nervously cleared his throat. "Are you threatening me, Ms. James?"

"I don't make threats, Mr. Petty." She smiled. "Well...not idle ones. You got my file." She stood and walked to the door. "You got one more day, Petty."

Family First

He picked up on the fourth ring. Tired of ducking her calls. Knowing he'd have to face her soon. Before he left for good. He didn't want to see her face. It would be too hard. But a call, he could do. "Good morning."

"I've been calling you. I came by. Where've you been?"

"I'm in Frederick. At my mom's. I needed to take some time."

"Well, why haven't you been answering my calls?"

"I dunno. I guess...I guess I didn't have anything to say."

Brandy hung up the phone.

They hadn't spoken in weeks. Not since the shooting and the night it happened, Tay didn't say much. He didn't ask much. Which was good because she didn't know much. Not at that time, anyway. At that time, she knew only what Aunt Pat told her. That the men that took Misa might come back, so she should stay away from Ridgewood and go to Uncle Edwards'. And she would have, but she couldn't bear to be under the same roof as mean old nosy old Aunt Carolyn, so she decided to head over to Tay's to kick it with him and TJ. They lived around the corner from Ridgewood. So technically she complied. How was she supposed to know there was a tracking device on Aunt Missy's car?

Her phone lit up. She picked it up before the end of the first ring. "Hello."

Tay spoke in a calm tone. "What if TJ would have been home?"

Brandy didn't speak, which annoyed Tay all the more.

He shouted into the receiver, "Hello!"

"Yes, I'm here."

"What if my son would have been at home, Brandy?"

"I know. I thought about that."

"Really?" he asked, facetiously. "Well I'm glad you thought about it. Because it's all I can think about now. I think about it every day. Every single day since it happened. Every time I look in his face I think what could have happened if he would have been home the night two gunmen busted through my front door, held me at gunpoint, and then started a gunfight that left my windows broken and a dead man lying on my living room floor. Brandy, why would you bring that shit to my house?"

"Tay how was I supposed to know that—"

"Look, I'm moving."

"What?"

"I'm moving. Back to Frederick with my mom. We're putting the house on the market. I'll be moved out by the end of the month."

Brandy sat quietly for a moment. Tay gave her that moment to digest. She swallowed hard before she spoke again. "When did you decide that?"

"About a week ago. When the carpenters were replacing my windows and pulling up the bloody carpet in my living room. When TJ brought me a got damn shell casing he found in the front yard."

Her voice cracked. "You know I never meant for any of this to happen."

"I know you didn't mean for it to happen. Of course you didn't. But it still happened. Brandy, you came to my house after you were told, *specifically* told, not to come back to the area because somebody might be looking for you. Somebody armed and…and fuckin dangerous. Then you brought that danger straight to my house and didn't say nothing to me about what was going on. You just left me in the blind. And if it wasn't for a little kids slumber party, there's no telling what would've happened to my son. TJ is all I have! And I'm all he has! The only reason I stayed here in DC *this* long was to let him be around his mother. And we see how well that worked out. I can't do this no more. I can't. I wanna raise my son someplace quiet.

Somewhere…safe. So we're leaving. There's nothing left in DC for me."

His words stung. Especially since he was the one thing keeping her in DC. After their last crazy night, she had a complete evolution of heart. There was no need to fight it anymore. No need to hide it. Her mother was right. She shouldn't let anything or anyone stand in the way of her happiness. She loved Tay and she was gonna let him know it. She'd come clean with him about her feelings. Tell him about the pregnancy. Really let him in. She'd get all the answers to all the questions she'd been holding on to for so long. So they could have a fresh start.

"Hello?" Tay called out into the receiver. "Brandy?"

She gathered her thoughts. "Yeah, I'm still here."

"I said it's time for me to go and pick TJ up."

"O…Ok. Well, do you think I could come—"

He hung up before she could finish her sentence.

Tay sat staring at the wall. TJ was in the next room asleep. He just didn't want to hear Brandy's voice. It hurt too much. A life with her was a dream – a beautiful one, but a dream just the same. Besides, did she *really* want him or was she toying with him like the others? Did it even matter? Her family was so messed up he didn't know if he or TJ could survive it. It wasn't worth the risk. What would happen the next time the James' had trouble. The next time someone was kidnapped for ransom or murdered in their bathtub. The next time Aunt Pat had a plan. His first priority was TJ. Period. Everything else….well…it just didn't matter. Not anymore.

Home Sweet Home

Missy opened her eye, rolled over and awakened Chucky with a kiss. "Good morning husband."

Chucky slowly opened his eyes and smiled. "Good mornin wifey."

They kissed and she snuggled into his chest. He wrapped his arms around her and kissed her forehead. She looked up at him and smiled, "It's good to be home."

"Yes it is."

"I still can't believe we did it."

"I know, right. And in Vegas. I'm still a little disappointed you wouldn't let me give you a real wedding."

"We've both already done the big wedding thing, and we see how well that turned out."

"I know, but you deserve so much better than the Graceland Chapel in Vegas. I don't know what I was thinkin. And why you let me dress up like that cracka. That shit was dumb." He reached down and rubbed his left knee. "Dumbass bellbottoms damn near handicapped me. My shit still hurtin."

She laughed. "Stop it. It was fun. I loved every minute of it." She hugged him a little tighter. "And I have what I deserve. What matters to me is right here...next to me."

"You know, last time you said that to me...I lost you."

Missy lifted her head, an incredulous look on her face. "Oh my God. You're right! Wow. That day in the car on the way to tell my husband I was leaving him for good. I sure got a rude awakening that day."

"That's a hell of a understatement right there."

"Right. That seems like ages ago. You know we've been through a lot to get here."

"Who you tellin. But we here now baby cakes." He rolled over on top of her, his early morning hardness pressed up against her thigh. "And ion know what it was you did to me the other night at Mii Amo. But I swear I can't get enough of your ass." He kissed her on the neck and pulled down the top of her nightie, exposing her right breast.

"Chuckyyyy...no."

He whined. "Come on now baby. We still on our honeymoon."

"No we honeymooned all night. I'm tired baby. And dehydrated."

"Yeah I bet. Drained all the juice right out yo ass, didn't I?"

She laughed. "You so nasty."

"Yeah, and you love it."

"I do."

"I can't get my dick to go down."

She sat up, rubbed her stomach and mumbled. "I think I need to take a laxative or something."

He shuddered. "Ugh. All right, it's down now."

She pushed him nearly of the bed. "Shut up!"

"So what we gon do today?"

"Well first I need to go over to Champlain and check on my girls, let them know they got a *new daddy*. Then I need to go and see Carmen. For some reason, my final payment for the show never made it to my bank account. I'm sick and tired of playing with her shady behind. I swear that girl will do any damn thing for a dollar. She'll sell out anybody to get what she wants – PJ, Aunt Pat. She completely threw me under the bus. And that shit she pulled with Kevin..."

"Missy don't bring that nigga up to me."

"Oh. You're right. I'm sorry."

"Fuckin Carmen. That bitch ain't your friend anyway. Scandalous ass." Chucky jumped out of the bed and threw on his pants. "Don't bring her ass around me again. That's all I'm sayin."

"Ok. I know you're pissed but I'm just venting. So calm down."

"No. Fuck her. I don't want her around. Point blank."

"Wait. Chucky, come on. It's not like Carmen is just my friend. She was also *your* friend."

"Friend?"

"Ok maybe friend is too strong a word, but you were definitely cool with her. Cool enough for her to get you to come on the show. Or was that all about the money?" Chucky glared at her, and she immediately regretted her comment. "I'm just saying. I've never heard you say anything bad about Carmen until now. I understand you're still pissed about Kevin, and I'm not exactly her biggest fan right now either, but no matter how much shit I talk about her, that's still my best friend. So you can't start that you don't want her around stuff. We're not doing *that*."

"You so sure about her huh?"

"Actually I am. We fight all the time, yes, but at the end of the day I know she has my back and I have hers."

Chucky sat on the bed beside her. There was a long pause before he sighed. "Ok I wasn't even gon tell you this...cause I don't really like bein in between no women's business...but...

The Deal

Petty laid a Cuban on his desk beside a rocks glass. He poured the glass about a third full of Scotch and waited for her to walk through the door. Aunt Pat closed the door behind her and took a seat in the desk chair opposite him.

She picked up the cigar. "For me?"

Petty smiled, as he puffed a ring into the air. "It's for you."

She examined the label on the stogie. "It's my brand." She turned the bottle of Scotch around and peered at the label. "John Walker. Nice. So I'm guessing we have something to celebrate."

"Indeed we do. I've thought it over, and I decided I'm gonna accept your offer, Ms. James."

Aunt Pat picked up her glass and raised it. They toasted. "Smart man." She took a sip. "Damn, that's good."

"Yeah I'd been saving this for a while. Waiting for something big."

"Well this is big. The biggest gift you ever gon get. Instant celebrity."

"I would have to agree with that. This will definitely change my life. But I'm not the only one that will be thrust into the spotlight."

"It's a small price."

"You ever thought about writing your memoirs?"

Aunt Pat sighed and rolled her eyes. "No."

"No? Ms. James, you have quite a story to tell. Surely you realize the value in that."

"Petty—"

"I reached out to a friend of mine this morning. He's a literary agent. He's quite confident that he could get you a six figure deal for your story. Especially considering...how the story ends."

"So you discussed our business with him."

Petty noted the serious tone in her voice, the grim look on her face. "No, no of course not. Well…not in so many words. Don't worry, I kept it hypothetical."

She laughed and shook her head. "You lucky I'm turnin over a new leaf."

He smiled. "Or what…you'd kill me?"

Her smile faded. "Yeah…I would."

He shifted, nervously in his chair and took another sip of scotch. "Can I ask you something?"

"Sure. Why not."

"Why are you doing this? Just doesn't make sense, to me"

"It don't need to make sense to you."

"I mean…I know you love your family but–"

"Aint no but. I love my family. I'll do anything for my family. Don't you have family?"

"Not really."

"Then I feel sorry for you. Petty, if you ain't got nothin in this world worth living for, or worth dying for, you ain't really alive."

He took the last sip of his drink and poured another. "Very poignant, Ms. James. But I do just fine."

"If you say so." She finished her glass and put out her cigar. "Aight, enough small talk. This is how it goes down."

Mrs. Melissa Wilson

Missy parked her car at a McDonald's about a half block from BET Studios and walked the rest of the way down the hill. She didn't want to risk her car being seen. Carmen's assistant Shae said she had a dentist appointment and wouldn't be in until around eleven, which pretty much meant Shae wouldn't be in until 10:45. So Missy had about a half hour to do what she needed to do.

She walked into the building and signed in at the front desk. The security guard was his usual chipper self. "Hey Ms. James. Good morning!"

Missy flashed her wedding ring and a cheesy smile. "It's Mrs. Wilson now."

"Ohhh, congratulations. That there is a nice ring."

"Thank you. So how've you been Stanley?"

"Well you know I seen better days. This old man just ain't what he used to be. Got arthritis, bursitis. And the left side of my hip…" Stanley went on and on about ailment after ailment. Missy wished she'd never inquired.

"Stanley, I hate to interrupt but I'm really in a hurry."

"Oh no, you go'on ahead Ms. James…I mean, Mrs. Wilson. You have a good day now, hear?"

"Thanks Stanley. You too."

She walked over to the elevator and pressed the up arrow. Then she eased past it to the door leading to the stairwell. The stairwell was empty, so she walked up to the third floor and peeked out. The reception desk was empty, just as she suspected. *That girl needs to be fired.*

Missy walked into Carmen's office and closed the door behind her. She sat behind her desk and powered the computer on. She could hear voices outside the door. Walking past. She hurriedly typed *D*e*s*t*i*n*y*1*9*9*5*. It was the password Carmen used for everything – the daughter Carmen miscarried back in college.

She gained access, and the display was full. Carmen never logged out of anything. Outlook, Gmail, Facepage and about 15 other pages including Hood Tube, and Xvideos were idling at the bottom of the page. Missy shook her head. *Nasty ass watchin porn at work.*

She went into outlook first. There was a folder for *Black Love*. Mostly business it looked like. Contracts and lawyer talk. There was a subfolder, *The Ex factor* and another *Contestants*.

Missy scanned through nearly all of the hundred emails in Carmen's inboxes, getting angrier by the click. She printed the best of the worst. For evidence. She clicked and she scrolled. Her eyes bucked wide and her mouth agape. Everything Chucky said was true; right there in front of her, in black and white. Some of it in color. She was stunned.

Missy couldn't help thinking, everything about their relationship was a lie. She really had no idea *who* Carmen was.

Missy looked at the time. It was 10:47. She heard Shae settling in at her desk so she got up and walked to the other side of Carmen's desk and took a seat. Carmen would be in soon.

Missy thought on what she'd say. How to approach the situation. She really had no clue how to handle it. But there was no doubt, it had to be handled. Now. She checked her watch. 10:54. Her palms sweat. Her breathing was heavy. She crossed one leg over the other, to stop it from shaking.

Shae walked in. "Hey. Ms. James. You didn't mention you were comin in. Ms. Lewis'll be here in a minute. You know, I saw the show last week and –"

"Thanks hun, would you mind getting me some coffee? Just a little cream, no sugar."

Shae paused for a moment before she answered. "Uh…yeah, no problem. I'll be right back."

Missy thought she caught a glimpse of an eye roll as Shae walked out the door. Just then she thought, *she better not mess with my coffee.* Missy had no time for small talk. She needed to save every ounce of brain power for her *friend.*

Shae brought the coffee back and handed it to her with a smile. "Here you go Ms. James." Missy thanked her and waited until she walked out to take the lid off. She looked inside to see if anything weird – lint, a little funny foam – was happening. Then she sat it back on the desk. *Never mind.*

Minutes later Carmen walked in. When she saw Missy she had a curious look on her face. "Hey girl. What you doin here? I been meaning to call you. I got your check in my desk. If you want–"

Missy jumped up and slapped her hard across the face, backhanded, knocking her into the wall. "You dirty bitch! I knew you wanted my fuckin life but not *this* bad. All of them Carmen? All of them?!"

Carmen grabbed her face. "What the hell are you talking about?! Are you crazy!"

Missy pointed a finger in Carmen's face. "You know what, yeah I'm crazy. Crazy to think you were my friend. All these years. All these fucking years!"

"Missy! Wha–"

"I went through your fucking email!" Missy picked up the stack of paper off the desk and rattled off the offenses one by one, balling up the pages and throwing them at Carmen when she was done. "To Hector. *Thank you for last night. That dick is just as good as it used to be. Can't wait to see you again. With your crazy ass.* To Ian. *Where did you learn to work your tongue like that! I'll be over this weekend for more.* To Andre. *I'll be home at 7:00. Can you bring some papers when you come? I got us some of that good purple haze you like. You know you gotta fuck me right if you wanna get on the show.* Oh and to Chucky. *You don't know what you're missing. Here's a little preview.* Missy held up a picture. *You* sent *my* man a picture of your saggy ass, droopy ass, big nipple titties. She balled the page up and threw it in Carmen's face. When he told me about the picture, I didn't believe him. Not at first. I was like *hell no. Carmen is my girl. My best friend. She would never disrespect me like tha*t. He insisted, but he didn't have the picture. He told me he deleted it from his phone right after he got it. So I came here to see it for myself. And sure enough. It was right there, still in your sent items. With your stupid ass.

"Wait, ok listen..."

"Listen to what?! To you lie?! Tell me Carmen. How long have you been having my leftovers? Huh? Trying to be like me. Following behind me and picking up my scraps. Since when, high school? College? I know these aren't the only ones you've been with. Low self-esteem having ass. You know Chucky told me he took a poll in the house. They talked about you. Real bad. From your big man hands and feet to your stankin hair weave. He said he asked how many had been with you, and every single hand was raised, *except* his."

Carmen smirked and looked Missy directly in the eye. "You sure about that?"

"What? Bitch don't you even try it. I saw the emails you sent him, and I saw his responses. My husband wants no parts of your nasty ass."

"Your husband?"

Missy held up her left hand. "Yes bitch, my huzzzband."

"Since when?"

Missy ignored the question. "He told me you came on *strong*. And you kept coming even after he turned you down, multiple times. *You* said, you don't know what he sees is my bougie ass?"

"No, I never–"

"Yes you did. Carmen don't even sit here and try to deny it. You ain't shit, you never were and ain't never gonna be shit but a hoe. And you tried it right here, in your office. Called Chucky in here. Tried to turn him against me with this bullshit with Kevin, then you bent over and showed him your flat, wide ass. But he wasn't with it, was he? Turned your little nasty flat, stank ass down flat."

Missy snatched her purse and headed for the door. Tired of being insulted and berated, Carmen decided to strike back. Hit one last nerve for the road. She smirked. "Oh, he turned me down flat. *That's* what he told you? Hmm."

Missy stopped and turned back around. Her face washed

with annoyance. Carmen knew she had her. So she went in. "Tell me something. How's Georgetown? Does he still sprinkle baby powder under his sheets?"

Missy screamed and threw her bag at Carmen's head. She lunged at her bestie, grabbing her by the hair. Carmen latched on to Missy's hair, and they locked in. They swung wildly at each other, screaming and cursing, knocking into office furniture as Shae looked in through the glass panel, watching and waiting for Missy to draw blood. She wanted to see Carmen get her ass whooped, bad.

They tussled until Carmen finally got Missy to the floor. "Bitch! I'm tired a your ass!" She threw a hard punch landing at Missy's right eye. Missy kicked and screamed, pushing Carmen off of her "My face! You dirty hoe!" She threw an overhand left, her hand slightly open, scratching Carmen across the face and throwing her into the desk. The desk, with the large Styrofoam cup that flipped over, dousing them both with its scalding hot contents. They both screamed bloody murder as piping hot coffee soaked through thin fabric and burned their skin.

Shae rushed in to help. She grabbed the box of tissue from Carmen's desk and doled them out. With her slow DC drawl, she asked. "Oh my gawwwd! Wuss goin awwwn in heeeeere?!"

Missy scowled at Carmen as she held her aching right eye. Carmen hissed at Missy as she dabbed the blood that seeped from the deep scratches in her cheek. They were both still stinging from the coffee burns. It was the first time their fighting had ever gone beyond words.

Carmen picked herself up from the floor and straightened her dress. "Shae. Will you leave us alone please?"

"Huh?"

"Leave the room."

"Oh. Ok." She smiled. "Y'all gon be aight?"

"Shae."

"Okayyy."

She left the room and closed the door behind her. Carmen grabbed a few more tissues from the box and handed them to Missy. She extended her hand, offering to help Missy to her feet.

Missy took her hand and the arm of a nearby chair, pulling herself up off the floor. She smoothed her soiled dress down.

Carmen sat on the edge of the desk. "Missy, I've never been with Chucky. I just said that shit to make you mad. You're the one that told me about the powder on his sheets. I just needed to get that out of the way first. The others…yes. I'm not gon lie." Missy huffed. Carmen pleaded. "Look, I know you're mad and you have every right to be. What I did, betraying you like that. It was unforgivable. So I don't expect you to forgive me, but just hear me out…please…"

Carmen went on to apologize. Profusely. Sharing things that she never had. A history of abuse and neglect. Depression after the miscarriage in college. Her never really having any friends. Except Missy. She could tell she was getting through; Missy's heart was softening. She could see it in her eyes. Missy never could stay mad. No matter what they went through. Carmen wrapped it up nicely.

"…and the truth is, you're the only person who has ever really truly loved me." A tear escaped her eye. "Sometimes I think…more than I love myself."

Missy sat quietly. She'd learned a lot about her friend in the very short span of about ten minutes. Some of which she suspected but much more than she imagined. Carmen was damaged. She was hurt, so she hurt in turn. Disregarded and disrespected so many people. She'd sabotaged relationships and trampled over feelings. She'd been doing it for years. But considering all she'd been through, it made sense. Perfect sense.

Missy pulled another tissue from the box and dabbed her friend's face. She laid a gentle hand at her cheek, nudging Carmen's face toward hers. After everything she'd seen and everything she'd heard, there were only two words she could bring herself to utter – "Bitch. Please."

She threw the tissue in the waste paper basket, snatched her purse from the floor, and walked out of the office, slamming the door behind her.

Shae giggled. *"Bye Ms. Jaaames."* Then she walked over to Carmen's door and stood staring in, thinking how unbelievably lucky she was to be in Carmen Lewis's employ.

Just three months earlier, Shae was a temp, with no experience, making $13 an hour to answer phones and fetch coffee. Three weeks earlier she'd been hired permanently by the studio and assigned to be on Carmen's messy reality show detail. Just three minutes earlier, she'd stumbled upon the meal ticket of her life.

Flipping through a stack of freshly printed department store coupons while her boss and her boss's friend sorted out their differences, she happened upon the most gasp-worthy material she'd ever seen. *Oh. My Gawd.* At the end of the stack there were copies upon color copies of "saggy ass, droopy ass, big-nippled titties" and some very racy, very personal emails from what looked like the boss lady's personal account.

Shae snatched them up quickly, stuffed them in her purse, and smiled. *Look like somebody gon be gettin a lil raaiise.*

The Last Supper

The sweet dinner rolls were the last thing out of the oven. She piled her plate high and ate heartily, though she knew she'd never keep it down. Just moments later, crouched over porcelain, she purged every ounce of the perfectly seared filet mignon, every bit of the succulent Maine lobster tail, and every drop of the expensive French champagne. The label warned not to take the pills on an empty stomach, but they wouldn't let her keep anything down. She pondered, was it even worth it?

Prior to coming home and preparing her last supper, she'd spent the afternoon tying up her business affairs. Afterward, she sat at the bar, nursing a glass of cognac, as she explained to Rocky, finally, what was ailing her. A brain aneurism, diagnosed late because she'd continually ignored its rapidly progressing symptoms.

They wanted to operate. The doctors recommended an emergency craniotomy, lest the aneurism would rupture and very likely kill her. But that was four months ago. Before the James girls required rescuing, again. So there was no time to consider herself, again. Besides, she wasn't about to let them cut into her head. She thought, if the Good Lord meant for her to go by popping a vessel in her head, then so be it. If that be her karma for all the killing she'd done, then it was ordered. She'd live with it, until she didn't. It made sense, at the time.

She grabbed the box of Epsom salt from under the bathroom sink and drew herself a hot bath with a few drops of lavender oil and a few sprinkles of baking soda. That would surely put her body to good rest for the night. And the rest was well deserved. Her mind constantly raced. Her body constantly ached and her soul was truly tired, exhausted of the very air she breathed.

Sitting on the toilet, puffing a stogie, she held the book in her hand – a journal with a picture of her and a very young PJ affixed to the front. The book was among PJ's belongings that Rocky packed up and brought to her house after the funeral. PJ kept a small box full of journal's dating back to his teens. Some small tattered notebooks, a few composition books. The later journals were neater; more refined. Covered in fabric with satin ribbon bookmarks.

Aunt Pat didn't want to read them. She felt like it was invading his privacy. But she couldn't help wanting to know more about her son. She'd missed so much. She decided to open just one. At least for now. The one with her picture. That one seemed ok.

There was only one entry. The first two pages filled in. It was dated about a month before he died.

> *Dear Diary,*
>
> *Today was a good day. A great day actually. I did some things that I know will get me cussed out, but I'm hoping she will understand that I did it in love. I love my mother so much but she's so stubborn sometimes. She has way too much pride. She doesn't think I know what's going on but I hear just a much out in these streets as she does. There's no way I'll see her hurting. No matter what she says.*
>
> *I just wonder how long it'll take her to find out all her bills are paid. The mortgage company has got to send her a satisfaction letter for the house and the bar. I wonder if the utility companies will start returning her checks soon. I can't wait for her to say something so I can come clean. That will be well worth getting threatened and cussed out.*
>
> *I know she feels guilty about not being there for me. And I know I didn't help matters when she came home. But all of that has changed. None of it matters now. I forgive*

her. I just need her to forgive herself. I owe everything I have right now to her. She sacrificed everything to do the show with me. I'll never forget that and I'll never be able to repay her for it. But I'll try. Even if I have to keep it all a secret. For a little while.

Well let me take my beautiful behind to bed. Tomorrow is another day and I plan to make it a fabulous one. Until then...

PJ

Aunt Pat put out her cigar out and set it on the sink. She walked downstairs and made herself a glass of ginger ale, then she pulled a month's worth of unopened mail from her desk drawer. She sat in her recliner and flipped through for a while before coming across the first letter from Industrial Bank. The mortgage on the house, Satisfied. The loan for her business, Satisfied. The lease on the bar, paid to the end of its term. Her landlord sent a thank you card for the check.

She went through the stack of PJ's unopened mail in the box. Clearly he had reverted to some of his old ways to open a joint checking account in his and Aunt Pat's name. He'd deposited every dime of his money in that account and began paying her bills from it. Surely no one would question a payment made from an account with her name on it.

She opened the last statement he received, and *they* had an account balance of more than $200,000. That account was attached to several others, also with large cash amounts. She wept.

She held the papers in her hands and she wept for her child, thinking, after all he'd gone through, after all she'd put him through and after everything the world had taken him through, he had more good in him than anyone she knew. Her son. Generous and compassionate and forgiving and full of love. He was her greatest joy. And he was gone. And she didn't know him. That hurt more than anything.

After a moment of reflection, she decided there was no time like the present. So she reached back up to the top of her closet and pulled down his box of journals. She organized them all by date and began at the beginning. It was every bit of the closure she needed before doing what she had to do.

2 Cute for You Bitches

Chucky looked up from his newspaper. "Damnnnn! What happened to your eye?"

Missy rolled her swollen eye. "Carmen."

"She punched you in your face?!"

"We fought."

"Whaaat. For real? Well...did you hit her back?"

Missy yelled, "Of course I hit her back, Chucky!"

He giggled. "Okay, okay. I was just checking. What happened?"

"I don't wanna talk about it."

"Don't be like that."

"I said I don't want to talk about it."

"You sure?"

"I'm sure."

"Ok. I made some tacos. You want me to fix you a plate?"

"No, that's ok. I'll make my own."

The doorbell rang. Missy set her plate on the table. "I'll get it."

Chucky stood from the table. "No, go head and enjoy your taco, mamita. I'll get it."

He opened the front door and his heart nearly stopped. It was Tomeka, Ev's wife. Her eyes were red and swollen.

"Chucky, what happened to my husband?"

*****

Missy sat at the kitchen table, eating a taco, going over the day's events in her head. Carmen was something else. Never would she have imagined her best friend doing her so dirty. She'd done it to others. Yeah. Many times she'd been caught with somebody's man. A colleague. A friend. Even a cousin. But somehow she thought Carmen knew better than to try it with her.

Carmen was the closest thing Missy had to a sister. Her best friend, confidant, her shoulder to lean on. She was there when no one else was, so cutting her off wouldn't exactly be easy. The loss would be felt, for sure. Just thinking about it made Missy tear up. She was sad, and she was hurt, but more…angry.

How dare Carmen think that she could just shit all over her because she had a rough childhood. Everybody had to deal with something in their lives. That wasn't an excuse and definitely not a license to go around hurting people! But then again, Missy thought, what would her life had been like if her stepfather molested her? How would she act if her boyfriend threw her down a flight of stairs causing her to miscarry a child? What would her outlook on life be if she'd been raised by a junky mother that turned tricks in the alley for the whole neighborhood to see? Sometimes right in front of her.

Missy felt a little bad, but she couldn't just excuse what Carmen had done, especially when it came to Chucky. The rest of those guys meant nothing, but Carmen knew better than anyone what Chucky Wilson meant to her. On the other hand, she couldn't begin to understand what it would be like to have endured what Carmen had. Suddenly she felt guilty about leaving all those pictures and emails on the printer for Shae to find. That was uncalled for. But it seemed reasonable at the time.

Missy's phone dinged and illuminated. She picked it up from the table. An email. From Carmen.

I really don't know what else to say, other than I'm sorry. Deeply, truly sorry. I pray one day you'll find it in your heart to forgive me, Missy. I really do. Until then, I've decided to finally follow your advice and get counseling. I'm finally going to deal with my shit. If we never speak again, please know that I love you. Sincerely. Take care of yourself.

Missy sat there with her phone in hand, drafting and redrafting a reply, typing and deleting, trying to craft a response that would convey her feelings without sounding totally insensitive to the girl's pain. Missy thought, she might forgive her...someday. But not today. Today she would fire off this email and put all things Carmen Lewis behind her. She had plenty more to deal with. A brand new husband, piecing her family back together, trying to figure out exactly how the hell she was gonna deal with the "Kevin situation."

She thought of the perfect response. It was short and sweet. Concise. She couldn't give Carmen anymore of her time.

She hit reply and started again. In the middle of typing she just happened to look up at the email address. Something clicked.

To: 2cuteforyoubitches@zmail.com

Cc/Bcc:

Subject: Re: I'm Sorry

Carmen I have to be honest with you. When I saw those

Missy thought, *Oh HELL no!* Steaming mad, she hit the backspace key and started again.

To: 2cuteforyoubitches@zmail.com

CC/Bcc:

Subject: Re: I'm Sorry

Wow. Carmen. I've been sitting here for the last twenty minutes trying to find the right words and I thought I had them, until I looked up at your email. 2cuteforyoubitches huh? It just dawned on me. It was you. My bachelorette party? The videos? The pictures? You posted those videos. You sent Ray those pictures. You tried to sabotage my wedding.

Now I think back to all those times Ray knew where I was and what I was doing, damned near before I did. I guess I don't have to wonder anymore. With everything I learned today, I shouldn't be surprised. Guess it's just par for the course with you, huh? And the funny thing is, I would have forgiven you. For all of the other dirty shit you did to me, I would have forgiven you.

There is so much I can say to you right now. SO much. But I won't. At this point, what would it matter? It's funny, and pretty damned ironic that my ex-husband always used to say, what's done in the dark always comes to light. It's the one thing he said that always rang true. I get it. And pretty soon Carmen, so will you.

Sincerely,

Mrs. Melissa Wilson

P.S. I really hope that you get the help you need. I hope that wasn't just another lie. You take care of yourself.

Missy took a couple minutes to block Carmen from her phone and all of her social media. That was it. She was done. She got up and cleared the table. "Babe! You are not going to BELIEVE this. Then again, you probably will. Babe!" It dawned her she hadn't heard from Chucky since he went to the door. "Baby!" He didn't answer so she walked out into the hall. He stood outside the front door. "Chucky?" She opened it just as Tomeka turned to walk away. Puzzled, she asked, "Who's that?"

He turned to her. His face was wet. His voice cracked. "I have to tell you somethin."

The Last Days

It was almost time. Aunt Pat had spent the last couple of days tying up loose ends. At the bar, at the bank, on the street. Now it was time to come clean with the family, so they wouldn't be blindsided when the shit hit the fan. Figuring it would be better to inform everyone at once, she sent out a group text that morning.

To: Missy, Edward, Carolyn, Bessie, Brandy, Rocky

Text Message
September 15, 2016 7:36 am

Pat

I know this is short notice, but I need everybody at my house at 1 pm today. And please don't be late. I have something very important to announce.

Carolyn

What's going on Pat?

Edward

We'll be there.

Bessie

Can you come and get me? Floyd drove my car today.

Rocky

Ok

Missy

Why haven't you been answering your phone?

At 1:17, Aunt Pat sat in her rocking chair, waiting. *Motherfuckers always late.* 1:39pm everyone was seated in the living room except two. Aunt Pat snapped. "Where's Brandy?"

Missy rolled her eyes. "She's not coming. I'll talk to you about it later."

"Where Bessie?"

Aunt Carolyn chimed in. "She said *you* was comin to pick her up."

"What? Bessie no damn well I ain't tell her that. I ain't even talk to her today." She checked her watch. "Anyway, I ain't got a lotta time now. That's why I asked y'all not to be late. I called y'all here to let y'all know the real deal, before the shit hit the news. I wanted y'all to hear it straight from my mouth. As of tomorrow I'm gon be–"

"Police! Get down! Get down! Get down!"

Batter rams crashed through the front and the back doors. Police swarmed the house, guns drawn. One by one the James family hit the ground. Aunt Pat stood tall. Confused. "What the fuck?!"

Three officers grabbed her and yanked her around violently, before they threw her to the ground. Rocky kicked and yelled, "Get the fuck off her! She sick muthafucka!"

Aunt Pat calmed herself. This wasn't exactly how it was supposed to go down. But clearly things were already set in motion. She would deal with Petty later. "Rock, I'm good. I'm good."

One officer put the cuffs on her. Several others began ransacking the house. Missy laid on the floor, confused and afraid. "Aunt Pat, what's going on?"

Two officers yanked her up from the floor by either arm. "Y'all was late," she said. "So I guess I'll talk to y'all later. Just stay by the phone."

Uncle Edward called out to her, "Pat! I'll be down there soon as I can, hear? We gon post your bail."

She turned to him. "Don't worry bout that, Edward. It ain't

gon be no bail."

They pushed her outside into the blinding sunlight. The news cameras were already waiting. Cameras flashed. The neighborhood stood at attention. Tyrone Petty stood on the front lawn, waiting for his soundbites. They locked eyes just as she was pushed into the backseat of a squad car. Aunt Pat's glare was so icy a chill went down Petty's spine.

He'd deviated from the plan. They were supposed to have picked Pat up from the bar that afternoon at 4 p.m., not in front of her family. And definitely not in front of the cameras. But Petty couldn't resist. She'd totally sold him on the plan, and he wanted to make sure she didn't fuck around and get cold feet. So he had her tailed and the moment his people told him she was sitting still in her house, he pushed the go button. He called in the cavalry and tipped off the news. He'd already had everything he needed – a signed confession, a fresh haircut, and a killer necktie that would read GQ smooth on camera. It was show time.

Too Little Too Late

Missy opened her front door. She looked him up and down. He stood with a dumb grin on his face, drenched in cologne, holding a bouquet of flowers in one hand, and the little Misa-lookin-boy in the other. The boy was dressed just like him, which irritated her all the more.

"Hi...Miss James. Is Brenda home?"

Missy scowled. "Why?"

Tay frowned, confused. "Excuse me?"

"What do you want with her?"

"Oh. I'd just like to speak with her. If I can."

"Well you can't."

"Why not?"

"Because she's gone."

Missy closed the door before he could inquire further. She couldn't have answered any of his questions if she wanted to. According to the letter Brandy left on the kitchen counter, she was leaving and she wasn't coming back. The letter was long and it was harsh. Scathing and unnecessarily hurtful. But Missy was too angry to cry.

After all she had done for her. After all she'd done and sacrificed to keep the family together. To be called manipulative. Conniving. To be accused of stealing Misa for her own satisfaction. Because she couldn't have her own children. To be accused of ruining Brandy's life. It was unfair. And cruel.

Missy threw the letter in the wastebasket by the door. It wasn't the first time Brandy had threatened to leave home and probably wouldn't be the last. She didn't take many clothes from her closet, so she wasn't going too far. Probably to the beach with her friends or somewhere to clear her young silly head.

Maybe max out her credit cards and waste money Missy didn't have. Missy had no intention of looking for her and when she came back they were going to have a very serious conversation about that letter. Enough was enough.

She was hardly in the mood for any more drama and any more mystery. She'd had her fill. The news feeds were going crazy after Aunt Pat's arrest. She'd made international news for things she claimed she didn't do. Some of the most despicable, heinous acts one could imagine.

Chucky was behaving strangely. Ever since that woman, Tomeka had darkened their doorstep. He was quiet and withdrawn. He didn't even want sex. She didn't know what to make of it.

Kevin had suddenly and mysteriously gone missing. The day after he posted bail, he was released on home confinement but never made it home. His ex-wife reported him missing. A warrant was issued for his arrest. A week later, the police found his car parked near a riverbank with the front doors left open. It had been cleaned so there was nothing with DNA on it, and there was speculation of foul play. Considering everything he'd done and all of the death threats he'd gotten, there was no telling what had happened to him. Missy wasn't sure how to feel about it.

She locked up the apartment and headed over to the jail. She really needed to see her sister. To download all the craziness. She needed some of Brenda's downhome common sense wisdom. Some good sound motherly advice on how to handle her little drama queen and some good sisterly advice on how to deal with her man.

The guard checked his manifest. "Looks like Ms. James is in court today."

"Court? Why?"

"I'm sorry ma'am, I don't have those details. But you can call back tomorrow and see if she's taking visitors."

"Ok, thanks."

She sat in the jailhouse parking lot. Not really knowing where she should go. She thought, *what the hell is going on?*

...The Shit's Chess

The body count was piling up. She'd already signed the confession. Petty had teams out dragging the Potomac River and the shallow ponds at the Arboretum. Hazmat teams fished through putrid debris at the Blue Plains sewage plant looking for any signs of remains. The K9 unit released a half dozen pups sniffing through the foliage in Rock Creek Park. At last count, there were thirteen bodies, enough to technically classify her as a serial killer. It was front page news. But it wouldn't be the last headline. Tyrone Petty had no idea who he'd fucked with. But he'd find out. In due time.

Meanwhile she went forward with the plan. She was charged with every murder she told Petty about that day in his office. She gave detailed accounts that lined up perfectly with the forensic evidence. As a special request, Petty got her sent to the Fairfax County Detention Center first. And as her cell door slammed shut, several others buzzed opened.

Brenda Elaine James-Cohen, inmate 13-37759, Fairfax County Detention Center, Fairfax, Virginia; charged, first degree murder. Freed due to insufficient evidence.

Bobbi Lynn James, inmate 3764709-3 Rikers Island Correctional Facility, East Elmhurst, New York; charged, two counts aggravated assault, two counts kidnapping and extortion, one count of intimidating a Federal witness. Freed due to lack evidence.

Earlene (Early) James, Inmate 705-266591, San Quentin State Prison, San Quentin, California; charged, two counts of extortion, one count making terroristic threats, one count possession of an unregistered firearm used in the commission of a crime, two counts grand larceny. Freed due to insufficient evidence.

Millicent (Milly) James, inmate 271-98084, CDCR California State Prison, LA County California, charged, two counts of pandering, one count possession of a firearm, one count conducting a continuing criminal enterprise. Freed due to insufficient of evidence.

Petty kept his word. The important part of it. Her people were free. So she'd keep hers. For now.

Epilogue

Missy went to great lengths to make sure that her accommodations were perfect for a perfect delivery. A private room in the best hospital with the best doctor's money could buy. Money was most certainly an object these days, but nothing was too good for her beautiful, bouncing baby boy.

She laid him on her chest and cooed. Stroked his hair; thick waves of brown with the slightest hint of blonde at the base of his tiny little scalp. Brenda lay beside them, smiling as the effects of the epidural were just beginning to wear off. Missy placed him gently back onto Brenda's chest.

"Brenda, he's perfect. I can't believe you had a boy." She kissed him lightly on his tiny nose.

"I was hoping for a boy. Maybe I can do it right this time."

"Don't say—"

"Stop Missy. I don't need you to say anything. Just let me own it."

"Well…have you talked to MJ?"

"No. Not since he left. I keep up with him through Uncle Joe. He's doing ok. But he still won't talk to me. He won't talk to anybody."

"Sometimes, it takes time."

"Yeah. That's what mama used to say."

"She was right. So what are we naming him?"

Brenda grabbed onto the bed railing and pulled herself up. "Name him jughead. That boy big ass head almost ripped my ass apart."

Missy laughed. "Girl, stop it. Seriously. Have you thought of any names yet?"

"Well…yeah. I was thinking…maybe…James?"

"Yeah...James is a good name. Strong. But if that's his first, what would his last name be?"

Brenda laughed. "Oh...yeah. Ok, then Jesse."

"Really Brenda?"

"You're right. No sense in starting him off on the most wanted list. Ok I got it – "

"David Lee." Evelyn Cohen walked into the room unannounced. "David Lee Cohen Jr."

Brenda grimaced as she tried to sit up on the bed. "Evelyn, what are you doing here?"

"Well hello to you too, dear. I'm here to see my grandchild of course." She peered over at the child and smiled. "And I'm here to give you something." She handed Brenda an envelope. "Consider yourself served. Good day ladies."

Brenda motioned to Missy, and Missy took the baby from her arms. She opened the envelope and stared at the paper. Her eyes welled and soon tears began to stream her face. She hurled the papers across the room at to the door.

Missy shouted. "Brenda! What is it? What's wrong?!"

"She's tryna take my baby."

*****

His bank account was being drained month by month. After his bills, child support, spousal support, helping Missy with her bills...then paying Tomeka not to expose the video from the surveillance camera that was set up in the yard, across the street from Gi's grandfather's house. The camera that caught Chucky walking up to Ev, tasing him in the side of his neck and knocking him to the ground. The camera that captured Chucky getting into the back of a cargo van and leaving Ev for dead in the middle of a suburban Jersey street, convulsing until his body finally became still. Chucky was near tapped out.

Ever since that day sleep evaded him. He dreamed of Ev nightly and the dreams were so horridly vivid he was forced to just find ways to avoid it. Sleep. And Ev. He went from black bean espresso to Red Bull. From over the counter No Doze to behind the counter Adderall. Eventually, it all stopped working and then one night on one tour in a remote part of Utah, one scruffy white man handed him one vial of white powder and every problem he had was solved in one sniff.

So he was up he was hyped and he was ready. Up meant no sleep and therefore no bad dreams. Ready meant more shows which meant more money. And he needed money. Things were falling back into place.

Now Chucky wasn't green by any means. He'd seen the damage drugs could do. They'd gotten his father and his mother's father. A couple uncles and few cousins. But on the other hand he'd never been in the situation he was in, tormented every time he closed his eyes and stressed to the hilt every waking moment. The powder made him feel strong. Capable of handling anything that came his way. He handled it all, until he couldn't.

Missy came home on cloud ninety-nine. Her new baby nephew was gorgeous and instead of being sad, she was suddenly and enthusiastically inspired to give that 10 percent chance a chance. She'd just gotten waxed and plucked and the lacy black crotchless teddy she'd just picked up from Frederick's was sure to put Chucky in a baby making mood.

She walked through the front door and could hear the TV blasting from the basement. She yelled down, "Babe, I'm home." Then she ran upstairs to get into character. Twenty minutes later she walked back down the stairs, made up, oiled up, and tossing the hair from the infamous long black wig over her shoulders. Channeling Michelle Devereaux, a sexy dark haired French femme fatale who performed burlesque at the Moulin Rouge. Missy knew if anyone could summon an appearance from the one and only Chuck Nasty, it was most certainly her.

She scaled the steep basement steps carefully in her stilettos. Leather whip in one hand and a bottle of champagne in the other. 'Baaaby....'" He didn't answer. She called out to him. "Sa Michelle." Still no answer, but she heard faint noises coming from the spare bedroom. She tapped lightly on the door. "Mon amour? Elle cherche Chuck mechant." She set the champagne bottle down on the floor and adjusted her crotchless crotch before she turned the nob and pushed the door open to something she never thought she'd see. Not from him. Not from her husband.

The feeling of ecstasy completely overwhelmed him. He didn't even notice she was there.

"Chucky!"

*****

Paris was a lot less romantic in the winter, with no money and no half-Haitian bilingual roommate to translate. Aunt Missy closed her credit card account in an attempt to bring her back home. But Brandy was determined. She was putting all things DC far behind her.

She'd taken a job as a barmaid in a seedy tavern in Pig Alley. Her boss wasn't too happy she didn't speak any French, but she looked the part in micro mini, and the patrons took a special liking to the pretty chocolate American girl, so he kept her on.

She'd been working double shifts for over a week. Just trying to catch up. Her one night off she planned to rest but her roommate Kelsey had convinced her to have a girl's night out. She had tickets to see an American band that was playing for one night at the Palladium. When Brandy scanned the tickets and saw that it was Young Budda, a local semi-conscious rapper from the DMV, she was all in. She dolled up quickly and they were off to paint the town rouge.

The girls stood down front by the stage, dancing and carrying on. Brandy rapped every song word for word, and she was especially pleased that Young Budda was showing her some special love. He handed her the microphone, and she commenced to showing the French how they did it in DC.

The party was jumping, the drinks were kicking in and her bladder was screaming but she was waiting on her song. Two songs later she had to give it up and go. Kelsey followed her through the tight crowd of rowdy drunken Parisians. Kelsey stood in the mirror holding Brandy's bathroom stall door closed with one hand and reapplying her lip gloss with the other. Brandy had barely squatted before she heard the baseline to her jam. "Shit!"

Kelsey squealed. "Hurry up girl! We gotta get back out there!"

Brandy hurried out of the stall, rinsed, and shook her hands dry. They ran out the door singing.

When they rounded the corner, they heard a *pop*, then a whizzing sound and Young Budda tumbled forward off the stage. Screams echoed throughout the concert hall as three men armed with high powered rifles began shooting into the crowd. The girls turned back toward the bathroom and ran.

The crowd stampeded in every direction, as shots rang out. Brandy reached back for Kelsey's hand, but she wasn't there; though she could still hear her screaming her name. She turned and saw a man fall to the floor behind her. He'd been hit.

There was a loud ping, and then another as bullets struck a metal duct above their heads. Kelsey was lost somewhere in the crowd. But there was no turning back. The shooters were getting closer.

The bathroom door was blocked as the entire crowd tried to push their way in. Brandy forged ahead of them, trampling over a young woman who'd been trampled, down the hall toward an exit. The exit door was locked. She yanked at it furiously until she noticed a narrow door off to the side. A storage closet. She slid inside.

Gunshots echoed loudly, only a short distance away. Screams of terror pierced the air. Brandy tried to calm herself and she fumbled around in her purse for her phone. Her hands shook almost uncontrollably. She found her phone, powered it on and dialed.

Waiting for a ring felt like an eternity. *Please, please answer the phone.* There was no answer. She called again. Voice mail. She whispered through frantic tears. "Aunt Missy. Please. Please pick up. I'm in trouble."

*****

Sitting alone in her cell, drinking a carton of low-fat milk, Aunt Pat reflected on her life on the outside. So much had transpired in a few short years. Some of it good. She liked to think she'd done *some* good, although at the moment, the James Girls shit was in complete shambles.

PJ was gone, Brenda had lost yet another child through the courts, Missy's second marriage was another no-win situation and Brandy was wandering the streets of Europe like a dirty gypsy. *Guess you can't fix everything.*

She'd stopped taking her medication. What was the point? It only made her feel worse, and she needed to keep her strength up. Twenty-three hours in a cell could make you stiff, so she was sure to get in a little exercise every day. Mostly shadow boxing, she wanted to stay sharp, because on the inside, one never knew when one would have to check a bitch's chin.

She moved from one side of the tiny cell to the other. In a boxer's stance, jabbing and upper cutting furiously at the imaginary enemy until she worked up a sweat. Yesterday she'd gone so long she nearly passed out.

Marsha wheeled her cart down the hall, collecting the empty dinner trays from all the dames so unfortunate to be living in solitary. She came to Aunt Pat's cell and banged hard. "Aye Pat, let me get that tray back, babe." There was no answer. She knelt down and peeked through the narrow slot. She shouted, "Guard! Help! I need some help in here!"

Two correctional officers rushed to Aunt Pat's door and frantically searched for the right key on the crowded ring. They opened the door to find Aunt Pat lying on the floor in convulsions, shaking violently and foaming at the mouth.

By the time the medic arrived, the shaking had stopped. Aunt Pat was nearly out of it but coherent enough to explain her ailment. They wheeled her up to the infirmary.

The prison doctor wanted to transport her to the hospital for more tests, but the warden wasn't on board. Aunt Pat was way too high profile a prisoner to leave the jail without cause, and since her vitals were stable she'd just have to remain in the care of the prison medical staff.

Doctor Biermann was furious, but her hands were tied. She thought the least she could do was have a look at the patient's medical records before she went back to the warden to plead her case. So she put in a call to Aunt Pat's primary care physician at the Hospital Center. Apparently they'd attended medical school together.

Aunt Pat started to cough. The coughing was dry and loud. "Don't mind me, Doc. I probably just need some water."

Doctor Biermann absentmindedly poured her a cup of water while she waited for her colleague to come on the line. As soon as the doctor engaged on her call Aunt Pat started coughing again. Louder. The doctor turned to her. Aunt Pat signaled that she was fine and took a sip of her water. Dr. Biermann walked into the exam room, away from the noise, to finish her call.

As soon as she walked out of the room, Aunt Pat detached the sticky electrodes from her chest and unplugged the monitor so it wouldn't sound, then she eased over to the exam room and locked the door. She coughed a few more times for good measure then she slid out of her room into the hallway.

She tipped down the hall and ducked into a room near the end. When she flipped the light switch, her dear old friend Karen Braxton's eyes bucked wide. "Pat?"

She closed the door behind her. "Wassup Brax?"

Karen stammered over her words. "H…Hey. Uh…when…when'd you get in here?"

Aunt Pat turned the lock. "Couple days ago." Then she pulled the plastic tubing off of a nearby IV stand and began wrapping it around her fists.

"W…w…wait. Pat. Listen, I swear to you…"

"Don't swear."

Karen's eyes welled as she cowered in her bed and pulled the bed sheet up to her neck. "Pat please."

"Look, I ain't got but a minute. You got anything you wanna say to me? Like why you thought it was ok to put your fuckin hands on my family?"

Karen whimpered. "But I didn't–"

"Don't lie. I don't have the time."

"But Pat you don't understand."

"Make me!"

Karen jumped at the sound of Aunt Pat's booming voice. She sobbed and sniffled. "I can't…I can't say…"

"Oh. You can't say? Ok." Aunt Pat walked behind her and wrapped the tubing around her neck. She yanked Karen's head back and Karen squealed.

"OKAYYY!!! Stop! STOP!" Karen pulled at the tubing with both hands and screamed. "It was Rocky! Ok?! It was Rocky!"

Aunt Pat loosened her grip. She walked to the front of the bed to make eye contact. "Wait, what?"

About the Author

F.J. Stevens is a creative writer, a native Washingtonian with an immense love for her city and a wildly vivid imagination.

She spent the better part of the last 20 years in corporate America, until the day that a corporate merger (and a fairly generous severance package) sent her home to her sofa, where she was able to exhale, put up her feet for a while and pen her first novel, the first in a series of gritty urban family sagas, "James Girls".

F.J. loves to hear from readers so please, visit her website www.fjstevens.com, email her at info@fjstevens.com and connect on social media for more info on the James Girls, upcoming projects, promotions and events.

https://www.facebook.com/F.J.Steven.books

www.ingramcontent.com/pod-product-compliance
Lightning Source LLC
Chambersburg PA
CBHW070615260626
47161CB00007B/2437